I0538945

Fire Scion III: The Imperium Plot
By Kathe Todd

The events in this novel begin approximately one year
after the end of Fire Scion II: The Flying Dead

Chapter 1: Schoolhouse

The children – most of them lanky adolescents, now – had just finished a snack break after morning chores and they were milling around. They sounded like a flock of gulls contending over a dead walrus. "All right, settle down!" Francois Lamonte commanded, and they quickly took their seats and pulled out their books.

The nursery at Drakespring House had been converted into a schoolroom, like nothing that the Waterdon area had ever seen before. Gerard Bouchard and his fellow workers at Arngeld and Sons Woodworking had crafted ten good-sized, freestanding wooden desks. Each had an inkwell and pen rack mounted above a hinged lid, giving access to storage space for books and writing paper, with a chair permanently attached to the desk.

For the first time in living memory, kids in Waterdon who were interested in an education that went beyond the basics of reading, writing, and shopkeeper math had someplace they could go without leaving town. Classes were held three hours per day, five days a week, and covered everything from history and literature to foreign languages and higher mathematics.

Places for students were few, as eight of them were already taken by the Drakespring children themselves. Mondi and five of his dragon siblings, now all human more often than not, were joined by Sigi and Meri. At thirteen, she was the eldest of the students and sometimes the guest lecturer, as there was much she could teach about the history and cultures of the leukalfar.

Francois smiled at the way the kids had quieted at his command. They were a good lot, he thought, and they seemed to be a little in awe of him. Only Meri, Mondi, and Sigi had known him when he was old and feeble, for he owed yet another debt to his daughter-in-law. Once again, she had given him a new lease on life – regressing his age to what he might have been at fifty-five had not a series of strokes before that time begun to erode both his mind and his physical strength. At eighty-one, he looked a more appropriate age to be the father of Andrion – who appeared to be in his early thirties.

Bernadette had brought his wife Christine along for the ride, and the two of them had (to the astonished delight of both of them) become lovers again after more than fifty years of marriage. The couple continued to live in the small house in Waterdon they'd bought a decade before, and Francois happily made the walk to Drakespring Farm each school day – both for the exercise and for the sheer joy of being able to do so.

"Everyone has of course now read *The History of the Guardians,*" Francois began. "Who can tell me what significance the Guardians had regarding the destiny of the Fireblood?" Zuunenwalt raised her hand. Darkest of the dragonlings, an intense and tomboyish girl, she was a fierce competitor at everything she set her hand to – including scholarship. Her siblings – along with a girl and a boy from Waterdon – gave her a Look that she was oblivious to.

"I know, M. Lamonte!" she crowed, and he nodded at her to continue. He felt torn between pleasure at having a bright, enthusiastic student and concern over the resentment she generated in others.

"Giselle of the Guardians knew that Mama had gone to see the Old Ones at Eberburg, and that they'd sent her to find the Staff of Zauber as final proof that she truly was The Fireblood. She staked out the monastery, and after the Old Ones had acknowledged that Mama truly was the one prophesied, she tried to direct her in the way that she thought the Fireblood should go. Because of that, she and Papa Erik found Adalbert, and it was he that gave them the clue about using a dragon spell to defeat Tarragin." These kids had a strange, personal take on history, since so much of it over the past generation had been created by their own family.

"And he wasn't the only one who helped them!" came a familiar voice from the direction of the hall. The door had opened, and an enormously tall, slim and muscular man with dark red hair and deep green, amber-flecked eyes came into the room. Behind him was a tallish young woman with dark blonde hair, lushly pretty, holding a red-haired infant in her arms.

The classroom broke back into chaos in an instant, as most of the students surged to their feet. Francois sighed, and accepted the inevitable. "Father! Father!" came a chorus of voices, as six of the adolescents clustered around the tall man for hugs. Then they converged on the woman and the baby.

4

"Gods, Gilda!" Schickhimseel exclaimed, "Ursula is getting so *big*! And she's so *cute!*"

Sneyagflug beamed down at them. When he had begun his relationship with Gilda it had been mostly out of curiosity, and an undeniable physical attraction. But their love had blossomed, and the birth of their child had been the most amazing experience of his very long life – somehow even eclipsing the soul-shaking bond he had formed with Schunmurte. This human thing of having only one helpless child at a time, and needing decades in which to raise them, demanded so much more of you and gave you so much more in return.

His link with Bernadette would never be broken – after all, they had eighteen living children together – and all of those children were now, as he was, capable of becoming human. They were all going to live a long time, barring mishaps, and he was looking forward to some sensational family reunions in the decades to come. But he had finally accepted that Bernadette was not, and never would be, his. And he had moved on. He was, literally, a new man. Instead of a dragon masquerading as a human being, Sneyagflug was coming to feel as if he were a human being who often became a dragon.

Indeed, being a dragon was how he made his living. He'd been launched full-fledged into human society without any of the education an adult usually had, and it had left him wondering how he was to support a wife and family. But Eorl Ormund had been happy to give them quarters in Wyrmshalla, and gold in plenty, in exchange for Sneyagflug becoming his personal air force. He flew reconnaissance, provided air travel for up to three adults, and carried messages faster than any human courier could travel – even with a magic map.

Gilda smiled in genuine affection as her husband's children gathered around to admire and coo at their half-sister. That he had been a powerful dragon since long before her ancestors had been born thrilled her to the core. That he had all these kids with another woman, one he was still friends with, was less wonderful – but she liked them, and their mother as well.

At least not all of them were around Waterdon at once. Currently six of them were studying at Eberburg while another five were engaged in the same campaign of improving dragon-human relations the entire brood had started several years before. Now that any friendly dragon could obtain the ability to become human, the human-dragon alliance was becoming stronger than ever. Gilda wondered how long they would have to wait to learn whether Ursula was fireblood. It was Sneyagflug's theory that any human child born of the union between a woman and a transformed dragon would carry the blood.

Francois' patience was reaching its end. The majority of his students were related to him, if not by blood then by a strong family connection. In the Drakespring family, it was not so much who had provided the genetic material for your birth as whom you loved, and where your loyalty lay. It was possible young Sigi might be his actual grandchild, but he had come to care for Bernadette's other children nearly as much. Still, it was time to get back to work. It wasn't as if they had all day! After lunch it would be crafts, farm chores, weapons practice, cooking, and other human arts – while the students who were not resident at Drakespring Farm would be dismissed for the day.

"Sneyagflug, Gilda, good to see you," Francois said somewhat peremptorily. "But I'm afraid my students and I have much material yet to cover this morning." Sneyagflug smiled. After having been human a good deal of the time for more than a year, his mastery of social skills was vastly superior to what it had been on the day of his first transformation, when he'd attempted to seize Bernadette as if she were merely a stag that had wandered into his draconic hunting range. He winced at the memory of that day, and how utterly clueless he had been.

"Couldn't resist stopping in," Sneyagflug said by way of apology. "If anyone wants to come and visit us at Wyrmshalla when you have some free time, we'd love to see you." He and his little family let themselves out the way they'd come in, going to visit with Bernadette and Erik for a little while longer before returning home.

Chapter 2: Practical Magic

"All right," Andrion said, "go ahead and engage the lever." Gylabris pulled the gleaming dypalfar metal lever down, as Andrion stood by ready to freeze the process in case anything went wrong. The core glowed red, gears began turning, and the half-scale dypalfar lift they'd constructed rose from floor level up toward the ceiling. Andi and Rezira watched, fascinated, as the platform glided swiftly upward.

"Now try to lower it," Andrion commanded, and the lift went down. Clearly, the basic concept was working. But halfway through its second trip to the ceiling, the red light winked out and all motion ceased. "The spell's wrong," Andrion said with a sigh. "I think we have the mechanical elements correct, but the power source is limited by time."

Rezira felt a flush of shame. As the only living representative of the dypalfar race of elves in this plane of existence (all of her fellows having escaped, millennia ago, to one in which they were the only sentient beings) she felt to blame, somehow, for lacking the knowledge to reproduce all of the technology/magic her people had left behind when they fled. The fact that she was only a teenage girl, and that as the daughter of her city's military leader her education had focused mainly on matters like history, weaponry, and battle magic, did not – in her eyes, at least – excuse her.

Andi, sensing her thought, put an arm around her and murmured into the top of her head, "Nobody's expecting you to be an expert on this, love." She squeezed him back. She, Andrion, and Gylabris, here at the Mages' Academy at Eisenstag, had been engaged in a project to root out the secrets of the robon power cells that were the basis for so much of what her people had wrought – the suppliers of energy that made everything work, in perpetuity.

Just so he could be with her, Andi had enrolled in the Academy as a student. Though only seventeen he was far above the level of most of the students, possibly even above the level of the instructors, in battle and healing magic. But there were other magical disciplines, and still much for him to learn. She too, though in a unique position as a representative of a culture that had vanished from Iscandia ages ago, had things to learn from the faculty of the Academy. She studied with them in her free time from the project the magister and his colleagues were engaged in.

Rezira and Andi shared a comfortable room in the student residence hall, which had been augmented by the replacement of the usual single bed with a double one – and the addition of a lock on the wooden door. The place could certainly have done with some better bathroom facilities (so both of them thought; being used to hot baths available at any hour of the day or night), but otherwise the accommodations weren't too bad.

As magister, Andi's father Andrion had immense control over the Academy of Eisenstag and the directions in which it went. For years he'd maintained an ongoing, wide-flung research project in which the brightest and most creative minds at the Academy had been encouraged to engage in experimental research (with safeguards in place), or try spells dug up from long-forgotten tomes in order to expand mankind's knowledge and understanding of magic. The latest direction this had taken was the Department of Practical Magic, housed in a new wing constructed off of the western side of the original Academy campus.

Here, Andrion and all who supported his initiative and were willing to give it some time were free to tinker with the link between the strictly mechanical and the magical – specifically, the technologies the dypalfar had developed before fleeing this plane of existence. These mechanisms posed a mystery that had haunted Andrion most of his adult life, and one that Rezira (who appeared well on the way to becoming his daughter-in-law) had been unable to answer.

Why, with all these wonders at their disposal, had the dypalfar not simply bought off their enemies with offers of technology every human would want – instead of burrowing underground, and then fleeing this plane of existence? Rezira, seeing the situation from the inside, was only able to speculate as he had: the dypalfar were turned inward, insular, convinced that they were surrounded by enemies. And they'd been unable to consider their place in the world as anything but that of a beleaguered minority – when, if they'd been less xenophobic, they might have become masters of the world.

"I suppose I'd better let you two go," Andrion said to Andi and Rezira. "You're supposed to be at the Enchanting class, aren't you?" Rezira smiled at him. Now that Andrion appeared to be less than twice the age of his son, the resemblance between them was so striking that she couldn't help warming to him. But where Andrion usually seemed dead serious and a little restrained, Andi combined that razor-sharp intellect with a sense of fun.

"Thanks, Papa," Andi said. "Sorry it didn't work out."

"What we need," his father said thoughtfully, "is somebody with a deeper understanding of conjuring than anyone I've ever encountered in Iscandia." Andrion had been magister of the Academy for more than eighteen years now, and he knew his faculty and their limitations well. It had been some years since he'd last consulted with the faculty of the University of the Magical Arts in Remus, though. Perhaps it was time to contact them once again.

Chapter 3: The University of the Magical Arts

In his comfortable chair in the magister's quarters atop the central tower in the University of the Magical Arts' campus, Sextus Garabaldi sat back and marshaled his thoughts. "Resume," he said, and the golden pen that was poised unsupported in air above the writing table dipped itself in ink and assumed a ready position above the roll of paper laid out beneath it.

"Therefore," he continued, "I am inviting you and your research team to join me and my own researchers here at the University of the Magical Arts for a group effort, that I feel confident should lead to the results both of us have been seeking. As this may take some time, I am leasing a house in the Pantheatos District of Roma where you and your assistants, as well as your entire family, may stay while our project is underway."

"New paragraph," the magister said, and the pen dipped again before hovering over a new line. Its spelling and calligraphy were excellent, and this was surely one of the most useful inventions researchers at the university had come up with in the past several decades. "I urge you to bring along your wife, your co-husband, and at least your older children, as I am sure they would be delighted to visit our city and to attend some of the social events it is famous for."

"There are art exhibitions, martial contests in the Coliseum, and a wide selection of shops where your wife and older daughter would no doubt find anything they might want to buy. Roma is also only a short distance from many points of architectural and archaeological interest."

"New paragraph," Sextus commanded, then went on "Your stay here will be enjoyed by all, and I will personally present you and your family to our new emperor. As you are no doubt aware, since your last visit the Convocation has declared Giorgio Augustino to be the successor to the late, childless, Gaius Albus. As his family is descended through the female line from the ancestors of the Salonius emperors, he has taken the name of Giorgio Salonius I and pledged to re-establish that highly successful line. I have told him much about you and your work at the Academy of Eisenstag, as well as your family's many accomplishments, and he and his wife are eager to meet you."

"New paragraph, last one" the magister said, noting that he was running out of room on the page. "Hoping that you will be able to accept my invitation and that I'll be hearing from you shortly so I can prepare for your arrival. Sign it 'Sincerely, Sextus Garibaldi, Magister, the University of the Magical Arts." The pen completed the writing of the letter with a flourish.

"Make a second copy," Sextus next commanded. "One should be addressed to the Magister of the Mages' Academy at Eisenstag and the second copy to Andrion Drakespring of Drakespring Farm, Waterdon. One or the other is sure to reach him." With that he rose from his chair, paced across the room to a glowing magic portal, and stepped through it into the chamber below – where he approached a young man who was standing as if in wait.

"How may I assist you, magister?" the young man asked. He appeared to be no more than twenty, of medium height and slightly scarred with the remnants of teen acne.

"You'll find two letters on my writing table, Scipio. "Please see that they are sent by fast messenger as soon as possible.

"Right away, sir," the youth said, and soon vanished into the portal. He returned in a moment with the two addressed and sealed letters, and exited via another portal to the ground floor.

Sextus followed him, and strode out through the doors of the tower to the steps beyond. It was a lovely morning. Roma got some of its nicest weather at this season, and he decided to take a little stroll around the grounds. The chemia garden was always a pleasant place. He felt as if a weight had been lifted from his shoulders. If he and Andrion Drakespring could combine their knowledge and skills, who knew what amazing things might result?

Chapter 4: Birthday Party

Bjorn and Lifa guided their son, walking beside him and gently holding his elbows as they led the blindfolded young man along. Edla, grinning from ear to ear at the fun, brought up the rear. They'd put the blindfold on Fjuri before leaving the house, spun him around several times in the street after descending from the front step at Brightsgate Cottage, and then taken him on the half-mile walk up and down hill, twice across the river.

It was silly, of course. He'd traversed this path from their home to Drakespring Farm, or to the Bathing Maiden beyond, thousands of times in his eighteen (just) years of life. But he went along with it in good spirits. It wasn't often his so-serious parents did anything this frivolous, and he wanted to show them that he appreciated it.

Fjuri knew from the smell that they were passing Drakespring Farm, the manure from their cattle pens always an element in the scent along this stretch of the road. Oh, good! If they weren't going to the farm then the party must be at the Maiden, which was a cut above. He'd have been happy enough with a gathering (outdoors, in today's fine weather) at the farm, with Riki, Andi, and their family. But unless his parents and sister were planning to walk him, blindfolded, all the way to Coldstein (just a little unlikely), there was shortly going to be music, dancing, and fine food at the Bathing Maiden to celebrate his attainment of the age that, in this part of Iscandia, meant he was now an adult.

Sure enough, they soon led him up the wooden steps onto the porch. His feet had trod here so many times he almost didn't need their guiding hands. The doors swung open, the small party stepped through, and Bjorn (now slightly shorter than his strapping son) removed Fjuri's blindfold to reveal the common room of the inn packed with his friends. "Surprise!" everyone yelled, and he grinned at them in amazement. What a crowd!

Riki was the first to come forward and give him a hug and kiss. In this mob, it was considerably more restrained than some she'd given him over the past year-plus, since they'd finally reached an understanding. She had grown a lot in that time, and was now only around seven inches shorter than he – both more slender and more voluptuous (in all the right places!) as her body matured. Though

12

Fjuri had gotten over a lot of the shyness he'd felt when he was younger, the sight of Riki in snug-fitting armor, or the nicely draped knit dress she wore today, still brought a flush to his cheeks.

"Happy Birthday, Fjuri," she murmured in his ear – then presented him with a small package wrapped in a scrap of velvet cloth and tied with a ribbon. "I made it myself, both the amulet and the enchantment," she assured him quietly. Riki's father Erik, despite being an enormous and muscular man capable of cutting a bullock in half with a well-placed blow of the khopesh that was his favorite weapon, also had a deft hand with jewelry – and clearly he had taught his daughter much. The amulet on its leather cord was beautiful and exquisitely wrought, yet masculine in design. After opening the package he handed it to her and bent his head so she could slip it over his neck.

Immediately Fjuri felt a surge of well-being, beyond the happiness he felt being here at the Maiden for his eighteenth birthday and surrounded by friends and well-wishers – including the beautiful Riki. "Wow!" he said, "what's *in* this thing?"

"Mom helped me learn the enchantment," she confided with a little smile. "It increases your health and stamina, and it also increases the rate at which they regenerate. You should be able to sling a hammer all day without getting tired, or mow down a few dozen bandits without breaking a sweat, as long as you wear it."

"*Thank* you, Riki!" Fjuri exclaimed, and folded her to him for a much more enthusiastic kiss and hug. "I'll never take it off!" he promised. The assembled crowd voiced a collective "OOOoooh!" at the gesture, embarrassing them both – but not for long. They had not yet become lovers, and that was a source of tension in their relationship. But Riki was still a few months short of her sixteenth birthday, after all.

What they *had* become was much better friends, two people who could talk to each other about anything. With Andi gone so often, first with the Leukalfar Initiative and now studying with Rezira at the Academy, Fjuri saw more of Riki than he did of his lifelong friend. It had drawn them much closer together.

Next Andi came forward. He, Rezira, Andrion, and Gylabris had all fast-travelled down from the Academy in order to be here for this special event. He enfolded his friend in a hug. Fjuri had overtopped him since they'd been old enough to stand upright, and apparently that situation was going to continue for the rest of their lives – though he stood only a couple of inches shorter. More noticeable was the muscle mass Fjuri had accumulated as he continued to do construction work while Andi had been busy running diplomatic missions and studying magic.

"Happy Birthday, buddy!" Andi declared. He peered up at his friend. "Are you still growing?" he asked suspiciously.

"I think this is it," Fjuri said, gesturing at his nearly six foot five inch, two hundred-thirty-pound frame. "Unless you've got some spell to make me bigger?"

"Gods forfend!" Andi declared. Then he added, "Hey, I made you something."

Of the Drakespring children only Andi so far had taken up smithing; but his many other interests had prevented him from developing the level of mastery he would have liked. Then for the past two years a lot of his time had been consumed in working with the Leukalfar Initiative. That project was pretty well complete, now – with all of the tribes contacted and many of them now operating the dypalfar ruins they occupied as a source of revenue – acting within Iscandia's human society, instead of hiding beneath it and being killed off by treasure-hunting adventurers.

Andi had therefore gotten a lot of help from his mother in making this gift for the young man who had been his best friend from the time of his earliest memories. He had labored on it in his spare time for most of the past year, and it was by far the best work he had ever done. While it seemed likely that Fjuri might end up becoming a builder instead of a soldier or an adventurer, this gift was a token of the love the two of them had always had for the old tales of valor, and of the adventures they'd shared.

Fjuri looked around. The frisson of added vitality Riki's amulet had provided still had him feeling on top of the world. "Well, where is it?" he asked. The crowd parted and a troop of Andi and Riki's adolescent siblings stepped forward, carrying among them a complete set of daimonic armor. Fjuri gasped. Such a thing, if one could find it at a shop (unlikely in Waterdon), would cost several months' wages for a construction worker. And this had been lovingly hand-crafted to his precise measurements by his best friend! No *wonder* Andi was concerned about whether he was still growing!

Fjuri enfolded Andi in a bear-hug, to a creaking of ribs. "Thank you! This is magnificent!" he roared. It was almost enough to make him want to go kill off a few bandits, or join the Brave Company, just to put it into use!

Remy Caron, the inn's head innkeeper, stepped forward at this juncture and said, "Food and drink are waiting outside, folks! Come on, let's party!" More people from the crowd, many of them Fjuri's fellow workers on Hegmar's crew, surged around him with back-slaps and raucous congratulations, and he was swept along with them on a wave that spilled out the Maiden's back doors onto the deck.

One of the Maiden's semi-portable cooking tables had been set up along the south side, and a wonderful smell of grilling meat filled the air. Beside that another table was laden with every sort of food – fruit, pastries, fried potatoes, breads – and the crowd began milling around them in a hungry throng as bottles of chilled ale and mead were dispensed, wine was offered, and a group of musicians stationed in the far corner struck up a lively tune.

Fjuri could scarcely remember seeing his parents so relaxed and joyful. The Steadfast family had a good and comfortable life, and Lifa and Bjorn weren't without humor. But the pair of them had always possessed a certain gravitas, a reserve, that he hadn't seen much at Drakespring House except occasionally from Andi's father Andrion. And even *he* was a positive party animal by comparison with Fjuri's own folks.

Fjuri was completely oblivious to how much he shared those traits, of course. Even his sister Edla, a bright little soul, had chosen Meri Drakespring as her best friend – a girl from a race of elves that were famously reserved and formal. Though Meri, of course, was considerably less so than most of the leukalfar.

Everyone ate and drank, danced and sang. Many people hugged Fjuri and congratulated him, and there were numerous small hand-made gifts presented. Birthday celebrations (or any celebrations at all, really) were rare enough in Iscandia that this was the party of the year for most of the participants. After everyone had eaten their fill and then danced it off again there was cake, and ice cream (a rare treat usually only available here at the Maiden).

Fjuri was sitting at the Owner's Table with Andi on one side, Rezira sitting beside him, and Riki on his other. They were holding hands, and glowing with happiness and pleasure. This had been the most wonderful celebration of his life! As they sat now digesting their dessert, and feeling wonderfully content, Lifa and Bjorn arose to stand in the area of the mezzanine between the Owner's Table and the one next to it. Then Bernadette, Erik, and Andrion joined them. They were all facing toward Fjuri.

Oh ho, what was this? In the confusion Fjuri had scarcely noticed that neither his parents nor their very wealthy friends and one-time benefactors had given him any gifts. If he even thought about it he'd assumed that this party, which had obviously taken a lot of work to put together and cost a significant amount of gold in food, drink, and the closing of the inn to its usual afternoon custom, was their gift to him – and he was perfectly content with it.

Though all five of them were standing up there looking pleased as punch, it was Bjorn who took the role of spokesman. "Son," he said in a commanding voice that reached throughout the room and halted the chatter of the crowd, "eighteen years ago we welcomed you into our family, and you have been a joy to us ever since." Small hoots and cheers were heard around the room – everyone was feeling pretty mellow. "For the past three years," Bjorn went on, "you have been learning the builder's trade with us on Hegmar's crew (more hoots and cheers), and you have learned well. I think that I am not alone in saying that you have truly become a journeyman builder, and we are proud to have you on our team."

A chorus of "Yeah!" and "Fjuri!" was heard around the room, coming from his fellow builders. Bjorn waited for the noise to die down, then continued: "Now that you are a man, there is one thing that you have yet to do, the masterwork that will prove to the world that you are truly a master of our craft: and that is to build your own home." Fjuri's eyes widened. Build his own home? He'd been fantasizing about doing so for much of the past year, since his relationship with Riki had deepened. But the money to buy land and materials, and time free from work (the income from which, once he left his family's home, would be needed for little items like food), were things he wouldn't be able to have for years yet.

All five of the older people standing near the table were now looking at him with pleasure and anticipation. Riki, gazing up at him to see his reaction, squeezed his hand. She had an idea what might be coming, though she had not been let in on the plot. Bjorn went on, "Thanks to help from the Drakesprings, Fjuri, your mother and I are pleased to present you with this gift." With a flourish, he took the rolled paper Lifa had handed to him and spread it out before handing it over to his son. It was a deed!

"This is the deed to a ten-acre plot just west of the current bounds of the city of Waterdon," Bjorn explained. Fjuri knew the area well. He and his father, and the rest of Hegmar's crew, had been erecting houses out there during most of the time since he'd begun working construction. "This plot has a little bit of elevation to it, and a small year-round stream runs through it. It will be suitable for a little light farming, if that is what you – and whoever you will share it with – want to do." With that Bjorn cast a glance at Riki, and she stiffened. Hey wait, who said I wanted to be doing farm chores for the rest of my life? Who said Fjuri and I are even getting *married*?

Fjuri was so caught up in looking at the deed, visions of his dream home spinning in his head, that he failed to notice Riki's less-than-enthusiastic response. He glanced up again, as his father began speaking again. "You also have this draft in the amount of ten thousand guilders, to be used for purchasing building materials and other necessities while you're building your home. I'll work with you on the drawings, and I'll be happy to volunteer some labor to help you when I have free time. I'm sure many of your fellow members of Hegmar's crew will be glad to assist when they can, as well." There was another chorus of assent. Though Fjuri could be a little intimidating at times, he'd been well-liked by his fellows on the crew.

Bjorn handed the second piece of paper to his son, beaming with pleasure. It was a draft on the coffers of the hold, which could be redeemed for cash on presentation to the eorl's steward. "Happy birthday, son," he concluded. Fjuri surged to his feet, tears in his eyes and a huge grin on his face, and hugged his parents, Aunt Berni,

Uncle Erik, and Uncle Andrion. This was a gift beyond belief, an amazing start to his new life as an adult! Then he turned to Riki, who was smiling somewhat fixedly, and swept her up in an embrace.

"We can build it together!" he said, emotion surging in his voice. "It'll be just like we want it!" Riki hugged him back, tears in her own eyes. Oh, Fjuri! What were they getting into? She loved him, truly she did – but she wasn't *ready* for this! She wasn't even sixteen yet, and other people were already writing the next chapter of her life for her? When was there going to be time for her to set responsibilities aside and just spend some time learning who *she* was, what *she* wanted to do?

Andi, as oblivious as Fjuri was to Riki's hesitation, rose to his feet, glass in his hand. "A toast!" he declared joyously, "To our friend Fjurbund Steadfast! Happy birthday, and here's to many more!" A fresh ale was put in Fjuri's hand and he took a big swig, delirious with happiness, as glasses were raised around the hall. What an absolutely wonderful, totally perfect birthday!

Chapter 5: Meri Goes Shopping

"I'll be back before suppertime, Mom," Meri promised, as she gave her mother a kiss on the cheek and shouldered her pack. Two years ago, she would never have dreamed of going into Waterdon alone, without a screen of friends and family to protect her from the adverse reactions of strangers. Now, here she was being sent by herself with a list of supplies to buy, and the thought that someone would see her and be afraid – or worse, hostile – did not even occur to her or to her mother.

Leukalfar, dressed in ordinary clothing and speaking the common tongue, now roamed freely above ground throughout Iscandia. They were still far fewer than the gatti and saurions, who had well-established communities; but most of the Norsemen, Galise, Afrans, Remans and the various other alfar races had now gotten used to seeing them as fellow humans with something to offer society at large.

There was even a small, but growing, leukalfar presence right here in Waterdon – a goodly distance from the nearest dypalfar ruin. Those ruins, throughout the province, were now being made livable – occupied and guarded by the leukalfar who had lived beneath them for millennia. They'd eliminated the trespassing bandits in most places, and people coming to the ancient cities seeking dypalfar artifacts and materials were invited to obtain them through trade.

As Meri went down the front walk her vision was caught by a flurry of wings as a troop of her younger siblings, in dragon form, took to the sky across the road. They'd finished their afternoon chores and were now having a little free time, a chance to engage in their favorite type of exercise. Amid the six medium-sized red dragons was one smaller one, burnished gold scales glinting in the afternoon sun.

Meri let a little sigh escape her as she watched them go. Once Sigi's fireblood status had been revealed (and *how* laid-back did a boy have to be, to reach the age of eleven before discovering that key fact about himself?), it hadn't been long before he'd gotten the potion that enabled him, like Mom and Andi, to go dragon at will. The dragon spells he had already memorized without realizing it, just from hearing them spoken by Andi.

It would be so nice to soar far above the land, to see the mountains laid out beneath you. But Meri doubted there had ever been, or ever would be, a leukalfar fireblood. They had been such an insular people, in their little tribes, that it was rare for any outside blood to enter the gene pool – let alone dragon blood. All of the dragons that she knew who'd gotten the ability to become human had become men, too – though alfar might have made more sense considering their lifespans. It was a mystery, and she mused on it as she set her feet on the path toward town.

Rolf and Jurgen were on the main gate, evidently intending to make the Waterdon City Guard their life's work. When she'd first met them, a couple of years previously, they had been young recruits and as ignorant of the leukalfar as everyone else in Iscandia. "Afternoon, Miss Drakespring," Rolf said politely. The two no longer reacted to her as if she were not quite a person, but they hadn't warmed up to her the way they had to her older brother and sister.

She smiled and nodded at them, and said "Good afternoon, gentlemen," before going inside.

Her first stop, of course, was Brightsgate Cottage. She waved to Riki's friend Julia, out working the forge while her mom leaned up against a post, then knocked briefly at the Steadfast residence's door before going inside. She found Lifa sitting beside the fire pit, which was cold at this hour in late summer. She had a basket of mending beside her, and was wielding a needle in a purposeful manner. Her family was comfortably well off, but that didn't mean they had money to waste throwing away perfectly good clothing just because of a little wear.

She looked up and smiled. "Hi, Meri," she said cheerfully enough. Then she raised her voice to carry upstairs. "Edla! Meri's here!" "Be right down, Mom!" came the reply; and in less than a minute Lifa's thirteen-year-old daughter came down the stairs dressed for town. Lifa got up and went to the table, where a purse of gold sat along with a list of items she needed to buy. She handed them to Edla.

"If you get all the items on the list and there's some money left over," Lifa told her daughter, "you can buy yourself a treat. But don't dawdle too long!" Edla rolled her eyes, though her face was turned away so that Lifa couldn't see.

"We won't, Mom. See you in a little while." Now that her big brother was officially a grownup, Edla couldn't wait for it to be her turn – but five years seemed like an eternity.

The two girls made their getaway and set off, laughing and chattering together, up the main street of Waterdon. A new shop devoted to clothing of the less-expensive variety had opened in one of the cottages on this side of Bernard's, and they went in there to look around. Meri, like the rest of the Drakespring family, had all of her clothes custom-sewn for her; but some of the styles here seemed appealing. She didn't *always* want to look wealthy and refined.

The proprietress, a Norse woman by the name of Bruna Ingesdottir, didn't mind the girls coming in to browse without buying. After all, these children had parents – and the strange-looking leukalfar girl's parents, she knew (though she had come here from Normarsh only a few months ago) were wealthy. She saw them off with a smile and a friendly "Come again soon."

Both girls had lists of items to be purchased at Bernard's, and they made a fair attempt at bargaining the now silver-haired Galise merchant down on his prices. It was like extracting blood from a stone, but his asking prices were fair enough. Edla didn't need anything from the Potent Potion, but Meri had several chemial ingredients on her list and they went in together. Both of them liked young Lucia, who was much more engaging than old Adele had been.

Her purchases tucked into her pack, Meri exited the shop with Edla beside her and they beheld the marketplace before them. It had a well in the center, the Flying Horseman on their right, and half a dozen small market stalls ringing the edges. They both had lists of items to buy here, but of course they had to visit every stall to chat with the merchants and see what unexpected goodies they might have to offer.

It was such *fun* to be out on their own, even if ostensibly they were performing household chores. It made them feel nearly like adults, and in Edla's case this was close to the truth. She had already had her woman's blood, and would be a woman in truth in only a few short years. Having been raised in a family of Norsemen and Galise (and dragons!), and especially given all the responsibilities that had been heaped on her during the time of the Leukalfar Initiative, Meri too felt that she was about to become grown up. Yet, though she'd already attained a lot of her adult height, her body had not even begun to go through the changes of adolescence. The alfar races were slower to mature.

They hoped to be able to go to the Horseman for a snack after they finished their shopping, so they started on the left and worked their way around. Both girls were familiar to the long-time Waterdon stallholders, though it was only recently they'd been allowed to perform these errands unaccompanied by an adult.

As they completed the circuit and approached the last of the stalls, Edla stepped close to her friend and whispered, "Look! Edynis has a new assistant!" Edynis' stall was the newest in the Waterdon marketplace, selling everything from dypalfar household goods to grilled mandimant on a stick. He had been one of Andi and Mothris's earliest contacts among the Chalkhrazana, the leukalfar tribe that had made its home in secret chambers beneath Mzalendtham and were now, in increasing numbers, occupying the city above as well. The boys had had their best success among the younger members of the tribes they'd contacted; but Edynis was an exception. His age was indeterminate, but they knew he had an adult daughter. He'd seized on the chance for a better, more interesting life with enthusiasm.

His wrinkled, eyeless face broke into a grin as he saw Meri and her friend approaching. He knew well that it was this girl, and the curious circumstances of her upbringing, that had made his new life and growing wealth possible. "Greetings, young Merelle!" he said in slightly-accented Common. Working as a merchant in daily contact with the public (and with few fellow leukalfar-speakers around) had quickly honed his command of the language used by nearly everyone throughout Agena.

She smiled back. Edynis' presence here was part of the reason that she could walk around town unaccompanied. While she had visited in town only occasionally as she was growing up, he was seen by almost every Waterdon resident on a daily basis. As they'd gotten to know him, they had come to realize that while the leukalfar were funny looking, no doubt, they were really just people.

A leukalfar youth, who looked to be perhaps fifteen or sixteen, was standing beside Edynis. He nudged the older elf. "Grandfather, aren't you going to introduce us?" His accent was considerably less noticeable, his speech mannerisms less formal than leukalfar standard.

"Merelle Drakespring," Edynis said, "may I present my grandson Jymandor. He is newly come from Mzalendtham to help with the stall."

The boy extended his hand, a friendly smile on his face. "Call me Jymi," he said, adding "When in Waterdon, do like the Norsemen do, eh?" Meri stifled the impulse to writhe in embarrassment or giggle out loud. He was *cute*, with those long pointed ears and a somewhat surprised look formed by the wrinkles below his brows. He seemed already to have picked up a little color, and was not as pasty blue-white as some of the deep leukalfar she knew. Agoraphobia was heavily entrenched among her race, and it was hard for some individuals to overcome; but clearly Jymi had no problems with it.

She smiled winsomely and said, "You can call *me* Meri. Everybody does." As Edla stood by with a little smile on her face, the two fell into a deep conversation that lasted for nearly a quarter of an hour. Finally, Edla felt she needed to drag her friend back to Terris, and nudged her gently.

"Um, Meri, don't you want to have a little snack at the Flying Horseman before we have to go home?"

Meri started. She'd been so utterly caught up in her discussion with Jymi, she'd completely lost track of time. Admittedly he was currently the only leukalfar boy remotely in her age range here in Waterdon, and she the only girl; but even so, they seemed to be hitting it off pretty well. "Grandfather," Jymi asked, "Would it be all right if I took a short break so I can escort these two lovely ladies to the inn for some refreshments? I'll be back within half an hour."

Edynis wore a bemused expression. He'd thought that bringing the boy here to Waterdon to work the market stall would be keeping him out of trouble at home; but he'd reckoned without the presence of an eligible leukalfar female. Merelle was clearly far too young to mate; but he supposed that in a few years it would be a good match – her family were wealthy and well-connected. He was never one to pass up an opportunity. "That's fine, Jymandor. Go off with your new friends for a while," he said with the air of a doting grandparent.

"Oh! I almost forgot!" Meri exclaimed. I'm supposed to pick up three dozen leukalfar flatbreads, the soft ones. And do you have any mandimant powder?" The meat of the mandimant arthropod, as mainstream Iscandia was now beginning to discover, had many uses. It was similar in flavor, appearance, and texture to certain kinds of ocean shellfish, and was often served with fiery sauces to spice it up. It could also be dried and powdered and added to soups to give them more body.

Meri claimed a waxed paper packet of the flatbreads, and a small pouch of the powdered mandimant meat. Then she paid Edynis, tucked her purchases into her bulging pack, and the three of them made their way a short distance to the steps leading up to the door of The Flying Horseman.

They got roasted nut confections and some chilled apple juice, and sat in a corner far from the door. This time Jymi made some effort to include Edla in the conversation, though it was clear that Meri was very much the focus of his interest. By the time they'd finished their break, Jymi had promised to come and visit her at home in two days' time, when he would have an afternoon off.

He returned to his grandfather's market stall and the girls walked back down the main street toward the gates. "By the gods, Meri!" Edla squealed. "I think he really *likes* you!" Meri was in shock, and didn't know what to feel. She'd gone through her childhood without any playmates who were like her, but now that she was practically a woman here was this boy, this very cute boy, and she wasn't sure what she was supposed to do about him.

Get to know him a lot better first, she supposed. Romance still seemed like something distant, something that happened to other people. Growing up around men and the other alfar races as she'd done, she was as likely to think Norse or sylvalfar boys were attractive. But there was something about a leukalfar boy that called to her blood – and she knew that she was very unlikely ever to find a

Norse or sylvalfar boy who would want to get romantic with *her*. Only the love and support of her family over the years had convinced her that she was worthy of love at all, when she looked in a mirror and saw how different she was. Meeting others of her race and spending time with them had been a huge help to her sense of self-worth.

It was getting late, and Meri needed to get home. She bid Edla farewell at the door to Brightsgate Cottage, then hurried on her way down the road toward the Brightwater. As she walked, it seemed as if the sunshine was brighter, the birds singing louder, the butterflies' dance a celebration of joy instead of just random fluttering. Whatever might be going on with this Jymi, she couldn't wait to explore it.

Chapter 6: Supper Time

After returning to Waterdon for Fjuri's party, Andrion and his little research team (Andi, Rezira, and Gylabris) had lingered at the farm for a few days. In fact, he was stymied. They'd been trying for a couple of months now to figure out the secret to creating robon power cells, the power supply for nearly all of the dypalfar's perpetually running machines; but there was something wrong with the spells.

As both Rezira and Jerzha had confirmed, dypalfar technology was a blend of mechanics and magic – and while they'd been able to replicate the first part of the equation quite well by reverse-engineering working examples, they had not yet found the secret of the spells necessary to forge a permanent link between the power cell and the alternate universe where, it was postulated, alien suns provided a continual flow of energy.

So, while waiting for inspiration to strike, they might as well enjoy some time at home with the family. It gave everyone a chance to visit with friends, a chance for Andrion to sleep with his wife (something that had become a lot more important to him since he'd abruptly gotten twenty years younger last year), a chance for them all to be together.

The Drakesprings, mostly Andi and Andrion, had worked closely with Gylabris over the years since they'd first met, and the collaboration had been enjoyable as well as profitable. The magic-block collars they'd developed were now being manufactured by the Mirskhrazana, most tech-savvy of the leukalfar tribes, and had been sold to guard forces all over Agena. It was the first time in recorded history that law enforcement had had the ability to permanently restrain a hostile mage without resorting to killing.

Gylabris was now bunking in Drakespring House's small spare bedroom, which had housed their farm hands often over the years the family had lived there. After the transformation of Bernadette and Sneyagflug's dragon children into humans last year, they'd finished the remaining free space in the basement and transformed it into a dormitory. Now the nursery functioned as a schoolroom and temporary storage for oddments, and all the kids slept below.

Riki was now sharing her basement room with Meri, which she didn't mind too much. It certainly kept Fjuri from getting any ideas about sharing it with her. They'd also had Hegmar's crew in to knock out the front wall and extend the dining/kitchen/living room area out toward the east – doubling the space. That allowed the family to bring in more tables, so that at times when everyone was at home all fifteen of them (including Rezira, who now shared Andi's room in the basement when they were at home, and the five extra dragonling kids who lived there at any one time) could sit down and eat a meal together without leaving the house.

Bernadette (and others in the household who shared culinary duties) had gotten adept at cooking for a small army. She sometimes blinked in astonishment as she considered that thirteen years ago, she'd been thinking how content she was with just two children. But at least it was finally possible for her to begin getting to know some of her other children as well as she did Mondi. As a dragon he'd never been exactly cuddly, and he and his transformed siblings were certainly too big to be so now; but she was able to interact with them as their mother at last – helping to expunge some of the guilt she'd felt at having never been a mother to Gotteluub, the boy who had died.

With the plan for rotating groups of the kids every couple of years, Bernadette was looking forward (and not without trepidation) to having a chance to raise some of them as older adolescents, and some as teens. Thank the gods, the fact that they'd been born as dragons seemed to ameliorate some of the worst effects of adolescence on their human forms.

The form you took had a definite effect on your outlook – something she knew all too well from the time when, for more than three months, she'd been trapped as a dragon – but her twelve-year-old dragonling daughters weren't going through nearly the emotional turmoil Riki (or she herself) had at that age.

Tonight both Bernadette and Erik were handling the cooking duties. Andrion would have been willing to help, certainly, but despite his vast and ever-growing knowledge of magic he had not yet found a spell that would turn him into a better cook then either of them were. Besides, space in the kitchen was limited. Meri had returned late with the supplies she'd been sent to get, and seemed to be extremely distracted for some reason. Fjuri had come over for some sword practice with Riki (whose skills were improving, now that her rapid growth had stabilized) and would be staying for supper. They'd be needing the extra table tonight.

The Drakespring kids who could turn into dragons (Andi excepted; he loved flying, but Rezira took precedence over that) had all returned from their expedition to the mountains east of the farm. Flying for any length of time raised a powerful hunger in a young dragon, and they'd eaten a couple of deer and a bear while they were out there. They'd also returned with a large elk, which Erik carried down into their cold room after two of the boys had gutted and bled it. They'd become adept at killing these creatures with dragon spells, frequently snapping the elk's neck when it tumbled before Gale; or with their claws as they stooped on it while it lay stunned.

They were all at the age where children are starting to take responsibility – and aside from Bernadette's desire to mother them as she had never done before, their lives at Drakespring Farm were all about learning the skills of humanity. Sneyagflug had taught them how to be dragons, and they'd done well at it. But in their human forms, there was so much more to learn. One night a week it was the five new humans, frequently assisted by their more-adept brother Mondi, who produced the evening meal. The rest of the family were learning to get used to it.

The sixteen of them sat, near six in the evening, to eat stewed meat and vegetables wrapped in heated leukalfar flatbread. Dragons didn't really have an adolescent growth spurt, though their growth was faster in their younger years and slowed down over the millennia. This was a good thing, as otherwise Mondi and his five age-mates, even as humans not dragons, might have eaten them out of house and home.

Gylabris tucked into the meal, enjoying the familiar flatbread. Since emerging from his lair at the bottom of Mrzhgradfendz he'd gotten quite used to eating unfamiliar foods, but it was still a treat to eat food prepared by leukalfar hands, in the manner he'd become accustomed to during his long life. Most of the rest of the family were happy enough to eat anything, provided it was wholesome and delicious.

While everyone ate, drank, talked, and enjoyed themselves the doors of the cook-fire had been closed for the baking of an enormous pan of bread pudding. The scents as it baked had even served to increase everyone's appetite for the meal, and there were scarcely enough leftovers for one person. This was pretty typical.

The pudding was done, but would need to cool before it was consumed – with a thin, sweet sauce and dollops of whipped cream. Erik had whipped the cream, skimmed from the morning's milking, and set it chilling in their cold chest before he'd begun assembling the stew. Everyone was relaxing, chattering, and waiting for dessert when a knock came at the door.

This late in summer it was already dark out, and they all wondered who it could be. Erik, sitting nearest the door, got up to see. A young man stood there on the doorstep, illuminated by the ever-glowing dypalfar lamp Andrion had installed eighteen years previously. He blinked, gazing up and up at the huge Norseman who stood before him, blocking most of the light from the room behind him. Erik cracked a friendly smile and said, "Welcome to Drakespring House. How can I help you?"

The kid looked to be no more than eighteen, and he had circles under his eyes that suggested it had been a long time since he'd last slept. "You a messenger?" Erik asked, guessing.

"Erm, yes, messenger!" The boy replied. This wasn't his first time in Iscandia, but he still wasn't used to just how *big* these Norsemen could be. He'd fast-travelled to Waterdon, his nearest available fast-travel point, and then used his legs and a set of explicit directions to arrive at the front door of Drakespring House. He had no idea what day it was, but his body was telling him he'd better get a meal and a bed before he collapsed where he stood. But first, his message!

Gathering his remaining scraps of energy, Giovanni drew the sealed message from his pouch. "I have a letter for Andrion Drakespring of Drakespring Farm, from Magister Sextus Garibaldi of the University of the Magical Arts!" he announced. Then he sagged. Erik grasped the boy by the shoulder and nearly dragged him into the room, then sat him down at the nearest dining table as he plucked the letter from the boy's hands and relayed it to his marriage mate. Andrion had risen from his chair between Riki and Rezira, and took it from him.

As Andrion opened the message and began reading it, still standing, Erik scraped up the last of the leftover stew. The flatbread had all been eaten, but there were some bread rolls around and he tossed a couple of those onto the plate. He popped open a chilled ale and set it beside the plate, on the table in front of the young emissary. "Eat!" he commanded.

A few of the people in the room were glancing at Giovanni, looks of amused pity on their faces. Most of them were all too familiar with the effects of fast-traveling, and from the look of this young man he had come a long way. The rest of them had their attention riveted on Andrion, waiting to learn what message was so important that it would require a messenger to drive himself almost to exhaustion – and arrive in darkness.

Andrion read it through, the lamps in the room and the still-flickering fireplace supplying enough illumination now that his eyes were young again. Then he lowered the paper and smiled around at the curious faces waiting for him to reveal all. "Sextus – Garibaldi, he's now magister at the University of the Magical Arts – has been working on the same problem we have," he said. He directed the statement to Andi, Rezira, and Gylabris. "And he's convinced that if we pool our resources we can find the answer we've both been looking for. He's inviting us –*all* of us – to come and live in Roma!"

Chapter 7: Opportunities

While the young messenger slept like one dead in the kids' dormitory below, the Drakespring family (and friends) discussed the wonderful opportunity that had dropped into their laps. Andrion was delighted. He'd been considering trying to get Sextus (whom he'd met years ago, on his first trip to Remus – when the man was not yet magister, but only an instructor at the university) to consult with him, but hadn't wanted to take so much time away from Berni and the kids. And now, he had the perfect chance to work on the project with all the resources both he and the university's staff had to offer – while having his family close at hand.

"We can't *all* go," Berni said with a worried expression. Families in Remus tended to be no larger than those in Iscandia, and while she was sure Sextus' offer was sincere, she doubted he was prepared to obtain them quarters large enough to house the seven younger children. They hadn't communicated with him in years, so he likely had no idea their household had exploded in size. "Besides," she went on, "I don't want to punch a two-month hole in the kids' education."

Meri spoke up, "I'd prefer to stay here in Waterdon, really. I'd be happy to pick up more of the chores and help the younger kids with their lessons." All three of her parents looked at her with puzzlement. Surely, a young teen girl would be eager to experience the thrills of the big city? Meri hadn't yet mentioned her meeting with Jymi to her parents or the rest of the family.

Schickhimseel was the next to chime in, "Tapferverd and I have already lived in Remus for years," she pointed out. Their brother Wissliiben, who had lived with them there, was among the group now studying at Eberburg. "I'd just as soon continue our classes here."

"I can probably get Mama and Papa to come and live here for the duration of our trip," Andrion suggested. Now that his parents had been rejuvenated, they were certainly strong enough to ride herd on the dragonling brood.

"What about the milking?" Riki asked. This had been her chore more often than not for several years now, and it was one that required a certain amount of strength – reminding the cows who was boss, hefting the full milk buckets from the milking shed into the kitchen and up onto the counter to be strained into containers for the cold chest, and so forth.

"We can do it," Langekiind assured her. "We just need to work in teams." From the chorus of assent to that, it appeared that all of the dragon children were in accordance with Schickhimseel's notion of staying home.

"What about you, Sigi?" Bernadette asked. "Do you want to keep at your studies, or come with us to Remus? Her youngest son grinned back at her. Despite his coloring – and his recently discovered abilities – he seemed more like Erik with every passing year.

"I want to see Roma," he said. "I'm having fun here, but I've never really been anywhere else."

"I'd like to come with you too, Mama," Mondi chimed in.

Bernadette nodded. "And it's not as if we can't pop back home for a visit every once in a while." She loved her "new" children and knew she would miss them – but the past year had quadrupled her work load at home. The idea of a little vacation, living in the lap of luxury and enjoying the high society of Roma, sounded very appealing.

"Andrion, Andi, Rezira and Gylabris *have* to go, I guess," Erik mused. "And if Berni, Riki, Mondi, and Sigi are going, I'm definitely in." The adults began discussing logistics and scheduling as the dragon kids began chattering about what fun they were going to have. Being left at home with only the Lamontes for adult supervision would mean they'd have to be doing a lot of the cooking and laundry. Even after being human whenever they wanted to for more than a year, the former dragons still found those chores, ones many people despised, a delight. The possession of strong, clever hands with opposable thumbs was such a gift, how could you not take joy in all you could make and do with them?

Fjuri's deep blue eyes had grown darker, and he invited Riki along with him out the front door and around to the veranda so they could sit on the settee there and talk. A couple of the ever-burning dypalfar lamps provided some illumination here. Looking into her summer-blue eyes and taking her hands, he asked "Really, Riki?

You're going to run off and leave me for two months?" She looked up at him a little guiltily. Though they told each other everything, she had not yet found the courage to burst his bubble about her reaction to his plans for them to build his home – *their* home – together.

She squeezed his hands and smiled. "Fjuri, it's just for a few weeks! How could I possibly pass up this opportunity? Think about it – invitations to dine with the emperor, gala balls, palaces? I've been dreaming about things like that since I was a little girl, and now I have a chance to experience it for real!"

Now it was he who felt sad and guilty for failing to share *her* dreams. Though Riki had the size, strength, and skills to be every bit the warrior his older sister Anja was, Fjuri knew that the life of a bold adventurer had never been one she hankered after. Given that, he'd thought she would be glad to know that he was putting aside his own dreams in that direction to pursue ones closer to home – a rising career, a house close to their loved ones, the sort of life most Iscandia residents were happy to embrace.

Fjuri kept forgetting how young Riki was, not even sixteen yet. No wonder she was still harboring girlish dreams of palaces and fancy balls. Wasn't that what every little girl wanted, at some point in her life? And how many of them actually got the chance to experience that dream? Of *course* she had to go. If only it didn't have to happen *now*, just as he was eager to get started on their home!

He leaned down a little (not much; sitting, she was only a few inches shorter) and kissed her deeply. Oh, the sweet aching that caused! He was so eager for her to be his completely, and so envious of Andi's relationship with Rezira. Not that he fancied the petite dypalfar girl, but he was envious of the fact that they got to spend every moment together, day and night. He dreamed of waking in the morning with Riki beside him, her red-gold hair spread out like a wash of flame across his chest, her firmly smooth body in his arms… Cut that out!

The two broke apart, gasping for breath, eyes wide. Riki desired Fjuri as he did her – though she had misgivings about plunging into a course of action that might lead her straight to marriage and children before she'd had a chance to explore life. But both of them were inexperienced, and so far she had been holding him at bay even though sometimes she just wanted to throw caution to the winds. It was probably time, she thought, to bring up the issue with Mom (again) about giving her one of those amulets.

Fjuri was the first to break the silence. "Oh, Riki," he gasped. "I love you so much. Of *course* you should take this chance. Go have tea with the Empress, and fill up your sketchbook with the sights of Remus! I'm sorry I was being so selfish." Riki's eyes widened. No wonder she loved him, he was so sweet!

"Thank you for understanding, Fjuri. It won't necessarily be two months, anyhow – just however long it takes for Papa Andrion and the rest of the mages working on the project to figure out how to make robon power cells that work. Once they do that, we'll all be rich and famous!"

She said that last facetiously, of course. The Drakespring clan was *already* rich and famous – even Fjuri himself had found a part in the histories when he and Andi had traveled to Mrzhandtham through the last portal and discovered what, truly, had become of the long-lost dypalfar. "What if they don't manage to figure it out?" Fjuri asked, still a little concerned.

"It's not as if the rest of us can't just come home any time we want, doofus!" She shoved him on the left shoulder with her right hand, hard enough to knock him back. Riki was a *strong* girl.

He looked sheepish. "You're right," he said quietly. "But I'll miss you an awful lot. Who will I have to kiss when you're gone?" She favored him with a mock glare, which he delighted in. Riki was so beautiful, there was no facial expression she could form that didn't make him want to kiss her.

"I suggest," she said frostily, "that you practice on your hand during my absence. You could certainly use the training."

He kissed her again, until they were both panting. "You *are* getting better at it…" she said weakly.

He turned serious then, and said "We have to get together again before you leave. Be sure to let me know when you're going. As soon as you're back for good we can get started on the house!" Riki sighed softly.

Chapter 8: Seat of the Empire

The day of departure had come. A consultation with young Giovanni (before they had sent him, rested and refreshed, back to his employers the next morning) had revealed that fast-travel time between Drakespring Farm and Roma was close to thirty hours – a useful interval. It had resulted in the messenger, who'd been sent on his errand in mid-afternoon, arriving exhausted after dark. But that was better than the ten-fourteen hour fast-traveling time gaps that separated Waterdon from most of the other cities in Iscandia. On this trip, they could leave in the morning and arrive in the afternoon of the following day – starving and tired beyond belief, but at least in the daytime – able to contact the magister and be conducted to their new quarters.

They'd sent Giovanni back with a message accepting the offer and letting Sextus know how many people would be coming and when. They planned to fast-travel directly to the university, then take a night at least to recuperate after their journey before beginning the work that was the reason for it.

Francois and Christine Lamonte were already living at Drakespring Farm, bringing most of their personal belongings with them and moving into Andrion's room for the duration of their stay. The younger kids all respected him and loved her. She'd been a frustrated mother hen with only one chick, and had taken to her unexpected pack of grandchildren with joy.

Riki had already ceded *all* of her farm chores to Meri and the dragon kids who were staying behind; and was pleased to see that they were performing them quite well. Not, perhaps, precisely as well as she herself would have done them – after all, she was the expert and they only the young apprentices – but adequately. No doubt they'd all be experts by the time she got back, happy thought, and she could spend her days drawing – or writing poetry, or perhaps taking long walks in the countryside. Or something.

She still had not revealed to Fjuri the true depth of her reservations about building a home with him. She supposed she might actually *want* to do that someday, in a few years – just not yet. But there was plenty of time to discuss the issue after she got back. No point in making him any unhappier than he already was at the prospect of weeks or months without her. For her part, Riki was somewhat ashamed to admit (to herself alone) that the excitement of spending some time living in Roma was so great she didn't even feel any regret at leaving Fjuri behind.

Julia and Sintra were wild with jealousy, of course. Here they were, utterly trapped in the lives their parents had set up for them – unable to go anywhere or do anything on their own. Yet Riki, a full year younger than they were, was getting an all-expenses-paid trip to the heart of the empire – there to attend grand balls and meet important people? It just wasn't fair.

Riki felt positively wicked as she realized the satisfaction that gave her. What kind of evil person was she turning into? Happy at the envy of her two closest friends, not even caring that she was leaving her sweetheart? Good sense told her it was just a touch of fever, and not to worry about it.

Jymi had paid a visit to the farm a couple of days after they'd decided to make the trip to Roma, which appearance had at last explained Meri's desire to remain in town. He'd been hugely pleased to meet Gylabris, whose fame had begun to spread among the more progressive leukalfar tribes. And for their part, Bernadette, Erik, and Andrion had been happy to see that their "other" daughter had made a new friend. They doubted they had anything to fear from this relationship, given that Meri was only thirteen and not yet in adolescence; and they gave her permission to spend time with him – provided their visits didn't interfere with the duties she'd imposed on herself.

Bernadette was wrestling with her two natures as the final preparations were made. In her youth she'd been a carefree person who had always expected that things would work themselves out. And they usually had – for her at least. And for those she loved, as well. But an ever-increasing brood of children had claimed more and more of her concern, and a lot more of her time.

Her supply of love had expanded to cover the demand – but time is a limited commodity. To be letting go of so many of her responsibilities had sent her into a frenzy of last-minute safeguards and instructions, and as the hour approached for them to leave she felt as if she were about to explode into a thousand shards, each needle-fine splinter of her being targeted to a particular worry.

Erik saw her starting to lose it, and stepped close to enfold her in his powerful arms. He was currently the eldest of them, it seemed, though she'd been unable to resist regressing him by around a decade to his mid-thirties. "Berni," he rumbled quietly as he pinned her in his embrace, "it's all right. Just let go." Held tight in his arms, she looked up into those blue eyes so full of cheer, quiet strength, and love. She smiled beatifically.

"You're right, love," she said. "Let's just get out of here."

An hour or so later goodbyes had been said, supplies and luggage had been gathered, and most of the older members of the Drakespring Clan – plus Rezira and Gylabris – found themselves standing just inside the courtyard near the front gates of the University of the Magical Arts. From the height of the sun, it was early afternoon. They were all so excited that the thirty hours of elapsed time had not truly caught up with them yet. But they'd had the sense to bring along a packed lunch, and all of them were munching on bread and cheese, fruit and pastries, as they made their way up to the doors of the magister's tower.

Alerted by the messenger to their expected arrival time, Sextus was waiting for them as they trooped inside the tower's bottom room. Andrion and Bernadette had both been here before, and recognized him immediately though it had been some years since they last met. But their host took in the group with a look of perplexity on his face. His eyebrows rose at the sight of Gylabris, then kept looking back and forth between Andrion and Andi.

Finally he spoke, hesitantly. "Andrion? Is that you?" Andrion smiled warmly.

"Heh," he said, "I had a little accident last year. This is just a side-effect of a healing spell, I'm afraid. Not that I'm complaining…" The Drakespring family, Bernadette especially, wasn't eager to have it widely known that they possessed the power of rejuvenation. She'd be spending the rest of her long, long life extending the lives of others, if it came out.

Brow furrowed, Sextus turned next to Bernadette. "And you my dear?" he asked. "You don't look a day older than when I saw you last… how many years ago was that?"

"Don't forget," Andrion cut in, "Bernadette is The Fireblood." There was a strong hint in his voice that anyone should of course know that The Fireblood would not age as did other mortals.

Sextus passed it by. The alfar races could be found in all walks of life throughout Agena, so it wasn't as if people who lived for centuries and aged slowly were all that remarkable. Shrugging, he said "Welcome to the University of the Magical Arts, all of you. I'm sure that you are all tired and will be wanting to get to your quarters and rest. I am Sextus Garabaldi, magister of the university. Might I be introduced to the rest of your party, Andrion?" His gaze had fallen on Riki, as lovely as a sunset.

Sextus was a middle-aged Reman of average height, as bald if not yet as graying as old Paolo up at Wyrmshalla. He had a little paunch, which was fortunately disguised by his magnificent mage robes, and looked as if he spent the great majority of his time indoors. Andrion smiled, and directed the magister's attention to each of his companions in turn.

"This is my son, Andreas, and my daughter Erika. My co-husband Erik, of course" – the enormous, powerfully-built blond man nodded and smiled – "Rezira here and our leukalfar friend Gylabris, along with Andi, are the members of my research team. Then we have two more of our sons, those young scamps hiding at the back – Drachmondien and Sigmund. We call them Mondi and Sigi, when we can catch them."

"My goodness," Sextus said mildly, "you really *did* bring the whole family. It's fortunate that the house where you'll be staying is large."

Bernadette twinkled at him. "Oh, no," she said. "Actually we left six of the kids at home. And another nine of them are studying abroad." He chuckled, assuming she had made a joke. A family with as many as four children was rare, and twenty would be absurd – especially since Bernadette scarcely looked old enough to be the mother of Andreas. She didn't disabuse him of the notion – just smiled at Sextus and winked surreptitiously at Erik and Andrion, who were also grinning. She was tired, and she wanted to go to bed – not spend the rest of the afternoon explaining her family situation.

Some of the university students were drafted to help them with their luggage, and they walked out the front doors of the tower and south through the gates into the Floral District. The ancient city, laid out as a perfect square in remote antiquity, had a dozen also-square districts surrounding the much larger square where the Imperial Palace sat. The main walls, thirty feet high, were pierced by four large gates to the east, west, north, and south; and flanked by the university's campus on the north and the Penitentiary, where criminals were housed, on the south.

Despite their tiredness, all of the members of the party who hadn't been here before found it hard to keep moving. They wanted to stop and gawk at everything – the magnificent architecture, the sculpture, the barrows of the flower-sellers. Bernadette, watching her children's faces, was amused as she recalled how impressed she'd been at her first sight of Sylvanian – Iscandia's own "Imperial City." That place was a country village compared with Roma.

Andrion let Bernadette, Sextus, and their volunteer porters lead as they circled around the market square packed with colorful offerings and turned left toward the gates leading into the adjacent Pantheatos District. He brought up the rear, chivvying them along lest anyone get left behind and lost. With the city's geometric layout, the enormous tower atop the Imperial Palace rising in the center, it was hard to get truly lost here. But one could certainly get terminally distracted.

The house Sextus had secured for them was quite large indeed, and only a short distance from the gates leading to the Floral District. It stood three stories tall plus an extensive basement, and was just to the east of the massive Pantheatos from which the district took its name. This huge temple to the six gods and goddesses still worshiped across most of Agena made its counterpart in Sylvanian seem small. Nor was it the only temple to be found here. A little further down the same main boulevard was a smaller, but still large, freestanding temple honoring Aderos in his aspect as a dragon.

Sextus presented the key to Andrion, with a second copy for Bernadette, and ushered them inside. After some exploring and working out where everyone would be sleeping, they had their young porters deposit the luggage in the appropriate rooms and then let them go back to their studies. As the rest of them were getting unpacked, Bernadette and Andrion accompanied Sextus to the door. "Thank you so much for your kind invitation, Sextus," she said warmly. Andrion shook his hand.

"We all need to get some food, and then a good night's rest. But Andi, Rezira, Gylabris and I should be ready to get started on the project tomorrow morning. Where and when should we appear?"

"Meet me in the lobby at nine, will you?" Sextus replied. "No need to bring a lunch – I'll arrange for us all to be fed while we're working. I've commandeered some space in the Enchanting Hall for this project, and once you four arrive we can all go over there and I'll introduce you to the members of my team."

"Say," Andrion said before the magister should leave, "any idea where we might be able to get an early supper? We brought some food with us, but it's not enough to prepare a meal."

"Oh, I almost forgot!" Sextus said with a smile. He led them toward the back of the house, which extended quite far, to what proved to be a good-sized kitchen. In it, a short and plump, fiftyish-looking Reman woman stood chopping carrots.

"Cornelia, this is Andrion and Bernadette Drakespring. You'll meet the rest of the family later, I'm sure." To Bernadette and Andrion, Sextus explained "Cornelia is your cook and housekeeper for the duration of your stay. She and Marta, your maidservant, have their quarters in the basement. They have evenings after eight off, and all day on Apoldtag, when you'll have to fend for yourselves." Cornelia produced a slight curtsy, as the two Drakesprings goggled at her. Servants?!

Blithely ignoring their stunned reaction, Sextus continued. "Cornelia's household and food budget is paid by the university, of course. If you have any special requests for meals or if you plan to dine out, you should let her know a few hours in advance."

Cornelia nodded at this, and put in "I sent Marta out after some groceries. If you don't mind, I thought I would be serving just a light meal this afternoon at around four – since you're no doubt tired from your trip."

Bernadette blinked, then stammered "Oh!... That would be wonderful… Uh, *thank* you Cornelia. Say, what's the chance of getting a hot bath?" The lack of the wonderful bathing facilities they had at home was one factor she hadn't really considered when jumping at the chance for this vacation.

Cornelia smiled. "I'll just run up to the roof and light the boiler, ma'am. Then you should have hot running water in the second floor bathroom. The top floor bathroom only has a cold-water sink and toilet, unfortunately."

My, they *were* in the big city. The flush toilet and septic system Andrion had designed for Drakespring House had not originated with him. But here, instead of a septic tank, the city had a network of sewers beneath it. Many of the nicer homes had running water from roof-mounted cisterns, some of which was used for flushing toilets. Bernadette hoped the house's cistern would prove adequate for their big group.

She smiled warmly at Cornelia, and said "Yes, please. Or if you like, you can take me up with you and show me how to do it myself so we won't have to bother you." Cornelia was puzzled. This woman was well-kept and well-dressed, but she acted like a peasant. You just didn't go around offering to help your servants with the chores. Well, maybe it was just that she was a provincial.

They thanked Sextus and saw him off, then while most of the family napped or rested Bernadette nearly fell asleep, sitting up to her neck in a large free-standing tub of hot water – with scented soap in it. Ahhh, delightful! Cornelia rang a bell to announce the meal and all nine of them gathered around an enormous carved-wood table in the formal dining room – which was when they met Marta. She proved to be a young Galise girl, perhaps Andi's age, with brown eyes and short-cropped medium brown hair tied up in a kerchief. She served them their food but seemed shy, particularly around Gylabris – though the little leukalfar did what he could to put her at her ease.

They had a large salad with a myriad of different greens and tomatoes chopped up in it, and pasta in a red sauce that included carrots, onions, several other vegetables, and mushrooms. Both salad and pasta were served with lots of hard cheese grated over the top, and crusty bread rolls that had been toasted with butter and garlic. It was all delicious, washed down with water or a full-bodied, slightly sweet-tasting red wine.

Everyone ate heartily, and were sure to let Cornelia know how much they'd enjoyed the meal. Then, soon, they all went off to fall into bed – the food having made them even more somnolent. It was quite a few hours before they awoke.

Chapter 9: The Mask

The smallish figure, his face shrouded within the hood of the cloak he wore, entered the Sailors' Rest Inn in Roma's Waterfront District and peered around the dimly lit room. He spotted a tall, similarly obscured figure seated at a small table in a dark corner, a flagon of ale set before him.

Walking up to the table, he murmured "The ale is good here, is it not?" "It tastes of death," came the reply –muffled by a cloth mask that obscured all but the figure's eyes. "Methinks the innkeep should check his casks for rats." The newcomer seated himself, and he and the masked man sat looking at each other across the table. So this was The Mask, he thought, the fabled mage-assassin. It had cost a small fortune in gold, delivered covertly to his underworld contacts, to set up this meeting – and he hoped he was not going to be disappointed.

The presumed assassin spoke again, his voice low. "I may assume that you are in need of my… *unique* services, then?" The shorter man nodded, the motion visible as his cloak's hood tilted down. He spoke as quietly, and hoarsely – hoping to disguise his voice lest any here recognize him. To be discovered in this was death, and worse: the ruination of his entire family.

"I need a man dead, and I need another man blamed for it," he said simply. "There must be no question that the victim has been murdered, and plenty of witnesses to the identity of his killer."

The assassin sat nearly motionless, with only the slightest of nods to reveal that he had heard. "And who is this murder victim?"

Though leaning across the table no doubt made the cloaked man look more suspicious to anyone watching, he judged that preferable to raising his voice. "You know of him. A man now childless, whose responsibilities weigh heavily on him. It would be a mercy to relieve him of them."

"Him!" his table companion hissed. He produced a scrap of paper and a stick of graphite from an inner pocket of his tunic and wrote a number on it, then passed the scrap across the table. Unseen in the shadows of the hood, the client's eyebrows rose. So much? But once the thing was done, the rewards to be reaped would be endless. "Do you agree?" the masked man murmured.

43

"Yes," he whispered hoarsely, "but it will take me a while to come up with the money." The masked man made a slight gesture and a wisp of flame leapt out and caught the paper scrap, burning it to ash in an instant. Though gloved, the assassin's would-be client dropped the scrap and started back, eyes wide. A mage, indeed.

"And who is it," the assassin asked quietly, "that will commit this crime?"

It needed to be an outsider, someone without a lot of political support in the court. But who, indeed? "I will tell you who when the time comes," he murmured. "For now, I must get together the money and consider the details."

"When you have deposited the money with Croaker, tell him where and when we will meet again. You can give me the details then. Obviously, the killer will need to be there when the deed is done." With that the masked man rose and exited the inn, leaving the cloaked man sitting alone at the table with the untouched ale. The assassin could hardly have drunk any, masked as he was; and his client felt in need of a drink. But he decided to leave it. Rats or no, he suspected that it would indeed taste of death.

Chapter 10: The Work Begins

Everyone had slept far longer than usual, making up the sleep deficit from their long journey. And for a change it was not Bernadette who woke first, sleeping with her head pillowed on Andrion's shoulder. There was no bed here big enough to contain the three of them, so she would have to take turns sleeping in ordinary beds with one of her husbands or another – as she had done for months before the three of them were wed. This was another drawback of going on vacation that had not occurred to her before making the decision to come here; but it wasn't without its compensations.

In fact it was Mondi and Sigi who were the first of the travelers to slip out of bed and get dressed. The two, so close in age physically if not mentally (those born as dragons had about a five-year head start on those born human), had become co-conspirators in a plot to have as much fun as it was possible to have, for a couple of nearly-adolescent boys far away from home and the responsibilities of their daily lives.

The fact that both of them could become dragons at will was secondary here. Being a dragon was fun in itself, though it came with a price – you couldn't fly around for long before you'd be hungry enough to eat an entire stag by yourself. And, no doubt, be required to kill it and cook it by yourself as well. Being human offered a lot of advantages, especially in this urban setting; and they had no immediate plans to go flying.

They'd dressed in the kind of clothes they would wear if they were at home: comfortable, practical, a little worn. Neither of them had ever harbored any dreams of wearing fancy clothes and being waited on hand and foot as they moved in the rarefied circles of high society. What they had in mind was something more elemental. The pulse of the big city called to them, whispering promises of exotic delights and unlikely encounters.

The upper two stories of the place were given over to sleeping quarters, for the most part, while the ground floor held the kitchen, pantry, dining room, and something that was probably a parlor. Both Mondi and Sigi had *heard* of parlors, they had just never seen one.

As they came down the stairs Cornelia met them, and herded them into the dining room for some breakfast.

These two were tall, taller than she was, and they appeared to be close in age – though the one with the flaming red hair seemed considerably older, somehow. The pair bore a slight resemblance to one another, while not looking all that much like brothers – but then, weren't both those men supposedly married to the redheaded woman? Probably half-brothers, then. This assignment had sent Cornelia's curiosity working overtime. Why did that tall, reddish-haired boy look to be nearly eighteen while his supposed mother seemed scarcely out of her twenties? Neither of her "husbands" looked much older. What sort of things were those savages in Iscandia up to, anyhow?

Used to eggs and bacon or sausage, griddle cakes, and other hearty northern fare Mondi and Sigi were surprised to be served mugs of hot milk with some kind of a flavoring in it (it was brown, frothy, and actually tasted quite good) and told to help themselves from a tray of pastries. Some of these were not dissimilar to the breakfast treats of Iscandia, but others were completely unfamiliar. There was plenty of it, though, and they ate and drank their fill.

Having stolen a march on the rest of the family, the boys had hoped they might actually escape the house and go exploring on their own; but before they had finished stuffing themselves other members of their party began to appear. Andi and Rezira came down together, followed by Gylabris, Riki, Erik, and finally Bernadette and Andrion. At home, she usually beat him out of bed by an hour or two; but this morning something seemed to have delayed her.

Mama seemed well-rested and in a good mood this morning, probably the result of extra hours of sleep and not having to get up and perform any household chores. As the family tore into the collection of pastries, with some fresh fruit alongside (and, to Bernadette's surprise, some of that *kaf* she'd sampled in Zahar with the Afrans back before her first dragon transformation) she eyed her two younger sons. "You two are certainly up early," she remarked. They grinned at her. There was no escaping the All-Seeing Eye of Mama. "I suppose you're eager to go exploring the city?" They nodded enthusiastically.

The dining room had a good-sized fireplace, cold now in late summer. On its mantelpiece sat a clock, of a similar design to the one the nascent Drakespring clan had installed in their home all those years ago. The things were certainly useful! Bernadette, sitting beside Andrion, nudged him and gestured at the clock. "Did you tell Sextus you'd be in his lobby at nine?" she murmured.

He glanced up, eyes widening. It was already 8:20, and walking over to the university grounds was going to take a few minutes. He was used to sleeping as late as he liked, frequently past ten, when he was at home. Sigh. He hastily stuffed one more pastry in his mouth and washed it down with the last swig of the heavily sweetened, milk-laden *kaf*. The stuff wasn't bad, really. Maybe they should try to get in a supply of it at Drakespring House, or at the Academy.

"We'd better get moving," Andrion said to his team members. They all hastened to finish their breakfasts and run upstairs for ablutions and last-minute preparations before leaving. Andrion had brought along a number of objects connected with the project, and Gylabris had brought still more. Andi and Rezira were traveling light, though.

Half an hour later they'd bid the rest of the family goodbye and were approaching the doors to the magister's tower. Andrion had to admit, the layout Sextus had here was really a lot more impressive than the arrangement at the Academy. A much nicer climate, too. He felt a twinge of professional envy. They found Sextus awaiting them, and soon they had threaded their way across the University grounds and into the Enchanting Hall, a building devoted entirely to the practice and study of enchanting. It was not a bad choice, as enchanting was certainly a key component in the power cells they sought to re-create.

On entering the building they encountered a middle-aged saurion woman wearing mage robes. "Ah, Magister," she said, "these are the team from the Academy in Iscandia?" She seemed very eager to greet them, as if she'd been waiting a long time for this opportunity. It made Andrion and the rest of his team feel important.

"Aphinea," Sextus said with a smile, "this is Andrion Drakespring. He's my counterpart at the Academy of Eisenstag in Iscandia. His team members are his son Andreas, Rezira... you are of the dypalfar, is that right my dear?" While Sextus had not contacted Andrion directly in a few years, there were rumors aplenty circulating around Agena.

"Rezira Bagrum, of the Mrzhandtham division of the dypalfar," she said coolly but with a slight smile, taking Aphinea's hand. The lizard-woman blinked at her. It was *true!*

"And this," Sextus went on, "is Andrion's colleague Gylabris. He is of the tribe of leukalfar who were first contacted by young Andreas a couple of years ago, and has been a key person in the efforts to resurrect dypalfar technology. I believe you have reactivated a talking robon?" he asked. Gylabris smiled and bowed slightly to him, and to the Saurion.

"Several, actually," he said deprecatingly. "As we discovered last year, most of the automatons that the dypalfar left behind had been intended to communicate verbally with their human masters. It was simply a matter of restoring that which had been disabled. The departing dypalfar did not wish the mechs they left behind to be taken over by their enemies – and they tended to see everyone as enemies, I fear."

Aphinea goggled at him. She had heard the stories, of course. Leukalfar were little-known in Remus, and she had lived here all her life. Her ancestors had come to Remus from Fendil generations ago. But she was a mage and a scholar, and had always believed that the leukalfar were some sort of humanoid animals, like trolls. The revelation that they were humans (which her own species were not, though saurions were certainly very human-*like*) with a language and culture of their own had been hard to accept.

Now the proof was before her eyes. She took Gylabris' hand and said, "I am very pleased to meet you, Gylabris. I thank you for coming here, and I look forward to working with you." Andi smiled. He hadn't met a great many saurions in his life, as they were rare in the Waterdon area and his travels hadn't been all *that* extensive. But though dragons were *not* truly reptiles, scaly but warm-blooded, he still felt a certain kinship with the lizard-people. Whenever he felt like it, he too was a great big lizard.

He refrained from mentioning this subject at the moment, however. "Well, shall we go down and see the facilities?" Sextus asked. Saurions' faces, like those of dragons, were unable to smile. But her body language told them Aphinea was pleased to lead the way, proud of what they'd set up.

They went through a wooden door and down a flight of steps to a surprisingly large, stone-lined basement. "These buildings originally had no basements," Sextus was saying, "but during the time of my predecessor as magister, in the reign of Gaius Albus II, we needed more space and decided to build down rather than up. Didn't want to disrupt the university's architectural lines, you see. Of course magic was employed during the initial digging, but now as you can see the upper two stories are well-supported by stone buttresses."

A young man with reddish brown hair, of a height with Sextus and wearing mage robes, was at work at a table partway down the room's length, where an apparatus of some kind had been set up. He looked up and gave them all a lopsided grin. "Almost ready, Magister," he said.

"This is Louis LeBois, the conjurer on our team," Sextus told them. "Andrion Drakespring and his son Andreas, Rezira Bagrum, Gylabris."

"Are you any relation of Diane LeBois Baudin?" Gylabris asked. He'd worked with Diane and her husband Georges off and on for the past couple of years. Louis smiled and shrugged his shoulders.

"She's my second cousin once removed, I think," he said. "I've never actually met her, though. She left Auverne before I was born, though I hear she's making some amazing discoveries up in Alfenstein. Uh, that would be with *you*, I suppose?" Gylabris smiled and nodded.

Sextus took charge then. "I thought it would be best for us to begin by comparing notes, so that each of us can learn what the other team has discovered and what problems we've been having. Andrion, did you bring along one of your test cells?" Andrion nodded and set his pack down. A Remus-style enchanting station sat nearby, and he laid the spherical device they'd constructed on its work surface.

"Rezira," he said, "if you will do the honors?"

She was the most advanced of them in the enchanting arts, having a perspective on it that was unique to the dypalfar – though as the young daughter of the city's military commander she had not been privy to the deepest secrets of its artificers. A glow arose around the sphere, then sank into it and ignited the red light at its core. The central dypalfar metal ball in which the light was mounted began to spin.

Chapter 11: Tourists

As Andrion and his power cell research team were getting caught up on the progress made by the team at the University of the Magical Arts, the rest of the family were preparing to set out on an expedition into town. Of the five of them only Bernadette had visited Roma before, and that was years ago. She was looking forward to it as much as the rest of them were, and was delighted to find as they stepped out the front door of their Pantheatos District house, that the sun was shining. Roma got even more rain than Waterdon did, though fortunately with its extensive sewer system and stone-paved streets it never became a mire the way little Iscandia towns like Normarsh did.

As the impressive Pantheatos was just across the road from their house, they stopped there first. Here, a couple of centuries before, Crispus Salonius – last of the Salonius emperors (until now, that is) – had transformed into a dragon and battled the daimonic lord who had launched a province-wide invasion of Netherworld demons in an effort to take over Agena – and eventually, all of Terris.

Crispus (bastard son of the previous Salonius emperor, Argus Salonius IV) had vanished after routing his foe – thus closing the dozens of portals the daimonic lord had opened. Supposedly this was because he had given his life to provide a conduit for Lord Aderos to manifest physically in his form as a dragon.

But Bernadette, Mondi, and Sigi, all of whom could also transform into dragons, stood looking at the commemorative statue that occupied one section of the temple's heptagonal Grand Cathedral, wondering: Could the last Salonius emperor have been fireblood? Still, it didn't seem possible that any ordinary dragon could have defeated a daimonic lord with the power of Nergal. Not when even Tarragin, a god among dragons, had been defeated by a mere six humans.

From there they went down a long boulevard lined with residential buildings, moving south, and through a gate to the central square of Roma. This space, four times the size of any of the twelve districts, housed not only the towering Imperial Palace but also the buildings wherein the day-to-day business of running the empire was conducted, the audience chambers where the Convocation met, a largish artificial lake surrounded by lush public gardens, and the historic Coliseum.

"Sigi, can you tell us who the emperor is?" Bernadette asked, unable to resist making this trip part of her son's education. He, Meri, Mondi, and the five other dragon kids had been well-schooled by Francois Lamonte in recent months. How much of it had stuck?

All of them were gazing in wonder at the enormous palace that rose before them. It was the broadest and also the tallest building any of them had ever seen. "The current emperor," Sigi said with a grin, standing up straight and parodying a rote recital in class, "Is Giorgio Salonius I. He took the throne in year 2110 of the Imperial Era, that is nine years ago, after Emperor Gaius Albus II was killed, while visiting in Iscandia, by an assassin hired by a group of conspirators seeking to bring about an imperial crackdown on the Norse partisans there. The Convocation selected him to rule – partly because his family, the Augustinos, was descended through the maternal line from the ancestors of the Salonius emperors. He took the name Salonius to bring back the line."

Sigi took a little bow, and they all smiled and applauded him. He was scarcely an energetic student, and could not hold a candle to his sister Zuunenwalt, but he was bright and knew a lot more than people realized he did. Mondi chimed in, "And the next emperor will have to take a new name, as well. Giorgio's only son and heir, Bruno Salonius, died in an attack by minotaurs while traveling between Roma and Seneca around five years ago. As his wife is now past the age where she might have another child, he has named his sister's son, Tiberius Appolonius, as the new heir."

"Show-off," Sigi chided – but with a smile. They all continued walking the broad road that led around the palace, going in an easterly direction. Riki was smiling serenely, her eyes alight with interest as she looked here, there, everywhere. Roma had so many amazing views, so much to see! Smiling fondly at her, Erik threw an arm around his daughter and kissed the top of her head. "Glad you came, Rikita?" he rumbled quietly. She squeezed him back, her strength something of a surprise. All that cow-milking and swordplay had laid muscles of steel beneath the smooth golden skin. "It's wonderful, Papa! Where will we go next?"

"I'd like to see the Coliseum, if nobody minds," Erik said. Bernadette gave him a tolerant smile. In the beginning months of their relationship they'd slaughtered foes side-by-side in many a bandit den, vampire lair, and aptrgangr-infested tomb. But decades of motherhood had mellowed The Fireblood a lot – even if she and Erik *had* been in the thick of a battle together just last year. Erik had proven to be a wonderful husband and father, as happy and cheerful working at the forge or shoveling manure as he was mowing down his enemies. But he was one of nature's warriors, and there was no escaping that he was damn good at it. Of course he wanted to see the Coliseum.

The Coliseum, built in ancient times, was some distance beyond the palace. One of the lower structures in Roma's central square, it was a three-story square building with a broad circular hole in the middle of it, offering stone bleacher seating through 360 degrees for viewing of the contests that were held in the circular arena below.

The building was flanked by heroic statues of Saint Cornelia (after whom, no doubt, their housekeeper had been named) and Tyrenius, and backed by more gardens. "They used to fight to the death here for the entertainment of the spectators in Crispus Salonius' time," Bernadette remarked. Riki shuddered. What a pointless waste of life, and how gruesome that people would pay money to come and see it! "For the last century, of course," her mother continued, "it's been more about skill at arms than blood. Contestants fight for prizes until one of them surrenders. The judges can stop the match, too, if it looks like one of the contestants is about to get killed. Some people still die anyway, of course, but you can get killed walking across the street I suppose. And the spectators still get to cheer on their favorites and bet on the outcome."

"Did you ever do anything like that, Papa?" Sigi wanted to know. Erik chuckled.

"When I was young and foolish, I got into a few informal contests. Nothing to the death with my friends, of course. And then your mom and I 'won' contests with more than a few bandits. The winners of those contests got to walk away, breathing."

"Oh," the boy said softly, reminded that the stories he'd heard all his life were more than just stories.

They walked around the grounds a little, then went in at the front of the building. It was now past ten, and they could hear crowd noises coming from the far side of the curving stone wall before them. A smiling elf in a leather jerkin and hose greeted them. "Here to watch the fights, are you?" he asked them. Family groups were a common sight here, these days. "It's three guilders apiece to come in, and if you want to bet on any of the matches I can sell you a scorecard for an additional two guilders."

Erik looked around at the group. The boys looked eager, Riki less so, and Bernadette's eyes were sparkling. She may have abandoned her former bloodthirsty lifestyle, but that didn't mean she had lost all interest in the excitement of combat. Erik paid the man and got a scorecard as well, not because he planned to do any betting (how could you bet when you knew nothing about the contests or the combatants?), but just so he could get a feel for this interesting part of the local scene.

They turned to the right and went through an ancient-looking wooden door up a stone ramp to the stands. At this hour of the morning there was plenty of seating available on the stone benches that ringed the arena. Down below, separated from the stands by a stone wall fifteen feet high, was a sand-paved circular arena fifty feet in diameter with a circular iron grating set into the center of it.

"What's down below the grating?" Sigi asked, and his mother replied "When this place was first built, more than a thousand years ago, they used to have wild beasts fight each other – or sometimes, be pitted against captive warriors. None of that has happened in centuries, but the basement below the arena still has the cages that were used for the lions and so forth."

As they entered the stands area they spotted a squat, middle-aged Reman woman standing with her back to the rear wall. She had a tray suspended by a strap around her neck and resting on her belly beneath her prodigious bosom. On it were gold guilders and slips of paper. "Place your bets here," she boomed. "Two to one on Morto Avenzio."

"No thanks," Erik said, and they took seats along a curving bench in the front row.

Across the Coliseum they could see a sort of box seat area with three figures in it, seated around a table and looking comfortable. "Those are probably the judges," Bernadette said pointing. A fourth person, a broad man holding a megaphone, sat on a chair off to one side of the box. As some helpers assisted a very battered-looking man off of the field and his opponent, an enormous blonde woman, struck a pose, he put the megaphone to his lips.

"Winner of the match is Louana the Lioness," he announced. "Please collect your bets. Next up, we have the current third division champion, Andreas the Gargantuan Galise, with warhammer, fighting challenger Morto Avenzio with short sword and dagger." The crowd cheered as the blonde giantess strutted off into a doorway that led into the fighters' dressing room, where wounds would be attended to. In this day and age, they would probably just get a health potion and a sponge bath.

From doors on opposite sides of the Coliseum two new combatants emerged. The one nearest them could only be the Galise – from his size, flaming red hair, and the warhammer he carried. "Andreas!" Sigi and Mondi exclaimed in unison, grinning. The rest of them smiled as well. "Wait'll we tell Andi we saw his namesake fighting in the Coliseum!" Sigi said, and the two boys stood up to press themselves against the stone railing for a better view.

Bernadette, sitting next to Erik, remarked "I notice that all of these fighters seem to have stage names." He grinned.

"Well, they *are* performers. I suppose having a good, tough-sounding name helps you get a following. It's probably not just the purses they're hoping to win. Wealthy patrons, free food and drink, adoring fans… I wonder what *my* name should be?" He winked at her.

"How about 'Erik the Excellent' or 'The Iscandia Smasher'?" she said, squeezing his bicep.

"Hmm," he mused. "Maybe 'The Norse Annihilator'?"

"Your choice," she replied. "Let's watch the fight." They turned their attention to the arena below, where a dark-haired, olive-skinned Reman wielding two blades was facing up against his much-larger opponent. No wonder the odds were two to one!

The darker man might have been shorter, but he was powerfully muscled and walked like a panther on the prowl, ready to explode into action. Both fighters were wearing the official Coliseum garb, issued to all in an effort at fairness – though they chose their own weapons. But Morto had opted for the light version, while Andreas had gone for the heavier, and more protective, armor.

Both Bernadette and Erik knew that was a good choice, as the warhammer (while devastating when it struck) was a slow weapon – and you needed two hands to wield it, so you couldn't fend off your opponent's sword strikes with a shield. It all hinged on whether Andreas was faster than he looked. The man, as near as they could tell from this distance and angle, was a little shorter than Erik but even wider.

"Let the match begin!" the announcer commanded, and the two fighters began circling one another. They were both standing on the iron grid, which in dry weather like today's would provide acceptable footing. Even Riki was watching intently, lower lip caught in her teeth, as the two prepared to close with one another. Andreas was now facing them, and they could see an evil grin on his scarred face. He was not a handsome man.

Morto feinted with his dagger, flicking out with his left hand, and then crouched and spun to come in from the side as Andreas swung his hammer. He had more than a foot of reach on the smaller man, between the length of his arms and the length of his weapon. It whistled through the space Morto had occupied a split-second before, but the Reman had already dodged out of the way – striking at the Galise with his short sword as he came near. The blade scored the bigger man's armor, but didn't draw blood.

Suddenly Andreas surged into action. He *was* faster than he looked, and he had more than one trick up his sleeve. One hand slid up the steel shaft of the warhammer, and he was suddenly wielding it like a quarterstaff. It was poorly balanced for that, the weight of the head throwing it off and making it hard to spin – but clearly the Galise had practiced this maneuver a lot. Avenzio danced around him, trying to get at him with his blades, but his strikes kept getting deflected by the whirling steel shaft.

The crowd was on its feet, chanting "Andreas! Andreas!" Clearly the Gargantuan Galise was a big favorite. Sigi and Mondi were shouting along with them. After all, they were both sort-of redheads and at least half-Galise. Plus this guy had their brother's name! The crowd gasped in unison as Morto slipped through with his dagger and scored a bleeding cut across the bigger man's knuckles. Ow, that must sting!

It seemed to infuriate Andreas, but he didn't lose his head. He was a veteran of these combats, and many more lethal ones in his days as a soldier and adventurer before coming here. He stepped back nimbly, out of the Reman's reach, and then letting both hands slide down to the far end of the warhammer's handle he thrust it straight forward into Morto's midsection as he was about to advance again. Oof!

The blow had just missed caving in his ribcage, which would likely have been fatal with the force that was behind it. As it is, it may have ruptured something inside – and Morto was doubled over in agony, dagger falling to the ground. Bernadette gasped. Her instinct was to dash down there and administer healing, but of course that was absurd. Just like all those bandits and renegade mages she'd killed, these guys knew what they were getting into and would just have to take what came to them.

Morto's dagger had landed on the iron grating, clattering against the metal, but he still held his short sword. As he began to straighten up, raising the sword as if to strike, the Galise brought his warhammer down head first, breaking both bones in the Reman's forearm. The sword dropped from lifeless fingers, and Avenzio sank to his knees clutching the injured limb.

"The bout goes to Andreas the Gargantuan Galise!" bellowed the announcer as the crowd went wild with excitement. Mondi and Sigi were still smiling, but they looked a little pale. So did Riki. It wasn't anything Bernadette and Erik hadn't seen before, hadn't *done* before, and they shrugged it off. But Bernadette was alert to what her children were feeling.

"Well, that was fun. How about we go see something else?" she suggested.

"Not yet, we want to see some more matches!" Mondi piped up, seconded by his brother. They *were* occasionally dragons, after all.

"I wouldn't mind staying for a few more," Erik said with his lazy grin. "Why don't you and Riki go over and look around the Mercantile District?"

"That's fine with me," Riki said. While she'd found the combat exciting, a whole district devoted to shopping sounded fine too. And less likely to spoil her appetite for lunch.

As the women stood up to leave, they saw Andreas, his warhammer hanging down, step over and help his fallen opponent to his feet. Then he walked off toward his own dressing room, looking a little subdued. You got the sense it hadn't been enough of a contest to really stir his blood. "Sure you can find your way back to the house?" Bernadette asked before they left. Erik pulled a folded map out his pocket and waved it at her.

"Found this in my nightstand this morning," he said. "Besides, I'm pretty good at making my way around – and I can always just use my Agena map to fast-travel back to the university and walk from there."

They both hugged and kissed him, then took their leave as another match was being announced. For Bernadette, it was one thing to be in a fight for your life because somebody was trying to kill you, or stop you from getting what you needed. But to go in front of a screaming audience and try to maim someone just for money and the adulation of the crowd, seemed distasteful somehow. She was a bit surprised when Riki remarked, as they were making their way southeast from the side of the Coliseum to the gate leading to the Mercantile District, "I'll bet Fjuri could have kicked that guy's ass."

Bernadette eyed her daughter. One of the things Riki and her sweetheart did for fun together was sparring with practice swords, and he certainly was a lot better than Riki was – though the regular practice had improved her skills, too. But banging on somebody with a stick of wood was a bit different from going up against someone who seriously intended to do you harm. She shuddered at the thought of that kind of harm being done to her friends' magnificent young son, just as she did at the idea of similar harm coming to any of her own children. She'd lost one child, and didn't ever want to lose another.

Bernadette smiled wryly. "Did you see how ugly that guy was, Riki?" she said. "It would be a travesty to put Fjuri in the Coliseum and spoil that face of his." Riki sighed slightly. Fjuri was that rare thing – an amazingly, utterly gorgeous guy who was completely unaware of his own good looks. Before they'd gotten together, he'd confessed to her, he'd been convinced he would never be able to find a girlfriend. Clueless, but she loved him.

It was late afternoon by the time Bernadette and Riki returned from their explorations of Roma's Mercantile District. Though each of the twelve districts, even the one housing the Pantheatos, each had its commercial strip with shops, inns, and taverns, this was the place to go if you wanted the widest selection of merchandise. The only people resident in this part of town were the shopkeepers who lived above their stores.

The two were weighed down with packages, "just a few things for the house while we're here," and found the entire group gathered in the parlor having a sort of "cocktail hour" before supper. The women were flushed with the exercise of walking back here, as well as the fun and excitement they'd had, and looked more like sisters than mother and daughter.

They also found, on a small silver tray sitting on one of the parlor's occasional tables, an invitation for the whole family to attend a dinner and dance at the city home of Duke Enzo Terentius of Brindis, in the prestigious Scintillio District this coming Maritag evening. Riki was over the moons, and Bernadette was seized with anxiety as she realized the party was only four days away – and none of them had anything to wear.

"I need to get everyone party clothes!" she exclaimed, biting into a little slice of cheese around which a paper-thin slice of a salty, fatty, smoked sausage had been rolled and washing it down with a swallow of wine.

"You know what size I wear," Andrion assured her. He had the feeling even his fairly fancy magister's robes weren't going to cut it for an affair of such splendor.

"Me too," Erik pointed out. The last time he'd enjoyed shopping for clothes had been when he and Andrion selected their wedding outfits at The Golden Thread in Sylvanian, nearly eighteen years ago.

"You can probably buy me clothes too, Mom," Andi said. "But actually I think Zira and I can get away from the project for a few hours and come with you. We haven't had a chance to see any of the city yet."

"Yes," Andrion confirmed. "Today we mostly compared notes and learned from each other what *doesn't* work. Then we brainstormed some possible solutions, but before we can proceed with actual testing we need to do some more research. It's too bad Papa isn't here."

Francois Lamonte was one of the foremost scholars Agena had produced in the last few generations. That the Drakespring children got to have him as their tutor was amazing good fortune – which they, for the most part, did not appreciate. But his son was no slouch at digging up nuggets of useful information out of old musty tomes, either. "It'll probably be a couple of days of nothing but reading and research, Andi," he said. "Why don't you and Rezira and Gylabris just take some time to explore?"

Gylabris was now literate, one of the first of his race to become so in thousands of years. But he lacked the practice at research of this type to be useful for the task at hand. He looked a little uncertain. "I suppose it'll be all right, if I come with you…" he said, addressing Bernadette, Andi, and Rezira. He was all too aware that the sight of a leukalfar wandering around Roma, however nicely dressed and articulate, might provoke negative reactions.

Bernadette took another canapé and another sip of her wine. Her mood of effervescent pleasure was returning. "That's settled, then. First thing tomorrow we'll mount a mass assault on the Mercantile District and get everybody fitted out with finery for Duke Terentius' party. Once that's done, everyone can continue exploring however they like."

Sigi looked at his mother. "Do we have to go?" he asked, with that innocent and loveable expression that had always been so successful in the past.

"Why not?" she asked, "You haven't even seen the Mercantile District yet. Aren't you curious?"

Sigi ducked his head, and Mondi chimed in, "After you and Riki went shopping this morning we watched a few more matches, and Papa Erik got us some lunch. Then he gave us his city map and let us go off exploring. We met a new friend, a boy who lives here, and we said we'd meet up with him tomorrow morning out at the waterfront."

Bernadette cast her extra-large husband a level look. "You just let them run off by themselves?" she asked sweetly. He gave her the full benefit of his blue-eyed, innocent grin, and shrugged.

"They're big boys," he said. "I gave them my map, and they didn't get lost. Or into any trouble. Come on, Berni, think about what this city is like for a twelve-year-old. And it's not as if they can't handle themselves."

He had a point, she admitted reluctantly to herself. They could both become fire-breathing, flying, scaly monsters bigger than two horses laid end-to-end, after speaking a few words. Or blow an attacker down the street with Gale while they ran for safety. They were both also becoming adept at healing magic, and could repair any hurts in a few minutes' time. Erik's easy-going attitude was one of the things she loved about him, so perhaps *she* just needed to lighten up a little. She took another sip of her wine.

"All right you two, I'll buy you party clothes without you having to participate. But use your heads and stay out of trouble. I don't want to be having to bail you out of the Penitentiary!"

The boys grinned. "Thanks, Mama!" The wine was making her feel more relaxed by the minute, and Bernadette turned back to Erik.

"Okay," she said, "what's *your* excuse for not coming on the clothes-shopping expedition?" He grinned at her.

"Tomorrow morning at eleven," he explained, "The Iscandia Slasher is having his debut match in the Coliseum."

Chapter 12: Loyalty

The duke ushered his most trusted advisor into his private study. The elf had served not only him, but his father and his grandfather before him. He could scarcely imagine a problem he would not put in the hands of this, his most trusted of servants. The two took comfortable chairs and sipped at tiny glasses of fine brandy, before his servant revealed the reason he had requested this consultation.

His ageless features, usually so cold and dispassionate, were alive with excitement. "We have him!" he exclaimed with satisfaction. "He is utterly done for, and the rest of his family will go down with him!"

"Are you sure?" the duke asked. They had stalked this foe for years now, and had been unable to get anything on him though they knew he was rotten to the core – as rotten as they were.

"He paid a fortune just to speak with me!" his retainer assured him. "And then he promised to deposit funds to cover the cost of doing the job. I told him I wanted double, and he didn't blink an eye. He wants somebody else framed for it, but he is definitely paying for an assassination."

The duke smiled. This was good news, at last – but it wasn't enough to satisfy his plans. "It's no good without any physical proof, and there's not going to be any. If you go ahead and do the job, there'll be no way to bring him down without you, without *us* being implicated. And if we just take what we know to the authorities, it will only reveal us to him as enemies. There must be another way."

"I have just the thing," the elf assured him. "With the illusion spell I've developed, we can do whatever we want. Not only will everyone see someone else as the killer, as he desires – but the victim will *also* not be as he appears. We merely acquire a stand-in – some beggar from down along the waterfront, perhaps – then we abduct the intended victim, and place a glamor on the beggar as well as on myself."

"You know who the 'murderer' is to be, then?" the duke asked.

"He hadn't worked out the details yet," the elf admitted. "I think he only recently decided to speed things along. In any case, he's to contact me again after the money has been deposited and give me the details. I'm guessing it will be soon, so we should have our plans in place."

The Duke sipped his brandy and sat, lost in thought, for a moment or two before speaking again. "So… The intended victim wears the semblance of the beggar, I assume, and we spirit him off. But then what?"

"I'll cast a paralysis spell on him initially," the Court Mage replied. "I'll need some help getting him out of the palace, and at that point we should already have the beggar waiting in the wings. Ideally it should be someone of a similar build, and we will switch their clothing. It will require much less effort to create a permanent illusion if I only have to do their faces and bodies and not the clothing as well."

He went on, after having another sip of his own brandy. Ah, how the stuff burned going down and infused his interior with warmth! "Our men will carry off our 'beggar' to a safe location. We'll keep him paralyzed, so we won't have to worry about him making noise. I'll take the real beggar, who will be under the Command spell, back into the palace. We'll have to use the secret entrance, of course. I assume the guise of the murderer, whoever that is, and will be seen stabbing the disguised beggar to death."

The duke leaned back, watching his retainer work. The man's mind was astounding, the way in which he thought through every detail. It was thanks in large part to his mage's clever plans, over the past century, that his family was where it was now. And soon, they would be able to obtain the pinnacle of their ambitions!

"I'll need to get a look at the 'murderer' before we get started, of course. There will have to be time for me to see him or her, then make my way to the secret entrance and Command the beggar. Probably best if our men bring the chosen beggar there with some blandishments – offer him food or drink or whatever, and have him happily waiting around with them until I appear. Once I've ascertained he's there, we will need two false messages to be sent – one to lure the 'victim' back into the area near the secret entrance so I can paralyze and glamor him. Then after the clothing exchange has been made, we'll need a second message to lure the 'murderer' near the area. It wouldn't do to have a dozen eyewitnesses swear they saw so-and-so standing next to the bandstand or whatever, while another dozen say they saw that person stabbing the victim."

"This seems a little unfair to the 'murderer,'" the duke remarked. He was merely a man who took steps to ensure the prosperity of his house, not some evil villain. Of course he was perfectly willing to see a nameless beggar die in the furtherance of his ambitions, but it hardly seemed fair to do anything that would benefit his political enemies – like frame a fellow member of the upper classes.

The elf smiled, an expression rarely seen on that somber face. "I haven't told you the best part yet!" he said. "As soon as we get our 'victim' to a safe and comfortable place, I will administer a potion I have developed. It will wipe his mind free of all recent memories. Then I will use a spell I've also been working on, that will enable me to implant new ones. In his mind, he will know that his abduction was carried out and his assassination staged by my would-be employer, who planned to hold him captive indefinitely – since he couldn't bring himself to kill a family member. He will now revile that man and all his family, but will cleave to you and yours – as it will be your men who have found and rescued him! He will shortly be naming a new heir, have no doubt of it! And the accused murderer will then be freed, as clearly the person killed was only a beggar – I'll release the illusion at that point, assuming the body is still lying in state. That will make the identity of the murderer, as attested to by the eyewitnesses, so suspect that the case will have to be thrown out."

The Duke looked at him coolly. "You can really *do* that?" he asked, though he didn't actually doubt it. He'd known this man his whole life. How could there be anything he *couldn't* do? "I think this will finally gain us what we've been working for all these years," he said. "Let me know as soon as you have the details." The elf smiled again, and downed the last of his brandy.

Chapter 13: Putting on the Ritz

Maritag had arrived, and as evening came on the house in the Pantheatos District was in an uproar. This was far and away the most prestigious party any of them had attended, and it was not just Bernadette who was in a tizzy. Erik was the calmest of them all, as usual – his unshakeable confidence and sense of himself ensuring that all was, of course, going to go well. What did any of them have to fear, really? It wasn't as if their position in Roma's society was going to have any effect on their *real* lives.

The boys were uncomfortable in their fancy clothes, and Gylabris was nervous about being introduced to a roomful of Reman bigwigs – would they despise him for his race? Or worse, regard his fascination with dypalfar technology as something to be dismissed? He'd certainly gotten his fill of *that* attitude during the first several decades of his life. But the Drakesprings were his friends, and he was willing to put up with this… affair, for their sakes. He was not a complete stranger to the connection between socializing and politics.

Bernadette had selected a gown that she'd been assured by the woman at the garment shop represented the height of current fashion – for a respectable matron. She still looked good, but it wasn't as if she was trying to attract a mate. And she was determined not to outshine her daughter. This trip was making memories Riki would treasure for a lifetime, or so she hoped. Erik and Andrion had suffered from having their party clothes bought "off the rack." Both of them were used to the perfect fit of the clothing (most of it rather utilitarian, as there were no fancy parties to be attended in Waterdon) crafted for them by Gerde Snowhair at home.

Cornelia demonstrated an unexpected talent, when she quickly produced pins and sewing supplies and was able to alter the garments so that – at least – they did not hang on the two big, muscular men like tents. Bernadette was satisfied with the result. It was through Sextus that they'd gotten this invitation, she was sure, and she was anxious for Andrion – at least – to show some style.

"The Iscandia Slasher" had fought in the Coliseum a couple of times a day for the past four days, before being forcibly retired. He'd finished his brief career as a gladiator undefeated and for the most part unharmed (nothing a dose of healing magic couldn't put right in a minute) – but his wife, after the second time she'd been asked to apply that spell, had put her foot down. Unless The Iscandia Slasher was planning on sleeping alone from here on out, it was time for him to lay down his sword and return his official Coliseum armor to the dressing room for good. At least he'd found the experience a lot more entertaining than shopping in the Mercantile District, even if not something he wanted as a career.

Andi had put a lot more attention into his outfit than Bernadette had expected, given her experience of the male sex in general. And by the gods, did he look sharp! His slim-muscular build was perfect for the snug-fitting doublet and hose that were the current Remus fashion. Rezira, who would look good in rags, was stunning in a long, deep blue-violet satin gown that fit snugly through the bodice and flared to a full skirt that hung nearly to the ground. It almost precisely matched her eyes, and her glossy black locks had been piled on top of her head and held in place with jeweled hairpins.

Finally all of them were ready to go, save for one more arrival. Riki had had her gown fitted at the shop, and Marta had been helping her get ready for the past hour. The rest of the family were growing impatient when she appeared at the top of the stairs at last, and stood looking down at the floor below where her family awaited her. Bernadette's breath caught in her throat, and she wished Fjuri might be here to see. Outshine her daughter? Impossible!

One manicured hand resting gracefully on the stair rail, Riki stepped carefully down to the lower level with her head erect, blue eyes sparkling. The looks on the faces of those waiting below told her that she looked every bit as fantastic as that mirror in her bedroom had shown her a minute before. She too wished that Fjuri were here. Though of course, *he* thought she was beautiful dressed in the frayed old clothes she wore for doing farm chores.

Instead of being dressed up, her mass of lightly-waving red-gold hair fell around her shoulders and down to her waist. Marta had applied touches of makeup to accentuate her blue eyes and rosy lips, and the overall effect was… amazing. She'd never been more excited in her life. Erik stepped forward and embraced her carefully. "Rikita, you are magnificent!" he declared.

He loved all of their children, but Riki was so clearly a blend of Berni and himself that he couldn't help feeling his heart soar whenever he was reminded of how beautiful she had become. It was if he, so unmagical, and she, with only limited magic at her command, had created a miracle – the ultimate expression of their love for one another.

Riki gave him a stellar smile, then hugged her mom and Andrion too. "Sorry it took so long," she said matter-of-factly, as if her insides weren't churning. "Shall we go?" There was no way the women in their velvet slippers were going to walk the better part of a mile to the address in the Scintillio District where the party was being held. Seven of their party squeezed inside the hired coach, while Andrion and Erik rode atop it. They didn't mind their party clothes getting mussed. While Andrion had always enjoyed being a prominent member of Iscandia society, and enduring events like this one was a requirement of that station, Erik would have been just as happy working at the forge.

The coach pulled up in the street outside the townhouse of Duke Enzo Terentius, and they all disembarked. The driver, whose employer supplied coaches for many such functions, knew exactly how to reach the coachyard around the corner. There he would wait until sent for to return his clients to their home. Andrion handed the man a tip as they made ready to go inside.

A large and imposing servant dressed in the duke's livery was standing at the door, greeting guests and checking invitations. The invitation had come addressed to Andrion, and covered his entire party. He'd checked with Sextus and learned that indeed, it had been through him that Duke Terentius had learned of their presence in the city. But it had not taken any urging on Sextus' part to get the duke's social secretary to send them an invitation. Rumors swirled around the magister of Iscandia's Academy of Magic, his wife The Fireblood, and the doings of their children and associates as well. Roma society was dying to back them into corners and pump them for first-hand information.

The duke's townhouse could not claim palatial status – no residence in Roma was more than a fraction as large as the Imperial Palace. But it was certainly far larger, and grander, than the large and comfortable house where the Drakesprings and their party were staying. They walked into a stone entry hall much bigger than the front room at Drakespring House, even after the recent remodel, and came to a short staircase with another liveried servant standing at its head.

Below them a large room spread out, the house's Grand Ballroom one would presume. Finely dressed people dotted it, forming conversational groups and snacking on delicate hors' d'oeuvres while sipping fine wines and other beverages. The servant took the invitation from Andrion's hand, and announced them. Sextus had made sure that all of Andrion's party were included by name, and it resulted in an impressive recitation.

"The Magister of the Academy at Eisenstag in Iscandia, Andrion Drakespring. His wife, The Fireblood, savior of Terris, Bernadette Drakespring. Their marriage mate, Erik Drakespring. Their son, Andreas Drakespring. His companion, Miss Rezira Bagrum, of the Mrzhandtham division of the dypalfar (a murmur of surprise was heard from the crowd below at this announcement – no one had met a representative of that long-vanished elven race in thousands of years). Their daughter Erika Drakespring, their sons Drachmondien Drakespring and Sigmund Drakespring, and Keeper Gylabris of the Mirskhrazana tribe of the leukalfar."

Chapter 14: Meeting the Elite

Talk about being put on the spot! Riki thought, as she moved with the rest of the group down the stairs – body erect and head held high. Now that they were actually here in this amazing place surrounded by the upper crust of Remus (and, by virtue of this being the seat of almost the entire continent's government, Agena), she found her anxiety giving way to a sort of triumphant excitement. I *do* look beautiful, she exulted to herself. And if you can't handle a beautiful woman who stands five feet ten, go hide in a corner and wait for someone shorter to come along!

Heads were turned all over the ballroom as the party descended the stairs. Gylabris was the least confident of them, and Rezira took one of his arms as Andi took the other. They would never have gotten to where they were now without his aid, and it was brave of him to be plunging into Roma society like this – the first of his race to do so since they were Changed and enslaved by Rezira's ancestors. He turned from side to side and smiled at them. "Thank you," was all he said.

Duke Enzo Terentius, who'd been mingling with his guests, made a beeline for the foot of the stairs as the party was announced. These people were so very intriguing, and he had staged a social coup by being the first among his peers to host them during their visit to Roma. How fortunate that they had arrived during the time when he and his family were in residence here, rather than back in Castle Brindis!

He was trailed by two of his three sons, Arturus and Flavius. Young Gaius, of an age with the two younger sons of The Fireblood (or so it would appear) was off somewhere, preferring his own amusements to socializing with his elders. As soon as the group had finished descending the staircase he swept them up. "Welcome, I am so glad that you were able to attend my little soiree," he said.

Enzo was tall for a Reman, dark hair going silver, with deep brown eyes in which a sharp intelligence glimmered. He was still a handsome man, though age had scored lines on his brow and around his eyes and mouth. His sons, very much alike, appeared to be perhaps eighteen and twenty. They too were tall and handsome, with olive complexions, glistening black hair, and smoldering dark eyes.

Both of them took in Riki with deep interest, though the older one seemed more drawn to Rezira.

"Arturus Terentius at your service, Miss," he said with a bow and seized Rezira's hand for a kiss. She was a bit startled, having had little experience with Reman gallantry. "I am so very pleased to meet you," he went on. "Ignacio said 'companion' – does that mean you and Andreas are not married?"

Andi, annoyed at being spoken about as if he were not standing there at Zira's elbow (not to mention the fact that this upper-class shark was making a move on his beloved), seized the young Reman's hand in a firm, very firm handclasp and said, "Alas, we cannot be wed without the permission of her parents. And they are in another dimension, which is no longer accessible from this one now that the portal has been closed forever. It's an old dypalfar custom, quite unbreakable. So we'll just have to live together for a few centuries."

The young man, heir to the ducal throne of Brindis they supposed, looked up at Andi with a trace of annoyance. He was about an inch shorter. "Centuries, Mr. Drakespring? Will your alfar girl be caring for you in your dotage, then?" Andi gave him a big, confident grin.

"Not at all. I'm fireblood, and have the power to turn into a dragon at will. That confers certain … benefits. I'm afraid that I can't demonstrate here, as there's really not enough room. Besides, I would briefly have to become naked, and that might not be considered proper in this polite company…"

Arturus looked a little sickly at that statement, but seemed disinclined to challenge it. He'd heard the stories, after all. After recovering himself he asked, "Then, turning into a dragon makes you immortal?"

"Not quite," Andi explained. "It just greatly shows the aging process. The more time you spend in dragon form the more pronounced the effect, of course. But look at my mom. She first turned into a dragon when she was twenty-nine, and now she's almost forty-three. Yet she has spent hardly any time in dragon form."

His aura of aristocratic composure abandoned, Arturus gaped at Bernadette where she stood with her husbands, the leukalfar gentleman, and his father. Those two adolescent boys seemed to have already made their escape – probably headed for the food table. The red-haired woman was unquestionably a looker. At his age he thought anyone over twenty-five was old, of course, and he could see the marks of life on her. But no way was she past forty! It had been several years since Duke Terentius' wife had passed away, and the duke was practically breathing down The Fireblood's cleavage while her husbands stood flanking her. The slightly shorter of the two was glaring at him.

"Is Andrion your father, Andreas?" Arturus asked. He'd been utterly shut down trying to get next to Rezira, but his curiosity had been piqued too much for him to simply excuse himself and flee.

"As if it weren't obvious!" Rezira chuckled. The resemblance between them was clearer the older Andi got. "But he doesn't look much past thirty, either," the young Reman said in puzzlement. "Is your whole *family* fireblood?"

"Oh, that," Andi said deprecatingly. He wasn't supposed to talk about the Renew spell, which he himself could now cast – provided he was wearing the Wissagleb mask. "It was an unexpected side effect of being healed from a horrendous injury last year. He's really in his early fifties. But some of my family besides my mom and I are fireblood. And a lot of my brothers and sisters are actually dragons, only most of them are learning how to be human now."

"Actually… dragons?" Arturus asked dazedly. He'd never even seen a dragon, spending most of his time in Brindis or Roma. And now he was, sort of, talking to one at a party.

"When my mom first became a dragon she was … convinced to lay eggs and have some baby dragons in order to be given the information she needed to become human again," Andi explained. It was a tale he'd told many, many times. "They were raised by their father, except for my brother Mondi. He's the kid with the carroty red hair… uh… Oh! Over there by the food table with my brother Sigi and some dark-haired kid."

Arturus looked. "Ah," he said, "that's *my* brother Gaius. He's named after the old emperor. My family were really close with the Albus family."

"Aha," Andi replied. "Cute kid. I can almost feel the waves of mischief coming off the three of them from here. Anyhow, up until last year Mondi was a dragon and he hadn't been able to live with us since he got too big for the house. Plus, you wouldn't believe how much food a dragon can eat."

"He looks about twelve now, so how old was he when he had to leave?" Arturus asked. "Five or six as I recall," Andi replied thoughtfully. "But when he came to live with us he was only a little over a month old, about the size of an eagle, and his mind was already approximately at the same stage of development as my own. I was five at the time."

In response to the young Reman's questioning look he explained, "Dragons' language and a lot of their intelligence was sort of built into their brains by their creator, Aderos. And Mom taught all of the dragon kids the common tongue too, while their native ability to speak the dragon tongue was forming. She was determined they would be friends to mankind. It wasn't until last year we learned there was a potion and some dragon spells that would let dragons turn into human beings."

Arturus smiled. He couldn't help liking this young hick from the sticks, even if the lad's girlfriend was *way* too beautiful for him. "Thanks for all the information," he said politely and shook Andi's hand again. "Please excuse me. I'm supposed to be mingling!" Duke Enzo had led the elder Drakesprings and Gylabris off to introduce them to some other people before continuing his own mingling. As the host, he needed to welcome every guest personally. It was at times like these that he missed his late wife the most.

Meanwhile, Riki's attention had been utterly monopolized by the second-eldest of the three Terentius sons, eighteen-year-old Flavius. Riki was entranced. He was a few inches shorter than Fjuri but still overtopped her by a reasonable margin. Both young men had raven locks and were devastatingly handsome. But where Fjuri was shy, thoughtful, and sometimes so reserved he was unable to express himself, Flavius was witty, charming, urbane, and extremely well-educated. She had never met anyone like him before, and he seemed to be enthralled with her. He had taken her hand and then not released it, as he stood filling her ears with gallant banter – all the while gazing into her eyes.

Andi and Rezira went over to the food table to get some refreshments and try to catch Mondi and Sigi before they and young Gaius got into any serious trouble, and Arturus joined his brother where he was talking with Riki. Flavius smiled at him brilliantly and stepped to Riki's side, putting an arm around her shoulder. My, the girl had some muscles.

"Sorry brother, I saw her first!" he said. Arturus smiled back. The two of them were unmistakably brothers, though Flavius was minutely taller and Arturus a little more muscular. Probably Flavius would fill out in another couple of years. Neither of them had a build remotely as powerful as Fjuri's and probably never would. But they certainly dressed a lot better than he did!

Arturus bowed, took Riki's hand, and brought it to his lips for a light kiss. Mmm, she thought, she could get used to all this courtly behavior. It certainly made her feel like something special – not just the Drakespring family's live-in farm hand and kitchen help. "Erika, is it?" Arturus asked smoothly. He was a little more sober than his brother, Riki thought, perhaps not as much fun to be around.

"Everyone calls me Riki," she explained with a little smile that revealed her perfect white teeth and dimples.

"Riki it is! What lies has this rapscallion here been telling you while I was speaking with your charming brother and his friend?" Riki rolled her eyes sideways at Flavius, whose own eyes were sparkling with amusement.

"Let's see," she held out a well-manicured hand and began ticking off items. "You're the eldest, right?" Arturus nodded. "I believe he said you'd been betrothed since childhood to a woman whose mother is well-connected but whose father was rumored to have been an ogre or possibly a troll; that he himself narrowly missed being named as the heir to Emperor Giorgio Salonius after the tragic loss of his son; and that your castle in Brindis has some of the most beautiful gardens in Remus."

A look of incredulity spread across Arturus' handsome face. "All true, surprisingly! Except that I believe the unfortunate young lady's father was actually a minotaur. Or maybe some species of daimon. We still get those around here occasionally." She peered at him, sure that both he and his brother were having her on. At least the part about the betrothal, and that heir-to-the-throne-of-the-empire thing. But why shouldn't Brindis castle have nice gardens? Clearly, the family of the duke had money.

Flavius removed his arm from around Riki's shoulder and took her arm in his. "Come, my dear," he said, "Let me introduce you around." Bernadette, Andrion, and Gylabris were now standing, drinks in hand, talking with a tall ljosalfar in mage robes and a somewhat portly Reman with an unfortunate moustache. He was quite finely dressed, though, so probably he was a lord of some kind.

Across the room, Erik had been cornered by a pair of plump, well-dressed matrons of a certain age. Riki steered Flavius in that direction, preferring the company of Erik over that of most of the other adults in the room. As they came up one of the women was gushing, "Oh, my dear! When that servant introduced your party at the head of the stairs I recognized you immediately! I'm often at the Coliseum, of course, it can be such a bore filling up the days when my husband is out of town, and I saw every one of your bouts! You were absolutely magnificent!" She rested a dainty hand, nails long and lacquered red, on his muscular arm beneath the fancy silk shirt he was wearing and batted her eyelashes at Erik. He had the good grace to blush, and looked up in relief as his daughter appeared.

The two women turned their attention from Erik to smile at Flavius. He was a very good-looking young man, if perhaps young enough to be their son or grandson. "Lovely party, Flavius," the taller of the women, whose hair was a dubious shade of red, simpered.

"Thank you, Madame Delarue," he replied. "And you, Signora Orsini, I trust you're enjoying yourself? May I present Miss Erika Drakespring, of Iscandia?"

Riki smiled and curtsied, a glint of mischief in her blue eyes. "Pleased to make your acquaintance, ladies," she said. "I see you've already met my father, Erik Drakespring."

"The Iscandia Slasher is your father?" Violetta Orsini gasped in mock horror. She put a hand to her breast as if she were having trouble catching her breath. "How absolutely marvelous!" Riki got the sense that these women regarded Erik (and by association, herself) as members of a lower social order, and it irked her.

"Gladiatorial combat is only a hobby for Papa," she assured them. "He just wanted to have a little fun while we're on vacation here. But he *is* one of the heroes who helped to slay the Soul-Devourer Tarragin, thus saving the planet we're standing on. I hope you're suitably grateful."

While the two women stood looking taken aback, Riki turned back to Flavius. "Flavius, this is my papa Erik. Papa, Flavius is the second son of our host. What do you say we go chat with Mom and my *other* papa?" She led the two men away, head held high, leaving the women looking rueful. To be snubbed by this (admittedly, large and beautiful) snip of a girl!

As they made their way across the room, Riki looked around. Andi and Rezira were dancing over in one corner near where the musicians were playing, though most of the party guests who'd arrived so far were talking, eating, and drinking. There was no sign of Mondi and Sigi, and she feared they were up to some mischief.

The Reman who'd been talking with Bernadette, Andrion, and Gylabris had wandered off, but Andrion and the tall ljosalfar in the mage robes were deep in conversation as Riki and her escorts approached. They'd been joined by Sextus, he who had arranged for them to receive this invitation. Bernadette smiled at them as they came up and gave her daughter a little squeeze, put her arm around Erik's waist, and winked at Flavius. "Talking shop," she said quietly, and gestured toward where Andrion, Sextus, and Gylabris were raptly listening to what the ljosalfar mage was saying about some branch of magic. It appeared that Gylabris was doing better in this social situation than he, and they, had feared would be the case.

Before the new arrivals had had a chance to be introduced the servant, Ignacio, spoke up to announce another party of guests. He had a fine, ringing voice that penetrated to all corners of the room and somehow managed to drown out the buzz of dozens of different conversations – and the music as well. The more so as the musicians fell silent at *this* particular announcement.

"His Imperial Majesty, Emperor Giorgio Salonius the first! His wife, Her Imperial Highness Lucia Salonius. His sister, Her Imperial

Highness Mariana Appolonius, with her husband Sir Davos Appolonius, and their son, His Imperial Highness and heir to the throne of the Empire of Agena, Tiberius Appolonius!

Holy gods, Riki thought – all the while maintaining her composure. The reactions of almost everyone she'd met tonight had bolstered her courage. She was a tall, commanding, beautiful woman wearing a dress any aristocratic female in Roma would love to be seen in, and there was no way she was going to dissolve into shyness like some provincial milkmaid because the *emperor of the entire freaking continent* had just walked in.

For years Riki had regretted her height, but now she was starting to enjoy it. It certainly gave one a lofty perspective from which to look down upon those she wanted to convince were lesser mortals! Duke Enzo Terentius, who had been circulating throughout the gathering continually since the first guests arrived, materialized and led the emperor and his party into the room.

"Giorgio!" he said jovially, as if the current emperor and he were bosom friends. They had indeed known each other for years, and were on friendly terms. "So good of you to come! We'll be going in for supper in just a few minutes I think." Now that this, his most important invitee, had arrived, he was anxious to move on to the meal. It wouldn't do to let the guests get too drunk before they were seated.

The emperor and his party exchanged greetings with their host, while all around the room the other party guests were watching. Brindis was scarcely one of the province's most prestigious duchies –indeed some thought the place a disgrace – but the Terentius clan had blood ties with the Imperial family, and enjoyed an enviable friendship with the reborn Salonius dynasty.

"There is someone I'd like you to meet, Giorgio," the tall duke said as his servants converged with trays to offer the new arrivals food and drink. He was leading the emperor and his party right toward the Drakesprings! Despite her newly-acquired unflappability Riki found herself standing up straighter and suppressing a gasp. Even Flavius seemed a little on edge.

The ljosalfar mage had broken off his magical discourse when Ignacio's announcement had been made, and now the party spread out to welcome the emperor and his small entourage. This was an honor indeed! As they approached, Riki took in the party with interest. The emperor, Giorgio, was a fairly typical-looking middle-aged Reman – of medium height and a medium build. He looked to be in his upper forties, and his dark hair was rapidly turning silver. His handsome face, while smiling, had a cast of sadness about it as if he'd borne some tragedy in the past. Recalling what Mondi had said about his son, Riki guessed it was that loss that haunted him.

His wife, a petite and slender woman who was still handsome in middle age, had a look in her dark eyes that suggested she, too, had not yet recovered from the loss of their only child. The sister, Mariana Appolonius, appeared to be somewhat older than her brother and tall for a Reman woman. The resemblance between them was unmistakable. Her husband was little taller than she, and a bit on the dumpy side despite his rich and finely-tailored clothing. He had the intent look of a man who knows what he wants and goes after it with a resolve. No doubt he was very successful in whatever enterprises he had taken up. Looking at him, Riki guessed that he was *not* the sort of aristocrat who sits around on his family's money playing games and idling away the time.

Their son, the nephew Emperor Giorgio had adopted as his heir after the tragic loss of his own son, was of particular interest to Riki – at least as far as her girlish fantasies of court life were concerned. Here she was in the presence of a *genuine prince*, and unmarried she had to assume since there was no young woman accompanying him. Actually, he appeared to be no more than about three years older than she was – a gangling youth. Regrettably, he also seemed to have gotten more of his looks from his father than from his mother. In addition, a bad case of teenage acne had not yet cleared.

Momentarily Riki tried to picture Fjuri as a prince. She sighed a little at the mental vision of his handsome splendor clad in the brocades and velvets of Remus's nobility. But then she tried to imagine him conducting political intrigues and making nice with people he didn't like for the sake of alliances, and the image crumbled. Fjuri was too shy, and too straightforward, ever to be able to tolerate the hothouse atmosphere of the Imperial Court. Now Flavius, on the other hand…

She broke from her reverie as Duke Enzo began making the introductions. He started with Papa Andrion, of course. It was his work with Magister Garibaldi that was the whole reason for their being here. The emperor's air of slight sadness evaporated as he put on his party face, smiling broadly at Andrion and shaking his hand. "Magister Drakespring, I am delighted to finally make your acquaintance," he said, exuding genuine warmth. No wonder the Convocation picked this man for the throne, Riki thought. He clearly had a talent for the job.

"Sextus has been keeping me informed about your progress," Giorgio went on. "This work has immense implications for the future of the empire, and I'm delighted that you are so close to penetrating the secrets of the dypalfar at last. Once we can make our own power cells, it will revolutionize the way people live. Hunger will be reduced as food can be stored safely for longer periods of time, everyday tasks will become easier, and eventually there may be no more need for conventional fuels, with power for everything from mechanical tasks to cooking and home heating being provided by endless energy from other dimensions!"

Andrion smiled as warmly. He hadn't known what to expect in this new emperor, and was delighted to meet a man who thought as he did, who shared his appreciation for the benefits that new technology could bring to everyone across Terris. "Thank you kindly for providing us with this opportunity to work together with the University," he replied. "My wife and family have been enjoying this little vacation away from our usual haunts immensely." He failed to notice the sour look on the face of Davos Appolonius.

Introductions made the rounds. Flavius of course was well-acquainted with the royal family. They were cousins of his, in a way, and as he and Tiberius were close in age they'd met frequently over the course of their lives. The young man, unfortunate-looking though he might be, was very interested to meet Riki – and this time Flavius refrained from laying claim to her. He'd imbibed politics with his mother's milk, she'd be willing to bet. And though the whole business was quite new to her, she seemed to have something of an inborn knack for it.

Putting on her most precious look of blue-eyed innocence, Riki gazed down at Tiberius. He was a couple of inches shorter than she was, and might not be getting any taller at his age. "Your Imperial Highness, I am so honored to meet you!" she said, letting him take her hand to kiss it.

"The honor is mine," he replied suavely. "Had I known that Iscandia bred such beauties as you, Miss Drakespring, I would surely have traveled there by now."

Riki had decided to make a game of it, and her anxiety had fled. Much as her trepidation had evaporated while she, Mothris, Meri, and Mondi had been taking down that undead dragon last year. You just had to get out there and *do* it, and not waste any energy worrying about things. She smiled shyly at him. "Iscandia is full of beauties," she assured the crown prince. "And they're not all walking around on two legs. You should see the mountains!"

Tiberius seemed charmed, and while there was a smile on Flavius' face Riki sensed that he was not pleased to have the prince cutting in on his action. She turned her head to the side and included him in her radiant smile, just to let him know he was not forgotten. She was surprised to see a flash of helpless longing in his dark eyes before she turned back once more to Tiberius.

The emperor and his party were moving on, greeting other guests, but Tiberius lingered for a while talking with Riki (and, technically at least, Flavius). He was, after all, an adult – not tied to his mother's apron strings. There were other lovely young maidens in Roma of course, many of them of high birth and the sort of noble connections that might give them some hope of a royal alliance. But Riki's beauty was of an exotic type: she was statuesque, a golden goddess, and those eyes! And she seemed to possess both wit and charm in addition to her stunning looks.

"I have heard that two of your brothers are fireblood," Tiberius asked. "Are you also, Erika?"

"Please, call me Riki," she replied with a hint of flirtation. Why did this seem to come so easily? She was a little surprised that the prince was this well informed. Neither Flavius nor his elder brother had had this much information about her family.

"Alas," Riki said, "The dragon blood seems to have passed me by." She lowered her eyelids for a moment, the long and surprisingly dark (considering her overall coloring) lashes nearly brushing her cheeks. "Though really," she went on, "the idea of turning into a gigantic scaly monster and devouring stags whole – and raw – doesn't appeal to me all that much." She smiled.

Tiberius' jaw (receding slightly, a gift from his father) nearly dropped. He felt a curious sensation rising up through his midsection. I'm in love! He thought, then stifled it. The chances that Mother and Father would permit him to marry into a family who were not only foreigners, and commoners, but possessed of a taint in the blood that could blur the line between human beings and dragons (and hadn't he heard that this beautiful, incredible girl had more than a dozen siblings who had actually been *born* dragons?) were somewhere between zero and not at all. He sighed.

Just then a servant appeared with a bell, announcing, "Dinner will shortly be served. Please go in to the dining room and take your seats." He walked through the crowd ringing his bell and repeating the message, sending eddies through the crowd in the ballroom as the party guests began to obey. Those who hadn't been stuffing themselves on hors d'oeuvres were more than ready to eat.

Riki gave Tiberius a brilliant smile, then took Flavius' arm. "I suppose we'd better go in and get seated then," she said. Tiberius followed in their wake, his eyes searching the crowd for his parents, uncle, and aunt. Duke Terentius would of course have arranged for them to be seated together, with him no doubt on the end with some daughter of the nobility, the flavor of the week, at his elbow. He sighed again.

"I'm amazed at how well you're doing, Riki," Flavius murmured into her ear as they stepped through the double doors into the enormous dining room. "Are you sure you've never done this before?"

"Done what?" she asked innocently. Followed a moment later by, "Oh! Where are we supposed to sit?" She really *was* a country bumpkin, Flavius realized. An incredibly beautiful, desirable one, but...

"There are placards on the table at each seat," he explained. "The seating arrangements were drawn up by Father's social secretary, and as you and your family are new in town she probably put you all together. Let's look for your parents."

Riki felt a burst of gratitude at Flavius' kindness. He was not just handsome and engaging, he was willing to help her along as she navigated the treacherous shoals of this new and beguiling environment. The room was full of individual tables, each no more than three feet by six feet, which had been joined together end-to-end forming a U shape. There were more than fifty guests at this party, and the bottom part of the U had two tables while each of the legs also consisted of two. People sat around both sides of each table.

They spotted Bernadette, Andrion, Erik, Andi, and Rezira taking seats up near one end of the U's central span. Wow, Riki thought, I guess we must rate. She was a bit surprised, not realizing what a big deal it was in jaded Roma society for some new, interesting people with actual accomplishments to arrive. She and her entire family were like an exhilarating breath of fresh air for these jaded aristocrats.

Riki and Flavius made their way up there, jostling with other guests as everyone tried to get into their seats (and felt pleased or offended at learning what position they'd been given and next to whom). She happily greeted her family members, and slipped into a seat opposite them, where her name had been written in elegant calligraphy on a small, tented piece of stiff paper. On her right, supposedly, was Mondi. And on her left, to her surprise and pleasure, was Flavius!

He pulled out the chair for her to get seated, then took his own. "Did you somehow arrange this?" she asked accusingly. It seemed to suggest some deep plot, that she should find herself seated beside the handsome young son of their host – who had been her constant companion since they had arrived. Flavius held up his hands, radiating innocence from his flashing dark eyes.

"I swear," he said with a believable grin, "I had nothing to do with it! Maybe Lucrezia has psychic powers, and knew that as soon as I laid eyes on you my heart would be lost forever!" The twinkle in his eye told her he was not – entirely – serious.

She grinned at him, and looked across the table at her parents. "Where's Gylabris?" she asked. Bernadette smiled back at her. "He's been quite the hit with some of the younger men here," she said. "Everyone wants to know all about the dypalfar automatons up in Alfenstein, and he's been regaling them with second-hand tales of the way the robons performed at the battle of Osteon Rise last year. From the details, you would think he'd been there himself!"

Riki smiled. She quite liked the little leukalfar Keeper, and had begun to think of him as a sort of eccentric uncle. After all, she'd had a leukalfar sister since she'd been only a toddler. Other people might find the leukalfar odd or even scary-looking, but to her they were just people who looked a little different from the usual. She glanced to her right, wondering if her younger brothers were going to show up. Letting them run wild at this party had probably not been entirely a good idea.

Just then, though, the two of them rushed up to the table and took their seats. They both seemed a bit flushed, as though they had run some distance to get here. Riki looked down at Mondi and asked casually, "Are you boys having fun?" Her dragon brother grinned at her, a remarkably foxy expression with his bright red hair.

"Tons of fun!" he said enthusiastically. "Gaius has been showing us the whole house, and you wouldn't *believe* how extensive it is!"

He glanced around Riki to where Flavius sat, eyeing him questioningly. "Oh, hi!" Mondi said, with his usual ebullience. "You've got to be Gaius' brother Flavius, right?" Flavius grinned back at him and nodded, eyes twinkling. "Hey," Mondi went on, "how come you're seated next to Riki and Gaius is way over there on the far side of your father?"

Lucrezia, Duke Enzo's social secretary, had put the youngest Terentius son down toward the end of the second table that made up the crossbar of the U, between two middle-aged widows whom she hoped might, someday, be candidates for Duchess of Brindis. In her opinion, it was not good for a man with three sons to remain unmarried for so long.

Flavius shrugged. He had a pretty good idea of what had been in Lucrezia's mind. He'd known the woman all his life, as she'd held her post since long before his mother's passing. But he doubted her efforts were going to be successful. His mother had been the only woman Duke Enzo had ever wanted to marry, and though there had been brief liaisons since her death Flavius doubted he would ever find himself with a stepmother. At this point an army of servants came in bearing trays of food, and all of the guests found their attention drawn to the steaming platters that appeared before them.

The meal was opulent beyond belief. Riki had enjoyed sophisticated food many times at the Bathing Maiden, the inn owned by her family since before she was born. But those were normal meals, with maybe an appetizer and perhaps a salad plus bread and a couple of side dishes in addition to whatever the main course might be. Here, the courses seemed endless – as if it were impossible for this rarefied breed of human animal to be fed on less than a dozen or two dishes – each more exotic than the last.

At their "home" in the Pantheatos district Cornelia had served them many Reman dishes, some of them familiar to Riki due to Uncle Lev's Remus connections. Long before he'd moved to this province with his partner, people in the Waterdon area had learned to enjoy pasta. Some other of Cornelia's offerings had been less familiar, but all delicious – and Riki had a good appetite. Even without the exercise of sword practice or farm chores she'd been packing everything away, and was beginning to worry about putting on weight. But this "little dinner" was to the meals Cornelia prepared as Roma's Mercantile District was to Waterdon's central area with its three major merchants and half a dozen stalls. She had trouble maintaining her composure.

The boys to her right were tearing into everything that looked good as if they were in danger of starving, but Riki was trying to pace herself. "Good idea, just take a taste of everything," Flavius advised. "There are going to be around two dozen courses, and if you find something particularly delicious take a little more – or leave it if it's not to your taste. But save room for dessert!"

She smiled gratefully at him, and took a second bite of a dish that seemed to blend broad pasta noodles with an incredible mixture of rich sauce, several cheeses, savory meats, and mushrooms. Ooh, she'd like to get the recipe for that! She'd been cooking more and more over the past year, and was really beginning to enjoy it.

Unlike meals Riki was used to at home there was no ale or mead offered as a beverage – just cold spring water, chilled fruit juices, and a profusion of wines. She found herself drinking more wine than she would usually have done, and by the time the desserts began to arrive (also accompanied by a selection of sweet, powerfully alcoholic wines) she was beginning to feel as if she were floating on a sea of happy repletion. By the gods, how much had she eaten? Would she be bursting out of this dress before the night was over?

After the last courses Duke Enzo stood and thanked all of his guests for attending, then invited them to dance on into the evening. Many of the older guests would probably be leaving soon, but Mondi and Sigi were off like a shot. Riki suspected they were not running off to dance, and she spotted them reconnecting with Gaius before vanishing from the dining room.

Flavius took her arm again, and murmured "As your brother said, the house is quite extensive. May I give you a tour?" She smiled at him and nodded, and they swept from the room. Despite feeling a little too relaxed Riki was alert to the possibility he might be hoping to show her his bedroom; but Flavius was a perfect gentlemen.

They surveyed the kitchen (an enormous room that filled Riki with envy, having been cooking over an open fire in an area with perhaps six square feet of counter space for years), then ascended a magnificent staircase to the middle floor. Here there were parlors, a music room, and a hallway along which doors opened to bedrooms. But he didn't offer to take her into any of those.

They came to another staircase, and Riki asked "How many floors are there?"

"Up those stairs is the top floor," Flavius replied. "There are more bedrooms up there and a glassed-in conservatory. When my mother was alive it was full of exotic plants, but it's fallen into disuse now."

"That's a shame," she said a little wistfully, sad to think of this all-male household and the boys growing up without a mother. She and her own mom might knock heads from time to time, but she couldn't imagine life without her.

"There is one thing up there I'd like to show you, though," Flavius said, and took her hand to lead her up the stairs. They turned down a hallway and went into a smallish sitting room, on the outer wall of which stood a pair of doors made from medium-size panes of clear glass. There was nothing like that in Iscandia, as far as she knew. Flavius led the way and opened the doors, which gave out onto a large balcony. Flowering potted plants stood on either side of it.

"Come on," he said eagerly. "The view of the city from here is wonderful." Delighted and intrigued, Riki stepped out onto the balcony and leaned on the decorative iron railing. This side of the house faced the city's center and there was a view of the Imperial Palace's tower. Though night had fallen there were many lights to be seen, and the view was entrancing.

She shivered slightly. Her dress exposed quite a bit of skin, and now in early autumn the nights were getting chilly – even this far south of Waterdon. Flavius put an arm around her shoulders and snuggled her close. "My home," he said softly, gesturing out beyond the balcony. "Isn't it beautiful?"

Riki leaned into him a little. She felt so languorous, and he did provide some warmth. The evening had been absolutely amazing! "I thought you were born and raised in Brindis?" she asked, confused. He smiled at her in the darkness.

"I was born in Brindis, and my ancestors have been dukes there for hundreds of years," he admitted. "But Mother was a Roma girl born and bred and she had us spend as much time as possible here in this house. I'm afraid the city of Brindis is kind of… run down."

This was the first time all evening that Flavius had let down his charming mask and spoken from the heart, Riki thought. It warmed her toward him, and as she turned her head to look into his eyes he cupped her face with his free hand and prepared to kiss her. Suddenly there was a small hail of pebbles falling on them from above, a scraping sound, and an enormous, leathery-winged shape hurtled down on them out the darkness!

As it came past Riki got a good look at it, and her panic subsided. They heard a whoop of exhilaration, and realized that there was a figure seated on the creature's back as it glided down to land in the street below. The mood shattered, Flavius stared down in disbelief. "What in all the hells was *that*?" he gasped. Riki leaned in and squeezed his hand where it had a white-knuckled grip on the balcony's railing. "It's all right," she said softly. "That was just my brother. And yours, I believe…"

Chapter 15: Longing

Fjuri sat down with a sigh, resting his back against the half-finished masonry wall, and began digging his lunch out of the pack he'd brought to work with him. He was eagerly sinking his teeth into a sliced bread roll heaped with cheese and cold roast beef, when a figure flopped down beside him.

"About time," she said in a hearty voice, digging into a small pack for her own lunch. "My stomach thinks my throat's been cut!"

"Mmrmph!" Fjuri acknowledged, then when he'd cleared his mouth said "Hi, Inge. I didn't see you today. Where are you working?" The tall, muscular young woman was just his own age, her long auburn hair caught in a braid down her back.

Women in the construction industry weren't common, but Inge had the skills to go with her strength and she was a valued member of Hegmar's crew. She'd joined them on her arrival in Waterdon a couple of months before, and had been one of the people toasting him at his birthday party a few weeks ago. She had a fresh, open face tanned from their outdoor work, with a spray of freckles across her nose, and more than one of Fjuri's fellow crew members had expressed interest in her.

Inge gave him a white-toothed grin, her emerald-green eyes sparkling, and said "Oh, I'm working with the framing crew at the new house on the far side of the development." Canny Hegmar had acquired a goodly stretch of the rolling prairie west of the city walls, and had subdivided it into parcels – one of which Fjuri now owned. As people came to the city and sought housing, his enterprise had doubled in size yet was still perpetually busy, erecting custom homes on the new lots.

Fjuri took another bite of his lunch and cocked an eyebrow at her. When he could speak again he asked, "You're working over there and you came all the way over here to eat your lunch? Why?" She grinned again.

"Because I felt like eating my lunch with *you*, Fjuri. I'd have thought that would be obvious."

Uneasily, he pretended to be lost in the enjoyment of his food rather than responding to her. He was not nearly as shy and tongue-tied around women as he'd been a couple of years before, but this was not the first time Inge had been forward with him and he didn't know what to make of it. She had guys chatting her up and asking her to spend time with them all the time – why pick on him, when he had a steady girlfriend?

Fjuri was, truly, clueless when it came to an understanding of the effect his looks had on women. The fact that he had a hard time holding up his end of the conversation meant nothing when compared with his tall, muscular body and handsome face. But until Riki had ambushed him in the front yard at Drakespring Farm last year, he'd been too shy to respond to any girl's advances.

It occurred to him that Inge had gotten a lot more aggressive since Riki had left. She'd been gone for a couple of weeks now and there'd been no word – not that it would have been easy for her to send any. It would cost the earth to hire a messenger, and days of time for her to return to Waterdon for a visit.

Inge broke the silence to remark casually, "So, your rich little sweetheart ran off to the big city and left you behind, eh?" Riki was certainly not "little," in fact she was the same height as Inge; but from her lofty vantage point of two more years of life experience, Inge regarded the Drakespring girl as little more than a child.

Fjuri smarted at the dig. Though the Drakesprings and the Steadfasts had been close friends throughout his life, the difference in the two families' financial status was undeniable. With her beauty and her family's wealth, Riki could make a much better match than a guy who was the son of a builder and a housewife. Perhaps even now, she was meeting some prince or heir to a duchy who would sweep her off her feet.

"I suppose *you'd* turn down the chance for a free vacation in Roma?" he asked her resentfully. Inge slapped her leather-clad thigh.

"Hah!" she crowed, "As if anybody would give *me* a free vacation anywhere. Unlike some people, I have to work for a living!"

"Riki's only fifteen," Fjuri pointed out. "And her folks may have lots of money, but they all work. Plus she's had to do heavy farm chores since she was old enough to lift a hoe. You shouldn't begrudge her the chance to visit with the upper-ups and see what it's like living in a castle with servants, and all. She'll be back home hoeing the cabbage patch again before long."

Inge smiled sympathetically at him and laid a reassuring (not so reassuring as all that!) hand on Fjuri's knee. "I'm sorry, Fjuri," she said sincerely. "I didn't mean to bad-mouth your girl. I'm sure in a few years, after she's had a little more experience of the world, she'll find something worthwhile to do with her time. Like raising a pack of your babies, eh? I understand her mom pops them out like bunnies."

Fjuri flinched. Truly, he did want to raise children with Riki someday. But the thought of all that responsibility when he wasn't yet nineteen years old, and the idea of an endless stream of babies, made him feel uneasy.

"There's plenty of time for that in the future," he said quietly.

"That's right," Inge said, squeezing his knee and sending a little thrill up his leg. "But in the meantime, haven't you ever wondered what it would be like to be with a woman, a real grown-up woman?"

He flushed. Oh gods, yes! Here he was an eighteen-year-old virgin, and his best friend – months younger – had been in an adult relationship with *his* beloved for more than a year. Andi hadn't talked to him about it much, for though they were close friends it seemed like a violation of Rezira's privacy to go into detail. He scarcely knew anything about the subject, his parents being as reserved as he was.

"I want my first time to be with Riki," he mumbled. Inge looked at him wide-eyed.

"You're both still virgins?" she asked, apparently shocked. Fjuri flushed again and nodded. "But don't you want to be able to thrill her, to make love to her skillfully her first time so that she'll enjoy the experience?" Nod. "Then you need to take some lessons, first! It's the worst idea in the world for a man to lose his virginity with his virginal girlfriend. You'd be clumsy, the experience would be awkward and painful, and she might think that was what it was *supposed* to be like." She shook her head. "Nope, nope, *bad* idea."

Fjuri stared at her. She had a point, he supposed, though Andi and Rezira had both been virgins the first time they made love and *that* had turned out all right. Was Inge feeding him a line, hoping to get her hooks into him? She had finished eating her lunch and now she leapt to her feet, dusting crumbs off of her thighs. She *was* a fine figure of a young woman, if not a patch on his Riki. "I've got a room at the Horseman, if you're interested in picking up a few tips," she said. Then she walked off, hips swinging, and left Fjuri gaping at her retreating back.

Chapter 16: Exploration

The morning after the party the family members who had partaken of wine the night before were slow to arise – but by midmorning they were all gathered around the breakfast table. It was Cornelia's day off, and she was already gone – visiting her married daughter and grandchildren in another part of the city. But she'd left them with a well-stocked larder and Erik, less hung over than the rest of the adults, had whipped up something for them all to eat.

After several cups of tea and couple of bread rolls with jam Andrion was feeling pretty good. Hell, when he thought back to how he'd been feeling a couple of years ago, he *always* felt good these days. The aches and pains of advancing age had all been left behind. He smiled benignly on his daughter, who seemed a little subdued this morning. Andi and Rezira, at least, were looking cheerful and alert.

They all had the day off from the university, but would be back at work on the power cell project tomorrow. The results of research by Andrion and his University colleagues had turned up an interesting new direction, but their experiments the past couple of days had been inconclusive.

"You'll all be delighted to know," he said to the group at large, "that the emperor himself has extended an invitation to all of us to attend a grand gala at the Imperial Palace next Maritag. There's to be another outrageous feast, and performances by some of the finest singers and musicians in Agena. Everyone who was at the party last night will be there, and quite a few others as well. Some of the aristocracy are traveling in from as far away as Alvenwald."

Bernadette looked at her daughter and, correctly assessing the problem, applied a brief jolt of healing magic to her. Riki looked up, startled, her color returning in an instant. Then she smiled brilliantly and said, "*Thanks*, Mom." She had actually heard what her papa had said, just hadn't fully processed it yet. Now she sat bolt upright and said, "Oh! I don't have anything to wear!"

The menfolk around the table looked blank. What was wrong with the absolutely gorgeous gown she had worn last night? The women rolled their eyes and said, nearly in unison, "We need to go shopping!" Mondi and Sigi had managed to avoid getting in trouble for their antics at the Terentius mansion, mostly because they had been aided and abetted by the son of their host.

They could hardly be faulted for going along with what their new friend wanted to do, could they? And once he'd shown them the way up to the house's garden roof, an experiment to see whether dragon Mondi was yet strong enough to fly carrying a passenger nearly his own age had been a reasonable thing to attempt.

"We told Gaius that we would come and visit with him today," Mondi said. As the elder of the two he was often their spokesman. Bernadette eyed them, and sighed. She knew it was hopeless to try getting them interested in the latest Roma fashions for young men, and at least they were making friends with the son of a duke. There didn't seem to be any reason to object. "All right, just stay out of trouble. We can have your outfits from last night cleaned and pressed for the emperor's ball."

They'd already eaten their fill, and soon darted off after delivering hugs to their parents and siblings. Bernadette looked around the table. Assuming she, Riki, and Rezira would be going shopping, that left Andrion, Erik, Andi, and Gylabris at loose ends for the day. "And what are you four going to be doing while we're gone?" she asked sweetly. She fervently hoped that the Iscandia Slasher was now well and truly retired. She'd spotted those two old she-cats rubbing up against Erik last night.

Andrion glanced around at Andi, Erik and Gylabris. While most of the family played, he, Andi, and Gylabris had been working most of the time since they'd arrived. The little leukalfar tinkerer was the first to speak up. "Uh," he said hesitantly. "At the party last night I was told that Remus has some very interesting eldalfar ruins. They tend to be haunted, of course, but the one nearest Roma has been pretty thoroughly explored and ought to be free of evil spirits. Do you think we might visit it?"

Andrion looked thoughtful. "Wylion, you mean?" he said. He'd visited this ruin on a previous visit, but he wouldn't mind another look. The architecture of the ancient eldalfar had an eerie beauty. Gylabris nodded.

"That was it. What do you think?" Erik grinned.

"I'm up for it," he said lazily. "Even if this place is well-explored, I'm assuming we should wear armor and take some weapons?" Bernadette rolled her eyes again. Erik's cheerful fondness for armed combat was one of the things that had attracted her to him in the first place. But sometimes, the man was just incorrigible!

"I don't actually own armor," the little leukalfar admitted. "And I don't have any weapons training. But I do have some useful spells." After a moment he added, "It's a pity I didn't bring Kziintke along."

"You should be perfectly safe with us," Andrion assured him. "Erik and I have been exploring old ruins for decades, and we haven't encountered anything yet that can get past the two of us."

"Um, *three* of us," Andi pointed out. Gylabris smiled, an array of sharp-pointed teeth gleaming in the morning light.

"Let's do it, then!"

Mondi and Sigi made good time, heading east down the boulevard through the Pantheatos District then turning south. They passed the Scintillio District, and continued on to the Mercantile District. Soon they arrived at a narrow door, where one of the district's least-prestigious merchants operated a sort of general second-hand store. You could buy almost anything here – all of it well-worn and on its last legs before it would be consigned to the rubbish heap.

A minute or two later the boys emerged from the shop carrying what looked like bundles of rags. Then they retraced their steps north, up through the Artists' Quarter to Scintillio and the home of Duke Enzo Terentius and his family. A yank on the bell-pull at the front door brought a manservant, who recognized them from last night's party.

"Ah," he said, showing far more aristocratic reserve than would most actual aristocrats, "The young masters Drakespring, I see. I believe that master Gaius mentioned you would be dropping by. Won't you come in?" He ushered them through the entry hall and into a side door, where one of the house's innumerable chambers was configured as a breakfast room. Gaius was just finishing his morning meal, and his eyes lit up as he saw them.

"Mondi! Sigi! Glad you could come. Thank you, Ignacio," he added, dismissing the servant.

"You brought it?" he asked, looking meaningfully at the bundles of seeming rags. The boys both grinned and nodded. "Come on, let's go downstairs. I know a secret way out." Some twenty minutes later three slight, raggedly-dressed figures emerged from a basement door in the foundations of the Terentius residence and made their way stealthily through the back gate into an alley that gave out onto the broad street leading west toward the Imperial Quarter.

Gaius grinned at his companions. This was such *fun*! Like his elder brothers he was dark of hair and eye, a beautiful boy who would grow to become a handsome man. Life in his family's Roma residence had been lonely for him until last night, when he'd met these two amazing visitors from Iscandia. Since his mother's death when he had been so small that he scarcely remembered her any more, they had lived in Brindis more often than not and all of his friends – few as they were – were there.

The three apparent beggar boys, appropriately dressed if suspiciously clean, made their way out across the Imperial Quarter, through the Produce Market, and thence through the city's western gate into the harbor area. The river Tyben, which flowed on either side of the island on which Roma had been built, ran deep and wide on this western side, and it was here – outside the city's walls from north to south –that Roma's docks stood.

It was also here that the thieves and beggars of the city made their homes. And here, Mondi and Sigi had befriended a beggar boy named Tullio. They spotted him at his usual corner, lurking along the curve of the harbor near the Imperial Trading Company's office.

He recognized them immediately, but didn't speak to them until after he'd looked around furtively to make sure they were not being observed by unfriendly eyes. The four of them had backgrounds so different it hardly made sense that they should all be in this same spot, dressed very similarly, and with a unity of purpose.

Mondi had spent the first eleven years of his life as a dragon, in the bosom of his human family at first but on his own, hunting like a wild animal, for at least five years before getting the ability to become human. Sigi had spent his entire life as the beloved baby of a family that had means but no pretensions to aristocracy. Gaius had started out as the beloved baby of a family both wealthy and powerful, only to find himself motherless and often neglected. And Tullio was the son of a barmaid with some unknown sailor, unable to afford even the potion that could so easily have saved her life when she caught a fever and left her son an orphan. He'd been on the streets and on his own from the age of nine.

He eyed his three recruits with skepticism. They might be dressed in rags, but they looked entirely too healthy and well-fed to be the beggars they were pretending to be. "When was the last time you three bathed?" he asked.

The boys looked puzzled. "A couple of days ago," Mondi and Sigi said, while Gaius responded "This morning, of course."

Tullio grimaced. "About six months too recently. Bend down and put your hands on the ground, then smear the dirt on your faces."

Three sets of bright eyes sparkled as they understood, and soon the beggar disguises were complete. Mondi, Sigi, and Gaius were still far too well-nourished and free of scrofulous afflictions to pass close inspection, but they'd do. They made their way down the street and turned into an alley leading to the beach that lay to the south of the stone harbor area.

Along the way they passed a drunken beggar, who was sitting with his back up against a lamppost and pretending to be crippled. "Good morning, Bronzo," Mondi said politely – blowing his cover. Nobody passing by paid him any attention, though. The old man (not so old really, perhaps fifty-five but the years had been hard on him) was a fixture in the waterfront area, as the boys had learned on their first visit here last week. He was a cheerful fellow as long as he was in his cups.

Mondi flipped the man a coin, another faux pas for someone who was supposed to be a beggar. Tullio grimaced, but inside he was smiling. He had a soft spot for old Bronzo himself, and had helped the old man on more than one occasion. There was no harm in him. He led his three followers on a twisting course down narrow alleys among half-ruined wooden shacks. This was Roma's least prestigious area – and also the home of one of its wealthiest citizens, though few realized it.

Finally Tullio produced a surprisingly long knife from somewhere about his person and pried loose a board in the fence surrounding the back yard of one of the shacks. He led the party through the narrow gap, then pulled it closed behind him. They moved from that yard through a passageway to the yard of the next shack over, where they saw a man of indeterminate age standing, as if waiting for them, beside a mound of rubble. He was curiously dressed in what appeared to be expensive finery – cast off from some rich man's wardrobe thirty years before.

He squinted at the four boys as they approached him. Tullio sketched a half-bow, and said "G'morning, Veletto." The figure eyed him with suspicion, then cast his glance around at the three "beggars" he'd brought with him.

"Scraping the bottom of the barrel, Tullio?" he asked in a world-weary tone. The boy shrugged.

"This is Draco, Felix, and…"

"Gaius," Gaius said, too distracted by the situation to think of an alias on the spur of the moment. This was all just a lark, anyhow – wasn't it?

"So," Veletto said, peering with suspicion at each of them in turn. "You want to become members of the League of Beggars, do you?"

Mondi did a passable impression of a somewhat-superannuated street urchin as he said, "Yes, sir. We're hungry." The man's gimlet eye took him in and rejected that statement as an obvious lie. He wasn't sure what these three were up to, but it was clear none of them had missed any meals lately.

"That may or may not be," he said. "But there's something you need to know, if you want to join our ranks."

"Draco", "Felix", and Gaius looked at him expectantly. Veletto continued his spiel, which he'd delivered to countless recruits during his tenure as the head of Roma's League of Beggars. "First of all, if you wish to beg within the confines of Roma, you must become a member of the League. We do not tolerate any beggars who decline League membership, and if you are caught begging without it you will… regret it. Should you live to do so."

Wow, Mondi thought. Was this guy really suggesting the death penalty for begging without a license? That seemed a little extreme. "League membership requires an initial payment of ten guilders,"

Veletto went on. "How you obtain this money is up to you, of course, but I do not recommend begging to acquire it. Once you are in the League, you are free to beg in any area of the city that is not already staked out as the territory of another League member. League dues are a mere ten percent of your take from begging, and you are afforded all the protections the League has to offer. We look after our own – with shelter, protection from the authorities, and emergency aid if you are unable, due to injury or other circumstances, to perform your usual begging activities."

Sigi, too, was incredulous. He'd spent his entire life in the loving and utterly sheltered environment of the family home where he'd been born. The idea that begging was organized to this advanced degree seemed ludicrous. In Waterdon, there were two or three citizens who were often short of funds and supported themselves (or their drinking habits) by asking spare change from anyone who walked past. But this? Veletto glanced around at the three of them, assessing their reaction to all they'd been told so far. "There is one more thing you should know," he said dramatically. "The League of Beggars is subsidiary to the Guild of Thieves, and answerable to its leader – The Night Walker."

Across town, Bernadette led her daughter and the woman she assumed would one day be her daughter-in-law on a hunt for sartorial splendor – and some groceries for supper. She'd had a full week off from the duty of cooking supper for the family, and was beginning to regard it as a fun project instead of an onerous chore.

They'd entered one of the smaller shops, tucked away down a narrow alley in the Mercantile District near the city's outer walls. They hadn't been in this store before, it seemed – though it was hard to imagine they'd missed anyplace over the past week. As Bernadette bent to examine a bolt of shimmering cloth that was on display, a voice suddenly seized her attention. "Berni? Aunt Berni!"

She whirled and was engulfed in a hug from a young woman considerably taller than she was, clad in leather pants and a soft linen shirt. Anja! "Aunt Berni – and Riki! What are you doing here in Roma?" Anja and Lars had been adventuring in Remus off and on for a couple of years now, and the pickings had been great. But they'd never expected to find these familiar faces from Waterdon, here so far from home.

After hugging the young woman who, as an orphan child of five, had led her to give up the life of a carefree adventurer for marriage and motherhood (ironic that Anja was now nearly the same age she had been back then, but showed no signs of wanting to settle down), Bernadette turned and gestured toward Rezira. "You remember Rezira, Anja?" she asked. Anja and Lars had been part of the rescue party that had ended up fighting to defend Mrzhgradfendz from an invading dypalfar army, more than two years ago.

Anja grinned. Her dark red hair was set off by a complexion well-tanned from years of outdoor life, brown eyes sparkling. "The dypalfar girl, right?" Rezira smiled at her. Though being characterized as "the dypalfar girl" was a little off-putting, Anja looked so much like Andi she might have been his older sister – and she had liked her at their brief meeting more than two years before.

Just then Lars entered the store, calling "Ani? Did you find what you…" He stopped short, eyes wide with surprise and face breaking into a grin. "Berni!" he said. He, Andrion, and Erik were the only men she knew who called her that, and she assumed he only did so because when she'd first rescued Anja she'd told the girl to call her "Aunt Berni." The tall young man, in his upper twenties now and superbly muscled, looked around and recognized Riki and Rezira. She'd made rather more of an impression on *him* when they met. No straight man could fail to take note of a young woman so stunningly beautiful.

"Have you eaten lunch?" Bernadette asked. It was now past one, and though they'd breakfasted late enough it felt like time for a break. Anja and Lars shook their heads. "Come on then," she said. "Let's all go grab something to eat at The Storekeeps' Inn, so we can talk sitting down. I'm delighted to have run into you!"

The party of five went around a few corners and came out on the Mercantile District's main thoroughfare, along which many of the more prominent stores were situated. The Storekeeps' Inn was the only one in the district, though the area could easily have supported a couple of others. So many people who didn't live in the district came here frequently for shopping. Fortunately the main lunch rush was past and they were able to get seated at a table together.

They ordered some of whatever was on the fire all around (like most inns, it offered hot dishes and bread plus a few basic foodstuffs and that was it), along with some wine, and began catching up on each other's doings. "Andrion, Andi, Rezira, and that little leukalfar fellow Gylabris whom you met a couple of years ago are engaged in a project to recreate dypalfar power cells," Bernadette explained. "Andrion's colleague Sextus, who's now the magister of the University of the Magical Arts, invited him and his team here to collaborate – and we all got to come along for a sort of vacation."

"Wow, that's great!" Anja said, taking a sip of her wine. "As you know, Lars and I have been here in Remus several times exploring eldalfar ruins and caves, killing off bandits for the bounty, and so forth. I miss the family, but it seems as if most of Iscandia has already been explored. It's getting hard to find a tomb with anything in it but old bones, these days."

"So you're in town picking up supplies?" Bernadette asked. Five bowls of mutton stew with vegetables in it, and a platter of bread rolls, arrived at the table and they all began to dig in. Anja grinned around a mouthful of bread roll. Though she'd been raised by Lifa and Bjorn, some of her less-than-ladylike mannerisms seemed to have been acquired from Aunt Berni. "We hit it big!" she said enthusiastically. "Found an untouched eldalfar ruin and got a ton of loot out of it, including a couple of Centrus Stones and an authentic pre-Imperial statue. In order to get the full market value we need to sell it off a little at a time, so we've been staying here and just enjoying life."

They all tucked into their food for a while before conversation resumed. "So," Bernadette asked, "have you heard anything about the adventure we had last year?" Anja looked somewhat blank. "We were all over the place last year but didn't make it up into Iscandia at all," she said. "Was there something about dragon attacks? I thought it sounded garbled. I was sure you and your dragon kids had done away with all the hostile dragons."

"Not quite!" Bernadette laughed. "Just the living ones…" That of course led to a retelling of the whole Meiskomtot crisis, their discoveries about the age-suppressing benefits of dragon transformation, Andrion's rejuvenation, and more. Riki and Rezira had quite a bit to contribute to that tale, having been on the scene for a lot of it. Anja and Lars just sat there, mouths open, taking it all in.

When the story had wound down and the landlord was beginning to cast annoyed glances their way for taking up his biggest table for so long, Lars said "I can't believe you were having better adventures than we were! Maybe we ought to go home more often!"

"I should think so," Bernadette said with a touch of asperity. "It's only a few hours away by magic map, after all – and Anja, you know your parents, brother and sister would all love to see you more often."

Anja looked a little sheepish. Like many young adults deeply involved in their own lives, she often forgot for weeks at a time that there were others out there thinking of her and missing her. "Oh my goodness, we still have to finish our shopping!" Bernadette said, rising to her feet. They'd talked half the afternoon away. "Do you have a city map?" she asked, and Lars pulled one out of his shirt. It was one of the sort you could buy all over Roma, with points of interest for travelers marked on it. Bernadette took a graphite stick out of her pouch and circled their house on it.

"Come to dinner with us this evening at 6," she commanded them. "I'm cooking, probably with some help from Erik. I know the rest of the family will be anxious to see you, and you haven't even seen Mondi yet in his human form."

Anja sighed. "I remember when he was the cutest little mini-dragon," she said wistfully.

She'd been a young pre-teen when Bernadette had first brought him home, at an age to find cuteness everywhere. "I can't believe he and all the rest are human now!"

"Not for more than a few hours at a time," Bernadette assured her, "except for Mondi himself sometimes. But now that Sigi can go dragon too, those two have become inseparable. I suppose Mondi is reliving the childhood he never quite had. Anyway, see you this evening?"

"Wouldn't miss it for anything," Anja and Lars chorused. Hugs and kisses were exchanged outside the door of the inn, and then they went their separate ways. Bernadette, Riki, and Rezira had not yet found gowns for the forthcoming ball, and they made a beeline for the area's foremost purveyor of upscale clothing. Bernadette designed all of her own clothing and much of the family's as well when they were at home, all of it made to measure by the superb seamstress Gerde Snowhair (or by her daughter and granddaughter, who had apprenticed with her in the trade). But now, they needed someone new.

Bernadette and Rezira were petite, slim but curvy – whereas Riki was built on a somewhat larger scale but proportionately the same general shape. They'd been able to buy gowns off the rack for the party yesterday evening, and they had only needed some minor alterations, and a little letting-out of Riki's hem, to be acceptably attired. But was "acceptable" good enough, for a grand ball at the Imperial Palace? This was very likely the only opportunity for such an event any of them would have in their lives.

So, after looking around at the gowns on display, Bernadette approached the proprietress. "May I speak with the person who does your sewing?" she asked.

"Which one?" came the reply. "We have half a dozen people supplying us, three who work out of our shop and another three who are independent contractors."

"Whoever is in charge of your shop staff, then," Bernadette said. She might look as though she was barely into her thirties but as the forty-three-year-old mother of more than a dozen children she could be authoritative whenever required.

The woman at the counter went through a curtain at the rear of the shop and returned with a plump, grandmotherly-looking woman in her sixties. The "sweet old lady" image was dispelled when she spoke however. "I have a great deal of work to do," she said brusquely. "How may I help you?" Bernadette decided it was time to speed things along.

"My companions and I have been invited to the Imperial Ball next Maritag," she said simply. "We want to outshine every woman there, and money is no object." The stern expression changed in a heartbeat.

"Well then, dear," the woman said sweetly. "Please, tell me exactly what you want."

Erik had packed them a lunch; and he, Andi, and Andrion were all dressed in light armor. He'd brought along his favorite khopesh, with which the Iscandia Slasher had so devastated his opponents during the previous week. The weapon was ideal for a man of Erik's size and strength to use for chopping his enemies into dog meat; but the hook on the end of it made it useful for disarming opponents as well – frequently without actually removing the hand holding the weapon.

Andrion had taken a few magical weapons with them on this trip, wanting to be prepared for anything, and he lent Gylabris a staff of lightning storms that would create a brief but fierce swarm of bolts in a fifteen-foot radius around the target –useful if your aim wasn't spot on. "Just point and shoot," he assured the little leukalfar, "but don't use it on anybody standing too close to us!"

"I won't," Gylabris said with a smile. He was frankly hoping there would be no fighting required on this field trip.

They made their way through the Floral District and out a nearby city gate, then walked along the shore heading west and then south. Roma was square, but it sat on a roughly lozenge-shaped, large island between the east and west forks of the River Tyben. The river on the west side was considerably narrower and shallower, and all of the commercial shipping docked along the waterfront on the island's east side. They had quite a little walk ahead of them, but it was a nice day for it and the scenery was attractive.

The shore was inhabited by a goodly population of crackclaws, perhaps a little smaller than their cousins in Iscandia but just as aggressive. "Huh," Erik said, eyeing one of these menacing creatures as it approached them with hostility. "A few of those might make a great basis for tonight's supper, but I don't want to lug around dead crabs while we're exploring this Wylion. Could you just zap him with a paralyze spell, Andrion?"

"Allow me," Andi said, halting the crustacean in its tracks. Not for the first time, he wished they'd been able to bring Fjuri along on this expedition. Adventuring with his papas was all well and good, but they tended to monopolize the action.

He'd brought along his bow, being a better shot with it than any of his companions. Still, like Gylabris, he wasn't really looking for a fight. They left a trail of temporarily disabled crackclaws and other hostile creatures along the riverside as they made their way over the island's rippled terrain and past the Penitentiary, a broad, rectangular three-story building with a walled compound. It stood due south of Southgate, and was where most of the criminals in Remus were incarcerated. There was also an office for the Imperial Army there.

The ruin stood just beyond there, on a broad headland jutting out from the island's southwest corner. A jumble of white stone marked its entrance. Like the dypalfar, Andi knew from his studies, the ancient eldalfar (first to found an empire on the continent of Agena) were a race of elves who had built both above and below the ground. Perhaps it was because the structures above ground were subject to harsh weather conditions, but usually the upper areas were considerably more ruinous while chambers and hallways below were frequently intact. These were often haunted by the semi-corporeal spirits of dead mages, undead in the form of skeletons or zombies, or more mundane creatures like bandits and daimlings – but one could often still find treasures inside.

Before going down through the stone doors they walked around the outside, admiring the architecture. Where had the ancients gotten all this fine stone to work with? Around a corner they came on a campsite occupied by a couple of bandits, one of whom got off a shot with his bow. It rebounded off of Erik's armor; and before either Andrion or Andi could react, Erik had rushed in and cut them both down.

"Uh, couldn't we just paralyze them?" Andi asked woefully. These might be cutthroat scum but they were still human beings, and so far he'd managed to avoid adding any humans other than the undead to his kill list.

"Sorry," Erik said, a little abashed. "My instincts got the better of me. But we've probably saved the lives of some innocent travelers by disposing of these two."

"You're right, Papa," Andi said after considering it for a moment. By living the kind of life these people did, hiding in the ruins and coming out to waylay travelers and kill them for their possessions, they had forfeited the right to any consideration. Andrion nodded.

"If we really want to explore this ruin, we're probably going to encounter some more of these bandits inside. We could paralyze them and tie them up, but then we would need to haul them in and turn them over to the authorities. That's a lot of work, just to avoid killing somebody who deserves it."

Andi thought about it some more. He was eager to explore this ancient ruin, but not eager to wade through human blood in order to do so. Then he had an idea. Rezira had given him an amulet that doubled the duration of timed spells, and it was around his neck now. The last of those crabs he'd paralyzed on the way up here was probably still immobile. "Let's go inside," he said, "and nobody do any killing. Let me handle it, okay?" His two papas looked at him questioningly, but they didn't just love him. Over the past two years, they had come to respect his abilities and his judgment.

The explorers opened the doors and crept quietly down the stairs. At the bottom, their path curved around before descending another staircase. They passed through a small anteroom littered with debris, and Erik carefully triggered a taut cord that ran, a few inches above the floor, across the doorway leading to the next flight of stairs. A pair of evil-looking steel balls studded with spikes swung down on chains from the ceiling, eliciting gasps from Andi and Gylabris – neither of whom had seen this sort of trap before.

When the balls had stopped swinging they carefully walked between them, then crept down one more flight of stone stairs to a tee intersection. In the hallway to the left of the stairs, a bandit sentry kept watch. Andi zapped him with a Command spell, one he'd learned in Mrzhandtham from Rezira. It was a spell that he didn't like much, because of its moral implications; but like his father, he wanted to perfect his craft. He had gotten a lot better at this particular spell over the intervening years.

Andi quickly closed the distance to the bandit's side, and spoke quietly to him. "Tell me your name," he said. Using the subject's name increased the effectiveness of both Command and Befriend spells. "Macatto," the man growled shortly. He was a rough-looking customer. "Excellent, Macatto, tell me how many people are in your band." Without a moment's hesitation, the bandit thug recited "Two outside at the campsite, then there's me and another three in here."

Hmm, Andi mused. Three others could be tricky, if they were spread out. He could cast the spell on all of them at once at a useful strength, only if they were clustered together. And the spell took far too much magical energy to be able to cast it repeatedly without a rest in between. He glanced around and spotted a pebble on the floor, no doubt fallen from the stone ceiling or tracked in from outside by one of the bandits. He stooped and picked it up, then handed it to the bandit sentry.

"This is an unusual gem, Macatto," he said firmly. Not only commands but statements of "fact" would be accepted by the enspelled person, if you did it right. "Do you see how it glimmers?"

"Yes," Macatto replied dully.

"I want you to take this into the room where your comrades are, and call them to gather around and look at what you've found. Don't tell them anyone else is here – I want it to be a surprise. All right?"

"Sure," the bandit replied. His weapon still hung at his belt, his hands cupped around the "gem," he went around the corner and into a large room ahead. Motioning his companions to stay back, Andi silently followed him. He peered around the corner at the highwayman as he made his way into the center of the room. "Hey Macatto, what's up?" one of the other bandits asked, observing the way in which his comrade held his hands as if looking at something precious. The band were comrades in arms, but they were as likely to slit each other's throats as those of the travelers who fell victim to them, if there was any suggestion that one of them was holding out on some special loot.

"You guys come here," Macatto said, "and take a look at this strange jewel I found. I wonder where it came from?" The other three hurried to cluster around, demanding to see for themselves – and perhaps snatch it away from the sentry if it looked valuable. As soon as they were in a tight group, Andi stepped out into the room and hit all four of them with the Command spell.

Now he needed to act fast. If he didn't, and the spell ran out, these four might be coming back here with murder on their minds. He didn't want to take the time for introductions. "Everyone, take off your weapons," he commanded, and there was a brief shower of knives, axes, swords, and one bow. "You have all realized that you have been living an evil life, and you are very sorry for all the death and pain you have caused." Looks of remorse appeared on all four ugly faces.

Hastily, Andi removed a piece of paper and a dypalfar fountain pen from his pack, and scrawled a note to the chief warden of the Penitentiary, only a short way from here. It read, "Dear Sir, I have found these four bandits lurking in the ruins of Wylion and have convinced them of the error of their ways. They have been instructed to turn themselves in to you, for whatever punishment is deemed appropriate for the crime of banditry. You may contact me via Magister Sextus Garibaldi at the University of the Magical Arts if you have any questions. Sincerely, Andreas Drakespring."

He had no sealing wax (and, for that matter, no personal seal), but he folded the note tightly and wrote "To the Chief Warden of the Penitentiary" on the outside. His magical energy had recovered, and he stood back a little to hit all four of the bandits with the Command spell once again. The previous one had not yet worn off, and the overlapping doses should assure that they were completely under its thrall for at least the ten full minutes.

Andi handed the note to Macatto. "Macatto," he said, "I'm putting you in charge. You will take this note and give it to whoever is in charge of the Penitentiary, and tell him that you and your companions wish to turn yourselves in." All four woeful-looking miscreants nodded sadly. "All of you, go with Macatto and get to the chief warden as quickly as possible. Run, run!" He shooed them off, and the four of them dashed past the rest of the party (who'd come into the room to observe as soon as Andi had all of the bandits subdued) and up the several flights of stairs, moving as fast as possible in a desperate effort to fulfill Andi's commands.

The four explorers watched them go. Then as the muffled "thump" of the doors at the top of the stairs slamming reached them, they all broke into uproarious laughter. "Andi, I do believe you have made *me* see the error of *my* ways!" Erik chuckled. "Why get blood all over my nice sword when we can just send the bandits off to turn themselves in to the authorities?"

Grinning from ear to ear, Andrion added "Are you sure the spell will last long enough?" He didn't truly doubt his son, but was too much the responsible adult not to ask.

Andi grinned back. "It should last at least ten minutes," he promised. "And at the clip those guys were going they should reach the Penitentiary with five minutes to spare. I'm hoping they'll have logged their confessions and be locked up in a cell before they come to." They turned to survey the room the bandits had been camping in. "Maybe we ought to just pick up these weapons and take them away," Andi suggested. He was sort of, completely, *mostly* convinced that his spell would last long enough to do the job – but why take chances?

They'd all brought full packs, so parceled out the collection of second-rate weaponry and each of them took a couple of pieces. Should the bandits somehow escape turning themselves in and return here in a fury, they would have only whatever weapons were on the bodies of their fallen comrades outside. The explorers weren't worried.

They wandered around the large space and explored side passages, as Andi, Erik, and Gylabris exclaimed over the architecture. It was worlds away from anything they had seen before – utterly different from both the ancient Norse ruins and the abandoned dypalfar cities of Iscandia. In those places, one usually found artifacts pertaining to the activities of daily life – left behind by the long-departed former occupants. Not here. Either the ancient eldalfar had packed all their belongings before leaving, or other intruders here, over the millennia since then, had cleaned the place out.

They found some chests on this level, but they contained little beyond items the bandits themselves had probably deposited. Going down a flight of stone stairs, they came to a set of curve-topped stone doors cut with the glowing representation of a sunburst. Aderos in his aspect as Apoldros, the sun god, had been the eldalfar's chief deity.

These led to a lower level of the ruin with an even more complex layout of chambers and passageways. "What do you suppose all of these alcoves were for?" Gylabris asked, as they traversed the largest of these rooms.

"I believe they once held statuary," Andrion replied, "though there is some controversy about that theory. No eldalfar ruin has yet been discovered with much of anything in the alcoves, but there must have been some reason for them to exist."

There seemed to be nothing living here. Likely the bandits above had only been camping within the ruin because it offered shelter, yet provided them with a base that was close to roads where they might prey on travelers. "Nothing living" was not quite the same as "nothing," however. The four of them, moving cautiously, had just entered a smaller, square chamber when they heard the ominous creak that signaled a walking skeleton.

Andrion, Erik, and Andi had all encountered these skeletal undead guardians before, in ancient Norse ruins in Iscandia. They seemed to be under a different spell than the one the dragon priests had used to produce the aptrgangr, one that did not preserve the body at all. And these guardians patrolled unceasingly, rather than lying at rest until aroused by the proximity of an intruder.

Gylabris had been bringing up the rear, and they spread out silently so he could get a good look. The ruins were lit by chandeliers consisting of spiky-looking metal baskets filled with the same blue-glowing crystals they had seen in a few of the older Norse ruins in Iscandia. That they should still be emitting light after all these thousands of years made Andrion wonder if they, too, might have some link to the extra-dimensional power source that he and the rest of the power cell team were convinced were at the heart of the dypalfar's technology. Perhaps successive groups of people had been re-inventing the same technique over and over again for millennia?

Of course without this source of light Gylabris would have been able to use his extra-ocular sight to see while the rest of them would have been blind, unless they used some illuminating spell. "Go ahead, Gylabris," Erik urged quietly. "Try out the staff on him." He assumed that re-killing foes who were already long-dead would not offend his son's sensibilities. The boy was Berni's son, sure enough.

A slight grin passed across the little leukalfar Keeper's features as he held out the staff. Never in all his very long life had he done anything like this, yet he felt completely safe with his friends around him. He aimed the staff in the direction of the skeletal archer, who had not noticed them, and fired it.

ZZZap! Lightning flashed between the staff and Gylabris' target, and coruscated in a globe around the skeletal form as it went rigid, dropped its bow, and collapsed with a rattle to the stone floor. The walking skeleton had not just fallen, but disarticulated – scattering its bones across the space.

Gylabris' face was lit with an expression of triumph. "Oh, my!" he exclaimed, delighted. "That worked very well! I wonder if I could somehow incorporate one of these into the armament of one of my robons…" Andi clapped him very gently on the back. He stood a foot or more shorter than any of them, and was far older than their great-great-grandparents, after all.

"Good job, Gylabris!" he crowed.

There was little here in the way of souvenirs to carry off, but they were all intrigued by the complex eldalfar architecture. Everywhere there were square pillars, niches, curious quarter-circle passageways. It was almost as if those ancient elves had striven to make it more difficult for anyone to pass from one place to another. It must have made daily life a hellish nuisance! This area seemed to a dead end, but in exploring the passageways (many of which dead-ended) Andi chanced to step on a pressure plate. He ought to have known better, but his experience of traversing ancient ruins was still fairly sparse.

There was a grinding sound and what they had taken to be a solid stone wall beside them began withdrawing into the floor. It revealed a broad chamber and a passage beyond, in the center of which stood a hideously maimed undead corpse. Andi's eyes were wide as Andrion and Erik swung into action. Andrion blasted it with dual-wielded lightning, and Erik followed up with a swift killing blow from his khopesh that severed the creature's animating magic.

Andi and Gylabris approached the now-motionless corpse with curiosity. It had no head, and was missing an arm as well, yet had managed to remain standing for… how long? "This thing has no weapons," Andi wondered aloud. The aptrgangr guardians in ancient

Norse tombs were at least armed and armored. "What exactly is the point of it being here?"

"Oh, they are more formidable than you'd think," Andrion assured him. "These are true zombies, raised by long-forgotten necromancers for some obscure purpose. Despite their apparent lack of armament they can attack with lethal force – and it's very hard to kill them with just conventional weapons."

His three companions, ignorant of such things until now, mumbled and nodded – and moved on. Beyond the passageway where the zombie had stood, another corridor led to a previously hidden staircase. They went down it, becoming ever more cautious, and came into another chamber. Then there were more stairs, and another apparent dead end.

As they wandered around exploring, somebody must have triggered another button. Suddenly they became aware of that grinding sound again, and another wall, in several sections, sank into the floor. Despite the obvious capabilities of Andrion and Erik (nor was Andi a slouch with battle magic) they were all becoming a little leery of this place. It seemed to hold more perils than treasures, and their enthusiasm for exploring it was beginning to ebb.

Beyond the now-vanished stone wall they beheld a good-sized chamber, full of the sorts of architectural elements that made it hard to tell exactly what it held. But they all spotted a dark, wavering figure hovering in the air near what appeared to be top of a staircase leading down. Andi stepped forward wanting a closer look, and Andrion held out a hand to restrain him.

"That's a sheda," he said *sotto voce*. Andi gave him a blank look. He hadn't had the benefit of the broad, in-depth education his younger siblings were now receiving from his grandfather. Andrion beckoned them all to back up a few paces, returning to the room where they'd been before. The other two were as ignorant, and looked at their mentor eager for an explanation.

"Their origins are lost in time," Andrion said, keeping his voice just loud enough to be heard by his three companions. "It's thought that they are the shades of powerful mages who were unable to prevent the eventual death of their bodies – yet through their arts they lingered on in a form half-corporeal, half-ethereal. They often haunt these eldalfar ruins and may be tied somehow to them – but they have powerful spellcraft and are very hard to kill."

"Will a magic-block spell work on them?" Andi asked, as quietly. His father smiled at him. He had loved Andi from the moment he first set eyes on him as a mewling babe, but his pride in his son had grown exponentially over the years. What a man he and Berni had produced!

"Good idea, son," he said. "Why don't you hit him with that and I'll do the battle spells?" Andi nodded, eager for the challenge.

Erik and Gylabris held back a little. Erik's preference was for non-magical, flesh and blood enemies – though he'd certainly halted his share of aptrgangr. Andi and Andrion stepped forward to the doorway and looked at the wavering, smoke-like figure hovering beyond. Andi hit it with a magic-block spell that, with his amulet, should last ten minutes. If they couldn't manage to take this thing down in that length of time, they might as well run home with their tails between their legs and go shopping with the girls!

There was no immediate reaction. As he thought on it, Andi realized that in the past, it was only when he tried to call on his magic that he had realized this spell had been used on him. Perhaps the sheda, suspecting no intruders, was completely unaware of its plight. Interesting. When he'd hit aptrgangr with the magic-block spell they had dropped in their tracks. But this not-entirely-corporeal adversary seemed unaffected – in *that* way, at least.

It certainly became aware of *something* when, a moment later, Andrion hit it with a blast of dual-wielded lightning. Lightning attacks sapped both health and magical energy from an enemy, and while the first might not be a factor against an enemy with no physical substance, the later most definitely was. It shrieked at them and flew backwards, disappearing down below the level of the floor. Had it been pushed to the bottom of the stairs?

All four of them rushed into the room and looked down the stairs, astonished to see that the center of the room, sunken below the level they were standing on by around twelve feet, was flooded to a depth of at least ten of those feet by a pool of clear water. The sheda continued to hover above the level of the bottom, but was completely submerged in water. How bizarre!

"Let's both hit him with lightning, Andi!" Andrion said, and blazing bolts of electrical power flew from their hands down through the pool to the sheda within it. The entire pool exploded in a blaze of blue-white light, energies converging and re-converging as they swept through and around the water, smaller bolts leaping from the surface in a chaotic frenzy and causing both mages to step back involuntarily. Whoa!

Their adversary was limned in the blue light for a moment; then a black shadow like a shroud fell to the bottom of the clear pool and lay motionless. "Got 'im!" Andrion said triumphantly. Then he added, "Wow – I didn't realize shooting lightning through water would have that effect." Andi was a little pale, but was staring at the pool bottom with a look of bemused delight.

"Wow," he echoed softly.

The four of them stood at the top of the steps and conferred. "I don't have any items enchanted with the power of water breathing, and I'm guessing none of you do either?" Andrion asked. Shrugs and shaken heads were his reply.

"I suppose I could hold my breath and dive down there, see how much water there is to get past before you come back into the air," Andi suggested. He and all the Drakespring children had learned to swim young, in the big pool in the rear deck at the Bathing Maiden.

Andrion eyed the water, which was still steaming, with suspicion. Then he gingerly bent to put a finger into it, and quickly withdrew it again. "Ouch!" he said. "It's still not much below boiling, I'm afraid. With the insulation of all this stone, it may be awhile before it's cool enough to be bearable."

"I for one," Gylabris spoke up, "would just as soon not be wandering in the depths of this ruin in soaking wet clothes in any case. What do you say we go back out, maybe drop by the Penitentiary and see if those bandits arrived safely?"

Andi was surprised that Gylabris' thirst for adventure had been quenched so quickly; but then even for an elf he was in late middle age. And this ruin hadn't offered much reward beyond some interesting architecture – no gems or magic swords or so forth as were supposed to be found when exploring such places. He was not five years old anymore, and he had never really wanted for anything (besides, possibly, respect) – but he still felt that by rights, if you went down into old places and fought bandits and arcane creatures, you should come away with something to show for it.

Nobody tried to talk Gylabris out of his notion, and they retraced their steps. Fortunately the sliding stone walls remained open and they didn't have to go looking for triggers on the other side. On their way out Andrion paused and used a short-lived telekinesis spell (another in the arsenal he'd acquired over his many years of studying magic) to lift down a glowing Lumos Stone from a metal sconce high atop a stone pillar. "Here," he said, handing it to Andi. "A little souvenir. It'll give you light if you don't feel like using a spell or a torch – or in a pinch, one of these will restore your magical energy from completely gone." Andi grinned at him and pocketed it happily.

They emerged from Wylion to find that midday had come and gone, but they decided to postpone eating their lunch until after they'd visited the Penitentiary. The area around the entrance to the eldalfar ruin was attractive enough as a picnic spot, but the proximity of the bandits Erik had killed dulled their appetites. At the large fortress, they went past the main gates and up a flight of stone steps to the main entrance of the Penitentiary itself.

An armed Reman sat behind a desk, and looked up as the four of them came in. He goggled a bit at the sight of Gylabris, but refrained from any overt reactions given that the little leukalfar was dressed in ordinary clothing. Andi stepped to the front, since it was he who had sent the bandits here. "May I help you, citizen?" the jailer asked in friendly enough tones. Andi suspected he was somewhat less friendly to those who came here in the custody of his fellow guards.

"I am Andreas Drakespring," he said forcefully. This pretense of being an adult in command was coming more easily to him, he found, as he got closer to actually being one. Imagine that. The jailer sat up straighter, taking him in from top to bottom.

"The Andreas Drakespring who signed the note delivered by those bandits an hour or two ago?" he asked.

Andi grinned, spoiling the stern effect. "They got here all right, then?" The jailer rose to his feet, smiling too.

"It was the oddest thing!" he said. "Four more obvious bandit scum I've never seen, and they rushed in here like all the daimons of the Netherworld were at their heels. Then the one passed over your note, and they all started talking at once – confessing their crimes. I had to bring in three helpers just to take it all down, before we marched them off the cells!"

He shook his head, an incredulous grin on his face, then went on. "Not five minutes later, after we'd locked them all up, they were yelling at the top of their lungs that they'd been tricked, that they 'hadn't done nuffing,' and so forth. How did you *do* that?" Andi had only the vaguest idea of the workings of Roma's criminal justice system, and he didn't want to see those bandits go free to harm innocent travelers again. So he hedged.

"After my companions and I had successfully fought off and killed two of their number, they became convinced that it was better to abandon their evil ways. I'm a little surprised, really, that they had enough honor to fulfill their pledge to turn themselves in."

The jailer eyed him skeptically, then shrugged. "Perhaps the reality of being locked in a cell overcame that honor, then. They certainly would now desire to recant, but with myself and three other witnesses to their confessions I doubt they will fare well when they come to trial."

"Trial?" Andi asked, hoping for the opportunity to relieve some of his ignorance on the subject of the Reman justice system.

"If they'd just been caught stealing, or admitted to it, they'd have been released after paying a fine," the jailer admitted. "Can't have a lot of petty criminals clogging up the courts. But all four of those you sent here confessed to murder – and murder is a capital crime. They'll be given counsel, assuming they haven't the coin to hire any, and in due course they'll be brought before the magistrates. Probably be months. The state will present its evidence, and the accused will answer. They're allowed to bring in any evidence or witnesses to support their claim of innocence, of course. No finer system of justice in the empire, than right here in Roma."

Andi smiled somewhat grimly and nodded. "Thanks for the information," he said solemnly. "I just wanted to make sure they got here all right."

"Those were the bandits from Wylion, right?" the jailer asked. Andi nodded. The jailer unlocked a drawer of the desk and handed over a purse of gold. "There's been a reward outstanding on those cutthroats for some time now," he said with satisfaction. "Thanks for your service to the empire."

Astonished, Andi took the money. As they were exiting the grounds of the Penitentiary and heading north again toward the western shore of the island, he said "I suppose you've earned some of this, Papa Erik." Erik shook his head.

"You keep it, Andi. All I did was cut off a couple of heads, but your quick thinking rounded up the leader and the rest of his gang."

Grinning slowly, Andi tucked the purse into his pack. Here he was, approaching his eighteenth birthday early next year, and this was the first time in his life he'd actually been paid gold for doing something. He'd quite envied Fjuri his job, even though he had no real desire to work construction.

The work he'd been doing for the past couple of years with the Leukalfar Initiative was something he had done because he had the necessary skills, and it was the right thing to do. There had been no payment. And he'd never wanted for anything. But getting your parents to give you things you wanted or needed, or asking them for spending money, wasn't the same thing as having a pocketful of money that was all your own, earned by your own actions.

The women were late arriving back at Pantheatos House, as they'd begun calling their temporary abode, having stayed at the dressmaker's shop for over an hour and then wandered the Mercantile District, buying groceries and generally frittering away their time. Coming from an area where there were few shopping opportunities, the three had rarely had the chance to enjoy the experience of roaming a business district rich with shops, and with hundreds of different items for sale.

When Bernadette and Riki hauled their packages into the kitchen they were surprised to find Erik and Andi in there, busily picking the rich meat from half a dozen enormous crackclaws that had recently been boiled and cracked. "Gods, Erik, where did all these come from?" Bernadette asked in puzzlement. Did crackclaws in Remus inhabit eldalfar ruins? (In fact they sometimes did, though not these particular crustaceans.)

Wearing one of Cornelia's aprons, a bit small on his enormous frame, Erik rinsed his hands off under the kitchen tap, dried them on a clean towel, and then came forward grinning to relieve Bernadette of her burdens. After which he folded her in his arms and bent her over for a deep kiss, which elicited whoops from his son and daughter. "Get a room, Papa," Andi said, continuing to remove crab meat from the shells piled before him on the kitchen table.

Erik released his wife and stepped back. "We caught these along the shore on our way back from Wylion," he explained. "They're all over the place along the western banks, and they're aggressive too. Andi just kept putting paralysis spells on them so they'd still be alive by the time we got back here to put them in the pot." The kitchen did boast one enormous pot, big enough to boil a whole crackclaw. *One* whole crackclaw.

Eyeing it, she remarked "One at a time?" "It only takes a few minutes to cook them," Erik assured her. "Andi kept the rest unmoving and it's taken about an hour all told to do the lot. But these should make a wonderful basis for supper." Bernadette's supper plans had been quite different, and she'd bought two large hams as well as an assortment of veggies and some potatoes. "Or maybe an appetizer," she said. "We're having two more guests for dinner – Anja and Lars!"

Erik's and Andi's faces both lit up. Anja had been like another member of their family in some ways, especially when she was younger, and it was always a treat when they got to see her. "So Ani and her man are still adventuring in Remus, huh?" Erik asked. Bernadette smilingly nodded. She owed the young woman a debt of gratitude for dragging her out of her aimless, hedonistic lifestyle at the tender age of twenty-three, and making her realize that life could be so much more fulfilling when you lived it for the benefit of others as well as yourself.

The young adventurers were the next to arrive, while Andrion and Gylabris were still relaxing after their somewhat taxing excursion. Then finally the boys showed up –disheveled and filthy beneath the oddly still-clean clothing in which they'd set out this morning. Bernadette eyed them suspiciously, and sent them up to bathe and change before coming down to eat.

They all had green salads piled high with the rich, savory crab meat and a spiced tomato sauce to begin the meal. Then there was roasted ham, nicely crisped roasted potatoes, and a medley of local fresh vegetables in a savory sauce, with platters of fresh bread and tubs of fresh butter. Both Bernadette and Erik enjoyed cooking, and they were thrilled at the experience of doing so in such an enormous and well-equipped kitchen. It made their kitchen at home seem like one step above toasting meat on sticks over a campfire.

For dessert Riki had baked a couple of apple pies, tart and sweet and delicious – especially with generous dollops of whipped cream. During the meal the conversation had been nearly nonstop, as Anja and Lars told of their recent explorations and adventures. Andrion was sorry they had abandoned their quest into Wylion so quickly, captured by the intrigue of these ruinous remnants of a lost civilization.

Bernadette, Riki, and Rezira chattered about the gowns they were going to be wearing to the Imperial Ball on the following Maritag. Each of them had to some extent designed her own, at least as far as selecting the cut and style, with amendments to current styles they felt would be more flattering – as well as the materials from which the gowns would be made.

They would all be going in for the final fittings in a few days' time. Bernadette was surprised to see Anja looking a little wistful at this tale. She'd eschewed nearly all feminine fripperies at an early age, dressing in leathers and a succession of sets of armor crafted by "Aunt Berni" during all the years between then and adulthood. Might she now be thinking about a different path in life?

"You know," Bernadette said to her, "if you and Lars are at all interested in going to the Ball we could probably wangle you invitations. The emperor seems to be very pleased by the research that Andrion and our team are working on with magister Garibaldi and his people at the university." Anja's eyes lit with excitement, and she failed to notice Lars' less-than-enthusiastic reaction.

"Really, Aunt Berni? Oh, I would *love* that! Just this once, to experience what life is like for the empire's elite! And *you'll* all be there, so it won't be like we're adrift on a sea of strangers."

She looked into her lover's eyes, and he was swept away. Lars and Anja had more or less grown up together, though he was three years older. He'd loved her madly since he was seventeen, though he'd had to wait years until she was old enough for them to be together. For an orphaned boy on the streets of Waterdon life had been hard; but she had been his rock, the center of his universe. For the past five years they had been together constantly, fighting side by side, sharing the ups and downs of life as adventurers.

And now she was eager to dress up in uncomfortable clothes and go to a fancy ball packed to overflowing with the kind of people who looked down their noses at people like her and him? It seemed insane, but if that was what she wanted, he was going to be there, by her side – dressed in an outfit he fervently hoped he would never have to wear again. Maybe he could sell it back, after the party?

Lars smiled at Anja, squeezed her hand, and leaned in for a kiss. "I suppose we'll have to go shopping for clothes soon, eh?" he asked. Anja's warm brown eyes brimmed with happiness.

"I love you, Lars!" she declared. Bernadette had a hard time keeping a maniacal grin off her face. While adventuring had been fun for a few years when she was young, it wasn't the kind of life for the long term. At least Anja, at twenty-three, didn't have *two* lovers to juggle the way she had done.

Andrion, Erik, Gylabris and Andi had a marvelous tale to tell of their visit to Wylion, and the story of the bandits Andi had Commanded had everyone at the table roaring with laughter. All of the adults except Gylabris had been adventuring and had to deal with bandits at one time or another, and Andi's novel approach was so… apt. It wouldn't have worked in most cases, of course, as the majority of bandits didn't set up camp within short walking distance of the Imperial Jail; but still…

After touting Gylabris' defeat of the skeletal sentry with the Staff of Lightning Storms, Andrion and Andi told of their brief and surprisingly spectacular defeat of the sheda, and the trip to the Penitentiary afterward – to more laughter around the table. They were digging into slices of the still-slightly-warm pie with many murmurs of appreciation, when Bernadette turned to her younger sons.

"Mondi, Sigi," she said around a mouthful of pie (middle age had failed to turn her into a lady, though she *had* become a force to be reckoned with), we haven't heard a peep out of you since we sat down to eat. How did you two spend your day with Gaius Terentius?" Sigi looked up, an expression like that of a trapped animal briefly crossing his face. The opportunities for him to get into mischief had been increased enormously by their trip to Roma, and he was not used to dissembling.

"Oh," Mondi said, after swallowing a delicious bite of pie and cream. "Today, we sort of joined the Guild of Thieves."

Chapter 17: Plans

Once again the smallish cloaked figure, face hidden within the cloak's hood, approached the door of the Sailors' Rest in the city's waterfront district. His furtive behavior drew the attention of more than one of the area's denizens, but none of them were city guards. This area of town, outside the city walls, was full of people whose business wouldn't bear close scrutiny.

He entered the tavern and quickly spotted the tall man he knew as The Mask sitting at the same table as before. The assassin must have some arrangement with the inn's management, he realized. He wondered if the masked man used this place for all his assignations (which might offer him some leverage) or if it was only with himself that it was used. His small experience of dealings with the underworld left him at a disadvantage he did not like. In his own world, he was a master.

No code phrase was needed on this occasion, as The Mask clearly recognized him and beckoned him to sit. "You have delivered the funds to Croaker as requested," he said so quietly no one could have heard him from further than five feet away. "The balance will be due after the task has been performed, and you can pay it to him as usual. Will you now provide me with details?"

Stifling his resentment at being treated with so little respect by a member of the lower classes, the cloaked and hooded man murmured, "Yes."

"On Maritag," he went on, "Half the province will be at the Imperial Palace for the emperor's Grand Ball. That is where you will do the deed." The masked man sat silently, staring at the table for so long that he began to wonder if he had been heard.

"Yes," the assassin said finally, "that will work nicely. With so many there, doing the killing before witnesses will be easily achieved."

The cloaked man sighed in relief. Every one of his few underworld contacts had assured him that this man, and no other, could be trusted to carry out his every command and do the job he wanted done flawlessly. A vision of the future, once that one little obstacle was removed, stretched before him. He was jolted from this reverie by The Mask, who asked "And who is it, from among the guests at the ball, that the witnesses will see doing murder most foul?" He spoke sardonically.

"Ah, of course!" the assassin's client replied. "It is that mage from Iscandia, that Drakespring fellow." "The elder or the younger?" the assassin asked, for both father and son were known to be mages.

"The elder," came the reply. "None other than the Magister of the Academy at Eisenstag will be seen driving a dagger into the heart of the emperor."

Chapter 18: Playtime

Marta came to the door, and her face lit with pleasure as she saw the tall, incredibly handsome young man standing there. "Yes sir, how can I help you?" she asked, showing her dimples. He smiled back at her, and handed her an elegantly printed calling card.

"Thank you, Miss," he said politely. "I am Flavius Terentius, here to see Miss Erika Drakespring."

Marta blushed, then recalled her manners. "Oh!" she said, and stepped back to gesture the young man inside. This was the son (admittedly, a *younger* son) of one of the empire's most prominent families. She could hardly leave him standing on the stoop. She ushered him into the front parlor and bade him take a seat, then rushed off in a tizzy to tell Riki about the visitor.

The house was a hive of activity, as the younger members of the family were preparing for an outing. Riki, astonished and pleased by Marta's announcement, hurried down to the parlor. Flavius had been idly looking around, admiring the room's furnishings. He knew, of course, that this house did not belong to the Drakesprings. But that it had been provided to them by the university, with the cooperation of the emperor, was a sign of the favor they were in.

When Riki came into the room Flavius rose to his feet, then stood gaping at her. She was clad shoulder to toe in some nicely-styled and quite effective-looking armor, her mane of red-gold hair caught up in a braid down her back, with a superb-looking sword – halfway in size, it seemed, between a longsword and a short sword – hanging in a tooled leather scabbard at her hip. She smiled radiantly at him, and took his breath away. By the gods, she was magnificent!

"Flavius!" she caroled, "so good of you to call." He momentarily lost his customary poise.

"Uh, you look beautiful!" he blurted out, then got a grip. "I was hoping maybe we could spend some time together today," he explained. "I can show you some of my favorite places in the city, and perhaps we can lunch at one of the better restaurants."

Her face fell. "Oh, that sounds wonderful," she said regretfully, "but I'm busy today. My brothers and I and some friends are going to go explore an eldalfar ruin."

"That explains the armor, I guess," he said. "I thought you were stunningly beautiful in that ball gown last Maritag, but this suits you even better. You won't need to pull that sword to slay me, I fear – I am already fallen at your feet."

Riki gave an unladylike snort. Something about being dressed like this made her feel more free, less worried about manners or how people perceived her. She felt more herself, somehow, not masquerading as a debutante. "Would you like to join us?" she asked hopefully. It might be great fun to have Flavius along on this expedition, and give her a chance to get to know him better. She sensed there were depths to this charming and gorgeous young man that she'd barely begun to plumb.

His face lit up, dark eyes sparkling. "How soon are you leaving?" he asked eagerly.

"Probably within the hour," she said thoughtfully. "Our friends haven't gotten here yet, and we're still packing to get ready. They're taking us near the place we're going with their map, but they haven't ever been to this ruin before. We may be back pretty late, or not get back until tomorrow what with the map-travelling time loss, so we're packing plenty of food."

"I'll just run home then and get dressed, and pack a few things to take along – and tell Father what's up. He pretty much lets me do whatever I want, so there shouldn't be a problem getting permission. See you within the hour!" Flavius took her hand and kissed it before hurrying out the door, leaving Riki standing in the parlor. She felt as if a whirlwind had just passed by. Her Reman suitor (if that's what he was) was certainly a man of action!

Riki went back to filling her pack. She wanted to take everything they might need on this trip, but still leave some carrying room in case she found any treasures to take home for souvenirs. Like Andi, she had never had a paying job. Upstairs, she found Andi, Rezira, Mondi and Sigi in the midst of their own preparations.

Andrion and Gylabris were already at the university this morning, doing more research on the power cell project – but they and Sextus' team had agreed that the young people could be given a couple of days off. They valued their input, but five people should be enough to carry on with the work they were doing. Andrion thought that they were close to making a major breakthrough, and both Andi and Rezira hoped that breakthrough wouldn't happen while they were gone – but they couldn't pass up the chance for this fun expedition.

With his recent experience in Wylion, Andi was aware that the expedition could be dangerous as well as fun – but if two seasoned adventurers, two mages with battle experience, a well-armed and well-trained young woman, and two adolescent boys with a full range of offensive dragon spells at their command couldn't take down a few shedas, skeletons, or whatever else was lurking in this ruin, he'd be mightily surprised.

Clearly Bernadette, Erik, and Andrion weren't concerned about the dangers. It had been Bernadette's suggestion, in fact, that Mondi and Sigi come along on the trip. She seemed to have been less than enthusiastic to learn what they'd been up to in the waterfront district, and wanted to get them involved in something less unsavory. Bernadette and Erik had decided to leave the excursion to the young people and have some time to themselves, for a change. It had been years since they'd spent time together without any kids around.

Anja and Lars, fully armed and armored and also carrying large packs, arrived only a couple of minutes before Flavius returned. All who were joining the expedition had gathered in the entry hall, milling around as they double-checked their supplies, when the young noble came in through the front door. The entire party turned to stare at his magnificence.

He was clad head to toe in a beautiful, glistening armor that Riki barely recognized as Glissande. It was almost too pretty to go adventuring in! Bernadette, administering kisses and last-minute admonitions to her children, was on him in a moment demanding to inspect the details of its construction. The style of Glissande armor found in Iscandia was different, not nearly as dazzling to behold. Nor was there much demand for it. Most Iscandia residents in need of armor wanted the cheap but effective steel – and those willing to pay top prices wanted daimonic.

Erik, whose work at the forge brought in a fair amount of the Drakespring family's regular income, was also fascinated. They got Flavius to give them the name of the Terentius family's armorer –

the smithy along the main street of the Mercantile District as it turned out – before saying their goodbyes and standing together, arms around each other's waists, as the adventuring party spilled out into the road and prepared to depart.

"So where are we going?" Andi asked, his arm around Rezira. She was clad in her own leather armor and looked positively dangerous, despite her small stature. Anja pulled out her map, and pointed with a finger to a spot about halfway between Roma and Remus's western border on the coast of the Nether Sea.

"This is Durash," she said. "From here we walk west into this blank area on the map. A gatti trader came through last week and we bought him a drink at the inn. He said he'd encountered a couple of adventurers when he was in Licras a month ago. One of them was a Norseman named Ragnar, and his companion was a Ricard somebody – a Galise I'd guess. Anyhow, they claimed that they'd discovered an eldalfar ruin without any buildings above ground to mark it."

"But they didn't get inside and loot it?" Mondi asked. He was at an age when the lure of treasure from plundered ruins had a romantic appeal, and Sigi was the same. "According to our gatti friend," Anja went on, "they *did* get in. They'd gotten caught in a storm and sheltered in what they thought was just a cave – but when they went further in, they discovered doors leading into an underground eldalfar ruin. But it seems they found themselves a little outnumbered by the denizens once they got inside. They'd decided it wasn't worth getting killed for, so they left and ended up running through the storm to get to an inn in Licras."

Andi's warm brown eyes glinted with amusement and a hint of avarice. An un-plundered eldalfar ruin! What wonders might it hold, aside from the possibility of rich treasure? Riki grinned at him, and at Flavius – who had the same expression in his own eyes. Clearly his family was at least as wealthy as theirs, but who wouldn't be excited by hidden treasure?

Urging them to gather around, Anja touched the marker for Durash and after a few seconds of blackness they found themselves standing on a wooded slope in front of an extensive pile of white stone – soaring arches, columns, and staircases in the typical eldalfar fashion. From the position of the sun, a few hours had elapsed since their departure.

"Well crew, let's get moving," Anja said and headed off in the direction of the westering sun. She had sometimes done babysitting duty for the Drakespring family when she was a young teen, but it had been quite a few years since she'd had such a large group of people to wrangle. She hoped Mondi and Sigi were going to behave themselves and stay out of trouble. From what Aunt Berni had told her, they'd been highly creative in their mischief since arriving in Roma.

Andi and Rezira, next-eldest of the party after Lars and Anja (not counting their last-minute guest Flavius), brought up the rear so they could keep an eye out for attacking bandits or wildlife, and make sure that the two boys didn't get distracted and wander off. They hiked vigorously for some forty-five minutes through the wooded hills, and Andi defused a bear's attack with Calm along the way. Flavius was impressed, though the trick was old hat to the rest of them.

At last Anja slackened her pace and began looking around. She was relying on second-hand instructions (the gatti trader's tale had not even triggered a quest marker on her map) to find a place that had apparently escaped the eyes of casual passersby for thousands of years. Of course they were nowhere near any of the major roads, so such passersby would have been few. She spotted a dead tree standing bare and tall amid the greenery ahead and off to their left, and pointed. "That's my landmark, I hope. Let's go…"

Lars strode beside her, the rest of the party bringing up the rear. He had come to rely on Anja's excellent navigational abilities, an inborn talent of hers that had gotten them through many a confusing labyrinth. She continued leading them in a southwesterly direction, dodging among the trees and undergrowth, until they came out onto a rocky outcrop. It stood no more than a dozen feet above the ground beneath, which was clear of trees in a swath perhaps eight feet wide, and they picked their way down its eastern side.

"There!" Anja said, pointing in triumph. Where two of the boulders of the outcropping leaned together, there was a good-sized triangular opening. It was plenty big enough for a large man like

Lars, as tall as Andi and broader, but even a dragon the smallish size of Sigi could not have squeezed through.

Many caves in Remus had been taken over as residences by daimlings or bandits, and might have wooden doors at their entrances and even pit props inside them. But this had the look of a completely natural opening that might be no more than six feet deep and unlikely to shelter anything besides, perhaps, a bear or some smaller wild animal.

Anja approached cautiously, sword out, and stuck her head into the opening for a sniff. The air inside was cool, and from the feel of it the cavern inside was a lot bigger than you might expect from the size of the entrance. It smelled musty, but there was none of the rank odor of bear or cougar.

She pulled a Lumos stone from a pouch at her side and held it out, illuminating a small area around her as she stepped inside and the rest of them quietly followed her. "Let's get some better light, shall we?" Andi said to Rezira, and she nodded with a smile. In an instant, two bright globes of light, a little bigger than a person's head, rose to the ceiling and floated along – each above the head of the mage who'd cast it. Rezira was wearing an amulet the twin of the one she'd given to Andi, so the light from these simple, low-magical energy-cost spells would last for a full two minutes before it had to be renewed.

Lars grinned at the two and said, "Thanks. Stumbling around in the dark when you don't know who or what is sharing the cave with you is one of my least-favorite activities." Sword in hand, he joined Anja as they moved forward, exploring the cavern and looking for the eldalfar doors Ragnar and Ricard had reported to their gatti drinking companion. Rezira stayed beside Anja, giving them light, while Andi brought up the rear.

The cave turned out to be more extensive than they'd expected, branching into multiple tunnels running back beneath the hillside. They found a few animal bones, and ancient droppings suggested that bears and big cats both had denned here in the past; but there was no sign of recent occupation – and little or no evidence of humans, either.

Finally after hitting a dead end and backtracking, they came to a second cul-de-sac. But this one had a pair of familiar-looking marble doors standing at the end of it. Jackpot! Their elation at finding what they'd sought was followed, a moment later, by rising anxiety. What "denizens" were on the other side of those doors, that had been enough to drive off two doughty adventurers?

The doors opened easily, well balanced on their hidden hinges, and the party began moving down a broad staircase. They found the familiar metal basket chandeliers filled with glowing blue crystals here, so Andi and Rezira were able to let their light spells expire and concentrate on being ready to shoot a paralysis spell or something more lethal at whatever might be going to attack them. Zira had become considerably more adept at battle spells during her time in Iscandia.

The staircase continued a long way down, then opened out into a cavernous white stone room, glowing eerily in the blue light from the chandeliers. It was also lit by a great number of Lumos stones perched in metal prong brackets atop pillars. There didn't seem to be anything stirring. "Ooh look, Centrus stones," Anja said pointing up toward the towering ceiling. At either end of the room were complicated metal cages suspended by chains, and inside them were enormous glowing crystals.

"What are Centrus stones?" Andi asked. "I'm not sure what they actually are or how they were created," Anja said quietly. Even if nobody was around, there was something about this enormous, silent room that encouraged you not to make a lot of noise. "But they are very valuable. They'll fetch around a thousand guilders apiece in Roma. Or, if you have a lot of enchanted weapons, you can use one to recharge every piece of enchanted weaponry on your person at once. Like having half a dozen filled magical essence vials."

Andi nodded, impressed. At this point Mondi spoke up: "Hey, is anyone besides me starving?" The time lags of map travel seemed to affect the young more than they did adults, and in any case he and his younger brother were at an early stage of adolescence. They rarely went more than three hours between meals if they could avoid it. "There don't seem to be any adversaries in this room," Andi said, "why don't we sit down on this dais and have a picnic?"

There was general agreement, and they all seated themselves around the edges of a platform perhaps twenty feet wide and ten deep that stood three steps above the main level of the floor. It had a stone counter similar to the ones you sometimes saw in dypalfar ruins in the center of it, and on that a long, dome-lidded chest of some kind. Andi was eager to get his hands on that chest, but it seemed appropriate to eat first. His own stomach was rumbling.

The boys, ravenous but excited by their unfamiliar surroundings and eager to start exploring, wolfed the lunches they'd packed and then ran off together down to the far end of the room to see what was back there. The rest of them were eating and talking quietly together when they suddenly heard a deep bellow, followed a moment later by a "Kraf-Luft-Struung-Wund!" coming from Sigi.

All the rest of the party dropped what they were eating and were on their feet in a moment, weapons drawn. As they dashed en masse to the far end of the room, where the boys were hidden from their sight by a wall, they heard another bellow – this time one of agony, mixed with a roaring sound. They rounded the wall to find a broad corridor with a couple of doors leading out of it. One enormous figure, singed and blackened, was down on the floor and Sigi had his bow out, pumping arrows into it. Mondi, as dragon, had a second of the creatures in his jaws and was shaking it like a rat.

As his friends and siblings arrived, Mondi dropped the figure in his jaws to the stone floor, where it landed with a crunching thump and began leaking blood. It did not move. He turned around and said, cheerfully, "Oh! Thanks, but I've got this!" In his guise as a lanky adolescent boy, it was easy to forget that Mondi had been a dragon on his own for years before he'd ever taken human form – and that his mental age was much closer to Andi's than to Sigi's.

Though the danger had passed, Mondi remained a large scaly monster for the time being. "We were just going to walk down to the end of the corridor, when these things came in through that door over there," he indicated with his head. "What the heck *are* they, anyhow?" Lars had only to glance at the seven-foot tall humanoid forms – massively muscled, with a bull's head, a man's chest and arms, and lower body like a bull's but modified for bipedalism.

"Those are minotaurs," he said.

Andi had heard about them but never seen one before, and he was intrigued. He stepped forward for a close look at the unburnt one, which seemed to have a broken neck. Two warhammers were lying scattered on the floor where the creatures had dropped them, so they were probably at least as intelligent as trolls and must have access to smithed weapons, somehow.

Mondi's interest was of a different nature. "Half man, half bull, huh?" he said cheerfully. "Are they any good to eat?"

"It never occurred to me to try eating one," Lars said with a half-grin, "but I don't see why not." The burnt minotaur was as dead as its companion, and Sigi had retrieved his arrows from it.

"If you don't mind," Mondi said, "I'll just test the theory. Fighting in dragon form always gives me a ravenous appetite."

They stood back as he toasted the fallen creature some more with Holocaust, until it was crackling and a rather delicious smell was filling the corridor. Then he sank his jaws into its leg and ripped off a hunk of flesh. After gulping it down, Mondi declared, "Delicious! It tastes just like beef, only a little gamier!"

Sigi, on the far side of the corpse from Mondi, said eagerly, "Ooh! I want to try it!" and quickly transitioned from clothed to naked, boy to dragon. In dragon form he was little smaller than his brother, there being less than a year's difference in their ages. The two of them made short work of the corpses with draconic ferocity, as the rest of the party backed off and returned to the platform in the center of the room. They all seemed to have lost whatever appetite they'd had left.

Rezira winked at Andi, saying "Aren't you curious, too?" Andi gave her a sickly grin. His enjoyment of the dragon form had more to do with flight than with draconic eating habits. "No thanks," he said. "Those monsters look just a little too humanoid for my taste, at least while I've got something else to eat."

Flavius was a little shaken. He'd seen Mondi in his dragon form before, though just a glimpse in the dark as he'd been about to get Riki (or so he'd hoped) into a clinch at the party last week. The well-lit reality of this beautiful young woman's brothers transforming into twenty-odd-foot scaly monsters left him with mixed feelings. He sensed that he was falling in love with Riki, and as he was only the second son a liaison between his family and hers – foreigners, true, but wealthy as well as being celebrities throughout Agena – didn't seem out of the question. But was he prepared for fire-breathing in-laws?

They all tucked any uneaten provisions back into their packs. The plan was to take a few hours on this trip and return to Roma, but who knew how extensive the ruins might prove to be? This enormous room, with multiple passages running off of it, suggested the place might be huge. Dragons eat fast, and the rest of them had only just gotten ready to move again when Mondi and Sigi, human once more, emerged from around the corner where they'd demolished the minotaurs.

Flavius looked at them in wonder as they came. They appeared to be just a couple of skinny, cheerful striplings. Sigi in particular was a sweet kid who charmed everyone who met him. Hidden depths… "Let's see what's in this chest shall we?" Andi asked rhetorically as he hopped up onto the stone platform.

"Do you need any lockpicks?" Anja asked him. Chests in eldalfar ruins, firmly locked, were usually the only place to find any items of value – not counting the Centrus and Lumos stones.

Andi gave her an impish grin. "Nope," he said, "Papa Andrion taught me his Unlock spell." This was a sign of great parental trust on Andrion's part – how many parents would give their teenage sons the power to open almost any lock? A pale glow emanated from Andi's right hand, there was a quiet click, and the rounded lid of the chest sprang open. The rest of them had their attention riveted on what he was doing, and when they saw the look of awe on his face, their excitement rose.

Mondi leaped up onto the table to see for himself. "Wow, Andi!" he said with enthusiasm. "Awesome!" The chest, which surely must not have been plundered in all the millennia since the eldalfar departed, contained sablium armor and gold coins, and a mixed pile of jewelry. Andi sensed these items bore enchantments, but he wasn't sure what they were. Perhaps even some lost spell from antiquity? He scooped the chest's contents up with both hands, and at the bottom of the pile was a magical staff of some kind. Quite a haul!

131

Mondi seized the staff and the two of them let themselves down off the platform, the chest now standing empty. The rest gathered around to examine the items with awe and pleasure. Like Riki and her siblings, Flavius had grown up in a wealthy family that paid little attention to money or the things it could buy – no more than fish noticed the water in which they swam. But there was something about entering an ancient, hidden place and uncovering treasure from eons ago that made it all so much more interesting.

The rest of the party clustered around, smiling excitedly. It was precisely this thrill, along with the challenge of pitting themselves against deadly foes, and being their own masters with no one's schedule to keep but their own, that had sucked Anja and Lars into this lifestyle some five years before and kept them doing it. Now Anja was starting to think about a more settled life, and the chance to watch her baby sister grow up before it was too late; but they needed a really big score first – something that could set them up with a house and an income.

Lars' father had been a hunter, dividing his time between stalking game on the plains and selling the fruits of his hunts in a stall in Waterdon's central market square. After his mysterious disappearance, Lars had tried to take over the family business and had barely managed to make a living at it. If he and Anja were to settle down, they needed to find something that was less hazardous and more rewarding.

Therefore, Anja had invited the Drakespring kids along on this expedition with the understanding that each of them could claim one item from whatever treasure they found, but that the rest of their plunder would belong to her and Lars as the organizers of the expedition. She didn't plan to be hard and fast on this agreement if it turned out the pickings were rich – the Drakesprings were like family, after all.

They spread the chest's contents out on the surface of the dais where they'd so recently eaten their lunch. Andi, as the most accomplished wizard among them, took charge of sorting out the magical items. The staff, a rather handsome-looking thing carved of a dark wood that resembled sablium, emitted a blazing fireball that exploded against a nearby wall with a resounding "whoosh!" Not all that valuable, then. It emulated a lower-level battle spell, and was probably far less effective than a bow against enemies.

"Anybody want this?" Andi asked, and got no takers. He set it aside.

"What's going on?" Flavius asked Riki *sotto voce*, and she explained their agreement with the adventurers. He grinned. Not only had he gotten a last-minute invitation to a fun party, but there were to be party favors as well!

All there passed on the armor, as well. It was clearly valuable, but everyone in the party already had armor fitted to them – and refitting found armor would cost money. Andi set that aside, and the pile of antique gold coins went into Anja and Lars' coffers, as well. "This is just the first room," Andi reminded them. "Unless there's something in this pile of jewelry you've got to have, we'll move on and see what else the place has to offer."

He spread out the tangled pile of jewelry, which glittered with gold. There were some silver pieces as well, but these had become tarnished over the millennia that they'd spent entombed. He put on a necklace consisting of a cabochon emerald set in gold, hanging on a slender gold chain, and his vision went blue. Everything around them was glowing as if lit from within by bright moonlight.

"Darksight!" Andi exclaimed. This spell, familiar in Remus, had taken years for Andrion to discover and acquire. With it, you had vision similar to that of the leukalfar – except that in normal lighted conditions, you might have trouble picking out detail amid the dazzling blue light. It was certainly useful for navigating in the dark, though.

Andi already had the spell, and hadn't had all that much use for it. Again he had no takers, and he set the necklace aside. Next he slipped a tarnished silver ring onto a finger of his left hand – and vanished. Everyone gasped. "Blend!" Rezira called out. She'd witnessed Andrion's casting of this spell more than a year ago, when they had needed to hide Ehrgeizig and the dypalfar robons from the view of Meiskomtot before the Battle of Osteon Rise. There was a sort of shimmering in the air that gave away Andi's shape if you knew what to look for – but had he remained motionless, he would have been nearly invisible.

"Me! I want that!" Mondi cried. Removing the ring from his finger, Andi stood working out the consequences in his mind. The dragon spell that sent your clothes and other possessions away allowed them to continue to exert any magical effects they had on your person, even when you were in dragon form. With this ring, his younger brother could become… a stealth dragon! Gods save us!

But he loved and trusted his younger brother enough to hand the ring over. Mondi seized it and slipped it onto a finger. The ring seemed to have an additional magic, that it adjusted its size to fit whoever wore it. The tall boy vanished from their sight, only a slight perturbation of the air revealing his whereabouts. He lifted an arm to look at his hand, and whooped. "Yeah!" Then he removed the ring, reappearing in an instant, and slipped it into an inner pocket of the tunic he wore beneath his fitted leather armor.

The rest of the cache of jewelry ended up in the pile that would be Anja's and Lars' to keep, and was soon tucked into their packs. "Time we were moving on, folks" Anja said. "Shall we go see where those minotaurs came from?"

"Maybe we should explore the whole room first," Andi suggested. He had a more intellectual, analytical approach to adventuring now that he was older, and would probably have excelled at it if it had been something he really wanted to do with his life.

They explored the other end of the room, and found a couple of metal grates blocking access to two relatively small rooms. Andi unlocked them with ease, and they gleaned some Lumos stones from each room - and some more of those antique gold coins from a chest standing in a recess at the back of one of them. Before they left this big room, they looked around for a way to release the Centrus stones from their cages – but found no obvious buttons or levers. "Sometimes they're hidden two rooms away," Anja explained. "Time to go, I guess."

They found little left of the two unfortunate minotaurs. Whatever intelligence those man-beasts had possessed, it was unlikely that they'd had any expectation of encountering monsters out of legend – monsters far too large to have gotten inside here in the first place – in their lair. At the far end of the corridor were two more of those small rooms behind metal slat doors. The further doorway on the right led to a flight of stairs leading up, the closer one (the one from which the minotaurs had emerged, according to Mondi and Sigi) to a stairway leading down. "We're not all that far below ground here," Anja said, her years of experience in eldalfar ruins coming to the fore, "so that's probably a balcony or something up there. Let's go down."

She might be three years younger than Lars, but clearly she was the boss of their little operation. She had the advantage of being the eldest child of a substantial family, the missing first five years of her life (about which she'd never recovered any memories, even after visiting the ruined farm where her birth parents were buried) notwithstanding. In addition to loving her, he had a huge respect for her skills and her intelligence.

So, they descended the stairs. Anja and Lars took the lead, and the rest of them followed – weapons at the ready, moving stealthily. Whatever other "denizens" lurked here, it would be far better if they could surprise them – instead of the other way around. Flavius found himself distracted by Riki as she moved gracefully at his side. For a tall, powerfully-built woman she moved like a will-o-the wisp, almost gliding along silently. She held that sword as if she knew what to do with it, too.

The stairway came to a right-angled junction leading to a doorway on the left, where they found themselves looking out at a room even huger than the one they had left behind. The ceiling far above them was supported by many tall, graceful square stone columns, with shorter ones bearing Lumos stones spaced at intervals on either side of a broad central aisle. They spilled out of the stairway and spread out along the wall, just staring at the huge space.

Mondi sidled up to Anja, who had been his babysitter on several occasions when he was still a small-enough dragon to be living at home. "Let me put on my ring, and sneak down through the middle of the room to see what's there. Then I'll come back and report," he said quietly. She grinned at him. She'd already gotten used to the dragon child she had known and loved being a human boy, and she liked him a lot.

"Go for it," she murmured softly. "We'll wait here."

Anja looked around at them and put her finger to her lips as Mondi vanished from sight. He crept, in his soft boots, down the center aisle peering from side to side. Like most eldalfar places, the room was full of alcoves, pillars, and other architectural elements amid which dozens of enemies might be lurking; so he moved slowly and cautiously.

Mondi had gotten around halfway down the room's length when he spotted a tall, angular figure – a wood sprite! He'd encountered them often enough in the wilds of Iscandia, and he wondered what one was doing here, far underground. They were forest spirits, usually to be found in close contact with the trees they resembled. He froze in place, but despite his near-invisibility she had sensed his presence. With the wave of a branch-like hand, she summoned a black bear – and it was coming straight for Mondi!

He did what he would have done, in his human form, if confronting a charging bear – cast the Calm spell. The bear kept coming. Perhaps this summoned creature was not a natural bear? He was armed with only a bow, and didn't think that was going to stop it, so he turned and fled, running back down the center aisle toward his companions.

"Andi!" Mondi shouted as he ran, "There's a bear after me! Use your paralyze spell on it!" The party spread out, ready to face the attacker, and as Mondi joined them Andi stepped forward and sent the paralysis spell at it. It had no effect! Was this really a flesh and blood creature, or some kind of apparition? The bear was almost on them, and the four members of the party armed with swords – Anja, Lars, Riki, and Flavius – stepped forward to surround and attack it. It couldn't maul all of them at once.

The animal (if that's what it was) gave a howl of pain as Lars sliced its nose with his longsword, even as Riki ran her own sword into its side and Anja chopped into its back from behind. It groaned and spurted blood, just like a real bear – but as it dropped to the floor it vanished. Its summoner, the wood sprite, had emerged from her hiding place among the columns and was coming toward them down the central aisle, hurling magical attacks that left them feeling as if they'd been struck with clubs.

Rezira stepped up and fired a magic-block spell at the creature, and the attacks ceased. But she was still around seven feet tall, with long arms and claw-like fingers, and she was continuing to advance on them. Andi, his magical energy recovered fully, hit the wood sprite with dual-wielded, concentrated fire and the bolt sizzled through the creature's midsection. Flames erupted as she uttered a thin wail and crashed to the floor.

Riki looked at her blade and saw that it was clean – the bear's blood had vanished along with its corpse. Flavius was gazing at her with a look of intense admiration, his own blade hanging point down and forgotten. What a woman! Andi quickly provided healing to anyone who needed it, and after an examination of the wood sprite's body they proceeded together – carefully – down toward the far end of the room.

There were no more wood sprites or other foes, but several of the room's alcoves held chests. Andi opened each of them, adding a considerable amount of gold to their growing coffers. Anja looked back behind them and gestured above, where a balcony ran the width of the room. "That's where those stairs go," she said. "Andi, want to come with me and see if there are any chests up there?"

The rest of them waited, exploring the room carefully, while Andi and Anja went back out and up to the balcony. After disappearing from it again they failed to reappear for some minutes, and Rezira was beginning to get anxious by the time they rejoined the party, looking smug. "Not only was there a chest full of gold up there," Anja said, "but the lever operating the Centrus stone cages was there too." She proffered one of the stones for the rest of them to see. It was several inches long, glowing white, and shaped somewhat like a chandelier crystal.

At the room's far end were two of those sets of stone doors with a glowing stylized sunburst on them, both of them leading to staircases going down. They chose the left ones at random, and on reaching the next level saw that apparently the right doors' staircase had led to the same place. Ahead of them was another broad hall, with a rectangular pool of water in the center of it. On either side of that, metal cage doors lined broad stone aprons.

137

Andi leaned up against the bars and peered inside. There was a chest in there, but he also observed that the room in front of him had a side door that connected to the room next to it. There were three of these cage rooms, each with its own front door and side doors that, if left open, would make them one big room. The next door over contained another of those grotesquely maimed zombies, though this one still had its head.

Moving to that cage's front door Andi hit the zombie with a magic-block spell, and it toppled to the floor of the cell – temporarily lifeless. "How did you do that?" Anja asked.

"Oh," he grinned, as he let himself into the first cell and began rifling the chest, "Fjuri and I discovered this last year while we were in an ancient Norse tomb complex. If you use magic-block on the walking dead, it temporarily severs their connection with the magic that animates them. This guy won't wake up for another six minutes, since I'm wearing my amulet" – he cast a grateful look at Rezira, who smiled back fondly – "and by then we can have him locked up again and be out of here. No need to permanently kill him."

"I'll be darned," Anja said thoughtfully. Neither she nor Lars, both pure Norse with little aptitude for magic, had ever considered such a thing. And zombies were hard to kill. They raided the chest of some gold and another magic amulet.

"Hey," Andi said in surprise, as he held it up. "It looks exactly the same as the ones Mom makes." He had two amulets slung around his neck, the one Rezira had given him that doubled the duration of his temporary spells, and the one his mother had given him almost two years before. It was identical to one she'd worn constantly for the past decade and more, and was the reason that Sigi, recently turned twelve, was the youngest of his siblings.

"Can I have that?" Riki blurted, then flushed a remarkable rose color. Flavius had no idea what was going on, though Anja and Lars (and Andi) certainly did. Bernadette had given one of these to Anja for her eighteenth birthday. She seemed to have a double standard when it came to what constituted an appropriate age for young people to take charge of their own love lives.

The boys didn't seem to be aware of the implications of Riki's request, or they'd have been sniggering. Andi handed it over to her with an inquiring look in his eyes. Surely she was not planning to give herself to this young aristocrat, with Fjuri waiting for her back in Waterdon? He loved his sister and respected her right to make her own decisions – but he also loved his best friend, and he knew that Fjuri felt things deeply. It would destroy him to lose her. Fjuri might be nearly the same size as Erik, but it would be hard to imagine two more different personalities.

Riki snatched the amulet, but did not put it on. Instead, she tucked it deep into an inner pocket of her pack. They all moved on without comment, leaving the still-motionless zombie locked in. There were steps leading down into the pool of water, which was clear as glass, and they could see that there was a passageway leading out of it. Unless that proved to be the only way to continue exploring, they weren't likely to go that way – but Mondi volunteered to check it out.

With an impish grin he said, "Cover your eyes, ladies!" before spelling away his clothing, pack, and bow. They all continued to stare at him, of course, causing him to flush beneath his tan (though his hair was carroty red, including that which had recently begun to sprout in his armpits and crotch area, his natural skin tone was a medium bronze) and hastily dive into the pool.

He swam down to the bottom and through the opening, as some of them chose to down packs and sit on the floor while Sigi went off to scale a nearby pillar and pluck the Lumos stone off the sconce mounted in its top. He'd worked his way around the edges of the pool and pocketed six stones, by the time his brother came back up out of the water, shook himself briefly and then hastily regained his clothing with a spell.

As a dragon he'd had no such feelings, being still many years away from the time in his life where mating would become a concern (and since all the female dragons in Agena were close relatives of his, it was unlikely he would *ever* find a mate in his draconic form); but as an adolescent human, Mondi had begun to experience the unsettling effects of pubescence and he found it actively embarrassing to be standing naked in front of good-looking young women – even if one of them was his sister.

His usual ebullience restored now that he was properly clad again, Mondi reported. "There's a staircase leading up into a smallish room, and a labyrinth of passageways beyond it. We might want to check it out if it turns out there's no place to go from here otherwise, but let's try to find out what's beyond that door at the far end first, huh?"

Before leaving the room they skirted the pool and checked out the three cages on the far side of it, mirrors to the ones on this side. The center cage there also contained a zombie, and they disposed of it in the same way as before – gleaning some more gold for their trouble. This was shaping into a very profitable excursion, Anja thought with pleasure. Might this be the trip that would buy them out of the adventuring business for good?

The door at the far end led to more stairs down, and a labyrinth of corridors and interconnected rooms. They began to encounter animated skeletons on patrol, easily dropped by Andi or Rezira before the others hacked them apart to scatter the bones and relieve them of their weapons. Then things heated up as the rooms they entered were guarded by ghostly undead warriors. The magic-block spell would prevent them from blasting you with magic, but they still had magic staffs or other weaponry – and magic-block did not render them unmoving as it did for the lesser undead.

The party, beginning to tire after hours of roaming the ruins (though they were all happily well-laden with loot, now), came at last to another long, rectangular room lined with columns. Anja was visually surveying the room, Mondi staying close by her side as he wanted to be the first to see whatever there might be *to* see, when she grasped him by the shoulder and hauled him back as he was about to step on the section of stone floor immediately ahead of him.

"Trap, Mondi!" she warned, and pointed upward toward the ceiling. A square recess above matched the size and shape of the stone in the floor below, and enormous spikes could just barely be seen within it – the tips gleaming slightly in the room's dim light. Once he was standing well clear of the edge she stood on one leg, reached out a booted foot and brought it down hard on the edge of the stone, before leaping back again. The entire block, some twenty feet square, rose up from the floor (seemingly an enormous solid pillar lifted somehow from below) and the top of it disappeared into the recess with the spikes.

Mondi's reddish brown eyes widened, as did those of everyone else in the party except Lars. He'd seen these before. "Whoa!" Mondi said, his vivid imagination picturing the damage those spikes could do. The surface of the stone, when it came back down again, was free of bloodstains – probably only because they were the first living creatures to come here in millennia.

They detoured around to walk on the far side of the columns, away from the center path and any possible traps. This area seemed like it might be a tomb, and there were broad, short corridors leading off of it on either side with stone platforms and wall recesses. "I half expect to see aptrgangr bursting out these recesses," Andi said quietly, and Lars nodded.

"They reminded me of ancient Norse tombs too when we first started questing in Remus a couple of years ago," he said. "At least the zombies here mostly don't have weapons or armor."

They relieved a long chest in a recess at the back of the first corridor of its contents (including a very nice sablium longsword), then returned to the central room and moved to the next corridor. Anja was in the lead and after peeking around the corner she dodged back and put a finger to her lips, motioning them all to be quiet and stay back.

Then she beckoned to Andi, and he came silently forward. "There's a sheda down at the far end of the next corridor," she murmured in his ear. "Can you block his magic before I start shooting?"

"Sure," he murmured back. He had an arrow nocked to his bow, though the bow wasn't drawn. He held arrow and bow in his left hand and poked his head around the corner silently, then used his right hand to cast the magic-block spell on the menacing figure floating eerily a foot above the floor some thirty feet away. Unlike the sheda they'd encountered in Wylion, which had looked more ghostly, this figure resembled a floating, fully armored undead warrior.

The magic-block spell didn't alert the sheda to their presence, fortunately. Now Andi and Anja both took aim and let their arrows fly into the creature's swirling cloak at the same time. It gave a hollow shriek and wavered in the air, then began firing at them with a magic staff, bolts of lightning flying out to shock them and steal their magical energy. All of them except Mondi and Sigi (who had only daggers in addition to their bows and their arsenal of dragon spells) rushed the creature with blades swinging, trying to swarm it under and disarm it. Rezira was wielding the sword they'd found in the first corridor, but it was way too much blade for her – very nearly as long as she was tall. She had a wiry strength though, despite her slight build, and was able to lift and swing it if without much finesse.

They encircled the sheda and hacked at it, a blow from Lars' longsword knocking the staff from its non-corporeal hand. Just then Mondi and Sigi shouted "Look out!" and Andi, who had his back to the rear wall of the corridor and was trying to thrust his sword through the undead creature's half-solid body from the rear, looked up and saw an armored skeleton wielding a sword and shield as it advanced and swung its blade toward Rezira.

This warrior must have been summoned by the sheda, which meant that it had somehow resisted his magic-block spell. And after the experience with the summoned bear, Andi couldn't assume that casting magic-block on the animated skeleton would work, either. "Zira! Duck!" he yelled. The lithe dypalfar girl fell to her knees, evading the blow, just as Anja, fighting beside her, swung her sword from the sheda to the attacking skeleton. The bow was her preferred weapon, but she wasn't too bad with a blade.

The women left the sheda to Andi, Flavius, and Lars as the three of them concentrated their attack on the skeleton. This thing was tough! Realizing how ineffectual she was with the oversized sablium sword, Rezira dropped it to the floor and dual-wielded a blast of flames at the skeleton as Anja and Riki swung at it with their blades. The thing collapsed in a heap of bones and then winked out of existence – weapons, armor, and all.

They turned and renewed their attack on the sheda, hoping to stop him before he could summon any more assistance. With a wail, the creature finally expired and the six of them stood panting. "It resisted my magic-block spell!" Andi gasped. "How could it do that?" Anja looked concerned. As she had never tried to use magic on anything or anyone, she hadn't realized that shedas could be resistant to spells.

"Sorry Andi, I had no idea. But I guess we'd better assume that they might not stay blocked the next time we encounter one. This is clearly a higher type of sheda than the ones we fought earlier." He nodded thoughtfully. This adventuring stuff went a lot more smoothly when you had experts along, but he doubted his papas could have provided any more information. They were *all* outside of their usual areas of expertise.

They were able to look across the room to the matching corridors on the far side and see a chest or two, and no shedas. Mondi looked up at the ceiling and assured himself that the smooth, unbroken stone above them had no suspicious recesses in it. Unless the hitherto harmless basket-shaped chandeliers were suddenly to turn lethal, it should be safe to walk straight across. Mondi had no Unlock spells at his disposal, though his draconic heritage gave him as great an aptitude for magic as Andi's Galise ancestry. Perhaps Andi's unusually powerful natural mage abilities stemmed from a combination of Galise (alfar) and dragon blood? What Mondi *did* have was a pocketful of lockpicks.

The rest of the party, Sigi excepted, stood watching Mondi anxiously as they were still recovering their strength from the battle with the powerful sheda. None of them was a lightweight, yet it had taken six of them to bring him down! Sigi wished he had his brother's boldness, but Mondi had a mental edge on him far greater than the difference in their ages. He stood watching with admiration as Mondi went first to one corridor, then the other – liberating the contents of the chests at the backs of each of them and then strutting back across the floor to join the rest of them with a triumphant grin on his face. Anja suspected that whatever those chests had contained, Mondi would not be dropping the proceeds into the common pot. There'd been so much wealth already that she didn't mind. What a kid!

From where they stood, clustered a short distance down the middle corridor on the left side of the long room, they could not see any of the left corridor immediately before the impressive-looking double doors. They could see partway into the corridor opposite it, and there was nothing there. Had that one (admittedly powerful) sheda been all that was guarding this room?

Andi took it upon himself to sneak out of the corridor the group was standing in and down the room a few paces to where the next (and final) corridor opened to the left. Nothing there, thank the gods! He was feeling more than a little tired from the hours they'd spent walking and fighting, and while adrenaline still kept him on his toes he was beginning to get that creeping feeling – a bill was coming due, and his mind and body were going to have to pay.

Andi crept a little way down the empty corridor. It contained another of the stone platforms, so reminiscent of the catafalques in ancient Norse tombs. But no coffins, no bodies – and no chests. Now he had a good view of the corridor opposite, and his heart sank. Hovering in air near the far end of it, in front of a small chest, was the translucent form of one of the lesser types of sheda.

These, at least, seemed mostly to succumb to his magic-block spell. He was tired of this, ready to go home to Pantheatos House and sleep until the Grand Ball on Maritag. It had been fun, but even fun could begin to wear you down after a while. He hit the floating figure with magic-block, which he hoped would take, then applied a magical energy poison (identical to the one he'd used on Meiskomtot last year, with great effect) to an arrow and fired it into the sheda with a burst of flames for added damage. The daimonic bow he was using was enchanted to cause its targets to catch fire briefly.

"Sheda in the corridor over there!" Andi shouted, and charged. He'd already examined the ceiling to make sure that the stretch of floor between here and there was free of likely traps. The rest of the group burst from their hiding place and attacked, edged weapons swinging. In these close quarters all the extra help almost became a liability, as the archers couldn't shoot into a swirling crowd and the mages were afraid to fire bolts of battle magic lest they hit their friends.

The boys held back as their elders closed on the undead creature. It had failed to resist Andi's magic-block spell and was unable to use any magic whatsoever as it was surrounded, and soon destroyed, by half a dozen lethal fighters. Riki, who was beginning to feel a little tired too, felt a thrill of triumph as the thing fell to them. She had the sense that they were approaching a culmination, that the doors before them led to something big – after which, they'd finally be able to rest. Rest was beginning to seem like a great idea.

As they recovered from the brief fight and prepared to go through the doors ahead, Flavius gazed at Riki – a warm glow overlaid on his sight. Never in his life (all eighteen years of it) had he fallen so utterly, hopelessly in love! His misgivings about her draconic connections were utterly forgotten as he had watched her in action – fearless, competent, determined. How was it possible that this magnificent woman was not yet sixteen? He planned to demand that Father arrange a marriage contract between them as soon as they got back to Roma – though a small voice murmured in the back of his mind that perhaps he ought to broach the subject with Riki, first.

The double doors ahead of them were… different. Anja and Lars, who had plundered more than a dozen eldalfar ruins since they had first come to Remus more than two years before, had never seen their like. They were stone, like the outer doors you commonly saw at the first entrance to a ruin. But while those were usually plain, with only a single engraved circle in the center, these were carved in a complex filigree pattern. And they were very firmly locked.

Andi stepped up to them. Like his sister, he sensed triumph awaiting them on the other side of these doors – if he could just get them opened. Trained by both his father and his mother in fine control of spellcraft, a skill that was still not common among the mages of Agena, Andi was able to use the spell to send his mind down into the lock, to see its tumblers and its intricacies. An ordinary mage, simply casting a spell and relying on the magic to do the work, would have failed to get through this lock. But he directed the power where it needed to go – and with a rolling sequence of clicks, it yielded to him and the ornate doors swung open.

There was an audible sigh as everyone watching him let out their breaths at once. Yay, Andi! He caught Rezira's gaze, and her blue-violet eyes bored into his with gratitude, admiration, and love. He had a sudden desire to scoop her up and take her into the nearest corridor while the rest of the party proceeded into the room ahead – a desire he successfully stifled. There'd be time enough for love when this quest was finished.

145

They found themselves walking into a large room. Not the biggest they'd encountered, but it seemed cavernous because it was unbroken by any architectural features at all. The ceiling was perhaps thirty feet above their heads, the room a stone box with the doors they had come through at one side – and an enormous throne, close to five feet wide and a dozen tall, standing up against the wall on the opposite side of the chamber.

There was a hushed silence as they took it all in. On the throne a tall, wasted figure sat. It was mummified, preserved by the cold dry air of this sealed chamber for thousands of years. From the height of the corpse, which sat stiffly as if presiding over a court, this person must have stood nearly seven feet tall in life. It had clearly been an elf, one of the eldalfar who were ancestors of the ljosalfar, and the rest of the alfar races as well.

The figure was clad in glistening armor – breastplate, greaves, gauntlets, and boots – wrought of elvengild and heavily inlaid with gold in an antique design. On his head (this had to have been a king of some sort) was an intricately fashioned gold crown, set with dazzling gems. Anja gazed on him, seeing her future life before her eyes. Wealthy collectors would be lining up and bidding against each other for the chance to possess these astonishing treasures, and the fortune she would realize from their sale, suitably invested, would mean she and Lars never had to work again. They could settle down in Waterdon and enjoy the remainder of Edla's childhood, perhaps start a family of their own!

There was a polished stone plaque carved into the top part of the stone throne, and Rezira was drawn to it. It was graven with sinuous runes, incomprehensible to every other person in the room. But she had been raised in an ancient elven culture that had remained essentially unchanged for thousands of years – and the writing looked familiar.

They all watched her as she approached the throne, crowding unheedingly close to its mummified occupant. "I can almost read this!" she said in wonder. "Here lies… no, I think it's more like 'remains,' Indalato, last king of Sindalo. Though the high elves may fall, yet his memory… no, maybe 'deeds' will live on." Anja, eyes shining, couldn't wait any longer. She stepped to stand beside Rezira

146

and reached up, seizing that amazing crown where it rested on the withered, mostly skeletal head. Rezira continued, alarm rising in her voice. "Wait! It says 'Let none disturb the rest of Indalato, lest the guardians'…"

As Anja lifted the crown, the chamber was filled with a rumbling sound. To their left and right, broad sections of stone slid down into the floor, opening doorways to chambers on either side of the room. And within those chambers the guardians waited, awakened at last for the task they had been set eons ago. Rezira screamed, as they flooded in.

There were so many of them! At least half a dozen shedas, and another half-dozen of the fierce skeletal warriors they were able to summon. Andi decided to skip magic-block and try some of his lethal blended battle magic on one of the skeletons, which was closing fast – and found that he, himself, had been blocked. He ripped his sword free of its scabbard and swung it in an arc, driving the skeleton back. But while he'd studied swordplay for most of his life, magic had become his weapon of choice. He was good, but he was going to need to be great if they were to defeat these undead foes that outnumbered them two to one!

So he cast a dragon spell. These spells were undeniably a form of magic, yet they did not draw on one's own magical energy – instead being powered by the stones he had absorbed into his being. You could still use them even if your normal magical energy had been blocked. He stood naked for a moment, then spelled again and became a dragon approaching twenty-five feet from nose to tail. Sigi and Mondi, whose only weapons were bows and daggers, quickly took Andi's cue and did the same. They kept their wings close to their bodies, though the room's ceiling was almost high enough to allow them to lift off.

As Andi surged forward and snatched one of the walking skeletons in his jaws, causing it to explode in a shower of bones, Rezira cast him a fierce grin and ran to the throne. She climbed up it, balancing on its top above the plaque, and began taking careful shots with her bow as the melee unfolded below her.

The skeletal champions remained scattered on the stone floor, not vanishing – so they must have been among the guardians waiting for the chance to defend their fallen king, rather than summonings of the shedas. Riki and Flavius stood back to back, swords in a blur, as they fought shedas also armed with swords.

All that sword practice must have given her more than a lithe body and some fun, Riki realized, as she actually managed to disarm the sheda facing her and run her sword through its body. Mom had given this "bastard sword" a fire damage enchantment, and the undead creature seemed to be vulnerable to it. It fell to the stones, and another of the skeletal warriors, one that had recently appeared, fell with it.

The young dragons had soon destroyed all of the original skeletal champions. It was harder for them to attack the shedas, but they had only to get one of the animated skeletons into their jaws and they flew apart like an exploding bundle of kindling. Andi had noted how effective fire damage was on the sheda Riki had killed, and he backed one into a corner and incinerated it with Holocaust. The dragons had to be careful in this confined space, lest they toast their friends as well as their adversaries.

Anja and Lars, too, fought back to back – as they'd done many times before. Rezira, on her perch atop the throne, had mostly escaped attack as the shedas' attention was concentrated on the people confronting them on the floor. She continued to pick her shots carefully, firing only when she had a clear shot – and if none of her arrows actually killed the target, they were wearing them down and distracting them so her companions could kill them.

Lars slashed down, cleaving the withered body of the sheda before him from shoulder to pelvis, and the undead creature fell to the stones. He whirled to assist Anja as she fought another sheda, and just then Sigi came up, a deep golden dragon looking darker in this dim light, and engulfed its head in his jaws. It was already floating a foot above the stones, but he lifted it still higher and shook it, until the body ripped free from the head and was flung to one side. Anja and Lars, eyes wide, stood panting as Sigi spat out the head with a "Bleah!" and turned to look for another opponent. There were none moving.

Looking around the room and realizing that all of the guardians were down, Andi spelled himself back into human form – then re-acquired his armor and weapons. "We did it!" he crowed, and the rest of the party responded with whoops and cheers. Mondi and Sigi quickly returned to human form, and Rezira agilely hopped back down off of the throne.

She made as if to dust herself off, then continued pedantically in her translation of the plaque. "As I was *saying*," she said, "'Do not disturb his rest lest the guardians be aroused, and destroy you.' You might have let me finish!" She grinned, showing she wasn't serious. They had screwed up, but they had triumphed. All was well!

Anja smiled back, and picked up the crown again from where she'd dropped it when the attack had begun. "Thank you, Rezira," she said. "Sorry I got greedy and didn't listen 'til the end before grabbing!" She began removing the long-dead eldalfar ruler's vestments. "With this, we can quit adventuring and sit around on our asses for the rest of our lives!" Anja declared. "Or do something we really want to do, without worrying about whether it puts food on the table. Right, Lars?" He gazed into her eyes, hypnotized. He'd sensed this change coming for a long time, and some part of him welcomed it. Adventuring had its rewards, but it was a hard, dangerous life – and he didn't blame his beloved for wanting to move on.

Instead of answering, he stepped close and took Anja in his arms. They were both heavily armored, but it didn't stop him from squeezing her tightly, bending her back for a deep, deep kiss. Flavius, his heart still pounding from the excitement of the past few minutes, was inspired. He locked his dark brown gaze on Riki's startlingly blue eyes. Then he seized her in an embrace that ignored the armor both of them were wearing. "You were magnificent!" he breathed, before kissing her passionately. Coming up for air, he murmured "I love you."

Chapter 19: Temptation

Fjuri and a group of his fellow workers on Hegmar's crew came into the Flying Horseman in high spirits. Today, they'd finished the job they'd been working on for the past several weeks, and it was a job well done. Furthermore, they'd been paid – and the satisfaction they were all feeling was enough, for the moment at least, to lift Fjuri's spirits and drive away the loneliness and frustration that had set in since Riki had left. She'd been gone for three weeks now, and it seemed like forever. He didn't think he could bear it if she was really gone for the two full months that had been mentioned as a possibility when she'd first dropped that bombshell on him.

He wanted her to be his forever – married in the Temple of Marmira in Lakedon just as his parents had been, living in the beautiful new house they would build together. But were his dreams just so much foolishness? He sighed, pasted a smile on his face, and lifted a tankard of ale with his fellows as the buxom barmaid brought a tray of drinks to their table. There was no point in brooding about things he had no control over, and he put his mournful thoughts away with an effort of will.

They were on their third round of ale, boisterously singing along with the house bard, when Inge Redmane walked in with a couple of their fellow construction workers from Hegmar's second crew. Unless somebody else opened up another construction firm in Waterdon and gave him some competition, Hegmar might soon need to expand to a third crew to keep up with demand. The three of them took seats at the table next to the one Fjuri and his comrades were sitting at, waving and calling out mock insults. Construction workers tended to be very serious about their craft, and not at all serious about anything else.

Soon Inge and her party were working to catch up on ale consumption, joining in the joking and laughter and singing loud and strong on "The Swordmaid of Normarsh" – one of their favorite humorous ballads. Then Inge picked up her ale, and sauntered over to Fjuri's table – lips parted in a smile and a look of lascivious mischief in her eyes. "Scooch back at little, Fjuri!" she commanded; and he, feeling no pain, pulled his chair out from the table a little.

Then she plopped herself down on his lap in her tight leather pants, and a chorus of hoots went up at both tables.

Fjuri stifled the urge to rise to his feet and dump her on the floor. Now that he was an adult, he felt it was time to work on his personal issues – to be more easy-going, one of the guys. He really did enjoy that feeling of belonging, and when he wasn't silently brooding his co-workers seemed to like him a lot. So instead of reacting like a scared rabbit, he put an arm around Inge's waist, his other hand raising his tankard to his lips, and leered at her.

It was all an act, but it fooled Inge and the rest of Fjuri's co-workers – and a look of annoyance briefly crossed her face. What fun was it to tease someone who refused to rise to the bait? On the other hand, she would just *love* to get this wonder-hunk into her bed. And who knows, perhaps pry him away from that hifalutin' blonde goddess of his. Wouldn't he be better off, really, with a woman of his own class, someone who shared his enthusiasm for building? And Fjuri was wealthy and well-connected by the standards of Inge's social circle – he'd be an excellent catch even if he *wasn't* good-looking and sexy beyond belief.

"That's a pretty big hunk you've bitten off there, Inge," Berand said, "Do you think you can chew him up?" He was not among those of Hegmar's workers who'd shared Inge's bed – being past thirty, a little on the short side, and ill-favored with a receding hairline and an overly large nose. She liked them big, young, and pretty. "I don't know if I can chew him up, but I think I can swallow him," she said with a leer. Both tables exploded in laughter at her double entendre.

Fjuri just grinned and took another gulp of his ale, emptying the tankard. He was feeling pretty good, actually, not afraid of Inge or much of anything at the moment, and called to the barmaid "Juliette! More ale all around!" as he gestured at his table and the one Inge had been sitting at.

The revelry went on for some time, and eventually Inge climbed down off of Fjuri's lap so he could go and use the privy. She pulled up a chair beside his. They all got some supper, then continued their drinking on into the night. Fjuri rarely drank enough to get a buzz, but he was well and truly soused now – and positively enjoying himself. He was disappointed when his friends began to drift away, heading for their homes.

Inge ran her hand down his thigh under the table stroking and squeezing, and he felt a sensation go through him like lightning – momentarily clearing his head. He wanted her! And wasn't what she'd said to him before only wisdom, shouldn't he have a little experience under his belt before he and Riki made love for the first time? He wanted it to be special for her, a happy memory not an embarrassment, and how could he manage that when he barely knew what went where?

Her hand still on his thigh, Inge leaned close to his ear. "Looks like we're the last ones here, Fjuri," she murmured, and then took his earlobe gently between her lips and sucked on it slightly. Another thrill ran through him. "Would you care to take me up on my offer of a few tips?" she went on. "My room's just right up the stairs there…"

He finished his ale. How many had he had tonight? "S-sure, why nah?" Fjuri replied, surprised at how hard it seemed to be to make his lips and tongue work right. His mind was drifting on a fuzzy cloud, while his body was urging him to go with Inge, now! They got to their feet, and Fjuri nearly fell over. Inge was not nearly as drunk, and she put an arm around his waist and let him lean on her as they walked to the back of the room and up the stairs. The few remaining patrons, most of them staying here at the inn, watched them go.

They made it into the room and Inge let Fjuri down to sit on the bed. His head was spinning, and he felt a wave of nausea. It was just possible, he thought, that he might have had too much to drink. "Ya gotta shamberpah?" he croaked out, and she hastily pulled the chamberpot out from under the bed. Fjuri suddenly heaved, half-filling the ceramic pot with the contents of his stomach, as Inge looked away in disgust. This was *not* what she'd had in mind!

Feeling much better, Fjuri tucked the pot back under the bed and grinned at Inge sheepishly. "Sorry," he said, "think I had too mush to drink…"

"No kidding," she said wryly, and handed him a glass of water. "Rinse your mouth out, will you?" He did so, then sat on the end of the bed weaving slightly.

"All better," he announced. "Now whah?"

She sat down on the bed and kissed him, gently, on the mouth. When he began to respond, she slipped her tongue into his mouth, running her hands down his chest and undoing the laces on his shirt. Then she broke away, and commanded him, "Pull off your shirt." He obeyed her, revealing his magnificently muscled arms and chest. He had some dark hair on his chest and belly, but his skin was remarkably smooth. Inge's desire rose, and she leaned close to run her hands over the bare skin of his torso. Mmm!

She kissed him again, and he kissed her back – but he was just resting those big hands on her shoulders. "Touch me here," she directed, and put his hand on her breast. He seemed nonplussed.

"Uh, okay…" he said, and did as he'd been told. Gods, the boy seemed to have no natural talent for this at all, Inge thought with annoyance. Or maybe it was just that he was so drunk…

She pulled away again, and once again he sat, hands at his side, swaying slightly and looking at her bleary-eyed. Inge sighed and rose to her feet. "I tell you what," she told her would-be lover, "why don't you just sit there for a moment. I'm going to get undressed." She was wearing much the same sort of clothing most of the male construction workers wore, though hers fitted her differently.

Trying to make it into a striptease, though she had little experience of the art, Inge strolled around the room for a bit, her body swaying as if to unheard music – and then she stood before Fjuri and put a booted foot in his lap. "Pull my boot off, please," she requested. When both boots were off and tossed to the floor she began working on her shirt, slipping it up over her head and throwing it one side. Her shapely, full breasts, which she regarded as one of her best features, bobbed free.

Inge was disappointed to see little reaction from Fjuri as her body was revealed. He was staring at her, or perhaps through her, and there was no sign of the excitement she'd been hoping for. Curses, she thought, I finally get the man into my bedchamber and he's too loaded to appreciate the experience! Well, maybe after she got the rest of her clothes off…

She began writhing, unlacing her tight leather breeches with their doubled knees, slowly pulling them down over her hips, peeling them down farther and farther… With a flourish, Inge stepped out of her trousers at last and stood naked with her back to Fjuri. She shook her well-shaped, muscular rear at him, then rotated to see what effect it was having. Fjuri had fallen over, legs still draped over the end of the bed, his upper body lying flat. His eyes were closed, and a none-too-gentle snore issued from his lips.

Chapter 20: Getting Ready

Bernadette looked into the full-length mirror and her mouth fell open. By the gods, she looked like a queen! Maybe she should dump Andrion and Erik and start looking for a prince to marry, she thought facetiously. The gown was of a shimmering silk fabric, a deep blue like the sky at the height of summer, and brought out the blue of her eyes (which were mostly a deep gray) while perfectly setting off her long red hair. The cut gave the illusion of being risqué, while actually covering her from neck to ankle. Frothy white lace peeked out from slits in the full skirt on either side, and her generous cleavage protruded above the bodice but was screened by sheer netting studded with glittering crystals. They were not real diamonds, she'd been informed – but for how much the dress had cost they might as well be.

Riki, Anja, and Rezira were clustered around her like ladies in waiting, oohing and aahing at the magnificence of her gown. They were next to get their own gowns fitted, each of them except Anja's custom-made. She had been fortunate to find a lovely (and reasonably priced; her thrill at attending the Imperial Ball had not erased her ingrained frugality, despite their huge score in Sindalo) gown on the shop's ready-made rack that flattered her tall, slim and muscular body while giving her a feminine air seldom seen on the young warrior woman since she had first taken up a bow at the age of six.

Rezira's petite form was given the appearance of extra height by a slim-skirted floor-length sheath in a deep purple shade, the bodice plunging to reveal her bosom – more ample than usual for a woman of the alfar races. She had a pair of high-heeled sandals giving her another three inches, and a choker necklace of sparking amethysts picked up the color of the dress – and of her eyes. She'd decided to let her mane of glossy black hair cascade down over her shoulders. Seeing those shoes reminded Bernadette of the red heels she'd worn to her wedding, all those years ago, and brought an internal sigh. She could have used a little extra height too, but had decided in favor of practicality and was wearing a pair of flat-soled velvet slippers instead.

Last to be fitted was Riki – and she outshone them all. Her gown was similar in cut to Rezira's, a slim floor-length sheath slit up the rear to allow leg movement. It was glistening cloth-of-gold lined with silk for comfort, and the bodice was cut more modestly – while the back plunged low. A full overskirt made of that same golden netting studded with glittering crystals softened the lines of the dress and rustled as she turned from side to side, admiring herself in the mirror.

Bernadette embraced her daughter carefully. "Oh, Riki!" she sighed, "You truly look like a goddess! Wait until that boyfriend of yours sees you in it – you're going to have to carry a handkerchief to blot up the drool…" My boyfriend, Riki thought, with a twinge. Fjuri was her first love, and had been her boyfriend for more than a year. He thought they were going to get married and start a life together, probably as soon as she turned sixteen. Did her desire to know more of the world before getting tied down mean that she didn't truly love him, didn't share his dreams? And what, really, were her feelings for Flavius? He was handsome, charming, rich, and a member of one of the empire's most prominent families – plus he was smitten with her. But could she love him?

In his private study at the family's townhouse in the Scintillio District Duke Enzo Terentius sat working on some correspondence. He much preferred staying in Roma over life in Brindis, but his ducal office was not a job he could entirely ignore. His steward managed things for him while he and the rest of the family were staying here, but there were many issues he had to address personally – if only by mail.

He heard a tap at the open door and looked up to see his second son standing there with a smile and an inquiring look. All three of his boys looked so much like their dead mother, it gave him a pang. "Papa, do you have a moment?" Flavius asked politely. Enzo set the letter aside. He was always happy to make time for his boys – even if two of them must really now be accounted men. "Come in, Flavius," he said, and gestured to a chair that stood on the other side of his writing desk.

Flavius, in contrast to his usual glib charm, seemed to be having trouble finding words. "Uh, Papa, now that I'm eighteen and all…

Well, Arturus already has a betrothal and he's the heir to the ducal throne but I'm just the second son…" Enzo's eyebrows rose.

"You've been squiring the Drakespring girl," he stated. It was hardly a secret, and more than one person had remarked on it to him as well. Flavius' eyes lit.

"Yes!" he said enthusiastically, "Riki! Papa, she is the most beautiful girl I've ever met, well-connected, and would give our family ties to Iscandia. I want your permission to ask her to marry me!"

Oh dear, Enzo thought. He should have seen this coming. Flavius, with his looks and his suave personality, had cut a swath through the maidens of Roma. But sooner or later one of them was going to get to him, and he was a good-hearted young man. How to discourage him, without breaking his heart or causing a rift between them? Later, of course, it wouldn't matter – but for now, he could not have his family involved with the Drakesprings of Iscandia.

Observing his father's expression, Flavius was getting a sinking sensation. Finally Enzo, an expression of concerned sympathy on his face, spoke. "She is a lovely young woman, I know," he said. "Though very young, of course. But I'm afraid that marriage with her is out of the question. There is a taint in her family's blood, a taint that would be passed to our own family if you were to ally with her."

Flavius' face took on a look of outrage. "But Riki doesn't have the dragon blood!" he exclaimed. "Her father is a pure, completely unmagical Norseman. Her mother has the dragon blood, without which I suppose I would never have been born since the entire planet would have been destroyed by the Soul-Devourer! But the dragon blood didn't pass to *all* of her children (two out of the three who were born human, he realized, plus there were the other dozen-plus who'd actually been born dragons… best not to bring *that* up). Our children would be free of any eldritch taint."

Enzo sighed. "It's not the actual dragon blood that is at issue, son. It's society's perceptions. When Erika's brothers go around turning into dragons it frightens a lot of folks, and people will talk. If you married her, your bride would never quite be admitted to society. She would be seen as a freak, as would you for marrying her – and everyone would be watching your children to see if they were going to sprout wings. I'm sorry, deeply sorry. Love her if you will, enjoy her while you can – but there can be no marriage with her."

He pulled the piece of correspondence he'd been studying to him again, eyes dropping to the page, by way of dismissal. Enzo's heart ached for his beautiful son and the sad fate of his first deep love – but there was no help for it. Such a marriage simply could not be.

Flavius rose to his feet, face pale, quivering slightly with helpless anger. He was a member of the aristocracy, and he had known all his life that he might not get to choose the woman he married. Look at poor Arturus, and his betrothal to that girl in Eraven. Her father had been the brother of the duke, actually, neither an ogre nor a minotaur; yet there was no doubt her beauty left much to be desired.

But he loved Riki so! Given enough time he supposed he might have coaxed her into his bed, as he had several daughters of the lesser nobility here in Roma. But he didn't want to make her his mistress, and he doubted either she or her parents would be happy with such a role for her. He wanted her to be his wife, but how could he convince Father that such a match would be desirable? Maybe if Andrion and his team at the University of the Magical Arts managed to succeed in their power cell project, the Drakesprings would be lauded by the emperor and society's opinion of the family would change? It was his only hope.

Draco, Felix, and Gaius were once again in their guise of street beggars, roaming the narrow alleys of the waterfront district and exploring. They'd all paid their initiation fee to the Guild out of the cache of gold Sigi had taken from the loot of Sindalo. That he might have that money for himself had been okayed by Anja and Lars, who were keeping all the rest of the cash to help fund their retirement from their careers as adventurers.

Likely the two would still explore a tomb or take out a nest of bandits from time to time just for fun, as Sigi's own parents had done rarely since he had been born – unless childbearing intervened. But with the huge riches to be realized by the sale of Sindalo's treasures, they could settle down with a comfortable house in Waterdon and enjoy life, free for a few years at least from the necessity to make a living.

Each of the participants in the Sindalo excursion who had not already claimed something chose a small item out of the pile of loot as a keepsake of the adventure after they'd returned to Roma and dumped out their packs on the dining table at Pantheatos House. But Sigi had little use for jewelry or other trinkets – and with the gold they could buy their way into the Guild of Beggars without having to explain why they were asking for the money.

It was all just a game to them, of course – three boys from wealthy families who were fascinated by the shadowy underworld and wanted to see how the other half lived. They had made no effort yet to find themselves begging spots – most of the good ones were already taken and would only be freed up by the death of the Guild beggars who had held them for years. And who wanted to stand around all day asking passersby for alms, anyway?

Now, Mondi was wishing that they had found *three* Rings of Blend instead of just the one. It would be so much fun if all three of them could become invisible, stealing quietly around the city and eavesdropping on the secret conversations of the thieves, assassins, and other plotters! Why, they might even manage to foil some heinous plot, and be lauded for their efforts! Instead they were engaged in more ordinary mischief, two of them watching while the third, wearing the ring, sneaked up and teased people – dropping a coin "out of thin air" into a beggar's hat, tapping people on the shoulder as they strode down the street, and so forth.

Sigi removed the ring from his finger and reappeared in the midst of his companions, his arms laden with apples from the cart of the street vendor across the way. He grinned slyly and passed one each to Mondi and Gaius, then sank his teeth into the third. He didn't tell them that he'd left payment on the cart. They walked off together, munching their treats. Somehow, "stolen" fruit tasted much better than the regular kind.

"So are you going to be at the Imperial Ball on Maritag?" Mondi asked Gaius. The boy's handsome face fell, before lighting again at the thought of the enhanced opportunities for mischief. "Yeah, my father's dragging all three of us there with him. I think everyone in Remus who is anyone will be there. You, too?"

The Drakespring boys grinned ruefully. Getting scrubbed up and into fancy clothes they were forbidden to ruin was a burden; and being forced to converse with snobby strangers who would patronize them and say stupid things, a positive torment. But they reasoned that, as at the party where they'd met Gaius last week, they would soon be able to make their escape. "We'll meet you by where the musicians are playing as soon as we get there," Mondi promised. "Visiting the Imperial Palace might be lot of fun."

Andrion, Gylabris, Andi and Rezira were gathered in the basement lab at the Enchanting Hall with Sextus, Aphinea, and Louis clustered around the other side of the workbench on which one of their prototype power cells sat. Its design was clean and simple, so it didn't look quite the same as one of the dypalfar originals. Ornamentation could wait, until they had solved the problems connected with making it work. And once they began manufacturing them, most would be hidden away inside the machines they were intended to power. Why bother with decoration, increasing the time and money needed for making them?

They had performed the spell forging this one's link to its power source three days ago, and it was still glowing red inside – the inner cage still turning. Presumably, they could have slipped this into a dypalfar robon – or perhaps, that refrigeration box Gylabris had devised with help from Jerzha in Alfenstein – and it would continually supply the needed power for operation.

"I'm really convinced this one is right," Andrion said, gesturing to the glowing power cell on the table. "Now we need to test our theory by bringing another one online using the same spell."

"It's my theory," Gylabris said," that quite possibly every power cell on Terris is connected to the same other-plane star for its power source. Whether we have tapped into that particular star, or another one in the same plane of existence, I can't be sure. But stars are huge beyond belief, many thousands of times bigger than our planet, and they burn for billions of years. It should be possible for even a medium-sized star to power millions of power cells without harming it or affecting its output of energy."

"Ah, but it's an issue of the precise location of that energy conduit, that minute portal through to the other plane and the star within it," Sextus said. "It may be necessary to record the exact positioning of the conduit for every core, and every one may need to be different from the last. Else a new portal may merely steal the energy from an existing one."

"I can't say for certain," Rezira admitted. "No one in my own city of Mrzhandtham, at least, had the making of power cells. We used the ones we had had for thousands of years, as they never wore out, and if any among my people knew the full secret of their construction it was not knowledge revealed to the general public. Our culture had become stagnant, I fear, with all of us smug in our 'paradise' and convinced that there was nothing left to learn, no progress worth the trouble of achieving it."

"Well, we can only try it and see what happens," Andrion said with a sigh. He was enjoying their trip to Remus, but beginning to think fondly of his home and of the other projects he'd left behind at the Academy. He missed Meri, missed the other kids, missed his parents. Berni's rejuvenation of Francois and Christine had made it possible for him to enjoy the relationship with them, as fellow adults, that he'd feared he would never get a chance to have. He hoped their team would soon have success here, and could return to Iscandia.

Andrion had a broader grasp of all schools of magic, and a greater fund of magical energy at his command, than almost any other mage in Agena. Yet even he needed a collection of enchanted items and a magical energy-enhancing potion to cast this spell with comfort. It was a variation of the magic that had been used to create the magical portals by which one traveled between floors of the university's Magister's Tower.

It was also akin to the spellcraft that had been used two centuries before to open enduring portals from various parts of the Netherworld to here in Remus – and millennia before that, from Iscandia to the world of Gaia where Andrion and Erik had contended against the immortal sorceress Luthia. All of those portals between Remus and the Netherworld had fallen when Crispus Salonius, in dragon form as the avatar of Aderos, had defeated the daimonic lord

Nergal. Yet the tiny portals within each of the dypalfar's power cells had stayed open for eons.

Andi watched eagerly as his father cast the spell. He knew it now, after watching it cast several times; but it would require a huge supply of extra magical energy for him to be able to cast it himself. As the spell took hold, the new power cell sitting on the table – the object of the spell – glowed red and its interior began to spin. As it did so the light of the one beside it, which had been glowing continually for days, winked out – and the motion inside it ceased.

Andrion sagged. The spell had taken nearly everything he had, and it now seemed certain that Sextus' theory was correct. You could *not* use the same spell to produce one power cell after another – each one must be recorded and calibrated, with a slight offset of the location of the far end of the portal for the next one so that each tapped into an energy locus that was not already in use.

Andrion had pioneered the fine-tuning of spellcraft in his generation, an art that might possibly have existed in some forgotten time and been rediscovered by him – or perhaps something he and he alone had stumbled on. His ability to control the precise target, size, and intensity of battle magic, interweaving two different sorts of spells like fire and lightning, had enabled him to use battle magic for such practical purposes as cutting metal, welding pipes, and cooling beverages. His wife, Bernadette, had extended what he had learned to healing magic, and been able to re-knit connections within the human brain to bring his father Francois back to his former self after a decade as an invalid following a crippling stroke.

So, Andrion was convinced that it would require only a little more research before they cracked this final obstacle. The attempt had tired him, and he felt the need of some rest and recuperation (and time to think it over) before they began again. "Sextus, I think you hit the nail on the head!" he said. "We just need to figure out how to pinpoint the exact geographical location on the sphere of our other-plane sun that was accessed by our basic spell, then adjust it so that a nearby but not identical location is connected to the next core. And so on."

Sextus nodded, pleased. They had made amazing progress in the short time that Andrion and his team had been here, completely justifying the expense of putting them all up. They'd all be millionaires, if they managed to put the cells into production – and the Imperial government, sponsor of their research, would benefit immensely from a monopoly on their sale.

"That's going to make manufacturing them a little more difficult," he said, "but once we work out the math we should be able to adjust the spell almost automatically. We're almost there!"

Andrion smiled tiredly at his colleague's gleeful enthusiasm. "I suppose you're all going to attend the Imperial Ball tomorrow evening?" he asked, and there were nods from Sextus and his university teammates. "I suggest we adjourn until Arytag, then. We'll see you all at the Ball, and then have Apoldtag to consider the best way to adjust the spell so that each core has its own unique connection to the star that's powering them all. Are we in agreement?" A quiet cheer went up from those assembled.

Chapter 21: The Grand Ball

The water system at Pantheatos House had been strained to the utmost bathing all of the members of the Drakespring family, along with Gylabris, Rezira, Anja, and Lars (no such facilities were available at the Storekeeps' Inn). Fortunately a rainstorm earlier in the week, one that had lasted for more than 24 hours, had replenished the rooftop cistern. Additionally, some of the friendlier members of the party had been willing to share the tub – or bathe in the same water left by the previous occupant.

Anja and Lars had joined with them and gotten dressed and ready at Pantheatos House some hours before the ball, so two coaches were needed to ferry them all through the autumn gloaming (and a light drizzle) to the Imperial Palace. The men were enduring this with stoicism mixed with a touch of excitement. Who could not be at least a little moved by the idea of hobnobbing with the emperor of all Agena, regardless of one's lack of social ambitions? The women were, generally speaking, over the moons.

Coaches were backed up for more than a block, waiting to deposit their occupants near the front entrance. A squad of city guards checked each party's invitations, then let them through to the ringed corridor that encircled the central chamber of the White-Gold Tower. For tonight, the ground floor and the one above it had been opened to the public, though the ball itself was taking place in the central chamber.

For this stupendous event, the year's lone must-attend party, nearly everyone of any consequence in the empire – or at least within Remus – had been invited. The Drakespring Family, so newly arrived, had been among the last of the attendees to receive invitations.

Bernadette, Riki, Rezira, and Anja found themselves the subject of lecherous – or envious – glances from all quarters as they came through the entrance hall and into the Grand Ballroom. The room did duty usually as an audience hall, where the emperor's throne sat when he was holding court. But for this event the room had been cleared of all its usual furnishings and seating for musicians now took center stage. Long tables heaped with food and drink flanked the room's sides, and the emperor and his party – his wife, sister, brother-in-law, and nephew/heir – stood along one side of the room's center line, ready to greet the guests as they arrived.

What an ordeal that must be, Bernadette thought as they stood waiting to be announced. Despite her fame and prominence in Iscandia, she'd never had the slightest desire to hold political power – or all it entailed. She had quite enough to do caring for her husbands and her twenty-two surviving children, and no wish at all to add the population of a province, or a continent, to her list of responsibilities.

As at the party the week before, a servant with precise diction and a marvelous voice that carried throughout the room announced each member of the party. Now Anja Steadfast and Lars (no surname given) were included in the announcement, though no one paid any attention. The two young adventurers were as important on the political scene of Agena as was the average greengrocer. Anja didn't mind. She was here, in the Imperial Palace, dressed in a magnificent gown and looking pretty damn hot, in her own estimation. Lars had been happy to add his own vote to that assessment. She expected it would be a night she would always remember, and tell her grandchildren about. Mama and Papa would be so impressed!

They walked forward from the doors to the reception line, and greeted the emperor and his family. "Magister Drakespring, so glad that you could attend on short notice!" Giorgio said urbanely. It was not just his family's ancestral connection to the Salonius dynasty that had led to his being selected as emperor. Giorgio Salonius (nee Augustino) was a consummate politician. And seemingly, a nice guy. "Later this evening I would really like a chance to talk with you privately about the progress of the power cell project," he went on.

"I think you'll be pleased," Andrion replied with a smile.

After the rest of the family had passed through and greeted everyone in the emperor's party, Mondi and Sigi peeled off. As they had waited for the grown-ups to finish their polite platitudes, they'd been visually scanning the room and had spotted Gaius' father, Duke Terentius, over near one of the food tables on the left side of the room.

Flavius had seen *them* entering, too, and was waiting to take Riki up with a chaste kiss on the cheek, and polite greetings to her family, before sweeping her away. Bernadette sighed as she watched them go. She'd always thought that Riki's relationship with Fjuri might eventually lead to marriage, completing a circle of some kind from the time when she had worked to create the Steadfast clan in the first place. Their descendants would be the culmination of that process. If that marriage ever came to pass, of course…

Riki was young, but Bernadette held a firm belief that she had her head on straight. She was not going to be dazzled by some young aristocrat's suave sophistication, and end up with a noble bastard in her belly. No one had told her Riki had acquired a birth control amulet, else she might have been both less – and more – concerned. If Flavius was sincere, and Riki reciprocated his feelings, maybe Fjuri was just going to end up the loser in the battle –never really fought, as the two were unlikely to ever meet – for her affections. It made Bernadette feel sad, but there didn't seem to be anything she could do about it.

Meanwhile Mondi and Sigi had joined forces with young Gaius, then went to stuff themselves at the food tables before going off to explore whatever other areas of the Imperial Palace had been opened to the public. Unlike the Terentius family's ball, essentially a cocktail party followed by a sit-down dinner, the Imperial Ball – with its many more invitees – supplied supper from the endlessly-refilled buffet tables on either side of the central hall. Later, there would be music and dancing in that hall – but the party had been expanded to selected other rooms on the ground floor and the one above it, where the guests could spread out to converse. Additional tables heaped with food and drink were scattered throughout the space.

The boys were soon gone, and Flavius was escorting Riki around the hall, showing her off to his friends and acquaintances. Papa might have told him that there could be no marriage liaison with the Drakespring clan, but he loved her beyond belief and she was far and away the most beautiful woman here. No one they talked with showed any fear or revulsion at the supposed "dragon blood taint" on Riki's family, but Flavius caught several of his friends' female companions eyeing her coldly.

Riki felt radiantly happy. This wasn't real life, and she was still uncertain of Flavius' intentions – or whether a life in Waterdon with

Fjuri was what she wanted. But tonight, she was a star. She looked magnificent in her golden gown, and all the men – old and young – were drooling over her, while all the women were green with envy. What more perfect antidote could there be to a life that, so far, had mostly involved farm chores? She had little formal education by comparison with these denizens of Roma, but she was intelligent and well-read enough to hold up her end of the conversation. She was a hit!

Anja and Lars had stayed together with Bernadette, Erik, Andrion, and Gylabris, as they knew no one else at the party. Bernadette, who was pleased beyond measure that her "niece" and her lover were planning to retire from adventuring and settle in the Waterdon area, was doing what she could to network on their behalf. "Anja and Lars have made some exceptional eldalfar finds," she would remark casually, "Are you a collector?" They eventually met several such from among the wealthy partygoers, and it seemed possible that they might soon get a bidding war going. Most of the treasures the two had collected in Sindalo were far too fine to be handled by the merchants of Roma's Mercantile District.

The food on the tables was sumptuous, and an entire balanced meal could be assembled from among the offerings if you felt like eating such. Plates were provided, but everything had been designed to be eaten with the fingers. Imperial guards pressed into service as waiters for the occasion (a duty they needed to perform only a few times per year), dressed in the livery of palace servants, circulated through the crowd with trays for collecting plates, fingerbowls for cleaning one's hands after eating, and glasses of chilled sparkling wine.

While the Drakesprings might have been outsiders here and some seemed to resent the favor they'd been shown by the emperor, other forward-looking Reman citizens were excited by the economic possibilities of the power cell project and eager to discuss it with Andrion. Others were delighted to meet the famous Fireblood, and a few even wanted to meet Erik – even if the Iscandia Slasher's career in the Coliseum had been a short one. The two old cats from the Terentius party changed their minds about swooping in after receiving a Look from Bernadette.

In the months before they'd become betrothed Bernadette had often split her time between Erik and Andrion, and when she was with Andrion Erik had slept with other women. She hadn't resented it – he was (at the time) a young man with a healthy libido, and it wasn't as if she had been exclusively with *him*. But that was then. Now, any woman who thought she might like to tumble her blond giant had better be prepared for a fight with the woman who had gotten all the credit for slaying Tarragin – and not without cause.

Some of Bernadette and Anja's time was taken up just looking around them, surreptitiously gawking at the garb of their fellow party-goers. The women were resplendent in their peacock finery, gowns in dozens of different hues – though none, perhaps, more magnificent than those worn by themselves and their party. The men were dressed in more sober colors – browns, blacks, burgundies – and each wore a fully functional (though ornamental) dagger at his waist. Not that they needed them for cutting meat at this particular feast.

Bernadette's forgework was famous throughout Iscandia and highly valued for its superb grace and functionality – but she did not ornament her weapons with jeweled pommels and such frippery. The jewel-encrusted daggers worn here by Erik, Andrion, Andi, Lars, and even Gylabris had been purchased for them in the Mercantile District especially for such occasions as this one, where for an adult male to be seen without a dagger would be to appear undressed. Bernadette was grateful no such demands were made of the women.

The tall ljosalfar mage who'd engaged Andrion, Gylabris, and Sextus in a technical discussion at the Terentius gathering the week before came up smiling, and greeted Bernadette and Andrion. Andrion smoothly took over introductions. "I don't know if you met my marriage-mate Erik?" he asked, and the elf shook his head. "And this is my niece Anja Steadfast and her friend Lars. People, this is Alderion, Court Mage to Duke Enzo Terentius of Brindis. He's very interested in the power cell project."

Alderion squeezed in beside Andrion, and shook hands with Erik and Lars. After taking in Anja from head to toe in an appreciative glance, he took her hand to kiss in Reman fashion. Anja smiled at him coolly, and asked politely "Court Mage? What exactly does a court mage do, Alderion?" Garimund, who'd been Court Mage in Wyrmshalla for as long as Anja could remember, seemed to spend all his time in research and rarely did any actual magic.

Alderion returned her smile, and said suavely "Many things, Miss Steadfast. We stop disease from breaking out in the duchy, work to prevent natural disasters, defend against incursions by renegade mages, and so forth. The Netherworld invasion was a little before my time, but I have served the Terentius family since the current count's grandfather was on the throne – and my predecessor did much to protect Brindis from the worst effects of the daimon invasion."

Anja gave him a look of bright appreciation. Evidently not all court mages were cut from the same cloth as Garimund. "It seems like the work you do is very important," she admitted. Alderion nodded, a twinkle in his eye.

"I do whatever is necessary to ensure the wellbeing of the people of Brindis, and further the interests of the Terentius family," he summed up.

The topic of conversation turned to the power cell project, and the emperor's support for it. "I'd prefer not to discuss the state of our progress with everyone here in detail," Andrion said, "but I can say that we are getting close. It may be no more than another couple of weeks before we have licked the last few problems and are ready to begin setting up manufacturing."

"So, the emperor is supportive of your work?" Alderion asked.

Andrion smiled, replying "Supportive in the extreme. It was he who arranged to invite my entire family and research team to stay here in Roma at his own expense, just so that we could collaborate with Sextus and his people at the university. And pooling our ideas has really paid off. We are much closer now than either of our teams has ever gotten before."

"Will the emperor invest in your manufacturing effort, then?" the mage wanted to know.

"I haven't discussed it with him, but perhaps so. In addition to the manufacture of the cells themselves, there should be a huge boom in devices that will use them as a power source. He indicated he wanted to talk with me later this evening, so maybe that will be one of the subjects on his mind." Andrion glanced around, and noted that the emperor and his party had left the reception line and were now walking toward one of the food tables. They'd be mingling throughout the party, but were probably ravenous after standing there, greeting arrivals, for the last hour and more.

"It's been good talking with you, but I must be off," Alderion excused himself. He eeled through the crowd, which was beginning to thicken, in the direction of the emperor and his party. On the dais at the rear the leader of the small orchestra stood forward, his voice rising above the murmur of the dozens of conversations that were going on inside the room. "We will now begin the dancing, so please clear some space."

Small tables with chairs were dotted around the room's margins on either side of the entry door. "If you don't wish to dance," the bandleader went on, "there are plenty of tables and chairs, and more refreshments, on the balcony upstairs." He gestured toward the hole in the ceiling, through which they could see the dome on the underside of the palace's central tower.

Andi and Rezira were among the first on the dance floor. They were having a marvelous time – two good-looking, well-dressed young people on the cusp of adulthood, and many in their age group had welcomed them into their circles. Gylabris' attention had been monopolized by some of the people he'd met the previous week, fascinated by his work with dypalfar automatons as well as by the renaissance in leukalfar culture that was taking place in Iscandia.

Anja dragged Lars out onto the floor, and she didn't have to use much force to do so. Growing up orphaned on the streets of Waterdon hadn't offered Lars to the chance to develop many social graces, but in the time they'd been adventuring together they'd learned to have fun drinking, singing, and dancing at inns all over Iscandia and Remus.

Bernadette eyed Andrion hopefully. He was a wonderful lover and a fantastic fighter, and dancing should certainly not have been beyond him. But he'd always shied away from such public displays. Sighing, she squeezed his hand and then took Erik's arm as he happily led her out onto the floor.

Left alone, Andrion looked around. Riki and Flavius were dancing too, though she seemed as though she felt awkward doing it. Flavius was a good enough dancer for both of them, however, holding her in his arms as he glided her around the floor. Dance lessons had been a part of his curriculum since he was a child, Andrion guessed.

Hmm, Andrion thought. Perhaps another drink, and then he'd see if he could find Mondi and Sigi. After the excitement at the party last week, and their recent revelation that they'd joined the League of Beggars, he felt those two needed watching. As he approached the table he spotted the emperor's sister, her husband, and their son standing nearby, talking with Duke Enzo Terentius. The emperor's wife, Lucia, he saw chatting gaily with some female friends a few feet away. The shadow of sadness he'd noted on first meeting her last week seemed to have lifted, at least for now. After all, it had been five years since they'd lost their only son. Of Giorgio, there was no sign. Perhaps he'd gone to use the privy?

Andrion was just reaching for another glass of that bubbly wine from a tray atop the food table when the imperial guard he'd seen escorting Giorgio and his family earlier approached him. "Magister Drakespring?" he asked politely, and Andrion nodded. "The emperor has requested that I bring you to him for the private consultation he mentioned earlier." Aha, Andrion thought. He supposed it made political sense, for the emperor not to flaunt his favor for Andrion and his projects too publically. The Drakespring Clan might find themselves in a storm of hangers-on seeking political favors, otherwise.

He left the drink on the tray and turned to follow the man, who led him out of the main hall and through the anteroom, then up a broad staircase and through a door to the space above. To their left was the entrance to the ring-shaped balcony above the main hall, also crowded with party guests; but the guard led Andrion to the right. There were relatively few partygoers here, most preferring to be in the thick of things.

The guard guided him around a corner, and then gestured for him to wait. "His Imperial Majesty will be with you shortly," he said with a slight bow, and left. Moments later Andrion, feeling slightly high from all of the wine he'd drunk this evening, saw a figure appear in the corridor to the left. It was the emperor, he could see from the garb, but he was stumbling as if in confusion. Had Giorgio himself had too much to drink?

As Andrion was about to go to him, another figure appeared in the corridor – holding a jeweled dagger. An assassin was attacking the emperor! Andrion attempted to hurl a paralysis spell and halt the villain in his tracks, but nothing happened. His magic had been blocked. He rushed forward, reaching for his own dagger, only to find it missing from his waist. When had he last felt it there?

Even as Andrion came within a few feet the attacker had seized the emperor by the shoulder and whirled him around, where he stood swaying in incomprehension. With one swift movement the attacker thrust the dagger into the emperor's chest, a slanting blow that came in from beneath the ribs to penetrate the heart – the stroke of a killer who knew what he was doing. "Stop, you!" Andrion cried futilely, as the stabbed man fell to the stones. The assassin met his eyes, and Andrion was shocked into motionlessness. He was looking at himself!

The killer turned on his heel and vanished around the corner, and Andrion rushed to the fallen emperor. The man lay lifeless in a spreading pool of dark blood, the dagger – his *own* dagger, Andrion realized – standing in his chest as he sprawled on his back. Suddenly there was an ear-splitting scream, and he turned to see that where before there had been no one, now the end of the corridor leading to the residential floors had half a dozen party guests standing in it. They were all staring at him in horror.

"He killed the emperor! I saw him do it!" one middle-aged woman shrieked, and then sagged in a faint.

"Guards! Guards!" a man shouted, and in seconds Andrion was surrounded by four of the imperial guards. He looked down and realized there was blood on his tunic. How had that happened? He hadn't touched the emperor, hadn't been anywhere near him until he was standing over his lifeless body.

Andrion briefly considered using magic to get free, perhaps cast Blend on himself and creep away – but his magic was still blocked. "He's a mage!" one of the kibitzing party guests shouted, and in another moment his magic was blocked for good – as a guard clapped one of the very magic-block collars he and Gylabris had designed, with help from Rezira, around his neck.

"It wasn't me!" he insisted desperately. "It's all some kind of Illusion magic – the real killer went down that corridor!" One of the Guards went down the corridor to check, and reported back. "There's nobody down there," he said. "Come on men, let's get him over to the Penitentiary."

Chapter 22: Reaction

Riki was not the weepy sort. She despised girls who burst into tears at the drop of a hat, and considered herself to be made of sterner stuff. But at the very moment when she felt on top of the world – dressed like a dream and whirling in the arms of her handsome, noble swain at the biggest social event of the year in the very heart of the empire, her world had come crashing down around her ears.

Her father, seen by witnesses murdering the emperor! Panic spreading as imperial guards flooded the room. Flavius (with a brief look of horrified longing on his face as he left her) handing her over to her remaining family and beating a hasty retreat. The Grand Ball had ended minutes after the emperor's heart had ceased to beat, as the entire Guard (including many dressed as waiters) spread out, searching for evidence and additional perpetrators. That the Magister of the Academy at Eisenstag had murdered the emperor could only mean a plot, they assumed – probably orchestrated by some of the Norse partisan holdouts who to this day refused to acknowledge the empire's sovereignty over Iscandia.

Certainly, it seemed unlikely he could have performed the assassination without help – so the Guard, having hustled the captured mage off to a cell in the Penitentiary, was scouring the environs of the Imperial Palace for accomplices. Two members of the Imperial Guard, including the man who'd been assigned as the emperor's personal bodyguard for the evening, had gone missing. Could they have been involved in the plot? The Captain of the Guard, Macchiatus Octavius, was investigating.

The family, including Anja and Lars, had taken their hired coaches back to Pantheatos House in the midst of an exodus of people from the Imperial Palace. Macchiatus had interviewed Bernadette and Erik and concluded that either they knew nothing about Andrion's plot to kill the emperor – or were doing a good job of pretending ignorance. Now was not the moment to put the screws to them, but he dismissed them with a warning not to leave town.

So, as they came through the front door of Pantheatos House, Riki ran into the parlor and threw herself down on a sofa, sobbing. It was all so insane! What possible motive could they imagine her papa would have for killing Giorgio? He had liked the man, was pleased at his support of their project to bring ancient dypalfar technology to the modern age. The rest of them were white-faced, still scarcely believing what had happened. The whole thing made no sense, and they were yet too dazed to see that a deep plot must have been at the bottom of it.

Andi came over and knelt beside the sofa where Riki lay face-down in her extravagantly lovely gown, crying her heart out. He gently stroked her shoulder. "Rikita, it's all right!" he promised, though he sensed that just maybe it *wasn't*. "Somebody has framed Papa Andrion for this crime, and in a day or two after everything has settled down the people in charge will realize that he had no possible motive. Then they'll start investigating, and pretty soon Papa will be out of jail and we can get back to normal life again. Don't worry!"

Riki's tears began to ebb, and she rolled over and sat up – dragging a hand across to wipe her nose in an unladylike gesture worthy of her mother. "You're right," she said, still struggling to breathe normally. "We need to figure out who had a motive for seeing the emperor dead, and why they thought Papa should be blamed for the crime. Once the authorities see that, they'll realize it's ridiculous. Papa getting rid of the emperor, in front of a crowd of witnesses, would be like cutting his own throat."

Bernadette, her face white with a combination of grief and fury, had been listening to their conversation. "You're both right," she said quietly. "There has to have been illusion magic involved in this, though not any spell that your papa knows how to perform. But he certainly knows how to do the Blend spell. Why in all the hells would he assassinate the emperor in front of witnesses, with a dagger everyone knew belonged to him, when he could have appeared as nothing but a moving blur? It's absurd. Why not just march himself over to the Penitentiary and hand them a signed confession?"

Her logic was inescapable, and they all nodded in agreement. Surely, in the light of day, whoever was investigating this crime on behalf of the empire would realize that Andrion's apparent guilt could only be the result of a clumsily-constructed frame-up that took no account of motive. They would probably have him sprung within a few days!

Chapter 23: Mobilization

The next morning as each of them awoke, the shock of the previous night's events hit them as they came to consciousness and cast a pall on the day. It was Cornelia's and Marta's day off and Erik, as troubled as the rest of them but hiding it well, got into the kitchen and scrambled up a mass quantity of eggs with herbs and cheese, a mound of crispy bacon alongside. There was something about preparing food – for himself, for his loved ones – that helped him to cope with the stress of intolerable situations.

Erik might have seemed like a big, strong, sometimes deadly and always amiable doofus to those who had met him only casually. He was most of those things. But he was no fool. He thought things through, when there was time to do so. When there wasn't, he often managed to find the right course of action anyway. And Erik sometimes had insights that brighter, quicker minds had missed.

But now, he was worried. He saw, in his mind's eye, a shadowy conspiracy orchestrated by people who swam in the waters of the empire's political seas like sharks among lesser fish. And he had the feeling that he and the people he loved most, including his brilliant brother Andrion, were mere Betanids – caught in their jaws and soon to be swallowed whole.

The family ate with surprising appetite. They seemed to have responded to Erik's loving desire to feed them, with a reciprocal desire to honor that love by eating what he'd prepared – and they were fortified by it. "I think Erik and I will go over to the Penitentiary this morning and see if they'll let us in to see Andrion," Bernadette said.

"What about the 'counsel' the guards mentioned?" Andi asked. He'd gotten a little insight into Remus' criminal justice system when he'd gone to check on those bandits he'd sent to turn themselves in.

Bernadette paused, thoughtful. The concept of "legal counsel" was mostly foreign to her. She'd stayed on the right side of the law throughout her life, and in Iscandia – where she'd spent nearly half of that life – justice was primitive. "Andi, do you think you could ask Sextus about that? I'm sure he's not going to believe your father is guilty of killing the emperor any more than we do, and perhaps he can put you in touch with someone."

Andi nodded, and inhaled another rasher of bacon. Something about this situation just made him want to eat. Bernadette next turned her eyes on the younger members of the family. "Mondi, Sigi, you have some contacts in Roma's underworld?" The boys nodded a little guiltily. So far they had been honest and forthcoming about their activities, and hadn't been punished for it. The three of them, Gaius included, had been engaged in the fun activity of dropping bits of food onto the heads of the party-goers from the second floor balcony last night, when the uproar had begun.

Bernadette looked her sons in the eyes, each in turn. The two of them might have reached the age where they were a pain in the butt more often than not, but she loved them deeply and she trusted them despite their tendency to get into mischief. "You two may have a better chance than all the rest of us to find out who really orchestrated this conspiracy," she told them seriously. "Get out there, talk to your League of Beggars contacts. Maybe you can even get the word out to all the beggars around the city to be on the lookout for anything suspicious. Somebody, somewhere must have seen something, or knows something. We will track these evil bastards down, and we will get your papa out of jail!"

There was a spontaneous mini-cheer around the table, and Bernadette realized she'd been orating. Oh crap, I *hate* that, she thought, and took another bite of scrambled eggs. Those people at the table (including Anja and Lars, who had put up in another of the huge house's bedrooms after they'd returned late from the Ball) not tasked with anything in particular began formulating their own plans. Somehow, they would prove Andrion's innocence and free him from the imperial prison.

Chapter 24: Eavesdropping

"Where's your friend Gaius?" Tullio asked, as Draco and Felix – looking a little grubbier and more hard-bitten than usual, came sloping up to him. "Detained," Mondi said shortly. He was angrier than he'd ever been in his life, at the events that had swept up his family. Sneyagflug and not Erik might have fathered him, and he had been a dragon for most of his life; but until now he had partaken of Erik's happy, carefree outlook on life and loved it. Now, he just wanted to find the people that had killed the emperor and framed his papa for the crime, incinerate them – and possibly, eat them.

"You heard about what happened at the palace last night?" Mondi asked Tullio. He needed information and he needed it fast. "The emperor!" Tullio said with a grim smile. "It's all over the city. That foreign mage, Andrion whatsisname, was the one who done it. A bunch of people saw him putting his dagger into the emperor's chest and then laughing over the corpse, so they say."

Mondi stifled the urge to go dragon and incinerate Tullio, as a warm-up. "You can't necessarily believe everything you hear," he replied coldly. "There's money says Andrion wasn't the one, that it was a set-up. Anybody who might have heard anything, seen something out of the ordinary, might be in line to make some gold if they tell the right people. That's what *I* hear…"

Tullio looked at him appraisingly. He, like all the denizens of Roma's underworld, was always on the lookout for the main chance. How had these two new recruits learned something before he had? He shrugged. "Aside from the news about the emperor, the only thing that's going around the waterfront district is what happened to old Bronzo."

Mondi's face fell. "Something happened to Bronzo?" he asked. He'd really liked the old man, even if he was something of a sot. He could easily imagine some mercenary, in an ugly mood, clubbing the old man to death on a whim.

"Abducted, disappeared!" Tullio said. "Some people saw a group of what looked like house soldiers, but without any badges, going off with him early yesterday evening. They'd passed him a skin of wine, and he was looking pretty happy."

Mondi and Sigi stood waiting for the rest of the story, anxious. Neither of them could imagine why a group of house soldiers should suddenly decide to treat the amiable old drunk to free booze, unless they planned some mischief for afterwards. Tullio went on, "Much later, past nine in the evening, he was seen again near the gate out of the Alfarien District. He was being hustled out by another or maybe the same group of anonymous soldiers, and he seemed completely incapacitated. They were just dragging him along. It seems like they must have taken him off the island!"

Sigi exchanged glances with his brother. This had to mean something. They could imagine a troop of house soldiers killing old Bronzo out of casual spite, or beating him up for being an old drunk; but there couldn't possibly be any reason to kidnap him! Who was going to pay ransom for a guy like that, or what secrets could be extracted from him? It made no sense, so there must be another reason they weren't seeing. Yet.

Mondi handed Tullio a gold coin for the information, eliciting a grunt of thanks and a look of speculation. He knew full well these two brothers (their relationship was unmistakable to anyone with eyes to see) and their friend Gaius were not really beggars. But what was their game? Reading Tullio's mind, Mondi said "I got a patron, somebody who's really anxious to find out what the real story was on the emperor's assassination and is willing to pay for it. There's more gold where that came from, for any information at all. Can you tell me who actually saw these soldiers take Bronzo?"

Doubting the truth of that but going with the flow Tullio said, "Talk to Megera. You can find her most days in the street near the Argus Salonius Hotel. She's been begging there since long before *we* were born, and she knows a lot about the city. That's all I can tell you now, but if I get any information I'll be sure to give it to you."

"Thanks, Tullio," Mondi said with a shadow of his old impish grin, "be talking to you later."

As he and Sigi started walking away, Mondi noticed a familiar looking, smallish and rather dumpy figure in a concealing cloak skulking along the waterfront in the direction of the Sailors' Rest. He seized his brother by the shoulder and pulled him into the shadow of an alleyway, as they stood watching the man go by. "I've seen that guy down here before," Mondi murmured, "but I think I've seen him somewhere else, too. Stay here, I'm going to follow him."

With that Mondi slipped his Ring of Blend onto his finger and became a hazy blur, imperfectly mimicking the background. He darted silently into the street and tailed the cloaked figure, being careful not to make any noise and equally careful not to bump into anybody. As the man entered the inn, Mondi crept in almost on his heels and then plastered himself up against the wall beside the door, watching as his quarry peered around the dimly lit room and then went over to a table in the far corner where a lone man sat.

The inn was relatively uncrowded at this time of the morning, and Mondi was able to make his way carefully over toward the pair's table without running into any other patrons. He parked himself nearby in the corner and stood watching them, trying to breathe as silently as possible. The person the mysterious cloaked man was meeting was Croaker! A fixture of Roma's underworld, the man was supposedly (according to wisdom received from Mondi's fellow beggars, most of whom were *not* really part of the Guild of Thieves) into everything. If you needed a particular item stolen, or a particular person removed, you talked to Croaker and he would arrange it – for a fee.

People relied on Croaker's discretion from both sides of the transaction. If you paid him, he made a point of not knowing who you were. The people he handed jobs to were known only by their aliases, and should the city guards take him in and string him up by his thumbs for a month, it would be unlikely he could tell them any real names.

He and the cloaked man were speaking quietly, but there was little background noise and Mondi's ears were sharp. "Excellent," the cloaked man said, "I am well pleased with the results." He passed a large leather purse across the table, its contents clinking slightly. Croaker made the purse disappear as if by magic, and smiled grimly.

"Glad you're satisfied," he replied shortly. "And now you're paid in full. Is there anything else?"

The man in the cloak seemed uneasy, as if paying off criminals in low dives was not an activity he often engaged in. "They've got the murderer dead to rights, right? No chance he'll get off?"

"I assure you," the underworld middleman replied with a hint of distaste, "he was seen committing the crime by half a dozen witnesses – all of them members of the aristocracy. That coupled with the blood on his tunic and the fact that it was his weapon virtually assures his conviction when the case comes to trial. You have nothing to worry about."

The cloaked figure lifted a hand to his face, wiping perspiration from his brow. And for just one moment, Mondi caught a glimpse of that face. He *had* seen this man before! Twice, in fact –both times in the company of the late emperor Giorgio Salonius. The cloaked man was the emperor's brother-in-law, Davos Appolonius.

Chapter 25: Unforeseen Circumstances

They arrived at the now-deserted mine and went inside, the four soldiers, the mage, and their helpless captive – dressed in rags. The paralysis spell he had been under when they dragged him from the city had worn off in the time lag from fast-traveling by magic map from the outskirts of Roma to this remote corner of Remus. The mage had let his illusion spell lapse as soon as he had exited via the Imperial Palace's secret door, though he now wore the mask that was part of his persona as the infamous assassin.

They shepherded their captive down through the mine's branching tunnels, heading for a room where they planned to hold him until the mage could perform certain... operations on him. Then the captors would become the rescuers, and their triumphant re-entry into Roma would spell the downfall of Davos Appolonius and his son.

They had cleared the mine of any lurking denizens (daimlings, for the most part) during the past week in preparation for this operation, this squad of the duke's most trusted household guard. As they were now in on the secret of what had really taken place, the mage had orders to alter *their* memories as well. Both the emperor and the squad of guards would be utterly convinced that they had come here on a tip and rescued him from captivity by Davos' hirelings. Killing them would be counter-productive.

The emperor had been paralyzed but aware as he'd been seized – after one of his own guards had requested his presence in a corridor on the palace's second floor, on the pretense of seeing something he thought odd and wanted Giorgio's opinion on. Once he was immobile, they had carried him away through a secret door and along a narrow staircase that wound around the circumference of the palace, to exit through an equally secret door at ground level.

His personal guard, he had been sure it was him – but now he suspected it must have been this mage in disguise – had renewed the paralysis spell on him and he'd remained inert, glaring at his captors, as they stripped him to the skin (the indignity!) and then re-dressed him in truly disgusting rags that reeked of the cheapest wine. Being unable to move, he had not seen what had become of his own clothing.

182

The soldiers had bound his hands before him and tied a rag around his mouth, preventing him from speaking in case the paralysis might wear off. He'd been quite unaware that he was now wearing another man's face. Then the seeming imperial guard had cast the paralysis spell one more time and returned inside the palace, even as the soldiers took him in hand and had begun hauling him away, staying in the shadows, down into the Floral District and on a zigzagging path to the Alfarien District.

They had dragged the emperor into an alley and waited in darkness for a few minutes, during which time the paralysis wore off and he had begun struggling and making muffled noises through the gag. "You want your throat cut, it's easily accomplished if you keep making noise," one of the soldiers murmured with a dagger pressed to his throat, and he lapsed into silence. He guessed they must need him alive or he would simply have been killed – his predecessor had died by an assassin's knife, after all – but he didn't feel like pushing his luck and held his silence. He felt exhausted.

A few minutes later the mage had rejoined them, now wearing a cloth mask that completely covered his face, and the paralysis spell had been renewed as he was dragged up the main road and out of the gates leading from the Alfarien District to the western river bank. The mage had then pulled out a magic map, and they'd traveled here.

They left Giorgio tied to the chair on which they'd seated him, but removed his gag. By now his fury and frustration were beyond bounds, and he immediately shouted, "I know you, Tertius! Did you think you could hold a dagger to my throat and I would not recognize you?" The Augustino and Terentius families had been close, and Giorgio had spent much time visiting with the Duke of Brindis. He knew many of Enzo's family retainers by sight.

Now he turned his head to the masked mage. "And you must be Alderion! I can scarcely believe that Enzo would betray me in this way. Since you evidently don't intend to kill me, you had better just let me go before there's hell to pay!" Deeply chagrined, angry at having his disguise penetrated, Alderion too let his tongue loose. But at least he had the sense to dismiss the guards first.

"You men, go to the quarters prepared for you and wait there for my orders," he said, and the four quickly left the room. Then the mage gave in to a sadistic impulse, knowing that anything he told the emperor would be forgotten in the next few minutes. He could say whatever he liked, enjoy the pain it caused, and not worry that it would ever come back to haunt him.

"Hah!" he said, ripping off the uncomfortable mask. "You and Enzo are such friends, are you? Yet it never occurred to you that one of his sons might make a better heir to the throne than that pathetic weasel Tiberius?" Giorgio was taken aback. This was about him naming Tiberius heir? It made no sense. "He's my own flesh and blood, my sister's son! Who else was I going to name, after the tragic loss of Bruno?" he asked.

"And who do you think orchestrated that 'tragic loss,' Giorgio?" Alderion asked – bile dripping from his words. The emperor was shocked. He had always respected and rather liked the ljosalfar mage, and thought that his long-standing loyalty to the Terentius family was laudable. He'd wished he had someone like that, who would put his master's family above all personal considerations. But this? "You...?" he asked hesitantly, fearing the answer.

"Oh, I certainly did my part," Alderion said with a sneer. "But my master Enzo gave the orders. It should have been him whom the Convocation chose to take the throne, not you. The Terentius family's blood ties to the long-dead Salonius dynasty are as close as yours." Giorgio's face went pale. Tonight had been an ordeal, certainly, but he remained confident that these people didn't intend to kill him. What shocked him was the revelation of just how badly he'd misjudged people he thought were his friends – and a fear of what *was* planned for him, if Alderion was revealing all this. If they didn't intend to take his life, they must mean to destroy his mind.

"Enough of this!" Alderion said coldly. He'd had his fun, enjoyed the look of anguish that had passed over Giorgio's face when he realized that a man he had thought of as a lifelong friend had commanded the murder of his only son. Now, with a slight gesture, he cast a Command spell on the emperor. This spell, used by the ancient dypalfar and lost for millennia, was one he had acquired only a year or so ago. It was so useful, he wished he'd had it decades before. And it was a pity that the effects were not permanent, as was the Spell of Seeming he'd developed. It would certainly have simplified the work he had before him.

To begin, he must erase the emperor's recent memories. Before he began to build the memories that would come, which would require a combination of potion, spellcraft, and careful direction, he must expunge any hint of the abduction, the journey here, the emperor's recognition of one of Duke Enzo's guards and himself, and above all their recent discussion. "Tell me how you feel, Giorgio," Alderion commanded his captive in a kindly tone. The approach one took was almost as important as the spell itself, when addressing the enspelled individual.

"I'm tired – and angry," the emperor replied. The Command spell had taken away his mental focus, but Alderion's question had caused him to seek within.

"I'm sorry you are not feeling well," the mage said soothingly. "Here, I have a potion that will make it all better. Drink it up, now." Better double up the dose, he thought. He regretted now that he'd spoken so freely, and he wanted to make absolutely sure that no trace of what had passed in the last hour remained in Giorgio's mind – perhaps to well up in dreams. "Drink both of these, I know they will help," he said.

The emperor, smiling slightly at the thought that he was in good and capable hands, obediently downed the contents of one bottle, then the other. It tasted delicious, quite refreshing. Soon a wave of numbness came over him, not like that… what was it that he had felt a while ago… was it a dream? What was I thinking? He smiled up happily at Alderion, still in the grip of the Command spell and pleased that he had done as requested.

Good, the mage thought. It seemed to be working as it should. This potion was of his own devising, and he had not had time to test it as thoroughly as he would have liked. One bottle, depending on the body mass of the recipient, would effectively erase the memories of one hour of subjective time. That was a little more than the amount of time that had elapsed since he had come in the guise of one of the emperor's personal guard – the man himself, stripped of his uniform, now lying dead behind a bush in the grounds surrounding the palace – to lure the emperor away from the party.

Alderion was reasonably sure that the amount of actual time elapsed should not matter, though he'd never tried the potion with fast-traveling thrown in. Since anyone fast-traveling only had memories of a few seconds passing during the transition, it stood to reason that the hour's worth of memories erased would account the passage as having taken only those few seconds. The double dose was just to make sure – and if it meant the emperor could not remember some of the people he'd met in the reception line during the hour before the abduction, he could rebuild those memories – just as he would be rebuilding the memories of the hour after that.

When the emperor emerged from the trance produced by the second potion and its accompanying spell, he would remember being seized by hirelings of the Appolonius family, who would have revealed Davos' plan to fake his assassination and put his son on the throne (which plot, minus the switch of victims, had indeed been Appolonius' intention). In Giorgio's mind he would have been taken here and left trussed up, then heard a fight that resulted in his rescue by the forces of Duke Enzo's household guard.

Bodies of the abductors, Appolonius tokens on their persons, were being supplied through the Spell of Seeming applied to beggars taken from the streets of Brindis. Davos employed no regular guards, so of course he would have hired these mercenaries to do his dirty work. The emperor's clear memory of the information they would have revealed to him – all of it implanted in his mind, permanently, by Alderion – would drive the last nail in the Appolonius family's coffin.

The plan was brilliant, if he did say so himself. When it had been accomplished, the happy friendship between Giorgio Salonius and the Terentius family would resume – closer than ever before, as Giorgio would also have been implanted with a desire to name Flavius Terentius as heir to the Reman Throne. The lad was handsome, bright, charming, and a fine figure of a young man – everything the unfortunate Tiberius, damned by his father's plot, was not. Enzo was determined that Arturus, his first-born, would remain heir to Brindis.

But first, before administering the second potion and beginning his long work of rebuilding the past two hours of memories in the mind of his emperor, Alderion wanted to make sure that the old memories had been thoroughly erased. Any conflict between the new memories and old ones from the same time period could have disastrous results. "Tell me," he said to his subject, "What do you remember from the past two hours?" While the Command spell was in place he could include a command to ignore the minute or two of time before the second potion was administered.

The haggard expression had faded from Giorgio's face, and he looked years younger. Still a little pale, but as though all of his troubles had faded. As so they should have, if he no longer recalled being forcibly snatched and spirited away, then informed that a man he had thought a friend had betrayed him most horribly. "Remember?" he said, seemingly puzzled. After a moment he said, "I have no idea. And who are you?"

This surprised Alderion. He should have been recognized, though the context for his being here would be a puzzle. "I'm Alderion, and I'm here to rescue you," he told his captive, beginning to build the story that would become part of the emperor's new memories. Giorgio's innocent brown eyes filled with happiness for a moment, then looked lost.

"Rescue me?" he said softly, "That's nice. But who am I?"

Chapter 26: Legal Issues

Andrion sat up on the heap of dirty straw that passed for a bed in his cell, and wondered what time it was. He had been brought here in chains in the middle of the night, his blood-spattered tunic taken as evidence along with his dagger that had been protruding from the chest of the emperor when he was arrested. They had removed the manacles from his wrists once he'd been taken into the cell, and provided him with a rough cloth shirt to cover his torso; but he was now wearing leg irons in addition to the magic-block collar they'd put on him.

He'd fallen into an exhausted sleep, only to toss and turn on the straw – his mind tormented by the image of seeing himself in the act of murdering the emperor. It stood to reason, he thought whimsically, that he could not possibly have that picture in his mind if he had *actually* stabbed Giorgio Salonius. But he couldn't deny, the circumstantial evidence was very compelling. The only thing missing was a motive.

Andrion had half expected his entire party, perhaps augmented by Sextus, to be down here demanding his release or at least lending him moral support and perhaps arranging for him to have an actual mattress and some food more appealing and nourishing than the stale bread rolls and questionably clean water that had so far been provided to him. Yet it must now be late the following day, and he had seen no one but the guards – who were in no mood to answer questions.

Oh, if he could only use his magic! He wouldn't even use it to try to escape, he was willing to swear – but for a man with a huge fund of magical energy, accustomed to using spells a hundred times a day, being cut off from his ability was a constant torment. There was no pain, just a continual unfulfilled longing with no relief.

There was absolutely nothing to do in here to keep himself occupied. There were no prisoners in any of the nearby cells, and he suspected that might be by the design of his jailers. He got stiffly to his feet and began doing some calisthenics. The cell was reasonably roomy, eight feet in either dimension, with the back and sides being solid blocks of stone and the front iron bars with a sturdily locked door. There was no window.

With his magic, he'd have had that door open in less time than it would take to pull out a lockpick. They'd searched him before throwing him in here of course; but in any case, a man with Andrion's skills didn't bother carrying around such objects as lockpicks. He wouldn't even have been carrying that dagger, if it hadn't been declared *de riguer* for a gentleman's dress ensemble.

Andrion wondered what other piece of evidence his unseen enemy would have used to frame him if the dagger hadn't been available. He also searched his mind, trying to recall the last time that he knew it was still at his belt. As it was not a usual part of his daily garb, he hadn't been aware of the missing weight.

He folded his elbows and leaned his forearms against the bars, resting his forehead on his hands and stretching out his back and legs. Thank the gods (well actually, the late Wissagleb and his beloved Berni) that he was now physically thirty-one years of age instead of his actual fifty-three. He had enough aches and pains from trying to sleep on the straw-covered stone floor as it was!

The bucket that had been provided for his wastes was beginning to stink, and the one containing water for drinking getting low. Andrion wondered how often the guards came by to service the cell. They had only come once since his arrival – was that going to be it, once every twenty-four hours? Ugh.

Andrion's ears pricked up and a surge of excitement rushed through him as he heard the sound of footsteps coming his way – coupled with the jingle of keys. When the food and water had come (was that this morning?) the jailer carrying the bucket and tray had been let into the cell by two armed guards, so jumping him and stealing his keys had been out of the question. But he was going crazy just sitting here, and the thought of any break in the monotony filled him with joyful anticipation.

He pressed his face to the bars and peered down the corridor, to see the same two armed guards (or two very similar ones) escorting a serious-looking man of around forty-five dressed in rich-looking robes. When they reached Andrion's cell one guard entered it and fastened manacles onto his wrists again. Then they led him out of the cell and down the corridor to an inside room that had a stout door with a barred window in it.

The man, whom Andrion guessed must be the legal counsel that had been mentioned, was searched before they were led into the room and seated at a plain wooden table. The table's legs were bolted to the stone floor, and Andrion's leg irons were attached to the table. They were taking no chances with the heinous assassin who had murdered the emperor, it seemed.

After the guards had left and locked the door behind them Andrion's companion rose and closed a wooden door over the barred window, providing them with a modicum of privacy. *Better than being taken out and summarily executed, I suppose,* he thought morosely. He still could not entirely believe he had gotten into this fix – what enemy had he made who hated him enough to frame him for murder?

The man returned to his side of the table, setting down a flat satchel, and reached across the table to shake Andrion's hand before taking his own seat. "Magister Drakespring, I am Marcos Benedetti. Your son Andreas contacted me through Sextus Garibaldi at the university, and has engaged me as your legal counsel in this matter."

Andrion couldn't help breaking into a big grin, even though he'd already guessed why the man was here. It was good to know, for one thing, that his counsel had been hired by his family and not assigned by the Imperial Court. "I am very glad to meet you, Signor Benedetti," he said sincerely. The lawyer wondered at the gravitas this man seemed to have, since he looked barely out of his twenties. But then he recalled that his client was Magister of the Academy at Eisenstag. He was undoubtedly older than he looked.

"As you are from Auverne via Iscandia I suppose that you are not entirely familiar with the justice system here in this part of the empire, Magister?" the counselor asked. "Please, call me Andrion," his client replied. He had the sinking feeling Marcos here might be the only person he would be allowed to converse with for some time yet to come, and formality became annoying after a while.

"Well then, Andrion... You have been formally charged with murder in the first degree of our emperor, Giorgio Salonius. As the emperor was a high government official this crime also carries an additional charge of treason against the empire. Either or both of these crimes is punishable by beheading, and it is my job to try to prove in court that you are not guilty."

Andrion looked at him grimly. "I assure you… may I call you Marcos?" A quick nod. "Despite appearances and evidence to the contrary, I did *not* kill the emperor. I liked the emperor, and he was very supportive of the work I'd been doing with Sextus at the university. I had absolutely no reason to wish him dead, and plenty of reasons to keep him alive."

Marcos nodded thoughtfully. "The facts are these. Half a dozen highborn witnesses, attendees at the party, say that they actually saw you stabbing the emperor. The dagger that was found in his body belonged to you, as several witnesses will attest, and when the palace guards were called they found you standing over the emperor's body with fresh blood on your tunic. There is no way to tell whose blood, of course, but it is reasonable to suppose that it is his. Macchiatus Octavius, Captain of the Imperial Guard, is investigating the case and collecting evidence, though it certainly seems that they already have enough evidence on which to convict you of the crime."

"Who hears that evidence?" Andrion asked. He'd never so much as been arrested and had no idea how these things were done. In many parts of Iscandia, serious cases were brought up before a magistrate, or even the eorl of the march.

"Capital cases are heard by a panel of three judges, appointed for life to the Imperial Court by the emperor. Currently two of these three are appointees of the late Gaius Albus II, while the third was appointed by Giorgio Salonius I."

"And all three must find for conviction?" The lawyer nodded.

"Execution is a serious affair, and we do not undertake it lightly." How civilized, Andrion mused. In Iscandia, you were usually free to kill anybody even suspected of a crime like banditry without fear of prosecution.

"And how much time do we have to prepare our case?" he asked next.

"The trial is set to begin ninety days from today," Marcos replied, "after which arguments will go on for as long as necessary."

Well, Andrion thought, if my family and I can't manage to find out who actually did the crime and prove it in that time, they can chop off my head for stupidity. "I take it I'm not allowed to have visitors here?" he asked. Marcos nodded. "Prison security forbids anyone but prisoners, jailers, and legal counsel in this area of the building," he explained. "But you can give whatever messages you want to me to pass along to your friends and family, and they similarly can give me messages to deliver to you. Your son said to tell you that they are conducting their own investigation, gathering evidence to find out who framed you. You see," he smiled, "*they* at least do not believe you committed this crime."

Andrion heaved a sigh of relief. He'd had little doubt, of course, that his brilliant and resourceful loved ones would immediately seize the initiative and begin trying to work out what had really happened. The idea of him as an assassin was ludicrous! Sure, he'd killed a few bandits… and renegade mages, leukalfar sentries, and other miscellaneous antagonistic sentients during his years as an adventurer before he, Berni, and Erik had settled down to family life. But he had never unlawfully harmed anyone.

"This has to have been an intentional attempt to frame me for the murder," he explained to Marcos, "presumably by someone who had reason to want the emperor dead. Possibly this someone was not happy about the project I'm working on at the university, which might take money out of some people's pockets while putting it into others' – and they thought to kill two birds with one stone."

"In fact," the counselor replied, "Macchiatus is convinced that you had accomplices in this, and that you are a member of a secret faction of Norse partisans still hoping to free Iscandia from the rule of the empire. He's been interviewing everyone, trying to find out if you'd been seen acting suspiciously before the ball. He even sent a messenger to the Academy at Eisenstag, to learn from your colleagues there if you've ever expressed any anti-empire sentiments."

"Gods save us!" Andrion cursed, "That is the most preposterous notion I have ever heard voiced. I'm not even a Norseman, for Aderos' sake. I'd expect that if there *were* a group plotting to kill Giorgio, might it not be the same people who did in Gaius?"

192

"Those people were all exposed, tried, and executed," the counselor assured him. "But Macchiatus is looking into that angle as well. He is a thorough man – and not an idiot."

"Perhaps his investigation will benefit me, then," Andrion said hopefully. He sighed. "Let me tell you everything I know. Then perhaps you can think of some more avenues to pursue." Marcos nodded, and sat ready with a notebook and a dypalfar fountain pen, to take notes on Andrion's deposition.

"My family and I attended the Imperial Ball at the emperor's invitation, which was relayed to us through Sextus Garibaldi. When we went through the reception line on entering, Giorgio Salonius mentioned that he wanted to discuss the power cell project with me in private. I assumed that he was hoping to work out an arrangement whereby the empire would invest in the technology and reap some of what Sextus and I anticipate will be huge financial rewards, once we're able to begin production."

"Are you close to that?" Marcos asked, more out of personal curiosity than anything else.

"Very close," Andrion replied. "Sextus and I thought it likely that we might be able to start manufacturing the cells within the next two weeks. Anyhow, along with the emperor and his family in the reception line were a couple of his personal guards, whom I'd seen at the Terentius party the week before. My family and I moved on and were socializing with various people that we had met previously, including Alderion, Duke Terentius' court mage. He and I have a lot in common, and we'd had a very interesting conversation at the Terentius gathering."

The counselor nodded and made a note. Alderion was among the most prominent non-University mages in Remus. Andrion went on, "My wife bought that dagger for me at a shop in the Mercantile District as part of my formal dress ensemble, and the night of the Imperial Ball was the second time I'd worn it. I wasn't really paying any attention to it, but I know I had it on when I got dressed for the evening. I didn't realize it was missing from its scabbard until I saw the killer stabbing the emperor, much later in the evening."

"You saw the killer stabbing the emperor?" Marcos asked, eyes widening.

"Oh yes," Andrion said bitterly. "You say there are six witnesses who saw me doing the murder. Add me to make a seventh." The lawyer raised his eyebrows at that, but let his client continue. "After the dancing started I decided to go looking for my two young sons, who had gotten away from us and were no doubt off about some mischief – they're both around twelve." The counselor nodded sympathetically. He, too, had a son of about that age.

"I had last seen them at the food and drinks table on the left side of the hall, so I went that way," Andrion went on. "On my way over there through the dense crowd I spotted Emperor Salonius' sister and her family, and also Empress Lucia. But the emperor himself was not in evidence, nor did I see either of the two guards that had been with him. Not finding the boys I was about to help myself to a drink when one of the emperor's personal guards whom I'd seen earlier came up to me and told me that the emperor wished to have the private discussion he'd mentioned before."

The lawyer wrote furiously for a moment, and Andrion had a thought. "It seems likely that in all that crowd, somebody might have witnessed the guard coming for me and leading me off. Perhaps you can suggest to Macchiatus that he ask that question." Marcos nodded and took another note. "We threaded our way through the crowd, the guard leading, and he took me around the corridor to the left and up the stairs to the residential wing. Then he left me standing in a corridor where there were no people, and told me that the emperor would arrive shortly – after which he left."

"I have to tell you," the counselor cut in, "that the body of one of the two guards assigned to the emperor on that evening has been found, stripped of his uniform, hidden behind some bushes near the Reman Palace. His throat had been cut. And the other has apparently gone missing." Andrion's face paled. This plot seemed to have caused more than one death, and he still had no idea why *he* should have been involved in it.

"The guard who drew me away must have been one of the plotters, cloaked in a glamor," Andrion said firmly. "It was clearly a ruse to put me in the same area where the emperor was to be murdered, because moments after the guard had left me there the emperor staggered into view, emerging from another corridor just ahead of me. He seemed disoriented, or maybe drunk, though he'd appeared sober enough when I'd spoken with him perhaps an hour before. He must have been drugged, or under a spell to slow his wits."

"And you saw the killer stab him?" Marcos prompted.

"Yes," Andrion said with a shudder. "It was the most horrifying sight I have ever beheld, and I've seen the Soul-Devourer flying straight toward me with a mouth full of flames. A second after the emperor appeared, the killer emerged from the same corridor he had come from, moving like a cat with the dagger that I only later realized was mine in his hand. And he looked exactly like me."

The counselor stared at him. "You witnessed the killing of the emperor, and the killer wore your face?"

"Not just my face!" Andrion said, "My clothing down to the boots, down to the empty scabbard where the dagger was supposed to be. It was a very disorienting moment. As soon as I realized the emperor was being attacked I tried to use magic to stop the killer, and discovered that my abilities had been blocked by a spell. Are you at all familiar with magic, Marcos?"

"I don't practice it myself," the counselor replied, "but I have made much study of it and its precedents in law. It complicates many legal cases."

"The magic-block spell is one of the most useful against mages, and was developed right here in Remus," Andrion waxed pedantic. "It's the same spell that powers this damned collar" – he yanked at it – "and prevents me from using any magic whatsoever. I was not able to paralyze the attacker as I'd intended. Unless the late emperor was an unsuspected mage, or one was hiding behind me, the attacker must have been the one who cast the magic-block spell on me."

"I'll check to see if any known mages were in the area," Marcos said, making another notation in his book. The energy with which he was taking notes filled Andrion with hope. Something *was* being done!

"As soon as I realized I had no magic available I reached for my dagger," Andrion went on. "That was the first time I realized that the knife was no longer in its scabbard. In no more than a second or two the assassin had thrust the knife he held – which I didn't recognize as mine until later – into the emperor's body and then run back down the corridor whence he came."

"Go on," the counselor said after jotting for another moment or two.

"I ran to see if there was anything I could do," Andrion continued. "The emperor was lying on his back in a pool of blood, with the dagger sticking up out of his chest. That's when I realized that it was the dagger Berni had bought me, and that's when the crowd of people turned up."

Andrion sat for a moment slumped in his chair, manacled hands resting on the table as he was lost in thought. Then he looked up at his lawyer, dawning realization in his eyes. "I saw myself kill the emperor, but I don't think those other witnesses could have. If they had seen what I saw, they would also have seen me standing between them and the scene that was being played out. I think they saw me standing over the corpse, and *assumed* that I was the killer. As no one else was in sight, that was a reasonable assumption. But a wrong one. I suggest you try to pin down the witnesses, second by second, as to *exactly* what they saw."

There was silence for a minute as Marcos continued writing down Andrion's words, taking his own notes as he did so. He was beginning, finally, to believe that his client might indeed be innocent. In the interim Andrion had time to consider some more, and he had more words to offer before their time was up. "One of the guards who arrested me acted on my suggestion that he search the corridor down which the assassin disappeared, and he reported there was nobody there. That might have been as simple as a Blend spell, which doesn't even require a mage to cast. Anyone can acquire a ring that can turn him invisible for as long as he likes."

The counselor nodded and wrote, then looked up again. "Anything else?"

"They should check that part of the Imperial Palace for a secret exit," Andrion said firmly. "While it's possible that this mage assassin and his cohorts all just disguised themselves as partygoers and mingled with the crowd, they may also have exited the building in another way. The palace is millennia old – who knows what secrets it hides?"

Marcos' eyebrows rose again. This client was a cut above the usual when it came to thinking things out. As he jotted down the suggestion, Andrion went on. "One more thing. I noticed the blood on my tunic after I came to stand in front of the body of the emperor. But I had not touched him, nor been within six feet of him when he was stabbed. That blood has to be an illusion cast on my tunic." The counselor pondered this, and nodded solemnly.

Andrion continued, "There are necromantic spells that will, in fact, tell you whose blood has been spilled, if the person died. For that you need liquid blood, but you can reconstitute enough for the spell from blood spilled on, say, a carpet – or dried on the blade of a knife – by adding a little water. I'd be willing to bet, though, that if you examine the tunic that was taken in evidence you'll find it still looks exactly as if fresh blood was just spilled on it. It will not have dried, and if you pour water on one of the bloodstains you will not get anything to show for it. I personally don't know of any illusion spells that long-lasting, but I think whoever framed me does."

Sensing that this was all the information his client had to offer, Marcos rose to his feet and once again shook hands with Andrion. He walked over to the window and raised the wooden door covering it, then called to the guards. They'd retreated a respectable distance away. After Andrion's leg irons had been unshackled from the table and the guards began to lead him back to his cell, he threw in, "Marcos, if there's any way a little… grease… could buy me a mattress and some better food, I would surely appreciate it. And tell everyone I love them." The lawyer laid a comforting hand on his arm.

"You've been very helpful, Andrion," he said sincerely. "I think we'll have you out of here in no time."

Chapter 27: The Investigation Proceeds

"Gods' blessing on you, kind sir," the ancient-seeming and rag-clad crone quavered, as she pocketed the coin that had been hastily deposited in her hand. A moment later her demeanor changed and she drew herself up, seeming both younger and stronger, as she saw Mondi and Sigi approaching.

"Whatta you boys want?" she asked in an unfriendly tone. "Don't be thinking you can beg here – this is my territory, and it has been for a long time." Sigi smiled at her, his sweet features seeming to reach into her soul and activate her inner grandmother.

"You must be Megera, mother?" He said politely, and she nodded. He slipped some coins into her hand, to her astonishment. "I'm Felix," he said, "and this is my brother Draco. Tullio said we might find you here."

The boys displayed the small tokens they'd received on paying their initiation fees to become members of the Guild, and she smiled at them. "How can I help you youngsters, then?" the old woman asked with considerably more amiability.

"We're trying to help in the search for Bronzo," Sigi explained. He was cuter than Mondi was, and they'd thought that he would make the better spokesman for this visit.

Megera's face clouded. Bronzo had been a friend of sorts, a friendly colleague at least, for decades, and the two of them were close in age. What had happened to him might be happening to her one of these days, the way things were going in Roma. Old beggars abducted, the emperor himself murdered in his own palace surrounded by a crowd of witnesses… Things were no longer as safe as they'd been in her day.

"People over in the waterfront district said that four guys who looked like house soldiers, but not wearing badges, picked him up at his usual corner and gave him a skin of wine," Sigi said. "They'd invited him to a party or something, and old Bronzo was always happy to go anywhere there was free wine. Then nobody saw him for hours, until you did. Can you tell us exactly what you saw?"

The old beggar woman nodded thoughtfully, and launched into her tale. "It must have been around 9:30," she began. "I'm not usually still out begging that late, but I got a late start yesterday morning and I thought that, what with the ball, some of the wealthy residents of my district might be coming home in a… good mood, you might say. So I was standing right over there, near the front of the Argus Salonius, when I seen this party come along."

The boys nodded, urging her silently to continue the tale. "At first I thought it was just a group of house soldiers, maybe let off for the night because of the ball, and that one of their number had had so much to drink that he couldn't walk on his own so they were helping him along. I stepped back out of their way. Soldiers don't often give alms, and they can turn mean when they're in their cups. Anyway, when they came past me I realized it was Bronzo they had. Two of 'em was carrying him along, like, while the other two was looking around for trouble, with their hands on their swords."

"And he was asleep, or dead drunk?" Sigi asked.

"No!" she replied. "That was the odd thing. He was completely unmoving, as if he were dead – but his eyes were open and you could see there was life in them. They had his hands tied in front of him with rope, and a piece of cloth tied around his mouth like a gag, see. But there was no mistaking it was Bronzo. I've known the man most of my life, and those were definitely his clothes. He only has one set, and pretty ripe they were too. I shrank back in the shadows until they'd gone past, then I followed from a distance to see where they were going. They took him right out the gate, out to the riverside."

"You didn't follow after that to see where they went from there?" Sigi asked, hopefully. Megera looked at him as if he were an idiot.

"Me, an unarmed old woman, go chasing off after four armed soldiers who seemed like they had an eye out for trouble? Not bloody likely!" Sigi gave her an apologetic smile.

"You're right," he said. "You did the sensible thing." He handed her some more coins and then, thanking her, he and Mondi took their leave.

They walked away in the direction of the city gate Megera had identified as the one Bronzo had been taken from. "What do you think, Mondi?" Sigi asked. "Should we go dragon and maybe fly up and see if we can spot them hauling old Bronzo along?"

"It wouldn't do any good," his brother assured him. "That was hours ago, and you can bet they got him out of sight long before the sun came up. If we had tracking dogs, we might find out – but even that wouldn't do any good if they had a magic map."

The things were a lot more common now than they had been fifteen years ago, as Andrion had trained others at the Academy in their manufacture. Mondi took a turn at the next corner and began leading Sigi back around the circle in the direction of the Pantheatos District. "Let's just go home and report what we've learned."

The boys found the whole family there, though several of them had been out and about on errands earlier. As they sat down to a lunch prepared by Erik and Bernadette, they shared their news. "Sextus is very upset," Andi said. "Of course he doesn't believe any more than we do that Papa Andrion stabbed the emperor, but he's worried that it's going to punch a hole in our work schedule on the power cell project. I promised him Zira, Gylabris, and I would be in tomorrow morning as usual."

"Anyhow," Andi went on after chewing up a bite of bread laden with spiced sausage and pickled vegetables, "He gave me the name of a reliable lawyer and directions to his house, along with a letter of introduction. Zira and I went right over and talked to this Marcos Benedetti first thing. He didn't seem to be at all put out about being called in to work on an Apoldtag. We gave him all the information we had and he promised he would go over to the Penitentiary to consult with Papa as soon as possible this afternoon."

"They wouldn't let us in when Erik and I tried to go this morning," Bernadette reported.

"No," Andi replied, "Mister Benedetti said that they don't let anybody except people who are recognized members of the Remus Guild of Legal Counsels go down to where the prisoners are kept. They don't have all that many magic-block collars, and think what a mage masquerading as a visitor could do."

While this discussion had been going on Mondi had been wolfing his food with the speed and enthusiasm only attainable by adolescent boys. He was eager to impart the riveting news he'd picked up while skulking, nearly invisible, in the Sailors' Rest this morning. Bernadette looked across the table at him and noticed that her dragon son appeared ready to burst. "Mondi, tell us what you learned from the beggars, will you?"

He was halfway convinced that this information would see Papa back with them by suppertime, yet he couldn't resist giving the story a proper buildup. "We met Tullio, our fellow member of the League of Beggars, and asked him if there was any news. He told us that Bronzo, an old drunk who begs down there along the waterfront, was abducted last night. It might seem like no connection, but for men who were identified as house soldiers to be seen luring a guy like Bronzo away, and then later dragging him – seemingly under a paralysis spell – out though the city gates, is awfully suspicious."

"House soldiers?" Erik asked. "Did anyone recognize their badges?" Mondi shook his head.

"According to Tullio, they were dressed in miscellaneous clothing and armor like mercenaries. But they moved, and worked together, like members of some noble's house guard. So they were undoubtedly in disguise. Anyhow, after we talked to Tullio I saw a familiar-looking figure, obviously trying not to be recognized, sneaking along toward the Sailors' Rest. So I put on my ring and followed him."

Bernadette heaved an internal sigh. She rather regretted that Anja and Lars had let that particular magical item fall into Mondi's hands. Why not just teach a fire spell to a toddler? Although now that she thought about it Andrion had taught Andi his fire/lightning metal-cutting weave when he was only five. As well, Mondi *was* older than he looked – and usually, when in Sigi's company, acted. Maybe something good would come of it.

Mondi went on, "I sneaked into the Sailors' Rest right behind him. He and I and the bartender, and the guy he was meeting, were about the only people in there at that hour. I was able to get over up against a wall, out of the way, and listen to their conversation without being detected. And I don't doubt for a minute, from what I heard, that the guy I'd followed was the one who had hired an assassin to kill the emperor. He was making a final payment to Croaker – he's an underworld figure who acts as a middleman for criminal transactions – and the guy wanted to know whether it was certain that Papa Andrion would be convicted of the crime! Then I saw his face – and it was that guy Davos whatsisname, the emperor's sister's husband. The father of the heir!"

Everyone around the table stopped eating for a few moments, and there were shocked exclamations. Finally Bernadette got a grip on her emotions and spoke. "It makes perfect sense! After his brother-in-law became emperor Davos must have thought his ship had come in. Then when his own son was named Giorgio's heir, he *knew* it had. But if he had no love for Giorgio, he must not have wanted to wait twenty years to see his son on the throne. He'd be an old man by then, and likely young Tiberius might have grown a backbone in the meantime. But at this point in his life, he's of age yet still definitely under his parents' thumb. So Davos hires an assassin, a mage assassin with the ability not only to commit the crime but pin it on somebody else so thoroughly there will be no doubt."

Mondi was grinning from ear to ear. Mama was so smart, probably the equal of Papa Andrion in brains if not the scholar he was. She'd figured it all out, and now all they had to do was go tell the Imperial Guard what he'd seen and heard, and Papa would be freed! To his surprise, Mama sighed. "If only we had some proof of this!" she said with frustration. "This Croaker you mentioned, Mondi, I don't suppose he could testify about the transaction?"

Mondi's face fell. Of course, if they went to the Guard with this story, who were the authorities going to believe – the husband of the late emperor's sister, a highly placed citizen of Roma, or some dubious foreign brat who was known to dress up as a beggar and frequent low dives? "I doubt that Croaker even had any idea who he was dealing with," he said reluctantly. "He usually avoids using names when talking with clients, and most of the thieves and assassins he works with are only known by their aliases. Even Sigi and I are 'Felix' and 'Draco.'"

"Thank the gods for small favors," Bernadette said with a wink at her son. She loved him so much; even if he was, at this point in his life, slowly driving her out of her mind.

Andi, who'd been finishing his sandwich with a frown of concentration on his face, washed the last crumbs down with a swallow of mineral water (another strange thing to be found here in Remus) and said, "This Bronzo fellow. I suppose there's no chance he's secretly the long-lost heir to the throne or something like that?" Mondi grinned at his big brother.

"We talked to an old beggar woman up in the Scintillio District who says she's known him almost all her life. I think it's safe to say he just an old beggar who turned to drink, or perhaps a drunkard who turned to begging – a long time ago. But he's a nice enough guy."

Andi spun out his train of thought some more. "Does anyone know whether Davos Appolonius has a household guard?" he asked. Mondi spoke up. He'd had the benefit, for most of the past year, of Francois Lamonte's wide-ranging and always-interesting lectures on everything from myths and ancient history to current political affairs.

"Emperor Giorgio's family, the Augustinos, was noble and wealthy but they were not dukes or anything like that. He and his wife had a townhouse in Roma and a smallish manor house out in the countryside, but when his sister married Davos Appolonius – supposedly for love, as his family had less money than hers did – they had only a well-appointed townhouse. So they've got servants, but I don't think they would have a force of house guards. Usually it's only dukes or counts that mount a military force."

"That's what I thought," Andi said. "So if we can reasonably assume that Mom's right about Davos' motives for wanting his brother-in-law dead, he would have absolutely no motive for abducting random beggars – nor the manpower for it unless he hired mercenaries. That means somebody else is involved in this, somebody with their own soldiers. So probably a duke? But why, and what is this duke trying to do? The fact of your friend Bronzo getting snatched right in the middle of the time period when the emperor was killed is too much of a coincidence."

All around the table nodded, knowing that Andi was right – but not having any inspirations with which to answer the questions he'd posed. Riki felt like a bystander. One of the most important figures in her life had been snatched away, and there didn't seem to be anything she could contribute to the effort to free him. She hated that! Mom had never stood by, letting other people jump into the fight while she held back playing the helpless female. Why couldn't Riki come up with some brilliant insight, a plan that would make this Davos guy confess his crimes and free Papa Andrion?

The meal concluded, the group scattered to their separate activities. Until they heard back from Papa Andrion's lawyer or came up with a plan to make the man who'd hired an assassin to kill the emperor confess, there didn't seem to be much any of them could do. Andi and Rezira went out, as did Mondi and Sigi. Bernadette and Erik retreated to an upstairs parlor with Gylabris, to talk about the power cell project and pump the leukalfar tinkerer for any insights he might be able to come up with on their current problem. Eccentric he might be, and a member of an obscure tribe that had only recently begun to interact with the rest of the world; but in his way, Gylabris was a genius.

Riki picked up a book on the history of Remus and flopped on a settee in the downstairs parlor, reading it. Perhaps if her education hadn't devoted so much time to things like archery and animal husbandry, she might be able to come up with something. She was feeling sad and mad and frustrated, and was surprised to find how interesting it was to learn of what had taken place in this ancient land thousands of years before she was born. Outside the weather, always changeable here in Roma, had turned rainy – and spending the afternoon reading seemed like a fine idea.

The doorbell rang, and Riki looked up. Oh of course, it was Marta's day off as well – and Riki was the only person in this part of the house. Setting her book down, she went to see who was at the door. On the doorstep, soaked to the skin, stood Flavius – looking utterly bedraggled, mournful, and apologetic. She let him in.

"Don't move!" Riki commanded, and went looking for a towel. There was a linen closet off the corridor leading to the kitchen, and she soon returned and blotted her erstwhile suitor dry. All the while she was doing this, he was looking at her with eyes that were alternately avid and haunted. She was beginning to wonder if he'd been delving into the potions.

When Flavius was dry enough that it was safe to bring him into the parlor without ruining Pantheatos House's fine carpets and gleaming wooden floors, Riki led him in and bade him sit down. He dropped to the surface of a well-upholstered chair with a sigh. Then he eyed her as if she was the victim of some immense tragedy. "Oh Riki!" he said, "I'm so sorry!"

She blinked at him. "Sorry for…" she prompted, hoping he would explain himself.

"That your family has had to undergo this ordeal!" he exclaimed. "To have your father, uh, your papa arrested for murdering the emperor! This must have been awful for you. And, I apologize for having to leave you so quickly when the news came. My own father demanded my presence, and I was not able to be with you…" He broke off weakly, looking anguished.

"Flavius," Riki said slowly, trying to work out exactly what was going on here, "did your father forbid you to see me anymore?" Andi might be the bright one in their family – and Sigi, Mondi, and the rest of the dragon kids were rapidly overtaking her in education – but Riki was no dummy. Flavius looked crestfallen.

"He did," he replied shortly, "but here I am. I defy him! I love you, Riki, and I don't care what people are saying about your family in Roma. I'm here to stand by your side."

Riki's heart surged with fondness at Flavius' declaration. She didn't know him as she did Fjuri, probably never could – being unable to remember a time when Fjuri was not a part of her life – but his sincerity shone through and she appreciated his support even as she regretted the attitude he was expressing. As it was probably the attitude of every person of consequence in Roma, he could hardly be faulted for it. Apparently, the Drakespring family had become social pariahs overnight.

Riki walked over to Flavius and took his hands, pulling him to his feet and enfolding him in an embrace. She was surprised to find tears coming to her eyes. Here in the bosom of her family, minus only one member, she had felt so alone! She pulled him over to sit beside her on the settee where earlier she'd been reading. "I don't know what you've heard, Flavius," she said, "But don't believe for a moment that my papa killed the emperor. It's all a setup."

His dark eyes limpid with love and relief, Flavius said "A setup? You mean your papa was framed?"

"That's right," Riki replied. "Somebody who wanted the emperor dead figured he could cast the blame on an outsider. We think he might also have reasons to want the power cell project stopped, but that's not going to happen."

"He?" Flavius asked. "You know who it is ?"

Riki gazed searchingly into Flavius' eyes. He was so beautiful, and she was so attracted to him. But how much could she trust him? His apparent sincerity won her over, and she decided to bring him in on what they knew. If he was playing her, what was the worst that could happen – he'd alert Davos that somebody was onto him? That might only trigger the late emperor's brother-in-law into actions that would further incriminate him.

"You can't reveal this to anyone," Riki said, squeezing Flavius' hands.

"I promise!" he said, "Whatever you tell me will go no further!" Glancing down briefly, she looked up again and said, "My brother Mondi saw Davos Appolonius paying off an underworld go-between this morning. He was making the last payment to an assassin for killing the emperor." Flavius' eyes grew wide, as he processed what Riki had told him.

Finally he said, "And this assassin wasn't your papa?" Oh gods, Riki thought. I never even considered *that* interpretation…

Chapter 28: Intimacy

Lucia Salonius had chosen to come alone to the quarters of the Imperial Undertaker. She often felt alone these days, though she had some friends whose company she enjoyed. But since the death of Bruno, her only child, some who had been her intimates in youth had been driven away by the devastating sadness that loss had caused. Others were no longer in her social class, now that she was empress of all Agena. Her parents were long dead.

And with the death of her husband, it seemed as if there was nothing left to her. She didn't care much for Tiberius, her late husband's nephew; and while she was fond of her sister-in-law, Mariana Appolonius, she had never liked the man she had married. Aside from his lack of physical appeal, he seemed always consumed by ambition. His air of triumph after Bruno had been killed and Giorgio had been forced to declare Tiberius his heir had struck her as repugnant.

Now she was here to say goodbye to the last good thing in her life, her beloved Giorgio. Oh, if only the blasted Convocation had chosen someone else! They had been so happy, so comfortable in their lives, hobnobbing with the aristocracy in the City for gala parties, then enjoying time at their country estate. There had been no stress, only pleasure in life.

Then Gaius Albus II had spoiled it all by getting himself killed by an assassin while on a visit far to the north. And Giorgio had pointed out that his family was tied to the long-gone Salonius dynasty through the female line, and should be considered for the throne since there were no more members of the Albus family around.

Stifling a sob, Lucia proceeded through the doors as they were held open for her by Onderion Nightpool, the Imperial Undertaker. He did not handle the preparation of all of the bodies of those who died within Roma, by any means; but all members of the royal family who died were within his purview, as were the victims of murder. He had performed these duties since before she had been born, and he was one of the empire's most trusted functionaries.

"I have laid him out as you requested, Empress," the elf said formally. "And the amulet enchanted with the spell of preservation

has been applied. Please let Cassia know when you are finished."
Cassia, a young Reman woman, performed menial duties within the
morgue. She nodded to him and murmured her thanks, then
proceeded into the chilly room.

The love of her life was laid out on a stone table as if sleeping.
His rent and bloody party clothes had been removed and the body
washed, then a beautiful amulet had been placed around the corpse's
neck while his other jewelry, all heirlooms of the house except for
the imperial signet ring, was removed for safekeeping.

A silken drape had been placed over his form, pulled up to his
armpits as if he were merely sleeping. He looked so peaceful, so
beautiful lying there that her heart caught and an unbearable wave of
grief flooded over her. Had there been any sharp instruments in the
room, she might have opened her veins on the spot and joined him in
death.

After sitting for a time on the padded chair that had been
provided for her with her head in her hands, heaving great racking
sobs as tears poured down her cheeks, Lucia began to pull herself
together. She wiped the tears from her eyes, blew her nose on a
handkerchief, and sat, more calmly, just gazing at the corpse.

They had not made love for nearly a week before the ball, never
dreaming that last time that it *was* the last time. How cold and lonely
her bed would be without him, she thought with a sigh. Tomorrow
the body, still wearing the amulet of preservation, would be clad in
the emperor's finest garments and laid on a catafalque in the
Pantheatos, where for a week all could see their emperor lying in
state and pay their last respects to him before he was consigned to
the flames. Then his heir Tiberius would be crowned as the new
emperor, and life would go on. For some, at least. For the dowager
empress, the prospect was bleak – as bleak as the weather outside.

Where minutes before Lucia had felt ravaged, tossed on storms
of grief like a tiny boat on the great ocean, now a calm had come
over her. Dry-eyed, she got to her feet and pulled away the silken
drape, exposing Giorgio's naked body where it rested on the stone.
"What did he do to you, my darling?" she asked quietly, running her
hand down the hard, cold flesh of his chest. Her heart was wrenched
with pity as she saw the knife wound, looking a little like a red-

rimmed eye just beneath the ribcage. Such a small opening, to let out a man's life!

Like many Reman men, Giorgio had had a good deal of black, lightly curling hair on his chest and torso. It was a manly attribute, and she had always loved running her fingers through it. She did so now, as if soaking up one last set of memories – memories that would have to last her for the rest of her life.

Stroking down from the navel, Lucia ran her fingers along the groin – where nestled just inside the line of pubic hair was a small black mole shaped like a little heart. He had not been born with it, he had told her on their wedding night, but it had appeared when they had first met – obviously a sign that in her presence, his heart and his groin were always linked! What foolishness the man could speak, she thought fondly with a wistful smile. Their love life had been passionate, Giorgio a wonderful lover, and it had always surprised her that she had only borne a single child. She ought to have had a whole brood of them like that Fireblood woman, she mused.

Her fingers rifled the hair along the groin line more frantically, seeking a last sight of the little heart that had been their secret and theirs alone. Where was it? It should be right… there. She spread the hairs apart with both hands, peering at smooth and unblemished olive skin. It was not there!

With a little wail, Lucia collapsed back into the chair and a sad keening rose from her throat as she buried her head once again in her hands. She had lost her only son. She had lost her husband. And now, she was losing her mind.

Chapter 29: Demands

"What do you mean, you need more time?" Duke Enzo demanded in exasperation. "He was to have been 'found' and returned safely to Roma by now, telling his tale of abduction at the hands of Davos' mercenaries! We need him back on the throne, and Davos Appolonius in prison on charges of hiring murder and treason, before the Convocation crowns Tiberius. It'll be much harder to do this, once Tiberius is entrenched, and it'd mean impeaching a sitting emperor. That's never been done!"

Alderion shuddered internally. That a mage of his age and experience should have screwed up so royally was something he could scarcely believe, himself. He had been over-confident, he realized now, assuming that his long trail of successes meant nothing could go wrong. Why should not doubling the dose of the memory-wipe potion merely double the span of time erased, as seemed logical and sensible? Who could have dreamt it would give the man total amnesia? Could the unintended result be a side effect of other spells or traumas that had been inflicted on him in the course of the abduction?

The elf might be castigating himself for his colossal blunder, but that didn't mean he had no pride. "I have failed you, Your Grace," he said stiffly, head bowed. "If you wish, I will tender my resignation immediately."

"Don't be ridiculous," Enzo snarled. "I need you, I've always needed you. And I need you to *fix this* right away!" After a moment he added, "You removed the Spell of Seeming from him, showed him his true face?"

"I did that as soon as it became apparent that more than the past couple of hours' memories had been wiped, sir. I had hoped that being restored to himself physically might trigger the regrowth of his memories. We cleaned him up and got him into some decent clothes, showed him a mirror, and he looked at it as if he was meeting some interesting stranger. He's very amiable and passive, and accepts everything that I tell him. I don't know what to do to speed the process along, though – anything I try might just make matters worse."

The duke rose to his feet and began pacing his study, his usually handsome looks spoiled by the deep furrowing of his brow as he tried to wrest a solution from his brain. This was a disaster! Instead of trapping that swine Davos and paving the way for Flavius to one day become emperor, he might merely have succeeded in elevating that chinless, spotty-faced Appolonius brat to the throne. And while Davos might be unaware of Enzo's machinations against him, there was already no love lost between them. With Tiberius as emperor, the Terentius family had better just go back to Brindis and stay there for good.

"We can't leave Giorgio penned up in a mine while we're waiting for him to recover his memory," he said at last. "Can you give him a sleep draught or something so that he'll be unaware while you move him to more comfortable quarters?"

"Certainly," Alderion said, thinking that he ought to have used that instead of the more-convenient paralysis spell when they'd abducted the emperor and made the switch in the first place. It would have lasted for hours, and they could entirely have avoided removing the previous hour's memories and gone right to implanting new ones. That and a Spell of Seeming on Enzo's guards so that Giorgio didn't recognize them… Was there no *end* to the mistakes he'd made?

"There's a small country estate that came to me after my wife's death," Enzo said. "It's up in the hills near Lake Trasimeno, out of the way, and I doubt many people know it has anything to do with me as she got it through an uncle on her mother's side. That whole branch of the family just sort of died out. Keep him comfortable there and guarded, tell him your story that you and my guards rescued him from the mine and that you're hoping he will regain his memories so he can tell you who abducted him. Tell him you're afraid to deliver him into the hands of his enemies, since we don't know what faction kidnapped him."

Alderion nodded. "I'll leave immediately. Giorgio seems to be very amenable to direction, almost as if he had been hit with the Befriend spell too many times in a row. I'll stay with him and spend our hours together reminding him of who he is and what we want him to remember. I'll also arrange for those 'mercenary' bodies to be left in the mine before we go, so we can discover the Appolonius tokens on them later. If worse comes to worst, we should have the emperor to a point where he can resume his duties, even if he still doesn't have any real memories of his former life. And I'll implant that gratitude to the Terentius family in his mind. And then of course, when we bring him in, we'll bring the 'evidence' that Davos was the one who orchestrated the abduction along with the faked assassination."

Enzo was still frowning, but he seemed to like the mage's suggestion. "Giorgio must be back in Roma and our story in place no later than five days from now," he warned. "Can any other mage undo your Spell of Seeming?"

"No," Alderion assured him. "Another mage who knew my spell or had a similar one of his or her own could lay another seeming on top of mine; and if I were to be killed, the spell would unravel in time. But other than that, the appearance of the person or object I cast it on will remain fixed – I would assume for as long as I live, though of course I only developed the spell six years ago before we used it to stage that 'minotaur attack' on Bruno Salonius."

"I think it likely no other mage has such a spell," Enzo said, throwing the elf a bone. Alderion had been a powerful, mysterious figure in his life from his earliest memories, and it disturbed him to see him so upset – even if he richly deserved censure for the mistakes he'd made in executing this mission. Was it possible for elderly alfar to lose their edge, just as old men did? "So no one will know that only the one who cast it can remove it."

He continued, "You will go to the Pantheatos after returning the emperor to the custody of his Imperial Guard, and remove the seeming in the presence of witnesses so all can see that the man killed at the party was some anonymous beggar, and not our emperor. Of course, if Giorgio recovers his memories less than five days from now, you can put this all in effect sooner. Just keep me informed." With that, Alderion was dismissed. He nodded curtly and left the room, hurrying to his quarters to gather some supplies before returning via map to the mine where the emperor was being held. Perhaps this would all work out, after all.

Chapter 30: Roadblocks

Marta opened the door to admit Marcos Benedetti, lawyer's satchel in his hand. A nice looking man, she thought – though far too old to be of interest to her, of course. She was half in love with the young Mister Drakespring (that is, Andi), though that young Lord Terentius wasn't half bad either. There'd been some mention of Miss Riki having a steady beau back in Iscandia, so perhaps she'd turn down Flavius and give Marta a chance. A girl could dream, couldn't she? On average, Marta fell in love with three to four different men per month – though usually, those crushes had slightly better prospects than did her current ones.

Marcos met with Bernadette, Erik, Riki, Mondi, and Sigi, as well as Anja and Lars (still living at the Storekeeps' Inn, but visiting for the day), in Pantheatos House's downstairs parlor. Andi, Rezira, and Gylabris were at the university working on the power cell project. The lawyer took some papers out of his satchel, along with his notebook, and addressed the assembled friends and family of his client.

"I'm happy to report that Andrion is in better spirits now that we've gotten him a decent mattress to sleep on and some improved food and drink," he told them with a smile. "I suppose I shouldn't be surprised at how amenable the imperial jailers are to bribery, but it concerns me a little as I wonder what else they might do if offered enough money."

"Think we could bribe them to just let Andrion go?" Erik suggested with a smile. It was driving him nuts, going slowly through legal channels when he just wanted to smash his way into the Penitentiary and free his brother with his fists and the odd edged weapon. His wife had pointed out that, at this time of their lives and with responsibility for more than a dozen children, it would perhaps be best *not* to become wanted fugitives. The empire's troops were all over Iscandia, and everyone knew where they lived.

Marcos took it for the joke it was intended to be and smiled slightly, then continued on a more serious note. "Unfortunately, we have run into some difficulties. I had Macchiatus' people examine Andrion's tunic, the bloodstained one that was taken in evidence when he was arrested, and they were very embarrassed to find that, two days later, it still appeared to be glistening with fresh blood. You can't raise a pink stain by pouring water over it, nor does the 'blood' come off on your hands when you touch it. The blood is an illusion!"

There was a murmur of excitement. Here, finally, was proof that illusion magic had been used to frame Andrion for the crime. "The dagger of course is real, and so is the hole it made in the emperor's chest. But there is no real proof of whose hand held it when it killed. I immediately made a petition to the Imperial Court for the charges to be dropped and Andrion released, since it seemed obvious that evidence against him had been falsified."

More excitement. But if he was here to announce victory, why did Marcos not look more pleased? "I'm sorry to tell you," he went on, "that my petition was denied. The heir, Tiberius, is devastated at the loss of his uncle and he is convinced that the killer is in custody. He thinks it possible that Andrion fabricated this obviously false evidence himself, in order to cast doubt on the eyewitnesses' testimony. And the judges agreed. Unless we can come up with irrefutable evidence condemning the true killer, Andrion may be forced to remain in prison until his trial. Though if we can get more evidence putting the blame elsewhere, there's a good chance he could be acquitted."

"I believe we know who hired the assassin," Bernadette said coldly, "and it goes far to explaining Tiberius' refusal to consider letting Andrion out of jail." Marcos looked at her with speculation. "We don't have any hard evidence, unfortunately, but my son Mondi is in possession of a Ring of Blend. Using it to become invisible, he saw and overheard Davos Appolonius paying off an underworld middleman in the Sailors' Rest down in the waterfront district yesterday morning."

The lawyer was stunned. A member of the imperial family, hiring the murder of his own brother-in-law? It horrified him, but past history of the empire and what he knew of Davos personally inclined him to believe it was not impossible. "This is a very serious charge, Madame Drakespring!" he said. "Is your son absolutely sure of the identification?"

Mondi spoke up. "The underworld character is widely known in the waterfront district. Sigi and I have been doing some…

undercover work among the beggars and thieves, and have established identities as beggar boys. The man's underworld alias is Croaker. Have you heard of him?"

Marcos nodded. His business, after all, was acting on the behalf of accused criminals – and not all of them were innocent of wrongdoing. He had interviewed this Croaker on two occasions, seeking information that he hoped would exonerate his clients, and found the man remarkably unhelpful. But he was known to be the man to see if you wanted to hire a thief, a murderer, or maybe just a thug to go round and intimidate your enemies into doing your bidding. "He is as you say," he responded. "But I was thinking more of your identification of Davos Appolonius. I assume, if it were him, that he would have made some effort to hide his face?"

Mondi nodded. His confidence was far beyond what you would expect for a boy of his apparent age, and Marcos found himself accepting what he had to say. "I met Signor Appolonius at very close range twice in the past two weeks," Mondi explained. "Once at the gathering at the Terentius mansion, and a week later at the Grand Ball. He was wearing a cloak with a hood, but I was standing not six feet away from him, and when he wiped his forehead his face became visible. There is no doubt, but also no hard evidence beyond my testimony."

"Which likely will not hold up in court," Marcos sighed. "Even if we are able to prove Davos guilty of hiring the killer, which would be treason and come with a death sentence, we also need proof that Andrion was not in fact that hired killer. I know it sounds ludicrous, to suggest that such a prominent and widely respected man as the Magister of the Academy at Eisenstag should hire himself out as an assassin; but the Guild of Assassins has often recruited from among the rich and powerful – people who had no need of the money, but killed by stealth for the thrill and power it brought them."

Everyone in the room looked horrified at the thought. Certainly, they had all heard of such people – twisted individuals who enjoyed killing for its own sake. Some of them even led quiet lives with wives and children, and when their hideous crimes were finally uncovered no one who knew them could believe the evidence. But even so, to accuse Andrion of being such a person? Ridiculous.

"We'll keep looking for more evidence," Bernadette promised, and there were murmurs of agreement all around the room. "Please tell Andrion what we're doing, and that sooner or later we will get him out." Marcos shook her hand and Erik's, gathered up his papers, and left. After seeing him out, Bernadette and Erik returned to find Riki, Anja, and Lars in a discussion with Sigi and Mondi about the fake "bloodstained" tunic.

"We've only been in Remus off and on for a couple of years," Anja admitted, "But I'm really surprised to hear that the authorities aren't making more use of magic in crime detection."

"Like using a Command spell to make criminals confess?" Mondi asked. That would certainly cut through a lot of red tape.

"Uh, not exactly," she replied. "I think you might run into some problems there, where you couldn't be sure that the person was telling the truth in their confession and not just responding to the spell. There'd have to be some hard evidence, too."

"Huh," Mondi said, "Andi got those bandits at Wylion to turn themselves in and confess using a Command spell a couple of weeks ago, and those guys are locked up awaiting trial for banditry and murder now."

"True," Anja replied, "and there's a pretty good chance that when their case comes to trial, their confessions won't be allowed and they'll be set free. But at least those particular guys aren't out killing anyone for the next three months. No, what I'm talking about is a spell of Detect Magic. It can be used as an enchantment on items like amulets and jewelry, and it works similarly to spells that detect life. But instead of putting a glow around living things – including animated undead – it puts a glow around anything that has an active spell on it. It would have saved Commander Octavius some embarrassment, when they took Uncle Andrion's tunic in evidence."

"I never knew there was such a thing!" Bernadette said, surprised. Andrion was the family's greatest authority on all things magical, and he was not available for consultation.

"I'm not sure where the spell came from," Anja admitted, "and I suppose it's not all that well known. I bought my ring from a gatti trader out near Salonno a little over a year ago. I just assumed that the imperial authorities would have access to such magic, if a random adventurer could lay her hands on it. It's endlessly useful when you're adventuring, especially in areas that have magical traps. And it helps you spot valuable enchanted weapons without having to have any magical abilities yourself."

A look of fixed excitement had come over Mondi as she was speaking, and a number of ideas were percolating in his brain. "Anja, do you think I could borrow your ring for a few hours?" he asked. "I promise I'll have it back to you by tomorrow." She looked surprised. Having loved Mondi as a little dragon child, and not gotten to know him very well yet in his recent incarnation as a mischievous human adolescent, she was not at all suspicious of him.

"All right," she said, "I'll get it. But don't lose it! Apparently it wouldn't be all that easy to replace."

Chapter 31: Two Can Play

After lunch Draco and Felix were once again wandering the streets of the waterfront district, dressed in filthy rags. It didn't take them long to find Tullio, who was lucky at his young age to have inherited one of the best begging locations in the area. The beggar boy was now beginning to have his doubts about these two. He'd helped them in their disguise, assuming they were just the sons of a wealthy family playing at being beggars – yet they kept coming back. Still, if they had money, why shouldn't he get some of it?

As usual, Mondi was the spokesman for their gang of two. He grinned at Tullio, an expression that for some unexplainable reason made the boy suddenly think of six-inch fangs, red slit-pupiled eyes, and glistening red scales. He hadn't eaten yet today, so perhaps he was hallucinating. Mondi slapped a wad of coins into Tullio's hand, and anxiety about getting a meal immediately vanished. Yes – whatever these two were up to, as long as he got paid he was perfectly fine with it.

"My patron was very pleased with the information we got from Megera," Mondi told Tullio. "And now he wants to talk with Croaker. I think he may need to have someone, uh… *removed*, if you know what I mean. How would we go about arranging an interview with Croaker?" Tullio felt a tightening run down the middle of his body. Anxiety, or just hunger? He really needed to go get something to eat, and soon.

"I'll have to talk with Veletto about that, but there shouldn't be a problem setting it up. Croaker is almost always around. Let me go get something to eat, and I'll meet you back here in a couple of hours with the details," he said.

The boys watched Tullio leg off, almost as if something was chasing him. "I hope we didn't put the wind up him," Mondi remarked.

"He knows we're not really beggar boys," Sigi said thoughtfully, "but as long as we have money to give him, and don't betray him or anybody he cares about, I don't think it matters." Sigi had a sort of purity about him, Mondi thought, an innocence that let him see things clearly – even when he was guilty as hell. He dearly loved his baby brother.

"Come on, Sigi," Mondi said. "We've got more than enough time to try out Anja's ring, while we're waiting to hear back from Tullio." The two of them set off to the northeast, leaving the waterfront district through the East Gate and then making their way west and north to the Pantheatos. The area was aswarm with people, as today was the first day of the emperor's lying in state. His body, held in stasis by a preservation spell, was on display in the temple for all citizens to come and see. They could pay their last respects, and say their goodbyes to the wise and kindly man who had been their ruler for the past decade. And it was great for reinforcing public support for the imperial throne.

It had not taken them ten minutes to jog here from Tullio's pitch, but Mondi was already beginning to wonder if he'd spoken too soon when he'd told Sigi two hours was more than enough time for their errand. The line of citizens waiting to pay their respects to the emperor ran from the temple's main door, off to the west and far along the perimeter of the seven-sided main cathedral – halfway encircling the building.

The boys got into the queue, where their apparent filth and ragged clothing repelled those around them. They were able to parlay this into an advantage, casting soulful eyes at their fellows in line and using whatever sad story would get them advanced a few paces along. Most people were happy to let them go ahead, hoping that they would soon move further and be out of smelling range.

Thus within a little more than an hour they were inside the building and approaching the central area, where the emperor's bier had been erected. Mondi briefly toyed with the notion that he and Sigi should go dragon and send everyone shrieking in panic from the building – but he knew it was a stupid idea. The emperor's body, clad in elegant robes and lying as if asleep atop a stone catafalque, sat near the center of the space. The central circle was cordoned off, and city guards in full regalia stood at attention, providing crowd control. How to get near?

Mondi handed Anja's ring to Sigi, and he slipped it onto a finger. It fitted itself easily to Sigi's right index finger. "What do you see?" Mondi murmured. The two of them were crouched at the very front of the crowd surrounding the cordoned-off area, between two of the guards. "He's glowing," Sigi replied as quietly, "but he would be, right? There's a spell on him to keep the body from rotting?" Mondi cursed silently. Of course, duh.

He glanced from side to side, and nobody but Sigi was paying him any attention. The guards stood stolidly staring straight ahead, doing their duty. And all of the people in the crowd were busy communing with their tragically murdered emperor. "I'm pretty sure it's an enchanted ring or amulet that holds the spell," Mondi hissed to his brother. "I'm going to go in there and take it off for a minute, and stand over by the far side of the circle. You give me thumbs up if he's still glowing, and thumbs down if not, okay?"

Sigi grinned at him slightly and nodded as Mondi slipped on his Ring of Blend and vanished from normal sight. Nobody else had apparently noticed, though of course to Sigi he was lit up like a beacon. He watched as Mondi slipped between the guards and up to the head end of the emperor's body. He was busy there for a moment, then pulled away from it again and retreated some distance away. The glow around the emperor's body continued, if slightly less bright than it had been.

Sigi glanced around to make sure that nobody was paying him any attention. He was just some random, filthy beggar boy paying his respects to a man who had never missed a meal in his life, and everyone else there was far too caught up in their own concerns to even glance in his direction. Surreptitiously, as if he were merely making a normal gesture, he popped a thumb up. In another minute or so Mondi had replaced the amulet with the Preservation enchantment on it back around the corpse's neck (wouldn't do to have the body start stinking!) and returned to Sigi's side, before carefully returning to full visibility. Then the two of them began making their way out of the crowd and toward the exit.

The two hours were nearly up by the time they made it back through the East Gate to the waterfront district. "Lit up like a candle!" Sigi averred. "That corpse had some whopping big spell on it, and it wasn't just to keep it from rotting or they wouldn't have bothered with that amulet." "You're right," Mondi said, as they hurried back toward Tullio's usual spot. "But why in all the hells is there a spell on the corpse of the emperor – unless maybe that's *not* the emperor?"

The conversation was interrupted as they spotted their beggar friend. He was looking a little more relaxed than the last time they'd seen him. "Hey ho," he greeted them cheerfully. "It's all set up for your patron. He's to meet Croaker at the rear table in the Sailors' Rest's main room at eight tonight. I assume he'll be in disguise, in fact that's the way Croaker likes it, so he'll wear a red rose pinned to his tunic and speak the code phrase, "'The harvest in Iscandia will be early next year.'" Mondi forked over another handful of gold coins, and they went on their way. As they walked along, Sigi murmured to his brother, "A red rose? Seriously? I'm a twelve-year-old bumpkin and even *I* think that's corny." Mondi shrugged.

Andi, Rezira, and Gylabris came home from a tiring day in the lab, only to be beset with the latest news on the Andrion front. As they sipped some wine and nibbled on some *antipasto* (appetizers, it turned out, another Reman thing that seemed to involve slices of sausage, cheese, and pickled vegetables) before dinner, the rest of the family filled them in on the day's events. They were in the midst of this when Flavius arrived, dry this time, and more or less invited himself to share supper with them. Riki vouched for him, so he was taken into their plots.

Everyone was interested to learn of Mondi and Sigi's visit to the corpse of the emperor. "You took away the Preservation amulet, and he was still glowing?" Andi asked, and got confirmation. The very concept of a Ring of Detect Magic was something he wouldn't have believed twenty-four hours before, had not Mondi lent it to him for experimentation. He cast a spell of Befriend on a volunteer, Gylabris, and saw for himself the effect. Why had not the whole world learned of this yet?

"Absolutely." Mondi assured him. "I put it around my *own* neck, so any effects of preventing rot should have been strictly focused on me. But Sigi saw the corpse still lit up." Like all of the dragon kids, he had an inborn gift for magic similar to that enjoyed by the alfar races and the part-alfar Galise. With a Galise mother, or was it a dragon mother, that gift was enhanced.

"Anyhow," Mondi went on. "I've arranged that my 'patron' – that's you, Andi – is going to go in disguise at eight this evening to meet with Croaker at the Sailors' Rest in the waterfront district. It's just a little east of here, north of East Gate. I'm sorry, but you're supposed to have a rose pinned to your shirt and use the phrase 'the harvest in Iscandia will be early next year.'"

Andi looked at him suspiciously, and Mondi went on, "Dumb, I know, but… I figure you know a spell or two that will convince Croaker to open up to you. We really need to know everything he can tell us about how long ago his client, Davos Appolonius, sought his services – and about the assassin he worked with to complete the contract. We need to get dates and times so we can pin down that Papa Andrion is *not* the assassin."

Andi washed down a delicious mouthful of sausage and cheese with some excellent red wine and snorted. "Papa Andrion, a professional assassin? Gods save us!" Cornelia called them for supper and they ate a simple but excellent meal – thin pasta noodles smothered in a tomato-rich sauce studded with savory mushrooms and little balls of seasoned minced beef, with an enormous basket of bread rolls toasted with butter and fresh garlic. Considering the assignment he'd picked up when he got home from work, Andi decided to take it easy on the wine.

There were roses growing in the yard behind the house, and Rezira had gone out and cut one before the day's light had fled. She pinned it onto the shoulder of Andi's tunic with a kiss, and a warning. "Stay out of trouble or I'll kill you," she said sweetly. Bernadette was concerned too, but she shied away from delivering any parental advice. Her eldest son might still be a few months short of his eighteenth birthday, but he was a man deserving of respect.

They all saw Andi off with good wishes around 7:45, then found themselves hard-put to simply relax for the remainder of the evening. Flavius lured Riki up onto the widow's walk atop Pantheatos House's roof, the weather having turned fine again. A million stars and the smallest of Terris' three moons did battle with the lights of the city as they gazed out from their promontory. He swept her into his arms and kissed her fervently.

"Ah, Riki, I'm so sorry for your troubles!" Flavius declared. "If only this tragedy had not marred your visit!" Deep inside he knew that Father's objections to a marriage alliance with the Drakespring family were such that, had none of this happened, he would still be forbidden to seek Riki's hand. But at least, perhaps, he would have continued to be able to see her – perhaps to make love with her. And now, after being privy to the family's discussions, he was convinced that her papa was truly innocent, and that some plot was afoot to blame him unjustly for the crime. Maybe, as a member of one of Remus' most prominent families, there was something he could do to help.

Andi had not had occasion to go to the waterfront district since they'd arrived here in Roma, but it was only a fifteen-minute brisk walk from the front door of Pantheatos House. Once on the other side of the gates, he found himself looking at a long, broad road running out to the riverside. The district was slightly longer than one of the city's sides, and three streets deep with the westernmost one running along below the city walls while the broadest, the easternmost, ran beside piers where ships and boats engaged in the river trade were moored.

As Mondi had instructed him he turned to the left after reaching the water and continued north to a narrow doorway on the left not far from the harbor area's northern terminus. This was the Sailors' Rest Inn. For disguise he'd put on the Meiskomtot Mask, a possession of the Drakespring Clan they'd acquired a little more than a year before. It certainly had its uses, and along with the Wissagleb mask had been packed for this trip. It definitely obscured his face, aside from its magical powers. Plus, it made it hard to see where he was going, and probably scared the pants off of anyone who saw him.

Andi had brought along a few other items to enhance his chances of making it through the evening. He was wearing a Ring of Darksight, which made negotiating the cluttered dockside road in the dim evening light less of a challenge; and he'd also brought along Anja's Ring of Detect Magic. It surely wouldn't hurt to know whether this Croaker guy was messing with him.

He opened the door to the Sailors' Rest and went inside. At this hour the place was crowded, but people shied away at his approach.

Tall, muscular, cloaked and wearing the frightening-looking dragon priest mask, Andi appeared to be someone to be avoided. If only they knew what a sweetheart I really am, he thought, as he looked around and spotted the table at the rear occupied by a hard-bitten, somewhat misshapen-looking character who could only be Croaker. Andi could see where he'd gotten the name – the man resembled a toad.

Not bothering to obtain a drink at the bar, Andi stalked across the room and slid into the seat opposite the underworld middleman. "The harvest in Iscandia next year will be early," he murmured, while fussing with the rose at his left shoulder. Croaker eyed him, and started slightly at the sight of the metal mask. Most of his clients were a little more... subtle.

"I understand you're looking to send someone away," the toad-like man murmured beneath the buzz of conversation in the crowded room. "Kind of surprised – you don't look like you need any help."

"Oh, but I do," Andi replied, as he gestured and silently cast a spell of Command over Croaker. He flinched a little as he did so. He had never been comfortable using this spell, but sometimes needs must.

"Tell me about the client you spoke with here yesterday morning," Andi said conversationally. "Tell me everything you know about him, starting with the first time you talked with him."

"Don't know his name," Croaker replied. "I never know anybody's name, of course – better that way. He learned about me through the grapevine, I suppose, but it was Veletto who arranged for us to meet. Must be..." he hesitated, trying to get it straight in his mind. Under the Command spell you would do your best to obey, but it didn't magically make you smarter or give you a better memory.

"Five weeks ago, that was it!" Croaker said at last, recalling the date. "It was back at the beginning of Sungold. He said he wanted somebody out of the way, but it had to be done in a way where there was no question it was a murder and somebody else had done it. Unusual, that, most people want it to look like an accident or natural causes, but not him. Of course at that time I didn't know whom it was he wanted dead, either." The man took another sip of his ale, perfectly at ease in the grip of the spell. To Andi's sight, augmented by the Ring of Detect Magic, Croaker had been dark when they first met. Now, he was lit up like a beacon.

"I knew there was only one assassin for a job like that," the middleman went on, "so I told him it was going to be five thousand guilders to start with. He blinked a little, but he had that much on him. Then he left." Another swig of the ale, and a wave of the hand to a barmaid to bring another. "You want one?" he asked, and Andi declined.

"So who was the assassin that you contacted for the job?" he asked. Croaker paled a little and shuddered slightly. "Feller called The Mask," he murmured. "Famous. Supposedly been in the business since before I was born, so he's got to be an elf. And a mage, obviously. But I *know* he's an elf, 'cause I've seen him without a hat and he's got the ears. Always wears a mask to hide his face, of course, but the eyes tilt up. Ljosalfar, I'd say, if I'm any judge…"

Ljosalfar, Andi thought, considering the ljosalfar mage who' been talking with his parents at the party a little over a week ago. Couldn't be, he thought. That guy had been a legitimate court mage for generations of the dukes of Brindis. He couldn't possibly have needed the money from being a hit man. And you'd think the dukes of Brindis would have noticed if their court mage kept disappearing on assignments that they hadn't ordered…

Croaker, set on his course by Andi's Command, continued talking after another downing another draft of ale to soothe his parched throat. "It took a while for me to reach The Mask," he said. "Sometimes you can't get him at all, like he's got some other job going on. A guy like that, he's probably somebody you'd never suspect. Anyhow, I finally got through to him. I'd already collected the initial fee, so he set up a meeting with the client. I don't know what they discussed, but I was told to collect another fee – a much bigger one – and leave a message for him when the money had been paid."

Trying to stay aware of the time, wondering when he would need to renew the Command spell (but by Croaker's glowing form, it was still in effect), Andi broke in. "How do you contact The Mask, anyhow?" he asked.

225

"Oh, I leave a note in a crock lying underneath a table in the abandoned shack out there on the far side of the island," he said, gesturing. "Cloak and dagger stuff, you bet!" he twinkled, and for a moment looked like somebody's jovial old uncle. Andi shuddered a little.

"And how do you know when he's gotten the message, then?" he asked. "He leaves a message for me in the same spot, of course!" Croaker chortled. The Command spell had a tendency, similar to the Befriend spell, to convince the subject that they were chatting with an intimate friend. "We have code phrases, of course. Rarely we actually meet, and we always change the code phrases then. It's worked for decades without any problems."

Huh, Andi thought. What else did he need to ask? He had the feeling he was running out of questions, but the ten-minute duration of the spell was still in effect. Croaker continued, still following the Command given to him. "After the client delivered the rest of the initial payment, I contacted The Mask again and arranged for another meeting. That was only about a week ago. I don't know what they talked about, of course. I always stay as far away as possible from my clients and the… operatives I hire on their behalves."

Andi nodded. Sweet gig, Croaker. All you do is talk to people and leave notes, transfer money around. No blame on you when people die and other people's lives are ruined. He stifled the urge to seize the man around the neck and strangle him. Seeing that Andi was looking at him expectantly, the human amphibian continued his tale.

"Apoldtag morning of course I heard what happened at the Imperial Ball, and it didn't take a genius to figure out that had to have been The Mask delivering on his contract with my client. I got a heads-up from Veletto to meet the guy here, and when he handed over the money he was all anxious about whether the other guy who'd been picked for the blame was really going to get convicted. Some mage from Iscandia, don't know why the hell anyone here would care. Maybe he was just a target of opportunity. But the client paid the final installment, and that was that."

"Did you see his face?" Andi asked.

"Can't say as I did," Croaker replied. Under the Command spell he would answer truthfully without being specifically told to do so. No doubt he'd had a long and happy career making a point of *never* getting a good look at his clients' faces. Well, that was that. Clearly Davos' plot had pre-dated the Drakespring family's arrival in Remus – and Croaker could be tapped to tell enough, even if he knew no real names, to convince the Judges that Andrion could not have been the hired assassin.

"Do one thing more for me," Andi Commanded Croaker. He passed over a sheet of paper, in case the man didn't have one on him. "Write a note to The Mask, telling him that a client has paid you for a… removal, and that he should meet me here tomorrow evening at eight. Then take it to your usual drop location in the abandoned shack. That is what happened this evening, and you don't remember anything else." A Command of this type often worked with the spell, continuing its effect after the magic had worn off – though it could be easily broken down under scrutiny. He hoped that there would be no reason for Croaker to question it.

Croaker pulled out a pen and a bottle of ink, and began writing on the paper. "I have to warn you, there's a pretty good chance The Mask won't get this note before your meeting. He hasn't been seen around since the assassination. But once he gets it he'll put in another note with a new meeting time. I'll check the crock every day. But how can I reach you?

"Uh, just leave a message with Tullio and my agents will tell me," Andi said. He had no intention of this game dragging on for weeks. If The Mask showed up tomorrow evening, he'd meet with him and put him under a Command spell, drag him back home. Zira had tucked one of their magic-block collars into her pack when they were getting ready for this trip, and it would only be poetic justice to put one around the neck of this ancient, "famous" mage assassin before they hauled him off to the Penitentiary, and demanded Andrion's release.

227

Chapter 32: Betrayal

Flavius had just hung up his cloak after returning home, his thoughts filled with Riki – and, a little bit, with how they were to prove her papa's innocence – when his father's manservant informed him that his presence was requested in the duke's study. Uh oh, he thought, wondering what was up. Father had been acting troubled lately, curt and distant. First he had seemed to be sympathetic with Flavius' love of Riki, though he'd forbidden him to discuss marriage with her or her family. Then, after the assassination, Enzo had told him to stay completely away from her and hers, lest any of the stink of murder and treason rub off on the Terentius family.

As soon as he walked into the room, he knew it was trouble. Duke Enzo stood rigid, seeming to quiver with suppressed fury, his face like a thundercloud. The lightning was soon to come. "Sit down, son," he ordered with a sharp gesture, and Flavius sat. As he looked up inquiringly, his father began to pace the room rather than taking his own seat. "I ordered you, did I not," he said in a quiet tone that failed to ease his son's fears, "to stay away from Erika Drakespring and her family?"

"Yes, Papa," Flavius answered, hoping that by reverting to the name by which he'd called his father when he was a child, he might turn away some of the wrath he could see on the near horizon. "But you did not, did you?" Enzo asked rhetorically. "I had you followed today, and you were seen entering the house where the Drakesprings are staying and remaining there for several hours. Are you trying to destroy this family?"

"No, Papa! Of course not!" Flavius said, looking abashed. That look had always worked on his late mother, but was less successful here. "Andrion Drakespring was seen murdering our emperor by half a dozen witnesses only a few days ago," the duke began his tirade. "It's true that his son and others of his team from the Academy are still working with Sextus Garibaldi on their dypalfar project, but the entire family have become social poison! Nobody, absolutely *nobody* in Roma can be seen having anything to do with them. And that most especially includes me, you, and your brothers!"

"My brothers?" Flavius asked. Was there some connection he'd missed?

"Your brother Gaius had been playing lately with the two younger Drakespring boys, whom he'd befriended at our party. I forbade him any contact with them as well, yet he was caught attempting to leave the house dressed as a beggar, planning to meet those boys in the waterfront district!" The Duke threw up his hands in disgust. "At least Arturus, my heir, has obeyed my command to have nothing to do with them. But you and Gaius apparently can't be trusted to do as you're told. I'm placing both of you under house arrest – Gaius is already cooling his heels in his bedroom, and you will be going to yours shortly. A guard will be posted to make sure you stay in there."

Flavius' father turned his back as to dismiss him. House arrest? No! How was he to help Riki, to show her how much he loved her, if he was locked in his room? He rose to his feet. He was an adult, after all – not some little kid to be ordered around. "Father, you don't understand!" he said, volume rising. "Andrion Drakespring is innocent! I've been trying to help them prove it, and we've already learned that it was Davos Appolonius who hired the killer. Plus, the bloodstains on Andrion's shirt were fake! Commander Octavius discovered that they were just an illusion. And soon we're going to find out who the *real* assassin was. We should be helping them stop this miscarriage of justice, not abandoning them in their hour of need!"

Duke Enzo whirled at this pronouncement, staring at his son, noticeably pale beneath his olive complexion. "That's enough!" he cried, infuriated. "Get to your room, and stay there!" He seized the disbelieving Flavius by the shoulder and handed him over to the manservant, who'd been waiting outside the closed door. "Ignacio, take my son to his room," he ordered coldly, "and see that he does not leave again. Nor is he to send any messages. You may bring him his meals there for the immediate future. And send Rodrigo to me at once."

Ignacio, whose duties including everything from running the household servants to acting as a bodyguard and enforcer for his duke, led the boy off. Flavius had enough sense to keep his mouth shut, as clearly raising any more protests was going to infuriate his father still more – but what had he said that was so bad, that had upset him so much?

Enzo was at his desk when a quiet knock came at the door and Rodrigo Fontana, the commander of the Brindis guard, let himself in. Rodrigo was an ill-favored fellow, looking to be the sort of man you would not want to meet in a dark alley; but he had come from a good family, and he combined many of the attributes of a gentleman with those of the worst sort of criminal. The duke highly valued his skills.

"What is it, sir?" he asked, standing at ease before the desk where Enzo sat. "It's those damned Drakesprings!" the duke exclaimed. "I have just learned from that recalcitrant young idiot, my middle son, that they have launched an in-depth investigation of the assassination for which Andrion Drakespring has been blamed. They have already discovered several facts I had assumed were unknowable, and I fear their prying will soon lead them to other facts that I do *not* want brought to light. Suggestions?"

Rodrigo pondered, cracking his knuckles. He was convincing as a thug, and had often acted the role. "There's half a dozen adults and a couple of kids Gaius' age, right?" he asked. The Duke nodded. "That's a lot of people to try to control," he went on. "You could whack one or intimidate them, but it would probably just make the rest dig harder, sure that the reaction was provoked because they were on the right track. Or, you might seed false evidence for them – turn them away from the truth. But you'd have to do that subtly, or they'd likely suspect your intentions if they're as clever as you say. You'd need a few days to do that."

Enzo frowned. He didn't have time for subtleties! If that damned meddling clan got onto his involvement in the plot, most especially his plan to interfere with the emperor's mind so that he'd not only cast aside Davos and Tiberius but cleave to the Terentius family and name Flavius heir, there was going to be hell to pay. But if Alderion managed to retrieve his error and restore enough of the emperor's memory in time, there'd be no further need for the Drakesprings to investigate – Davos would be arrested, Andrion freed (either immediately, or when the case came to trial), and everything nicely explained by the tale planted in Giorgio's mind.

As his duke sat glaring at the papers on the writing desk, lost in thought, another idea occurred to Rodrigo. "They're doing all this because they want to get that Andrion guy out of prison, right?" he asked.

"Yes," Enzo replied. "The family is large and clannish, and they really look out after their own. From what Flavius tells me, they had already organized the first stage of their investigation before going to bed, the night of the assassination."

"Well then, suppose something happens to this Andrion while he's locked up his cell, like suppose another prisoner helps him get loose and he's killed escaping? There wouldn't be much reason to investigate after that, would there?" Enzo looked up sharply, considering. He didn't have anything against Andrion Drakespring personally, and the success of the power cell project would be more likely to help than hurt his own enterprises – but he didn't have any great affection for him either. If the mage had to die to protect the Terentius family and further Enzo's ambitions to place a Terentius son on the Reman throne, well that was just too bad.

"It needs to be done immediately, tonight if possible," Enzo said. Rodrigo grinned, the kind of grin you might see on a smilodon just before you became its guest for dinner. "I'll take care of right away," he promised. "I have just the man for the job." With that he saluted and left, leaving Duke Enzo Terentius alone with his thoughts. Which were, "This had damned well better work!"

Andrion was resting on his mattress, and reading a book that Marcos had been allowed to bring him. A little entertainment made the hours pass so much more easily! The mattress was just a wool-stuffed pallet on the floor, and the supper he'd eaten with relish an hour before just the simple food eaten by the guards and soldiers here – but still way better than the slop the prisoners usually received. He could now expect to be left in peace and quiet until breakfast time tomorrow – and if he was lonely, and longed to embrace his children or lie in his wife's loving arms, there was something to be said for peace and quiet.

That peace was rudely snatched away as he heard a commotion coming from the corridor down to the left. There was a jingling of keys and weaponry, and shortly one of his usual jailers appeared –

followed by two armed guards who had a loudly-protesting prisoner held between them. He was dressed more like a rogue or charlatan than a bandit cutthroat, and it was surprising to see him being brought into the cells. Perhaps he had not had the money with which to pay the fine for thievery?

As he was shoved roughly into a cell one over and across the hall from the one Andrion was occupying, and the door locked behind him, he was shouting "I didn't do it, I tell you! I'm innocent! That lying bitch set me up because I threatened to have her arrested for robbery! You have to listen to me!" The guards laughed, having heard such protestations a thousand times before.

"Yeah, yeah, tell it to the Judges," the jailer said. He and his guard escort left the way they'd come in.

The freshly-jailed miscreant paced around his cell, inspecting the facilities and muttering to himself. Then he came up to the door and peered through the bars at Andrion, who was standing in the same position and looking at him. "I didn't think they were putting anybody else in this part of the jail," Andrion remarked thoughtfully. He'd been convinced that he was being intentionally isolated – though a small bribe to the jailers had markedly improved the conditions under which he was being kept, so perhaps not.

"I don't know why they put me here in particular," the man said, "but I don't belong in jail. I'm not guilty of the crime I was charged with, and I need to get out of here before that bitch who set me up finds my stash and steals it. Name's Ladrino, what's yours?" That sounded like an underworld alias to Andrion, a derivation of Old Reman for "thief." So what crime had he been charged with, that he *hadn't* done?

"I'm Andrion Drakespring," Andrion replied.

"Andrion Drakespring? What killed the emperor? Coo!" Ladrino replied, eyes wide. He was not a particularly large man, but looked wiry and strong and probably not much above thirty years old.

"I didn't kill the emperor," Andrion said resignedly. His "fame" was a depressing annoyance.

"Oh right, of course!" the thief (if that's what he was) responded. "You're innocent, same as me. But if you don't get out of here pretty soon, they're likely to chop your head off – ain't they?"

232

Andrion gritted his teeth. "Nobody's going to be chopping my head off for nearly three months in any case," he told his fellow prisoner, "and in the meantime my family is working with my lawyer to find out who killed the emperor and framed me. They've already found a lot of evidence in just a couple of days, and I expect they'll have figured out the entire plot before long."

"Maybe, maybe not," Ladrino said. "But wouldn't it be better to be outside, just in case?"

Truthfully, if they failed to gather enough evidence to prove his innocence Andrion did *not* intend to go to the headsman's block for this crime he had not committed. But the details of that hadn't even been considered yet. Wondering what the prisoner's game was, he shrugged his shoulders and gestured at the cell. "And how might I get out of here, anyhow?" he asked. "There are no windows, and I have no keys for the door. And then there's all those guards out there…"

Ladrino grinned at him and then dropped to the stone floor of his cell, taking off his right boot. "They never think to search the boots," he said gleefully. "I don't know why." In moments he had produced a handful of lockpicks and had set to work on the door of his cell. Evidently he was highly skilled at this, as less than a minute later there was a clink and the door swung open.

Andrion watched this performance with some surprise. Arresting a character like this, why *would* the guards neglect to search him thoroughly? "Oh good, you're out of your cell," Andrion remarked dryly. "But how are you planning to get past the guards?" Leaning up against Andrion's cell door, Ladrino lifted his left leg and removed that boot, then twisted the heel and pulled forth a wicked looking 8-inch dagger that had been cunningly hidden in the built-up sole.

"I'll just sneak up behind the one in the anteroom over there," he said gesturing, "and cut his throat. Then I'll get his keys and take his sword, maybe his uniform if it'll fit me. Poof." Andrion nodded solemnly as the thief, or perhaps more than a thief, began picking the lock on Andrion's own cell door. He readied himself in case the man was planning to cut *his* throat instead of the guard's. He was a lot bigger than Ladrino, and even unarmed and without his magic he should be able to overpower him.

But once he had the cell door open, his fellow prisoner remained friendly. "There you go," he said with a crooked grin, "Let's get out of here."

"Uh," Andrion said, thinking about the likely outcome once of the two of them killed that first guard, "Do you suppose your lockpicks would work on this?" He gestured with both hands to the magic-block collar locked around his neck. It was rather handsome, gleaming dypalfar metal with incised designs and a jewel-like indicator light that told you it was doing its job.

"Coo, that's pretty!" Ladrino said, his eyes lighting up. "Locked on so nobody can steal it?"

"I tell you what, it's kind of uncomfortable for sleeping in and the jailers kept the key," Andrion told him straight-faced. "If you can get it off, it's yours." The smaller man tucked the dagger into his belt, then began working with his picks on the collar's locking mechanism.

In manufacturing these for sale to guard forces all over the empire, the Mirskhrazana had used standard locks. They were high quality, not something you could open in ten seconds with a horseshoe nail; but this one yielded readily enough to Ladrino's high-level skills. As the collar came off, the thief gleefully holding it up in both hands to admire its beauty, Andrion felt the most ecstatic surge as his magic returned to him. Ah! He never wanted to be separated from it again!

As Ladrino walked out into the corridor saying "Come on, let's get out of here!" Andrion dropped the man in his tracks with a spell of paralysis. Then he stepped out of the cell long enough to reclaim the magic-block collar from Ladrino's limp hands and fasten it about his neck. With a deep sigh of sadness, Andrion pressed the locking mechanism together until the jewel glowed red again, his magic shut away. He took a moment to relieve Ladrino of his lockpicks, which he thoughtfully deposited in his own right boot. Then he went back into his cell and shut the door, which locked itself automatically. Only one thing left to do. "Guards! Guards!" he shouted, and listened for running feet.

Chapter 33: Success

Once again the power cell research team was gathered around the table in their basement lab. Andi was loaded up with magical energy-enhancing devices, and he thought he was ready to give it another try. His natural fund of magical energy had increased lately, with all the practice he'd been getting – and some types of spells seemed to need less of it in order to work. He was well on his way to being a world-class mage, but he wondered if he'd ever catch up with his father.

With Andi's dragon blood to enhance his own longevity and the Renew spell to keep Andrion young and fit, the two of them might go on almost indefinitely, he thought, constantly expanding the horizons of magic as they discovered new techniques. The one he was about to try had come to him last night as he lay nearly dozing, snug in bed with his arms around Rezira.

Both of his parents were amazingly skilled at using magic – two very different schools of magic – and it had suddenly occurred to him that Mom's technique for healing magic and Andrion's for battle both made use of a fine control that was beyond the ability of most practitioners of those arts. But while battle spells had an obvious effect that you could see and follow with your eyes, you needed to be able to send your mind into your subject's body in order to be able to fine-tune healing. He had also employed this in opening the lock on the door of the Last King of Sindalo's burial chamber.

The spell they had finally devised to create a link within the power cell to the sun in another universe, which would continue (presumably) to power it for millions of years, was a form of conjuring – but unlike any other spell in that discipline, you were creating a permanent link between planes of existence, a tiny portal through which energy – not daimonic creatures – would pass. Andi had heard, of course, about the portal below Gryndhaal his papas had gone through to another universe before he was born.

Before Andrion had been arrested, they'd been thinking that they needed to tweak the spell itself for each core, making it slightly different so that each device would draw its power from a different, centimeter-sized spot on the surface of that alien sun. You would have to keep track of what permutation of the spell was used each time, careful to use a new and different one for the next to be made. Recordkeeping would become a nightmare!

But what if you could take your mind inside the spell, and instead of changing the spell from one core to another just use visualization to focus it each time and lock the portal in place? No matter how the core – or the sun that supplied its power – moved in space, that link would remain fixed. Smashing the core to smithereens would disrupt the spell, with resultant small explosions at both ends of the link. But other than that, power cells were eternal.

Andi had explained his theory to Rezira and the rest of the team when they'd assembled for work this morning, and they knew that he had mastered Bernadette's visualization approach when performing healing magic. He could heal a cut in your finger while leaving your toothache untouched, should he wish to. Or root out a hidden illness and cure it, when you weren't even aware of being sick.

They had three of the cell blanks, as identical as large metal-and-glass peas in a pod, sitting on the table, and Andi had as much magical energy at his disposal as it was possible to obtain. He hoped it would be enough. Andrion had confirmed that the Link spell was horrendously costly, and he'd already been using magic on a regular basis for nearly seventeen years before Andi was born.

A hush fell over the room as Andi sent out his mind, first to the core in his hand and then questing out, using the same spell that had permanently linked their first successful prototype. But he rode along with it, visualizing – and nearly dropped the core, staggering slightly as he beheld the universe of the Source. It was vast beyond imagining, containing billions of stars and probably many inhabited planets as well; but the part of it that filled his vision was a red giant star that could have swallowed Terris and its solar system without so much as a ripple – and in his visualization, that star was enmeshed in tiny glowing threads.

Each thread was so small that he had to zoom in until he could scarcely see the curvature of the sun's orb, and even then they were like little hairs. Each one glowed faintly in the same red color as the sun, as the cells would glow once they'd been powered. His mind's eye soared in still closer to the sun's raging surface, where solar flares roiled and the burning gases heaved like a sea in torment.

But where each of the tiny threads touched the orb, there was a tiny pulsating spot as the power cell linked to that part of the sun's orb took on a steady flow of energy. And in these areas the surface was quiescent, as if the metaphysical connection somehow calmed its fiery turbulence. There were many, many threads – more than Andi would have thought possible. He personally had seen only a few dozen power cells – though it stood to reason there were many more than that here on Terris – and still more in the little pocket universe to which Rezira's people had fled.

But even though the connections were countless, they still occupied less than 1% of the huge sun's surface – and were presumably directly tapping energy that would merely have been released into space, were it not for the power cell's connection. Using the power cells' energy to do useful work in this universe was like getting a free gift from that other dimension.

Andi let the spell complete, directing the exact spot on the sun's surface where the connection would be made, and another thread appeared. Then his vision went dark, and his colleagues jumped in to catch him as he fell. "Andi! Are you all right?" Rezira cried, thankful that some of their fellow researchers were bigger and stronger than she was. Andi was beginning to fill out, and now weighed close to two hundred pounds as he approached his adult height of six-foot-three.

They laid him down carefully on the floor and put a pillow under his feet, and in another few moments Andi's eyelids fluttered and he came around. "Ooh," he said with a groan as he struggled to sit up, "I think I ran myself out of stamina there. Anybody got a stamina potion, or something to eat?" He downed the potion Gylabris handed him, and was soon on his feet again.

How could he have forgotten that stamina depletion was a hazard with this type of finely-tuned spellcasting? If he'd fainted a few seconds sooner, his connection might have fizzled out – or worse, been left flapping loose – possibly making the cell he'd been working on useless as anything but a paperweight.

He got back to his feet and saw, to his relief, that the cell's core was glowing nicely, its interior cage spinning. "What we need here," Andi said after a moment's thought, "is some multi-enchanted items

– rings, necklaces, maybe a circlet – just for this task, that will bump up your magical energy total, magical energy regeneration speed, and do the same for your stamina and stamina regeneration. Is there such a thing?"

Aphinea's reptilian eyes glinted for a moment. "I have the ability to lay multiple enchantments, though I've never placed those particular four properties on anything. But I have a goodly collection of inexpensive ring, necklace, and circlet blanks for the Enchanting department. There's a plentiful supply of filled magical essence vials as well. Perhaps the rest of you could take a break while I go produce the items you requested? You certainly look like you could use one, Andi." With that the Saurion woman went up the stairs to the building's main floor, and the rest of them retired to an area at the rear of the space that they'd set up as a sort of staff break room.

A couple of hours later they'd all eaten lunch and, loaded up with enough magical energy and stamina reinforcement to fly to the moons and back (or so he felt), Andi was ready to try again. This time, as he went on his mental journey to the universe of the great red sun, he felt sharper, clearer, less dazzled by all he saw. He found another unoccupied section of the surface to make his energy connection, and came out of the trance to find the second core glowing and spinning alongside the first. And he felt fine! A tiny bit fatigued, maybe – but his magical energy and stamina had already rebounded.

Andi took only a long drink of cool water before plunging back into the spell again, hooking up the third power cell in only a few seconds. When he returned to awareness of the room around him, his colleagues were cheering and slapping him on the back. "You did it, son, you did it!" Sextus crowed. This project was going to make his personal fortune – all their fortunes, in fact – and ensure that the university never lacked for funding again.

Andi put his arm around Rezira and gave her an affectionate squeeze, grinning in idiot delight at the three glowing, spinning power cells sitting on the lab table. "I guess all we need now," he said, "Is to find some apt conjuration students, load them up with gear like I'm wearing, and teach them the technique. Then we can start our power cell factory, and Agena will never be the same again!"

Chapter 34: Failure

Across town, a frazzled-looking Alderion appeared at the door to the duke's study. Duke Enzo was scribbling furiously on a piece of correspondence, looking as threatening as an ogre on a bad day. When he beheld his court mage standing there, his features darkened still more. No, no, he did *not* need any more bad news!

As was frequently his way when he was so angry he wanted to start smashing things, Enzo's voice became low, taut, and a little hoarse. "Why are you here, Alderion?" he asked quietly. The elf mage had known his duke since he was a wizened, red-faced baby at his mother's breast, and he had never feared the man – until now.

"For the past day I have been working with the emperor constantly," he began. "Trying to coax his memories to return, filling him up with the information we need him to report. But nothing works."

"You mean he still can't remember anything from before he took the potion?" the duke asked.

"If that were all!" the mage said bitterly, his tiredness showing in every limb as he stood dejectedly before the desk looking down at his master. "He can't remember anything, at all!"

Enzo's brow furrowed still more as he looked up at Alderion questioningly. "As soon as we had moved Giorgio to the manor house I told him who he was, that he was Emperor of Agena, and began telling him the story we concocted. Half an hour later he smiled at me and asked me who I was – and I knew who *he* was. I've tried the trance potion and memory spell that I was going to use to implant the false memories, but no matter what I tell him, he loses everything that was said to him within a few minutes. It's a wonder he still understands speech."

Enzo's heart sank. First, there had been the utter failure of the operative Rodrigo had planted in the prison last night. He had been supposed to lure Andrion Drakespring into an escape attempt that would have ended in him utterly forfeiting any claims to innocence or (so they'd hoped) being killed by the guards as he tried to get out of the Penitentiary.

The guards, who'd been bribed to place the man in a cell near Andrion's and not search him thoroughly, had been deeply embarrassed to be made fools of – finding the Drakespring mage locked in his cell, magic-block collar still in place, while Rodrigo's man inexplicably lay paralyzed on the stone floor of the corridor – a dagger in his belt. They'd tossed the man, Ladrino, back into his cell – stripped naked – and were throwing the book at him.

The duke decided not to mention any of this to Alderion. The mage had had no part in it, and though the blame had to lie with Rodrigo and his man, Enzo felt that he himself was also somehow at fault for underestimating his opponent. Those Drakesprings were too damn smart for their own good.

And now this. "Clearly," he told his court mage, "the double dose of potion has damaged his mind – damaged his brain. I have heard of this sort of thing before, cases where people suffered a major blow to the head and lost the ability to hold information in their memories. They were amiable enough, but less able than a toddler to fend for themselves. Have you tried healing him?"

"Of course!" Alderion replied in tired exasperation. "It was one of the first things I tried! It took care of all the little scrapes and bruises he'd gotten during the abduction, but did nothing to restore his mind. The healing arts have never been my main focus, of course." He gave his master a look that said, "You and the previous two generations of Brindis dukes haven't exactly been working me overtime to heal the sick when there were enemies to kill and dirty tricks to be played."

"No," Duke Enzo said with a little dismissive wave of his hand. "Your talents lie elsewhere. But I know who has the power to heal the emperor's mind, and she is right here in Roma. They say she brought her father-in-law back to himself from a near-vegetative state ten years after he'd suffered a major stroke. And you've seen her husbands! She is fireblood and that's supposed to slow aging – but those men are in their mid-forties or early fifties yet neither looks a day over thirty-five. It's rumored she acquired some lost, ancient dragon spell for eternal life during that thing with the dragon attacks in Iscandia last year. You must get Bernadette Drakespring to help you somehow. And soon!"

Chapter 35: Cutting Corners

Alderion stalked hastily along the thoroughfare leading from the Scintillio District toward the Pantheatos District, not quite muttering under his breath. He was exhausted from his efforts of the past few days, and he was not a young elf anymore. He had the horrid sensation that everything he had worked for, not just in the last few years but throughout his life from the time when he'd been a newly-minted mage happy to obtain a post at the court of Brindis, was about to come crashing down around his ears. It's just tiredness, he told himself. I'll get that Drakespring bitch to heal the emperor, dispose of her, fill up Giorgio's little mind with good things about the Terentius family, and then take a three-day nap.

Minutes earlier he had let himself out of the Terentius mansion, and before he stepped through the door he had placed a Spell of Seeming on himself. It always felt uncomfortable wearing the spell, as if he were wearing some kind of an insubstantial costume. Depending on the differences between his illusive appearance and his actual body, he might have to compensate for major differences in height, reach, and other attributes one gave no thought to while walking around undisguised. It would probably be a lot more comfortable, Alderion mused, as he hurried toward the house where the Drakesprings were staying, to be wearing a normal disguise consisting of clothing and makeup, and perhaps an artificial nose or some such.

Riki had been reading in the downstairs parlor again, and as Marta was busy doing their laundry out back she went to answer the door herself. Her eyes lit up with delight to see Flavius. She'd had her doubts about him, an older boy with a level of sophistication she'd never dreamed of acquiring, but it seemed clear that he cared for her and that his heart was in the right place. The fact that his family was rich and he was astonishingly handsome didn't hurt, either.

"Flavius!" she cried, letting him in. "I was afraid I was never going to see you again." The figure before her smiled sweetly, then cast a spell of Command over her.

"Tell me who is in the house," he said, in a voice that did not belong to Flavius.

"Cornelia's in the kitchen getting lunch ready, Marta's out back, and Mom is in the upstairs parlor reading," she replied cheerfully. "Everybody else is out and about."

"You are feeling very sleepy," the figure said. "You are going to go upstairs to your room. If you see anyone on the way, you'll tell them you think you'd like to take a nap. When you get to your room, lie down and go to sleep. You are so sleepy, you will sleep for two hours. When you awake, you won't remember anything that happened since you got up to answer the door."

This was pushing it, but Alderion had much practice already at using the Command spell. The spell would wear off in another couple of minutes, but with luck and a susceptible subject (as he judged this pretty young girl to be), at least some of his commands would be obeyed even hours later.

Riki smiled at him, so lovely he felt a pang. His firm position at the court of Brindis had somehow left him so busy that he had never taken a wife, and lovers had been few and far between. A little regret crept into Alderion's thoughts as he acknowledged the likelihood he would never know the love of a good woman, never father a child. But certainly, his life had other compensations. If he could just get through this…

He followed her as she went up the stairs, obedient to his Command, and down the hall to her bedroom. Now, where was this parlor? Oh, that must be it – the room with the door open, and light from windows shining into it. In the guise of Flavius, Alderion entered the room and stood looking at Bernadette as she bent over a book – searching for information that would free her husband, he'd be willing to bet. She too was lovely, though neither as fresh nor as lushly beautiful as her daughter. But she had a sort of commanding presence about her, a sense of substance – something he found more appealing than mere physical beauty.

She looked up, surprised to see him, and said, "Oh! Flavius… I didn't expect to see you. I thought Riki was in the downstairs parlor. Did you miss her?"

Alderion smiled with Flavius' face and said, "She decided to take a nap. But I'm here to see you, not her. I need your help." As she looked at him, puzzled, he cast the Command spell and she immediately became his bosom friend, eager to help him out with whatever he needed. If only the spell lasted a little longer, he thought, there were some things that he needed... or at least wanted... that he would love her help with. But, to business!

"The emperor has received a brain injury, and lost both his memory and his ability to form new memories," Alderion informed Bernadette. She looked at him alertly, waiting for a command. "You must heal him, so that he can lead the empire once again. Gather everything that you need, and we will leave."

Had Bernadette not been under his spell of compulsion, and had she not distrusted Alderion (as she had come to distrust most of the people they'd met in Roma, after Andrion's wrongful imprisonment), there was a good chance that she would have leapt to the task he'd assigned her anyway. She was a mother many times over, and she was proud of her healing skills. There was no way she would *not* have ministered to anyone who needed it. Though it probably would have occurred to her to ask why a dead man would need healing.

"I'll need the Mask of Wissagleb," she said. "That's about all. Should I bring a cloak?" Entranced, Alderion nodded.

"That might be a good idea," he said. The manor house where they'd stashed the emperor while trying to bring him back to himself was surrounded by mountains. He followed her as she went down the hall to one of the bedrooms and retrieved a pack. A very efficient woman, it seemed. A trace of admiration for her crept into his tired mind and he stifled it. After she'd solved his little problem for her, he would just Command her to take a double dose of the potion of forgetting – and he need never worry about her revealing any of this to anyone, ever again.

With Riki now asleep and both of the servants occupied in the rear of the house, it was easy for Alderion – still disguised as Flavius – to shepherd his charge out and into the street without anyone noticing. Renewing the Command spell, he took her along with him as he made a beeline for the Alfarien District to the west. From there they could exit West Gate to the riverside, and (as soon as he was sure that no one was watching) go by map to Duke Terentius' estate in the highlands north of Novaricce.

Mondi and Sigi were skulking along the main thoroughfare in the Pantheatos District, dressed in their beggar's rags. They'd been summarily turned away at the Terentius mansion when they'd asked to see Gaius, and told that he would no longer be associating with them or any other members of their disgraced family. Oh, well. Lunchtime was approaching, and they'd decided to go home and grab a bite before heading over to the waterfront district. They wanted to keep an eye on the abandoned shack Andi had told them about, and see if anybody might be going there to pick up Croaker's message to The Mask.

The figures ahead of them were quite a distance away, but the boys had sharp eyes. "That's Mom!" Sigi said, "And she's walking up the road with Flavius like she was hypnotized or something!" Sigi once again had the Ring of Detect Magic, and he slipped it onto his finger. The two stood off to one side, trying to stay inconspicuous. "I'll bet you anything that's *not* Flavius," Sigi said after a minute. He doesn't walk right, and besides that he's glowing like a firefly. That's somebody wearing Flavius' appearance, and Mom is lit up too. She's under a spell of some kind."

"Command, most likely," "Mondi said as he picked up the pace to draw closer. They were approaching the entrance to Pantheatos House. "Sigi, go on in the house. Tell anybody there what you saw, and wait for me to get back. I'm going to follow them." His brother nodded solemnly and mounted the steps. As he made his escape, Mondi glanced around to make sure nobody was watching him and then slipped on his Ring of Blend.

The crowds in the district were still thick, this second day of the emperor's lying in state, and Mondi had some problems slipping through them. There were many curses as people who had not noticed his presence collided with him; but "Flavius" and Mom continued to plow through the mobs of people – oblivious to any disturbances that were erupting around them.

After they got past the gates and into the Alfarien District the traffic thinned considerably, and Mondi was able to glide along silently behind them. He was glad his legs were long, as whoever was wearing Flavius' appearance was striding along as if his life depended on getting to where he was going in a hurry.

At one point Mom faltered, almost stumbling, and looked around her wildly as if she had no idea how she'd gotten there. Her companion turned to her, and Mondi could almost *see* him cast the spell again. There were many different versions of the same spells, he knew, with the differences mostly being the degree of the effect and its duration. Clearly this guy, whoever he was, lacked Andi's level of ability – or the amulet Rezira had made for him.

The person wearing Flavius' seeming must be at least as tall as the real Flavius, from the speed he was making. Mondi was getting taller by the week in his human form – and considering that his father's human form stood six and a half feet tall, he might someday tower over most of the people around him. But at the moment he was working hard to keep up without making any noise – and Mom, with her much shorter legs, was about ready to keel over from exhaustion. And she was in pretty good shape, for an old person.

Mondi stifled the urge to put the dagger he wore at his belt into the faux Flavius, and tell him to stop abusing his mother. He suspected that this person, whoever he was, might well lead him to important evidence in the plot that had jailed his papa Andrion. As the disguised mage and his enthralled subject exited through West Gate to the riverside, Mondi hastened (oh, so carefully and silently) to close up the gap between him and his quarries. "Flavius" looked around him, and saw no one near – at least, no one paying any attention to him and the woman who stood beside him, waiting for a Command.

When the mage pulled out a map Mondi knew his worst fears had been realized. If this guy carried his mom off with him by map and Mondi wasn't along for the ride, they would probably never see her again. That could not happen! Willing himself silent and unseen, Mondi crept close and took a fold of Bernadette's skirt in his more-or-less invisible hand. He'd had plenty of experience with map travel, and he knew that generally it was the map wielder's conscious acceptance of his or her companions that determined who went away, and who was left behind. He prayed to Aderos that his physical connection with Mom would be enough to include him in the party.

There were a few moments of darkness, and then the mage, Bernadette, and the approximately-invisible Mondi found themselves standing in a small valley surrounded by hills and mountains, looking at a nearby manor house. It was clearly later in the day, which Mondi took to mean that they had traveled to the east, as well as some distance from Roma. He had very little knowledge of Remus's geography and landmarks, and wished he knew more. Where were they?

The time lost in fast-traveling had caused the Command spell to expire, and Bernadette staggered and looked around her wild-eyed. Mondi almost expected her to get off a Gale dragon spell, or perhaps go dragon and have this disguised mage for lunch; but before she could get her bearings he (one presumed; could just as easily be she, eh?) had renewed the spell and Mom was once more under compulsion to do his bidding.

Mondi immediately dropped his mother's skirt and backed off a little. He really, *really* didn't want to tip off this guy that he'd been followed. Bernadette's abductor breathed a sigh of relief and in a moment the disguise had been shed. It was Alderion, that ljosalfar mage who worked for Duke Terentius! Did that mean the duke was in on whatever political plot had put Papa Andrion in jail?

Mondi felt like he was beyond his depth here. He might be sophisticated by the standards of Iscandia, but he needed someone older and wiser to guide him through whatever was happening here. The whole concept of bright, theoretically respectable people willing to commit a crime – any crime you could imagine – for the sake of enhancing their own political power, was utterly foreign to him.

Two armed guards stood at the manor house's main entrance, one on either side. They nodded to Alderion, then resumed their vigilance. Mondi, sweating now, drew as close as he dared behind the mage and his enthralled captive so that he could slip through the door before it closed, and not alert the guards to the anomaly. Fortunately Mom was oblivious, and Alderion seemed driven by some force that did not allow him to pay much attention to his surroundings.

They passed through the entry hall and into a spacious room, where a well-dressed man sat at a small dining table. He glanced up as the mage and his companion came in, and smiled at them like a baby. Mondi felt a frisson of excitement shoot through him. The emperor! Not the least of the reasons Papa Andrion was innocent of killing him, was that the man was still alive! Though he looked a little out of it…

Alderion, trying to keep himself moving while maintaining an awareness of the Command spell's duration, told Bernadette "Tell me who you see there." As she made to answer, he pulled a stamina potion out of a small satchel and downed it – immediately feeling better. He had been burning the candle at both ends for far too long.

"It's Emperor Giorgio," Bernadette replied thoughtfully. "You said that he has brain damage?" Alderion nodded.

"You will heal him now," he said. He had no idea what this woman's special healing spell entailed, or whether it would take longer than his Command spell would last. Had he known her better, he would have realized that she would have willingly undertaken this task immediately, with no compulsion needed.

Alderion sank into a chair, seemingly exhausted, as Bernadette got the mask Wissagleb from her pack and put it on. Mondi was unable to make sense of it all. The emperor was alive, but seemingly reduced to the mental capacity of an idiot or a small child. And the Terentius family knew this – but instead of rushing him to the capital for medical care, they had immured him in this (presumably) remote manor house and abducted a healer by magical force to minister to him. What in all the hells was going on here?

Mondi decided that it was time to turn the puzzle over to older, wiser heads. But how to get out of here? A couple more guards, whom he assumed must be house guards of Duke Terentius, were hanging around in the general area where the emperor was. But he hadn't seen any great force. He made his way stealthily up a staircase and found himself apparently alone on the house's second floor. Then he opened a window on the side of the house away from the main entrance and looked down. Could he do it quickly enough? Sure, why not?

Mondi very quietly spelled away his clothes, pack, dagger, and the ring that granted him near invisibility. Hey, he was still invisible. Cool! Then he crouched in the frame of the open window, looking out over the woods behind the house, and launched himself into the air. As he did so, he spelled again and went dragon, wings spread to stop his fall as he soared away above the trees. Yes!

Now, just exactly where was he? From the apparent amount of time elapsed they had traveled some distance – but not too far – from Roma, in an easterly direction. Unless of course they were now on some continent on the far side of the world, twenty-six-plus hours away… Nope, as Mondi rose higher he could see the spire of the Imperial Palace's central tower glinting to the southeast. Gods, how the thing dominated the land! If you could get a little altitude, it seemed, there was hardly any place in Remus from which it was not visible.

He took off like a shot, feeling as if every minute counted. There was a powerful freedom to his invisibility, up here. No crowds to avoid running into, only the occasional small bird to impede his progress. Below him, he spotted a fairly large lake and took note of it as a landmark as he fled through the air, on a beeline to Roma and "home."

Mondi flew over the city walls and used the domed roof of the Pantheatos, still mobbed with visitors, as a landmark to pinpoint the roof of Pantheatos House. He came in for a landing on the widow's walk, spelling himself back to human as he touched down. It was scarcely big enough to hold him, at his current dragon size.

After restoring his belongings and pulling off the ring Mondi opened the door to the house's top floor and pounded down the stairs, panting for breath and hoping he'd still find lunch on the table. He was starving! He found Sigi along with Erik, Riki, Anja, and Lars anxiously pacing around the downstairs parlor.

"You're here!" Sigi exclaimed, surging to his feet. "What happened?" Agony washed through him as Mondi tried to relate his urgent tale. The caloric requirements of a young dragon on the move could leave your human form ready to pass out from literal starvation. "Sigi, please, go get me something to eat! Then I'll tell you everything. We need to move fast!"

Sigi bolted from the room, heading for the kitchen. He, too, knew what it meant to be a young dragon. The high metabolism that fueled a dragon's fires required massive infusions of food – and as joyful as it was to fly free, the earthbound human form, insulated by clothing, was a much more efficient way to go.

Mondi collapsed on a settee and the rest of the family gathered around him. "Where's Berni?" Erik demanded. His usual easy-going nature had been set aside, and he looked ready to run fifty miles with his sword out, if there was the chance of drawing blood from whoever had taken his beloved away.

"Papa," Mondi panted, "the Terentius family is involved in this." Everyone in the room clustered around him, looking stunned. They had all trusted Flavius, Riki especially, and while they'd known that Davos had apparently hired the emperor's killer, they had never dreamed that anyone else was involved – especially not someone who wasn't allied with Davos.

Sigi came dashing back from the kitchen, bearing a plate on which sliced bread rolls heavily slathered with butter were stacked. Calories were the key requirement for a young dragon who'd gone too long without eating. In his other hand was a tall mug of what proved to be fresh milk. Mondi's eyes lit and he cried, "*Thank* you, brother!" before embarking on a campaign to inhale everything Sigi had brought.

The rest of the family, Erik especially, made an ill-concealed attempt to stifle their impatience as Mondi hastily wolfed food and drink until he began to feel like he was not about to fall over in a faint. Finally he slammed the empty mug to the tabletop, the plate holding nothing but crumbs, and took a deep breath. "That mage Alderion, Duke Terentius' court mage, had a spell on him so he looked like Flavius. But not really, he moved wrong. He had Mom in a Command spell and fast-travelled her away after they got outside the city gates."

Everyone was staring at him in astonishment, Riki not the least of them. She'd been roused from her Commanded sleep after Erik, Anja and Lars had come home, but she had very little memory of how and why she'd gotten there. Her last clear memory had been of answering the door and seeing Flavius.

"I came home and it seemed like nobody was here but Cornelia and Marta," Sigi explained. "But they thought Riki and Mom were here too, and then Erik came back with Anja and Lars and we went up and found Riki sleeping. She must have been Commanded to sleep, because it was hard to wake her up even after we told her Mom was gone."

"When the mage took Mom away with him by magic map," Mondi went on. "I was using the Ring of Blend, and neither one of them was exactly alert. By holding onto Mom's skirt, I was taken along with them. The emperor was there!" That one brought the house down. The emperor was alive?

"We went to what looked like a country noble's manor house, way up in the hills and mountains east-northeast of here," the boy continued. "It only seemed to take me about half an hour to fly from there to here, though fast-traveling appeared to take longer." "Fast traveling's time lag seems to be based on how long it would take for a person to walk," Anja said authoritatively. She whipped out her map. "Can you find where you were?"

Mondi studied the map, correlating it with his memories of the flight here. "Right here," he said, pinpointing a blank area somewhat to the northeast of Lake Trasimeno.

"I guess we haven't been there yet," Anja said somewhat ruefully, "but it's probably no more than a ten-minute walk from the lake, and we *have* been there. Let's get out of here!"

"No," Mondi said emphatically, "We need to run over to the university and get Andi and Rezira first. We need some mages on our side!"

"You're right," Erik said. Both Mondi and Sigi had natural magical ability and some training in it, but neither of them was yet thirteen years of age. He, Riki, Anja, and Lars were all Norse – with scarcely a spell among them. And they were going up against a mage who had been powerful enough to convince everyone in Roma that Andrion had stabbed the emperor – despite the fact that the emperor wasn't even dead, according to Mondi.

They hastened to gather up anything they thought might be needed, mostly weapons and armor with a few foodstuffs thrown in. They didn't want to see a repeat of Mondi's starvation act in the near future. Riki went into the room Andi and Rezira shared, searching for any useful items they might not have taken with them to the

University today, and discovered the Meiskomtot mask in among his things.

She didn't know he'd worn it to his meet with Croaker last night, and was surprised Andi had brought it with them – considering the bad associations they all had with it. But it *was* a powerful magical item. Better take it along – it would be useful against an opponent using magic. And what was this in Rezira's pack? A magic-block collar! Add that to the collection.

The party, now six strong, trotted through the Floral District and into the grounds of the University, asking directions to the Enchanting Hall. The found no one on the ground floor and made their way down into the basement, where they discovered Andi, Rezira, and their colleagues in the midst of a party. Eh?

The researchers were all jubilant, and though surprised to see the armed and armored party appear they welcomed them happily. Andi waved a glass and said, "Come on in! There's plenty more bubbly – and it's cold!" He motioned to a large dypalfar cold chest like the one Gylabris had put into service in Alfenstein the year before. "This chest is running on one of the power cells we activated today!" He said. From the air of relaxed happiness in the room, the team had gotten through quite a few of those bottles of sparkling wine already.

Rezira still had her wits about her, though, and she knew something was wrong. Erik, Riki, and the rest were grim and bristling with anxiety, not here to celebrate the research team's triumph. "Andi!" she said sharply, gripping him by the sleeve. "Can you use your healing spell to sober up?" Just her words went a long way toward sobering him, as he realized what she was getting at.

"Yeah, it's a form of poisoning, really," he said, concentrating for a moment. He was still wearing the magical energy and stamina-enhancing items Aphinea had crafted for him, which made the process easier. His head clearing, Andi looked around at the faces of his family and friends. "Where's Mom?" he demanded. "What's going on?"

Mondi, who knew more about the situation than the rest of them did, spoke up. "The Terentius family is involved with the plot against the emperor," he summarized. "That mage of theirs, Alderion, has the emperor hidden at a country manor out east of here, and he kidnaped Mom to get her to heal him. It seems like they did something to his mind."

"We need to get out there as quickly as possible and stop him before he can complete whatever evil scheme he's planning," Riki said. "Anja's map will take us within a few miles of there, but we need to hurry!"

"I need to get some things from the house, first!" Andi said urgently.

"The Meiskomtot mask and Zira's magic-block collar?" Riki asked. "Got 'em right here!" she indicated the pack she was carrying.

"Good job, Riki!" Andi said, then turned to the rest of the research team. "Gylabris, I think you'd better stay here. No point in you getting involved in a battle." The little leukalfar tinkerer acknowledged the truth of that with a solemn nod, though he wished he could help. To Mondi, he added "I assume there are some of the Terentius family guards there, too?"

"I saw four of them. Plus the mage, who seems to be awfully powerful."

"Okay," Andi said. "Let's be off. But we need to make one more stop before we go."

At the Imperial Palace Andi decided not to waste time trying to convince the guards (people in positions of authority so often feeling a personal need to mess with you just because they can) and cast a Command spell on the first guard he saw. "My party and I are very important people with an urgent message for your commander. You will escort us to Macchiatus Octavius at once."

The guard (who, fortunately, was the senior of the two on the doors) said sharply to his companion "I must take these people to see the commander. Hold your post until I return." The other guard saluted, and they set off at a fast walk around the curving corridor and up the ramp to the guard quarters.

Magic had gotten them in, but Andi was anxious that no magic should poison the evidence he hoped to deliver – evidence that would get Papa Andrion out of jail and justice dealt to the plotters. So he used no spells on Macchiatus – not even Befriend, which gave you a strong advantage when dealing with others yet left them still free to reject you.

"Commander Octavius, I am Andreas Drakespring." The guard commander, a vigorous-looking fellow in his late forties, nodded.

"I'm aware of your identity, sir," he said in neutral tones. "What is it that you want?"

"I'm here to report the abduction of my mother, Bernadette Drakespring, by the court mage of Brindis, Alderion. My brother was witness to this abduction, and using a Ring of Blend managed to follow them to a country manor northeast of Lake Trasimeno. He reports seeing a man who looks exactly like the emperor there, under guard."

Macchiatus' eyebrows rose. "So you believe that the corpse of the emperor, like the bloodstains on your father's tunic, was an illusion created by this mage – while he spirited away the real emperor for reasons of his own?" Andi nodded. "Yes, I do believe that. Mondi reports that there are at least four guards there at the manor, and we mean to go to Lake Trasimeno by map and then storm the manor, so that we can rescue my mother. But we want a witness from the Imperial Guards along with us, to see whatever there might be to see."

Macchiatus bolted up out of his chair, and took down a sword belt from a hook on the wall. Strapping it on, he said, "I too have reasons to suspect that the dead man we believed to be Giorgio Salonius is not. His widow... wife, came to me earlier today, distraught and fearful that she would be thought insane, to tell me that when she examined the corpse before it was laid out for the formal viewing there was an intimate detail that was not where it should be. Your mage, I think, would not be able to produce an exact illusion that included things he was not aware of. Let me get one more man, and we can be off."

Their party was already formidable, but it was not another man-at-arms that Macchiatus added to their number. A small man in Imperial Guard uniform but without the heavy armor and sword that was standard issue for the guards joined them, carrying a substantial satchel. "This is Junius Gregorius, our official Recorder," the Guard Commander explained, as they strode rapidly toward the front doors of the Palace. "He maintains a log book, recording statements, arrests, evidence brought in, and so forth. He will record what we see at this manor house, and what he reports will be admissible as evidence in Imperial Court proceedings." "Excellent!" Andi said with a grin. Maybe finally they would have a witness who would be believed – even against the word of members of the nobility.

Chapter 36: Reckoning

The party, now ten strong, shimmered into existence near the shores of Lake Trasimeno. "I'm familiar with this area," Macchiatus said. "I grew up near Novaricce, and roamed these hills hunting with my friends when I was a teenager. Is this estate the one that used to belong to the DiFabio family?"

Mondi shrugged. "Sorry," he said, "But this is my first trip to Remus as a human, and I haven't had time to explore much. It's off in that direction," he pointed, "and only a mile or two from here – I think. I got there fast-traveling by map to start with, and left flying." The guard commander eyed him questioningly. It really was true, then, that some of these ordinary-seeming people could turn into dragons? He shook his head.

Dusk was approaching now, as they made their way among the hills to the manor house. Most of the day, it seemed from Mondi's perspective, had been taken up in map travel – and he was already starting to feel hunger pangs again. As they walked, he and Sigi rummaged in their packs for bread rolls and dried sausages, munching while moving along.

Andi noticed his younger brothers, and thought he wouldn't mind a snack himself. Using the healing spell to cleanse his body of alcohol had left him feeling good, but hungry. Yet he was too anxious about the forthcoming confrontation to want to eat. What would they find there? Would Mom have succeeded in restoring the emperor's mind, only to be summarily dumped in an unmarked grave behind the barn while Alderion primed Giorgio to report that everything was fine? If they'd brought the guard commander and his Recorder here only to find that their enemies had covered all the bases, it would be too much to bear.

As they approached the house, just visible a quarter mile ahead, Andi stopped for a moment. "Riki, I need the Meiskomtot mask," he said.

"And I'll take the magic-block collar," Rezira added. The mask was scary-looking, and Junius wanted to know what it was for.

"It renders me immune to magical attack," Andi explained. "When we get down there and confront Alderion I anticipate that the first thing he'll try to do is block my magic, and I don't want him to be able to do that. We want to block *his* magic instead, immobilize him and then get our magic-block collar onto him so he won't be able to cast any spells. He seems to be better at creating illusions than any mage I've ever heard of."

"That's a thought, Andi," Anja said and rummaged in her pack. Sigi had returned her ring to her earlier in the day. "I have this Ring of Detect Magic, and I think Junius should be the one to wear it. He needs to be able to know if what he's seeing is really there, or just the creation of a spell." The little Reman seemed quite intrigued, taking it from her and slipping it onto a finger. It immediately adjusted itself to fit. Then he looked around.

"Aha," he said, "You, Mister Drakespring, are glowing. But nobody else here is."

"Try me now," Mondi said – slipping on his Ring of Blend.

"Oh, my!" Junius said, looking at Mondi and then pulling the Ring of Detect Magic off of his finger and looking again. He put it back on again, and said "Commander, I don't know where this young lady got her ring, but we really need to find out how to get one for our own force. This would have told us immediately that there was something wrong with that tunic we took in evidence." To Mondi, he added, "You are nearly invisible to the unaided eye, but with this ring – and I suppose a Ring of Life Detection would have the same effect – you are glowing like a beacon."

"I think I'll leave the ring on for the time being," Mondi said thoughtfully. "Might be helpful if the guards here think there are only nine of us." In the twilight, the ring was still more effective – rendering the boy nearly invisible. There were lights around the house, and they would have to cross a bare area in the front yard to reach the main entrance – where two guards were on watch. They wore a motley collection of armor, as if they were mercenaries; but they bore themselves like members of a regular force.

"How's your range on the paralyze spell now, Andi?" Rezira asked softly.

"Pretty good," he replied. Then to Macchiatus and Junius he said, "I'm going to cast a paralysis spell on both those guards, so nobody gets a crossbow bolt in the guts. Then we can sneak up there and tie them up or something, before trying to go into the house."

Erik found himself marveling at how easy it was to follow his son's leadership. Erik himself was all muscle and skill and catlike agility, but the boy he and Berni and Andrion had raised had grown into a man with an exceptional mind. Anyone would be happy to let him take the lead. He just hoped Andi was all right with the responsibilities his leadership conferred.

The rest of them held back while Andi cast his spell in an arc just broad enough to strike both guards down. They never even saw him coming, their night vision ruined by the lights near the house. Erik, Anja, Riki, and Lars surged forward then. In moments they had bound and gagged the immobile guards, then Erik and Lars each hefted one over his shoulder and carried them away into the darkness. Unless a wandering wolf pack found them, they should be safe enough and out of the way there.

As the group re-formed and prepared to go into the house, Junius remarked quietly, "I recognized that bald fellow. He's one of Duke Terentius' household guard force. He always accompanies the family whenever they're residing in Roma." There were grim looks and nods around the circle. It looked like the Terentius family were in this up their eyeballs, whatever "this" was. Riki was stricken. Had Flavius been getting next to her just so he could further his father's evil plans? It was hard to believe that about the charming young man, but she supposed that was what "charming" was all about – deception. Gods knew, Fjuri had none of that about him.

Before they opened the doors, Andi held the Meiskomtot mask in his hands and addressed them all – especially the two members of the Reman authorities – quietly. "I'll be wearing the mask to go in there, and depending on what we find I may be using paralysis, magic-block, or Command. Commander Octavius, are you familiar with the Command spell?"

Macchiatus shook his head. "Never heard of it," he admitted. "For the duration of the spell, and I can cast it to last ten full minutes, the subject will do exactly as I Command them to do and believe anything I tell them. In addition, I can ask them a question and they will answer truthfully even though I didn't specifically tell them that they must do so. Beyond my direct Commands, the person will be pretty much themselves and able to think about, and do, whatever they would normally be doing anyway."

"It sounds like the kind of thing that would make a confession inadmissible in Court," Junius opined. The things he had recorded had condemned many a criminal, and he was anxious that nothing he had a hand in would be tainted.

"It very much depends on the wording," Andi explained. "If I told you, 'confess to killing the emperor' you would respond with 'I killed the emperor,' but you would be unable to furnish any details since obviously you did not in fact do the crime. But on the other hand, I could Command you 'tell me everything you know about the death of the emperor,' and you would probably be busy for the next three hours reciting every detail that had been reported to you. Plus, if you secretly knew something about the plot, you would reveal it."

Junius pondered. "Three hours? I thought you said the spell only lasts ten minutes."

"True," Andi admitted, "and probably I would have to keep renewing the spell. But sometimes one can make a suggestion to a subject who is under their Command and they will continue to follow through with that suggestion after the spell has worn off. It depends on their attitude toward you, and how you phrased it. We believe that when Alderion came to the house and kidnaped my mother, he met Riki. She thought he was Flavius, Duke Terentius' son, because he was cloaked in an illusion. She remembers letting Flavius into the house, and then feeling very sleepy and going to bed. Sigi had a hard time waking her, even though Alderion's spell must have worn off a long time before then."

"Ah, I see," Junius said, making a notation in his book. He had a small, pocket-sized notebook in addition to the official Guard record book – which was far too heavy and unwieldy to be used for field work. "Very well," he said, "use whatever spells you need to prevent anyone in the house from doing us harm, but inform me what they are. This ring enables me to tell when someone is bespelled, but not in what way. And I'll be paying close attention to what you say, so mind yourself."

Andi grinned tensely at him. Clearly, he was going to have to be on his toes around the punctilious little Recorder. Donning the mask again, he had a thought. "Mondi?" he asked quietly, and nearly jumped out of his skin as his brother touched him on the elbow. Had he been there the entire time? "Why don't you be the first one in the door, and report what's on the other side of it?" he suggested. "And get ready to duck, if you have to – you'll be much more visible inside the house, with the lamps in there."

Mondi gave an unseen salute, then quietly opened the front door and slipped inside. The house was hundreds of years old, but they must have been keeping the place up. There was not even a slight squeal of hinges. The entry hall he'd seen on his first visit (was that only a few hours ago?) was empty, and in the dining area beyond the emperor was no longer to be seen. The room seemed empty except for a hulking guard, who was seated at the table shoveling food into his mouth. Mondi was glad he'd had a snack on the walk over here, as just the sight of the food on the plate brought a small rumble from his stomach. He froze, but the guard seemed oblivious to the noise.

Turning around, Mondi crept back out through the front door and removed the ring to deliver his report. He'd noticed that people found it unsettling to converse with him when he appeared not to be there. "There's just one guard in sight," he said quietly. "He's sitting at a dining table in the next room over from the one just inside the door – that's where I saw the emperor earlier."

"All right," Andi said, specifically addressing Junius. "I'm going to cast a Command spell on him as soon as he's in sight, and tell him not to attack us. Then the rest of the party can come through, and we'll ask him politely to tell us exactly what's going on here. Is that okay?" Junius glanced at Macchiatus, who nodded.

"That should be fine," he said. "It's not as if we're bringing this guard up on charges – yet. We just need to know what he can tell us so we don't encounter any surprises."

Andi stepped quietly through the door, having removed the mask again. It made it hard for him speak clearly, and limited his vision as well. He'd just as soon not use it when he didn't need to, though it had served well enough as a disguise during his interview with Croaker. The guard, almost finished with his meal, heard a click as the front door was opened and then closed. He had just turned to see if one of his colleagues was coming inside for some reason, when

Andi hit him with the Command spell and then immediately said, "My companions and I are friends, and we mean you no harm. Do not call out, and do not attack us."

The guard smiled and nodded. It had been lonely duty these past few days, and he was happy to see some friends. The rest of the party came in, moving quietly. Until they'd interviewed this guard, they didn't know how many people might be within hearing, hidden within the house.

They gathered around the guard, who sat smiling at them all, at his ease at the dining table and polishing off the last few crumbs of his supper. "Tell me your name," Andi Commanded, and he cheerfully replied

"Tertius. That's what everybody calls me." Andi smiled at him.

"Good, Tertius. First off, tell me who else is with you here on the estate."

"It's just me, Roberto and Carlo outside, plus Juan down in the basement with Master Alderion."

Ah, he took "with you" to mean part of his team, Andi realized. "And what other people are here besides the people you mentioned?" he asked. Tertius grinned. He so enjoyed chatting with his friends.

"Just the emperor, and that red-haired woman Master Alderion brought this afternoon. Don't know her name, but she was quite a looker. A shame, that."

Erik started up, fury written on his usually cheerful and friendly features.

"What…" he started, but Andi cut him off.

"Let me do it, Papa," he said quietly. "The woman's name is Bernadette Drakespring, Tertius. Tell me what happened after she got here." The guard looked a little sad, and Erik quivered as if he were about to leap over the table and rip the man's throat out with his bare hands.

"She was some kind of mage, it seems like, but Master Alderion had her under his Command. She'd brought a weird-looking mask with her and put it on, and then Master Alderion stood by her side while she worked doing healing magic on the emperor. I never saw anything like it! Ever since that night we took the emperor from the palace and brought him to the mine, he's been like a little child, or

261

something. He smiles and drools and can't remember who he is, or anything you tell him. But after that Bernadette person had been working on him for about ten minutes, you could see the lights come on. He sat up straight in his chair, and you could tell he was himself again. He looked right at Alderion and said 'Alderion, what are you doing here, and where am I?' so we knew he was, like, right in the head again."

Junius was scribbling furiously, the rest of them staring in open-mouthed awe – though they were also waiting for Tertius to get around to explaining what had happened to Bernadette. "Go on," Andi told him, mentally marking the time so that the spell would not suddenly expire without his noticing it.

"Master Alderion Commanded Bernadette to sit quietly, while he asked the emperor a bunch of questions. The emperor said he didn't remember anything since he was at the Ball last Maritag, which seems about right. Then Master Alderion got out a couple of vials of some potion he made, and told Bernadette to drink them both. He told her it was delicious and she'd feel better after she drank them. I've seen him Command people before, and believe me she'd have drunk it up and asked for more if it'd been fresh horse piss."

"So then what happened?" Andi asked. "Why do you keep referring to her in the past tense? Is she well?" He steeled himself against the answer, feeling Erik at his elbow doing the same.

"Well," Tertius said, considering the question. "She's *alive* right enough, not a mark on her. But now she's just like the emperor was before she healed him – smiling and drooling and can't remember nothing. Kind of gives you ideas, if you know what I mean…" He winked and leered, and Andi had to bodily restrain Erik from going after him. Not an easy task. Andi might be nearly Erik's height, but he was never going to have Erik's strength.

"Erik! Stop, please!" he begged, grappling with the bigger man. "I'm not through questioning him, and besides he's just an idiot underling. I don't think he would really *do* anything to Mom." Erik got a grip – but his face was still a mask of fury, golden complexion gone red.

Anja put a hand on his elbow, and murmured, "It's all right Uncle Erik, Aunt Berni will be fine."

Andi was having some difficulty containing his own fury – but his was directed, not at this guard, but at "Master" Alderion. "Tertius," he said, steel in his voice instead of the friendly and placating tone he'd been using to help the spell do its work, "Tell me where Bernadette is now, and then sit here quietly at the table until I come back."

Tertius, having not noticed the air of hostility in the room, smiled and pointed. "She's in the back room there, first door on the left. Nobody's with her right now, but she's safe enough." They dashed en masse to the door the soldier had pointed out, and found Bernadette sitting at a small table in what appeared to be sort of parlor. She was still dressed in the clothing she'd had on when she'd been abducted, and looked up as they came in – a faint smile on her lips. Before her on the table were the remains of some bread and cheese.

"Hello," she said sweetly, glancing around at all the people who had suddenly appeared. She seemed younger even than the thirty or so her dragon transformation had kept her at – maybe twenty-five or even a teenager, so innocent was her gaze. All her sharp intelligence, her awareness of the world, her years of experience, had been drained away. Erik gave a little moan. Berni, his Berni, so beautiful… and not there. All that remained was this attractive, utterly blank young woman.

He shouldered the others aside and crouched beside her where she sat at the table, looking confused. As he enfolded her in his arms, tears running down his cheeks, she wriggled in his grasp and said, "Who are you and why are you being so forward?" Erik sobbed and buried his face in her hair.

"The mask!" Andi shouted, "I can bring her back, just like she did the emperor! But I have to have the mask!"

He began trying to squeeze back out of the room, and Erik said behind him, "You all go take care of that son of a bitch Alderion, but don't kill him. *I'm* going to do that. I'll stay here with Berni and protect her until you get back."

They let Andi pass and then turned to follow him, but Riki stayed behind too. What business had she bearding mages in their dens? She did want revenge on Alderion for all this, and for his violation of her own mind earlier today. But right now, she wanted to stay with her mother – and with Papa, providing what comfort she could. In her entire life she had never seen Papa Erik so devastated, and it terrified her. He was their rock, the foundation stone of their family. He had to be strong, so they all could be as well.

As they cleared the room Andi heard Mom saying, "You're so pretty, dear! What's your name?" and his heart nearly broke. He had to get Mom back, just had to – but first, there was other business at hand. At least she didn't seem to be in any pain. First thing back in the dining room Andi cast the Command spell on Tertius again, sure that the ten minutes must nearly be up.

"What happened to the funny looking mask Bernadette wore when she healed the emperor?" Andi asked.

"Oh, Alderion took it downstairs with him. He said it's a powerful magical artifact and he was going to keep it for study, and not to tell anyone else about it." Just so long as he doesn't damage it, Andi prayed silently, before continuing his interrogation.

"Tell me what Alderion is doing in the basement," he Commanded.

"I don't understand any of that mage stuff," Tertius said, "so I can't tell you *exactly* what he's doing. He said he needed to work with the emperor for a few hours to help him get his facts straight about what happened to him at the ball, and afterward. It seems like there might have been a potion involved, not the forgetting one but one to maybe make you remember better."

Hmm, Andi thought. "Get his facts straight"? "Tell me what the rest of the plan is," he Commanded, and Tertius cheerfully complied. As with Befriend, repeated doses of the Command spell could have a cumulative effect that might takes hours or days to recuperate from.

"Once Master Alderion finishes working with the emperor," he explained, "we're all to pack up and go back to the mine. There's some bodies there under a preservation spell, and we need to set the stage. Then we fast-travel the emperor back to Roma, and reveal the plot by Davos Appolonius to fake the emperor's death so his son could rule."

"And the emperor would of course back this up with details?" Andi asked, as Junius wrote furiously.

"Of course," the guard replied. "That's what Alderion's doing with him right now."

"What about the body of the emperor that's lying in state at the Pantheatos?" Andi wanted to know. Tertius grinned slyly.

"That's some old drunk beggar we picked up in the waterfront district the night of the ball," he said – and now it was Mondi and Sigi that had to be restrained from doing him bodily harm.

"He was easy to lure away with a skin of wine," Tertius went on, "and he was about the same size as the emperor so the clothes fit. Master Alderion said that the illusion works better that way, less details to worry about. Of course we had to give him a sponge bath after we stripped him, or people would have been wondering why the 'emperor' smelled like a dead sewer rat. Don't think that fellow had had a bath in my lifetime!" His eyes sparkled, fingers held to nose, as the boys were held back by Anja and Lars.

"So are Alderion, Emperor Giorgio and your fellow guard Juan all together down there in the basement?" Andi asked, thinking about logistics.

"No, Master Alderion don't want nobody watching him work. Juan's standing guard on the door at the bottom of the stairway that comes out of the kitchen over there, and the other two are inside the room on the other side of the door."

"Sit quietly. You are feeling sleepy, and you don't notice anything that's going on around you," Andi Commanded. Tertius eyelids drooped, and in another minute his head sank to rest on his arms on the tabletop. He began snoring.

"Wow, that *does* work," Sigi remarked. It had not been easy to get Riki up this afternoon.

Andi looked at Junius and Macchiatus. "I think I need to use the Command spell on Juan too," he said, "because if I paralyze him he's going to fall down like he'd just been killed, and he might thump against the door and alert Alderion. I'd prefer not to have us met with a blast of battle magic or an ice demon or something when we open the door, even if I won't be affected thanks to my mask."

There was general agreement, and they all moved as silently as possible through the dining room to the kitchen, and then to a door they presumed led to the staircase Tertius had mentioned. They'd tied the guard's hands and gagged him, all without waking him, and he was currently sleeping peacefully on the floor in a corner of the dining room.

As he stood about to open the door, Andi pondered. He could have cloaked himself in illusion to look like Tertius, if only he knew any such spells. But as he did not, how was he going to keep Juan from attacking him on sight before he could get off a Command? Hmm. Well, it wouldn't hurt to try. Using the visualization he'd employed with such success earlier today Andi let his mind ride the Command spell, through the wooden door and down the stairs to where Juan stood alert, loaded crossbow in his hands and a sword at his side.

It was working, Andi could actually see him through the door! This was an exciting development, and he couldn't wait to tell Papa Andrion about it. When the spell engulfed Juan Andi could sense a relaxation. His expression softened, and he seemed less alert. But could Andi embed the Command without speaking it?

He looked around him and gestured to everyone to back up a few paces, then he did the same. "Juan," he sent his thoughts riding the Command spell, "Your friends are waiting for you in the kitchen. Set down the crossbow, because you won't need it, and come up the stairs quietly to greet us."

If this worked, Andi thought, it would almost be like that Joining thing the dypalfar did. Except here the range was about fifteen feet, which didn't seem very useful since you could just as easily speak aloud. He continued watching the guard in his mind's eye, as Juan looked around him and then stared down at the crossbow in his hands. He carefully released the trigger and set it down on the floor. There was an area only around three by four feet between the bottom step and the door he'd been guarding. Then, moving a little unsurely as if he wondered why he felt like doing this, he began walking quietly up the stairs.

As he opened the door and stood smiling at the crowd of people awaiting him, Andi's vision went from mind's-eye to real world, and he smiled back. "Hello Juan," he said. "We're having a slumber party, and I know you will enjoy it. Let's go back in the dining room and you can hang out with your friend Tertius."

266

"Okay," the guard replied cheerfully.

In another couple of minutes two snoring guards were trussed up on opposite sides of the dining room floor, and the group was once again preparing to storm Alderion's basement workroom. "That was amazing, Andi," Rezira said softly as they approached the stairs. "You have *got* to teach me how to do that. Do you think you can just find Alderion through the door and cast magic-block on him?"

"I don't see why not," Andi replied. But when he got to the bottom of the stairs he found himself unable to penetrate more than a little way beyond the door's inner surface. There was some kind of a gray barrier there, misty as fog and as solid as steel, beyond which his questing mind could not go. "He has some kind of magical barrier around him, it seems," Andi reported. "We're going to have to open the door."

Putting on the Meiskomtot mask, Andi carefully tried the handle. The door was locked. He used the Unlock spell on it, and there was a barely audible click. Then he put his ear to the door, but could hear no sound. Perhaps that magical barrier was there to prevent ordinary eavesdropping, not penetration by mages with powers that had only recently been discovered?

"Zira and I will be first in," Andi told the party. "Get your ward spell ready," he warned her, "but also try to magic-block him if you can. You've got the collar?" She smiled grimly and waved it at him. He pushed the unlocked door open silently, and they looked into the dimly lit basement room.

It appeared to have been used as a cellar for wines and root vegetables in the past, but Alderion had converted part of it for his purposes. There was a bed on high legs standing in the middle of the room, with candles on stands surrounding it. And on that bed lay the emperor, clad in robes that were of good quality without being ostentatious. His eyes were closed, but he appeared to be in a trance rather than sleeping.

Alderion, looking haggard and nearly ready to drop from exhaustion, was in the middle of reinforcing the spell that would lock the false memories he was supplying into the emperor's mind. The potion's effects lasted for thirty minutes, during which time the emperor would be calm and receptive to what he was being told without being aware of his surroundings. They had already gone through several bottles.

Repeatedly Alderion would recast the spell, then walk the emperor minute by minute through a set of events that, when he thought of them, he would be able to picture as vividly in his mind's eye as any memories of real events from his life. The mage had decided that, since their plans had gone awry and they'd had to keep the emperor for far longer than originally intended, that most of the time during the past few days would be taken up by confused memories of being repeatedly drugged into senselessness – with brief moments of consciousness when Davos' hirelings would have brought him food and drink and seen to his bodily needs.

He only needed to make crystal clear the events of the abduction, during which time the emperor would have heard the guards who captured him talking about getting paid by Davos, with additional conversations overheard in which the guards would reveal the plan to spirit him onto a ship and take him away to exile, "because Davos doesn't want his brother-in-law's blood on his hands," and then the final scene where the "mercenaries" were killed and Giorgio was rescued by Duke Terentius' guards, who'd stumbled upon his place of imprisonment by accident.

The last and trickiest bit was going to be the permanent implantation of the new attitudes Giorgio would have, toward Tiberius Apollonius and the Terentius family. His decision to exile his sister and nephew, and name Flavius Terentius as his new heir, must spring entirely from his own mind – after it had been carefully planted there by Alderion.

He gave a shuddering sigh, and reached for another stamina potion. His magical energy was holding up all right – a mage who had been using his powers for more than a century had a huge fund on which to call – but he had not slept in days, and he felt that his mind was beginning to tatter as his body consumed itself. Then he glanced up in the direction of the door leading to the kitchen stairs, and his face went white with shock and horror.

A tall apparition stood there, dressed in ordinary-seeming clothing, but wearing a hideous-looking metal mask that glinted a dull blue in the candlelight. Was he hallucinating? Where was Juan?

Then he spotted a much smaller figure beside the intruder, even as he felt a spell battering at the wards he'd erected. They were there to keep the help from hearing what he was doing with the emperor, but they also had at least some effect in warding off spells.

That was Rezira somebody, the dypalfar girl he'd met at the party! She was a mage, and so was her boyfriend... Alderion hurled a bolt of lightning at the figure who had to be Andi Drakespring. How in all the hells had they found him? The bolt slithered away without apparent effect, and in the next instant he felt a shimmering as spells crashed into his barrier from two sides and it popped out of existence. His magic had been blocked!

"No!" he screamed, and threw a dagger at the Drakespring boy. His aim was poor, and it hit his target's arm and then clattered across the stone floor without doing any apparent damage. In another second Alderion slumped to the floor, paralyzed. His mind was a raging torrent of fury and disbelief, as that slip of a dypalfar girl came over and clasped a magic-block collar around his neck. Doomed, he was utterly doomed!

Chapter 37: Consequences

Andi was glad that, in his haste to leave on the rescue mission, he had neglected to remove Aphinea's magic jewelry – though he *had* left the circlet behind. Between those and the Wissagleb mask, which they'd found lying on a table beside the emperor's bed in the basement, performing the Renew spell on Mom had been nearly easy. It was one hell of a spell and it could take a lot out of you – but he'd have done it until he collapsed on the floor, just to see the light come back into his mother's eyes as he took her back to the point immediately before the moment when Alderion had Commanded her to drink that potion.

He wasn't going to make the mistake (it was generally assumed she *had* done it mistakenly to Andrion) of regressing her into her remote youth, and had watched closely for signs of awareness. Actually, she stopped him herself by exclaiming "Andi! When did you get here?" when he'd reached the critical point. Though Alderion had kept her under the Command spell from the time when he'd abducted her in Pantheatos House until she had downed the potion, she had some peripheral memories of the afternoon.

"I think he must not have Commanded me to forget," she mused, as she sat between Erik and Riki on a settee in the comfortable manor house. "It seemed as if nothing was anywhere near as important as Alderion, like I was hanging on his every word waiting for the chance to please him by fulfilling his commands." She shuddered. "But I remember coming here, and feeling pity and horror when I saw what had happened to the emperor."

At the moment Giorgio himself was being interviewed by Macchiatus and Junius (who, still wearing the Ring of Detect Magic, had confirmed that the man before them was no longer under any spells yet still appeared to be, in fact, their sovereign emperor). Andi left his mom, sister, and papa snuggling on the sofa and went back into the dining room to listen in on the debriefing.

"After Mistress Drakespring had restored my mind to me, I remembered everything that had happened, from the moment I was incapacitated by a paralysis spell and hauled off by those thugs of Enzo's until Alderion gave me that potion," he was saying as Andi entered the room. "I felt better than I can recall feeling in years, and I immediately realized what Alderion was getting at when he asked me what I could remember. So I pretended that I was still hazy, and couldn't recall anything after being at the ball. I thought I'd gotten away with it, though I still didn't understand what he was up to. But then he put some kind of spell on me and suddenly I only wanted to do whatever he wanted. He took me down in the basement and commanded me to drink another potion, and I didn't even hesitate. It seemed like the most wonderful idea in the world. After that, things got fuzzy again but it wasn't like before."

Two hours before, when the paralysis spell had released its grip on Alderion, the elf mage had found himself securely bound to a chair – and spitting mad. Everything had been ruined – by those meddling Drakesprings, by Duke Enzo's greedy schemes, by Davos' murderous lack of familial affection. And yes, he had to admit, he himself might have made a few mistakes as well. It was all over, more than a century of power and plotting.

And suddenly Alderion's anger dissolved, slipping away from him like mist, and he felt more at peace than he could remember feeling in his adult life to this point. A sort of fatalism came over him. He was tired of running, tired of hiding, tired of plotting and fighting, manipulating and killing.

What he was, he ought to have realized, was just plain tired. He had been laboring for far too long without rest, and his mind had begun to unravel. Later, after he had had a meal and a good night's sleep, Alderion would come to regret opening his mouth and talking so freely to the Imperial Guard. But at the time, it had seemed that he was a celebrity being interviewed about his great accomplishments, and he was proud to reveal all – not to mention vengefully bringing down Duke Enzo Terentius, Davos Appolonius, and anyone else he could spill the dirt on while doing so.

Alderion looked around him. Commander Octavius and his Recorder were there watching him. The dypalfar girl, Rezira, was there with a couple of young people who seemed familiar. Perhaps he'd seen them at some party, though they scarcely looked the sort to be moving in *his* circles.

And there were those two Drakespring brats, the ones who'd been running all over the Terentius mansion with young Gaius. Their

271

older brother, the young Drakespring mage, had seized that odd-looking mask his mother had insisted on using and run from the room, evidently planning to use it to restore *her* mind. He'd thought, at the time he'd had her drink the potion, that nobody would be able to bring her back.

He and the guards would have left her behind when they took Giorgio (who would have been asleep at the time) back to the mine, and it was supposed that she would soon have starved to death or wandered into the woods to be eaten by a bear. He ought to have known she would have taught that spell to her son. The boy – not yet eighteen! – seemed to be one of the most powerful natural mages he had ever seen.

"I suppose you're wondering," Alderion remarked calmly to his rapt audience, "whether I am under any compulsion spell. I assure you I am not. The Command spell, which no doubt this young lady knows how to cast" – he gestured toward Rezira with his head, the only part of his anatomy that had free movement – "only works for the person who cast it. A person bespelled with it will be compelled to answer questions from anyone else truthfully only if they've been Commanded to do so."

Junius looked to his commander, who nodded. "All right," he said. "I, Junius Gregorius, Recorder of His Reman Majesty's Guards, Roma Division, am prepared to hear your testimony. Do you swear by Divine Aderos that what you are about to tell me is the truth?" A sardonic gleam came into the ljosalfar mage's drooping eyes. Such nonsense!

"I so swear," he answered tiredly.

Commander Octavius directed the questioning, as he walked Alderion through the story from the moment when The Mask had been told of Davos Appolonius' desire to kill the emperor, and all that had followed it. "You are certain it was Davos?" Macchiatus asked, wondering if there could possibly be any mistake.

Alderion barked a sharp laugh. "My dear commander," he said urbanely, "I have known Davos Appolonius since before he was able to grow a beard. I have been moving within the circles of the empire's elite since long before you were born. He wore a cloak, but it took no great effort on my part to see his face – assuming his voice, which he feebly attempted to disguise, were not enough for me to know him by."

Alderion was not content to explode the plot of Duke Terentius to put his son on the throne, which had included the murder of the young heir Bruno Salonius some five years past (Giorgio was able to corroborate that the mage had bragged to him of this, as well). He also revealed that for nearly a century he had been the legendary mage assassin The Mask, giving details of crimes dating back so long that none of the victims' survivors were left alive. He had often committed his murders at the behest of the dukes of Brindis, but had taken other commissions as well when they would not interfere with his masters' interests.

By the time they had finished interviewing Alderion, Junius had enough information in his notebook to assure that the mage's head would roll – as would the heads of Duke Enzo Terentius and Davos Appolonius – but additional evidence would be useful. The Judges were loath to convict on a capital offense without something beyond a single witness' testimony. Alderion was happy to suggest ways in which such evidence could be obtained.

When all of the interviews were over Anja had been able to take them all back to Roma with her map, dropping Macchiatus, Junius, the emperor, and their five prisoners off at the Penitentiary before taking the rest of the family to Pantheatos House. She and Lars had taken the spare bedroom they'd used before, falling into its bed without bothering even to clean their teeth. Everyone was exhausted.

Erik, Bernadette, and Andi had argued for getting Andrion out of his cell immediately, while they were there dropping off the prisoners; but Macchiatus had insisted that protocol must be followed. The officers of the Imperial Court were at home in their beds, and it would have to wait for the morrow.

First thing in the morning the entire Drakespring contingent (plus Anja, Lars, and Gylabris) were in the anteroom of the Penitentiary as the former prisoner Andrion Drakespring was led from his cell. He had not had a bath or been able to change his clothing in days, but he walked with a spring in his step and joy shining in his eyes as he came into the room and beheld them all waiting for him. As a cheer went up, Bernadette fell into his arms.

Though Alderion had come to regret his candor when being deposed by Macchiatus and Junius, he held to his word. If it was over, then let it be truly and finally over. And so, released from his magic-block collar and surrounded by city guards as well as university mages ready to block his magic again should he do anything untoward, he stood by the catafalque on which the body of "the emperor" rested, and restored the corpse to its true appearance. The funeral for Bronzo was held the next day, the body being interred in an honored grave in the central square's cemetery, with a stone that read "Here lies Benjamino Crucio, known as Bronzo, who gave his life for his emperor." There wasn't a dry eye in the house.

Lucia was ecstatic to find her beloved husband alive and well, beyond any hope she had held even after she'd discovered the missing mole. His sister Mariana was also happy to learn he was alive – and considerably *less* happy to learn that her husband Davos (what had she ever seen in him, anyway?) had hired an assassin to kill him. While she and Tiberius had not, as far as anyone could determine, been in on the plot, they had been tainted by it – and Giorgio exiled them to the countryside, to a manor house that had recently been confiscated from the estate of the former Duke of Brindis.

Andrion had been astonished, and pleased, to learn that his son had found a solution to the power cell problem in his absence. Had he really been incarcerated for only a few days? Sextus, it transpired, had been so confident of the combined teams' success that he had already set up a manufacturing facility in one of the Mercantile District's less prominent areas. Glassblowers and artisans in metal had been churning out power cell blanks in quantity, and were already working with plans for the devices they would power.

Andi found himself run ragged training mages with the aptitude to learn the conjuring spell needed to power the devices, and the ability to look within and visualize the path to the Source. Bernadette had pioneered this technique, though she had never employed it except for healing. She hadn't ever considered herself a mage, and beyond authoring the book that explained how she'd healed Francois Lamonte she'd never attempted to train anyone in her specialized technique beside her son. Now she was besieged with requests to act as a guide, as mages popped out of the woodwork begging for insights.

Another month had passed like a dream, and the Drakespring family were at last ready to set their sights for home. Riki had managed to send a letter to Fjuri via messenger, telling him of all that had happened and promising him that they would be home before too long. She had not received any message back from him, but then there was no mail service to speak of between Iscandia and Remus – and the Steadfast family was not rich. Messengers were expensive.

Of Flavius Riki had had little word. It had been confirmed that none of the three Terentius sons had had any notion of their father's schemes. Flavius would have been only thirteen when Enzo had plotted to have the Reman heir murdered, already planning his second son's future without his knowledge.

So he was innocent of his father's plots, Riki thought – why didn't he ever contact me? I thought he loved me, or at least that's what he said. It was probably just the heat of the moment, she guessed. Mom had been opening up to her a little more about such things, including the ways in which teenage hormones could perturb the thought processes.

She'd even admitted that by the time she was Riki's age – only a few months shy of sixteen – she'd already been in love three times and had *slept* with each of them! Without risk of pregnancy or disease, thanks to her amulet. Riki appreciated her mom's honesty, and had reciprocated by admitting that she now had an amulet of her own. Which, she was surprised to find, Mom advised her to start wearing immediately and keep it on. Evidently the pregnancy-prevention effects took a while to kick in.

Riki did so, but she was still having trouble getting over the shock of learning her mom had been – not to put too fine a point on it – a *slut* before she was even sixteen. It was so hard to believe that, considering the stable environment she'd been raised in. Mom loved Papa Erik, and she loved Papa Andrion, and she slept with both of them. And that was that. They all loved each other, and were there for each other, and this business of hopping from bed to bed just seemed absurd. Wasn't making love supposed to be about *being* in love?

The day had come, and they were all assembled with their luggage for the return to Drakespring Farm. The Imperial Technology Company's factory had begun selling the first of the Dypalfar Cold Chests, and they had been a huge success. No Dwelves had been involved in their manufacture, but the name apparently sparked a response in their target market. There would probably be Dypalfar Bath Systems soon to follow, and a few people had already been spotted tooling around the city on the Dypalfar Personal Transporter – something Gylabris had come up with that combined the hemispherical base of a roller with a comfortable seat and a set of controls. Who needed horses to get around?

The emperor and empress, with an escort of city guards, had turned out to see them off. They would be back, certainly – especially Andi and Rezira, who yet had much to offer the Imperial Technology Company. Gylabris was staying behind, for now. His fund of knowledge about the details of dypalfar tech was keeping the designers at ITC humming. Lucia came forward, and folded Bernadette in a warm embrace. She looked about twenty-five.

"Bernadette," she said, eyes lit with excitement, "I think it may already have worked! I missed my period a few days ago." Bernadette smiled and put a hand on her shoulder, delving her. Yes, there in her core was a spark of new life! "It's far too early to know for sure whether a child will result," she told the younger woman – only younger now thanks to her intervention – "but you have conceived. Take care of yourself!"

This had been the answer to Emperor Giorgio's conundrum regarding an heir, and Bernadette had agreed to it only on the understanding that this was a one-time deal. If he and his rejuvenated empress failed to produce a child of their own before Lucia was once again past her childbearing years, he would be back to figuring out Plan B.

As the last of their luggage was hauled out by the hired porters and they gathered in the street, ready for Bernadette to take them all back to Iscandia, Riki was stunned to see a familiar figure approaching. He was dressed all in black, which didn't suit him. Such dark and devilish good looks should be clad in red.

She stepped forward toward him, and they met in the street with everyone's eyes on them. But they only had eyes for each other. "Riki!" Flavius said, tears welling in his eyes, "I had meant to let you go without saying goodbye, but I can't do it!" Riki's own eyes glistened with tears as she beheld his misery. Flavius, so gallant, so vivid… he seemed like a shadow of his former self as he stepped forward to clasp her hands in his.

"I have nothing to offer you now," he said sadly. "Emperor Giorgio has confirmed that my brother Arturus may take the throne of Brindis, ruling in proxy now and for good once our father has been tried… and executed. But steep fines will be levied, and now not only the common people of Brindis will be impoverished. For Gaius and me, there is nothing – Arturus may be lucky enough to wed his troll bride, but it is unlikely that we will ever find a noble family willing to link themselves with us. Our family is disgraced, ruined."

Riki looked up at him, seeking his soul within the dark, sad eyes. "So that is why I've heard nothing from you these past weeks?" she asked, a flash of irritation showing. "You feel you are unworthy of me, now that your family has fallen? Or is it that your protestations of love were so much mist?" Now she was glaring at him!

Tears sprang from Flavius' eyes, running unheeded down his cheeks and dripping off the beard that had begun to grow. It seemed he had taken little care with his appearance over the weeks that had elapsed since she had last seen him. "No!" he cried, anguished. "I love you, Riki! I will always love you! But I truly am not worthy of you. You are a beautiful soul, a goddess among women, and I am nothing but the useless second son of an utterly disgraced, formerly noble family!"

Despite the tears and the apparent sincerity, Riki detected a hint of the dramatic. The rogue, he had seized the moment in his teeth and he was running with it! She leaned up into him and sought his mouth with a passionate kiss. "Don't run off and join a monastery just yet, Flavius," she murmured after releasing him. "The women of the empire would mourn your loss." He blinked at her, tears drying, as she turned back to her family. Bernadette brought out her map, and in another moment all of them were gone.

Chapter 38: Home Sweet Home

The Drakesprings, with Anja and Lars along for the ride, all shimmered into existence at the usual spot in the road below Drakespring Farm. As luck would have it, it was the middle of a dry and pleasant afternoon. Francois and Christine Lamonte were sitting on the veranda with their feet up, admiring the view. They jumped to their feet as the family appeared below them.

"Andi, you're back!" Christine called. Though she had taken to also calling her grandson by the pet name that she and Francois had used with Andrion in childhood, everyone knew whom she meant in this case. They had been gone for close to two months, and there'd been very little communication. The family left behind in Waterdon had not even been informed of Andrion's incarceration – considering it had gone on for less than a week.

Bernadette hugged her parents-in-law. "Thank you so much for being here with the kids and letting us have some time away!" she said warmly. She could hardly believe they'd been able to cope without her –but perhaps her children *were* growing up. "Where is everybody?" she asked, looking around. Other than the Lamontes, there seemed to be no one else in evidence.

"The dragon kids are all off flying," Francois said with a smile. "They promised to bring us some meat for supper. We can only hope it's not some old stag that barely escaped dying of natural causes!" Christine smiled at her husband. He'd become everything she'd loved about him when they first married and more, since Bernadette's rejuvenation of both of them. She felt like the luckiest woman in the world.

"Meri's up in town," she explained. "She goes there most days to visit with Jymi, when he's not coming here. I thought at first it was just a case of them being thrown together because they were only leukalfar boy and girl in Waterdon, but it seems to be something more. He's really taken with her, and she with him."

Bernadette glowed to hear Christine's tale. She had expected that as Meri came into adolescence there would be another crisis, one perhaps worse than the one that had led to their journey to the Eparchy two years before. Young humans wanted to get together and mate. It was part of basic biology, but it became a problem if you were leukalfar and the other human races around you regarded you as some kind of freak. How wonderful that Meri had found a beau, and furthermore a boy who was eager to embrace Iscandia's mainstream culture.

They were all tired from the thirty-hour, instantaneous journey from Remus, and gathered their luggage to take it into the house with some help from the Lamontes. Bernadette, Erik, and Andrion were looking forward to a nap in their enormous conjugal bed, and Andi and Rezira too soon excused themselves to go take a snooze in the basement. Mondi and Sigi were dead on their feet and joined them on their trip downstairs, planning to sack out in the dormitory. But Riki had something on her agenda that could not wait.

She'd hugged and kissed her grandparents, thanking them for being here, and then set off up the road to Waterdon. The excitement that vibrated in her core helped to stave off the tiredness that was creeping over her. Anja and Lars had already left for Brightsgate Cottage – almost as soon as they'd arrived, eager to tell Lifa the good news. They'd found competing buyers for the treasures of Sindalo, and they would be financially comfortable for years to come – maybe for the rest of their lives, with some sensible investments. It wasn't as if Iscandia offered a lot of opportunities for lavish spending.

Brightsgate Cottage was Riki's first stop, and she found Anja and Lars still there, enjoying a party of sorts with Lifa and Edla. "Riki!" Edla cried when she opened the door, and she was welcomed inside. It was too early in the afternoon, yet, for Bjorn and Fjuri to be home. Riki accepted a glass of celebratory wine, which helped to fortify her in her resolve, before excusing herself and going out again in search of the building site where Fjuri and his coworkers were currently deployed. Lifa was able to tell her that her message had been received, and that Fjuri knew she was on her way home.

She found him on the western outskirts of Waterdon, which seemed to be pushing farther out onto the plain with every passing year. Riki passed the ten-acre plot that had been given to Fjuri for his birthday, a nice little stretch of slightly rolling land with a small rivulet passing through one corner of it. Building had already continued beyond it, and soon it would be part of an area of homes (and a few businesses, as well) stretching off to the west, north and south of the city walls. Where were all these people coming from?

Riki found the site where a new home was rising, only a few dozen yards beyond. The two-story house stood on a small lot, just two acres – and while the foundation was already laid, and the walls of the ground floor in place, the second story was only now being framed in. She spotted Fjuri at work with a hammer on the upper floor, securing a section of wall timbers, and her heart almost stopped. He was so beautiful, such a powerful embodiment of manhood! She had missed him more than she had realized, until this moment when she saw him for the first time in nearly two months.

He seemed to sense something, somehow, and paused in his hammering to gaze down at her as she stood there, afternoon sun setting her red-gold hair ablaze. "Fjuri!" she called. "Fjuri! I'm home!" The hammer fell two stories, fortunately striking no one along the way, and in seconds he was by her side. "Riki!" he growled, his heart so full he could scarcely speak. He enfolded her in his arms, his lips pressed to hers, and they were as one for an endless moment.

"My my, what a touching reunion," a voice cut in. They broke apart, and turned to look at the tall woman with a dusty red braid running down her back, wearing rough construction worker's clothes, and glaring at Riki with contempt and hostility. "So the virgin girlfriend has returned from the big city," Inge Redmane went on. "What's the matter, didn't you meet a prince to marry?"

Riki stared at her in disbelief. She'd met Inge slightly at Fjuri's birthday party back in Sungold, but had scarcely paid her any attention. What was her *problem*? Inge strolled up and stood beside Fjuri, hipshot in her tight shirt and trousers, and laid a hand on his arm. "Fjuri and I have been having lots of fun while you've been gone," she purred. "Haven't we, Fjuri-love?" The hand left his arm and stroked along his hip, then went behind to squeeze his butt.

Riki couldn't believe what she was seeing. Fjuri had not brushed off this obscene slut in disgusted rejection, he had *blushed crimson* and now he was hanging his head! What in all the hells was going on here? She stepped up, eye to eye with the tall female construction worker, and gave her a look that would have withered a shri from twenty yards. Then she looked up into Fjuri's face. "What happened?" she demanded.

Fjuri stammered. "I felt so lonely when you left… I… I… she kept telling me I should have some experience before you and I made love for the first time…" He turned and looked down at Inge, anger in his eyes. "You knew I loved her, knew that she's the only woman I care about! Why did you keep trying to seduce me?"

Inge paled beneath her tan, but she kept her cool. "I wanted you, Fjuri. Wanted you, plain and simple. And *she* wasn't around. What difference did it make?"

Riki eyed her, a cool blue-eyed appraisal that seemed older than her years. Then she turned to look into Fjuri's deep blue eyes and asked again, more quietly, "What happened?"

"We were all having fun after finishing a job, drinking up our pay, and I had too much to drink," he admitted shamefacedly. "I went up with her to her room, and then… I don't know. I can't remember anything, and when I woke up in the morning I had the worst headache in my life. But I was there in bed with Inge and she was naked, and I had my shirt off. She wanted me to make love to her, but I just wanted to leave! And she's been telling everyone in town since then that I slept with her. I'm sorry."

Riki gazed up at Fjuri, sympathy flooding her soul. Oh, Fjuri. What a man, what a baby! She wanted to paddle his bottom and put him to bed without his supper, for his foolishness. Now Inge, on the other hand… She looked the woman in the eyes again. From the superiority of her adult status, she was trying hard to look down on Riki. But Riki could see her composure starting to crack.

She gave it a little longer, just letting Inge's uneasiness increase. Then Riki said in a low, cold voice, "You pathetic whore. You spread your favors around, but it's not just for fun, is it? You see something good, somebody like Fjuri, and you think maybe you can just step in and take him for yourself. Did you really believe that offering him sex was all it was going to take to pry my Fjuri away, when I've loved him my whole life? I pity you."

Riki took Fjuri's hand, and turned her back on Inge – planning to lead him away. She didn't actually intend to jump his bones in the next few hours, but soon. Inge stood there for a moment, face red, shaking with fury. "You stuck-up bitch!" she snarled, grabbing a handful of Riki's long hair and pulling her back. Riki dropped Fjuri's hand and turned to face her, anger flaring. "You can't talk to me that way!" Inge cried, and brought her arm back to slap her rival across the face. With her left hand Riki reached up and seized Inge's wrist in an iron grip. Then she balled up a fist, and decked her with a right cross.

Epilogue

The crowd nearly overflowed the small chapel in the Temple of Marmira in Lakedon, chattering quietly among themselves and then falling silent as Yusuf entered and it was time for the ceremony to begin. The aisle was too narrow for every member of the combined wedding parties to walk down at once, so Rezira had decided to cede precedence to Anja – accompanied down the aisle by her father Bjorn.

Then Rezira took her short walk, side by side with Bernadette, to stand before Yusuf (now graying, but still a handsome man) at the altar. To Yusuf's right were Bjorn and Lifa, the couple he had married here in this chapel more than eighteen years before. He smiled at them, and they beamed back. And to Lifa's right Lars stood, tall and good-looking and richly dressed. At his side, Anja looked absolutely breathtaking. Both she and Rezira had gotten their wedding gowns at the couturiers in Roma – the likes of which this rustic Iscandia chapel had rarely seen.

All of Rezira's living relatives were in another universe, unreachable now. But in the years that she and Andi had been together she'd come to think of Bernadette as a mother – a mother as fierce in a way as her own, but far kinder and more truly motherly. She stood with Andi to her right, marveling at how gorgeous he looked in his wedding clothes. They had planned this at his eighteenth birthday celebration a couple of months before, and there'd been plenty of time to get him outfitted in splendor that matched her own.

Bernadette remained standing on Andi's right, and Andrion rose from his front row seat to take his place beside her. There wasn't all that much room in the space before the altar, and Erik had cheerfully offered to remain in his front-row seat. Andi was his son as much as Bernadette's or Andrion's, but he could watch the ceremony just fine from here.

Also gathered for the ceremony were another nine of Bernadette's children – along with Fjuri, Meri's friend Jymi, Gylabris, Mothris and his betrothed Elsila, Sextus Garibaldi, Edla, and a few friends of Anja and Lars whom they'd known since childhood. Everyone who knew the couple were thrilled and disbelieving that, after cohabiting for more than five years, the young adventurers were finally settling down and getting hitched.

Fjuri, dressed in custom-sewn finery paid for by his big sister, put any imperial courtier to shame – and Riki felt proud to be sitting beside him, holding his hand. As the ceremony was about to begin, he leaned down and murmured in her ear, "Think it'll be us up there in another year?"

She grinned at him, but said "Don't be in such a hurry, love. I still have a lot more to learn about home-building before we can make our house together. And don't you want to see some of the world, first?" He squeezed her hand.

She was well into her apprenticeship as a builder. With the dragon kids doing so well on the farm chores, Riki had been freed from those duties for the first time in her life since she'd been big enough to pick up a pail. And Fjuri had been happy to donate half of his ten-acre lot to his sister and her fiancé. Since neither he nor Riki really wanted to farm for a living, they had no need of so much land.

Anja and Lars had paid for all of the materials, but the lot and much of the labor had been donated by Fjuri as an early wedding present. Riki had gotten her first lessons in the builder's art and had discovered both a talent and a liking for it. Making something beautiful with your own hands, something that would last for a lifetime and shelter generations of loving families beneath its roof, was more satisfying than she had expected.

Inge Redmane had moved on, having pretty well worn out her welcome in Waterdon. They heard she was now working construction in Normarsh, an un-walled town with plenty of room for expansion. Riki had not gone so far as to join Hegmar's crew as a paid apprentice builder, but now that Anja and Lars' house was completed that would probably be the next step. Though, she hoped that she and Fjuri would be able to spend some time together in Roma before they began working on their own house together.

Andi and Rezira, founding shareholders of the Imperial Technology Company along with Andrion, Gylabris, Emperor Giorgio Salonius and the team at the University of the Magical Arts, were making money hand over fist. The young couple could probably have retired before reaching their twentieth birthdays and spent the rest of their long lives just living on the royalties from the power cells that were being put into use to power new devices everyone wanted to buy.

With practice, the manufacture of the cells had become so efficient that the price had fallen to where even families of modest means could afford a cold chest to keep their food from spoiling. And the streets of Roma were beginning to fill up with people whizzing along on the Dypalfar Personal Transporters. Gylabris was now at work on a prototype for a family-sized carriage that would run on power from multiple cells.

But Andi and his bride-to-be weren't in the least anxious to retire. They'd bought a small townhouse in Roma and lived there about half the time. There was also a little cottage in Waterdon, near Brightsgate Cottage, that had been renovated for them by Fjuri and some friends from Hegmar's crew as a birthday present to Andi. Running back and forth between Waterdon and Roma by map was something of a pain, and Andi's new project at the university was the development of permanent human-sized portals that would allow near-instantaneous transport between the two cities – and eventually, other destinations as well.

Andrion had decided to leave the projects in Roma to others. He was still an insatiable learner, and no doubt he would go back there many times in the future. But for now he had an Academy to run, and a pack of engaging adolescents to raise. Life was good, he had his freedom – and he, Berni, and Erik had all the time in the world. Who knew, maybe after all of the current crop of kids were grown, they could have another baby.

The ceremony had begun, with Anja and Lars going first. They'd opted for the traditional ceremony, starting with "Our father Aderos created the world and all its creatures…" Everyone in the room was beaming with happiness as they concluded their vows, received their rings, and kissed. Then they remained standing as Yusuf began the ceremony anew for Rezira and Andi. It was simple, sweet, and powerful. In less than two minutes Andi, holding Rezira's hand, was looking into her deep violet eyes and pronouncing his vow: "I do, for the rest of my life."

The End

www.ingramcontent.com/pod-product-compliance
Lightning Source LLC
Chambersburg PA
CBHW071118170626
46809CB00002B/416